SHA

RH

More from Joan Swan in the Phoenix Rising series

Fever

Blaze

Rush

SHATTER

JOAN SWAN

BRAVA

KENSINGTON PUBLISHING CORP.

www.kensingtonbooks.com

BRAVA BOOKS are published by

Kensington Publishing Corp.
119 West 40th Street
New York, NY 10018

Copyright © 2014 Joan Swan

All Kensington titles, imprints, and distributed lines are available at special quantity discounts for bulk purchases for sales promotions, premiums, fund-raising, educational, or institutional use.

Special book excerpts or customized printings can also be created to fit specific needs. For details, write or phone the office of the Kensington special sales manager: Kensington Publishing Corp., 119 West 40th Street, New York, NY 10018, attn: Special Sales Department; phone 1-800-221-2647.

BRAVA and the B logo are Reg. U.S. Pat. & TM Off.

ISBN-13: 978-0-7582-8827-1
ISBN-10: 0-7582-8827-1

First Kensington Trade Paperback Printing: January 2014

10 9 8 7 6 5 4 3 2 1

Printed in the United States of America

First Electronic Edition: January 2014

ISBN-13: 978-0-7582-8828-8
ISBN-10: 0-7582-8828-X

For Paige and Alicia

Thank you for believing in
the Phoenix Rising series and my abilities.

ACKNOWLEDGMENTS

Deep gratitude goes out to my fabulous agent, Paige Wheeler, of Folio Literary Management, for her enthusiasm over *Fever* and the Phoenix Rising series, for believing in my writing abilities, and for taking me on as a client. And to Alicia Condon, my amazing editor at Kensington Publishing, for seeing the bigger picture, offering guidance and then allowing me to run with it. You both have enriched my life as a writer and I'm forever grateful.

Gracious appreciation to attorney Steven C. Burke, husband of the fabulous romance author Darcy Burke, for his input on the complex legal matters Mitch had to work around in *Shatter.*

A huge thank-you to readers for their enthusiasm for the series and their undying love . . . and lust . . . for Mitch. And a special shout-out to my critique partner, Elisabeth Naughton—who gave Mitch life at the very beginning of the series when I needed a brother for Alyssa in *Fever*—for getting me through this series with endless support.

Thanks to Russ Hanush, math, science, and physics expert extraordinaire, PhD, and longtime tutor to my daughters for taking questions like "How might my heroine control these crazy electromagnetic abilities?" and offering suggestions like "There's this thing called a ferrite bead . . ."

A shout to my street team, Swan's Sirens, for their support and enthusiasm. Thanks to my sisters, Jane, Clare, and Anne, who are always pushing my latest book into their friends' hands.

Last but never least, my husband, Rick, and daughters, Cassidy and McKinley, for loving me in all my quirkiness. And an extra shout to Cassidy, who is both my invaluable assistant and supplier of meals under deadline.

I couldn't have done this without you all. Each one of you owns a piece of this series and my success.

ONE

Heather Raiden sat on the floor of her darkened home on Lake Washington in Seattle and stared at the midnight blackness through her night-vision goggles. The man she'd been watching for two nights remained huddled in the compact speedboat he'd rented under the name Dane Zimerelli.

He'd dropped anchor in the perfect location to view Heather's living room, kitchen, and bedroom, all on the lake side of the property.

"I hope he's freezing his balls off out there."

At her elbow, Dexter picked up on the bitterness in her voice and whined. Lowering the binoculars, she ran her hand along the shepherd's silky-soft fur. His brows darted with his gaze, making him look truly worried. He was an incredibly sensitive animal, frighteningly intelligent. And her very best friend.

"Don't look at me like that. I can't just sit here and do nothing."

She reconsidered her options. Cops would brush her off. A private investigator would take time. Ignoring Zimerelli had potentially lethal consequences. And she'd spent seven long years preventing those lethal consequences.

Heather hurried through the darkness to her bedroom with Dex's nails clicking behind her on the hardwood. When she stepped through the door, he pushed past her, jumped on the bed, and lay in that alert pose, head up and watching every move.

"Everything I've done will be wasted if I don't act now. All my sacrifices . . ."

She stopped and closed her eyes, absorbing the weight of loss that always came with the thought. So many sacrifices. But only one she regretted.

Only one that haunted her.

Already dressed in black, Heather slipped on dark, lightweight running shoes and tightened the laces. In the bathroom, she wrapped her long hair into a bun. Her mind and body immediately slipped back into the training she'd gained. Training she had, admittedly, hoped never to use. Training that was still just training because she'd never utilized it in real life. But she'd also known deep down she'd need it some day.

Resigned, focused, she headed for the door leading to the garage and pulled her slim black jacket from the peg. She slipped it on, crouched in front of Dex standing faithfully at her feet, and hugged him tight.

"*Ya lyublyu tebya,*" she whispered, her throat closing tight around each Russian word, a reminder of the past she'd fought so hard to leave behind. "I love you so much, sweet boy," she repeated in English with more emphasis, because once just didn't feel like enough.

With a kiss to his muzzle, she stood, met his eyes, and firmed her voice when she commanded him to protect the property. "*Zashchita.*"

In the garage, Heather located her black canvas duffel at the base of the stairs. Adrenaline fizzed through her blood. The duffel's zipper ripped the silence and tension pulled at her skin. She clenched a penlight between her teeth, pulled the Heckler & Koch .45 semiauto from the bag, and checked the remaining contents—lock hacker, silencer, extra ammo, rags, bleach-laden wipes, latex gloves.

As she turned the key in the engine of her BMW, Heather experienced fear, resignation, the dark thrill of power. And anger over having to use such drastic and brutal measures to take back control over her life.

"Maybe there's more of my family in me than I thought."

She backed from the garage with the sick realization sticking to her like tar.

Heather left her sleepy Laurelhurst neighborhood for the streets bordering the University of Washington, still dotted with cars and pedestrians. Fear drummed its fingers on the back of her neck. What-ifs teased her mind into tangles. Her neighbors would take care of Dex if anything happened to her. She'd set up charitable trusts to receive her assets.

Heather located the stalker's rental and parked a block down and turned the car off. But as she waited, she realized that having her death in order didn't help her face the possibility.

Another deep shiver wracked his body, and Mitch Foster clenched his teeth around a growl. "My dick's turning into an icicle."

He lowered the night-vision binoculars and reached for the thermos of coffee, but it was empty. He chucked the container at the floor of the boat, glaring at the darkened house. "Screw this."

Halina Dubrovsky had turned out the lights over half an hour ago and he couldn't see shit. Her boyfriend, some dude named Dex, hadn't shown up for two days. Didn't matter. Even if the guy did appear, Mitch had enough information on Halina's daily activities now to confront her without running into him.

When Mitch cornered her, she wasn't going to have anywhere to turn. Anywhere to run.

Not this time.

He started the motor and crawled toward shore, holding his speed down for silence and warmth. Huddled behind the windshield, he pulled his phone from his pocket and hit the speed dial for Kai Ryder.

"What's new?" Kai answered.

"Genital hypothermia," Mitch said. "My nuts are buddying up with my kidneys."

"You have two? Balls, I mean. I thought you were down at least one."

"Shut the fuck up. How are Lys and Brady?" he asked, hating himself for missing the birth of his first nephew.

"Great. You'd never know Alyssa had a baby last week, and Brady and I are totally bonding."

"I hate you." He was only half joking.

Kai laughed, the asshole. "Was it worth it?"

"No." His teeth were starting to chatter. "No sign of the boyfriend. No friends. No activities. She rows in the morning, works all day, goes to the gym, runs with her dog."

And she played with her dog. And cuddled with her dog. And freaking *slept* with her dog. She was so damned *sweet* to that animal it made his teeth grind. And that was just one of the behaviors he found incongruent with what he'd learned of her over the last few days.

"Mmm," Kai hummed. "Bet she's got a killer bod."

"Ryder," he warned.

He didn't need any reminders. He'd been watching her for two days and she wasn't particularly discreet when it came to changing clothes. But then, under normal conditions, she wouldn't need to be. From the street, her home was virtually nondescript, the only entries the front door and one curtained window. Lakeside, the house was nearly all glass, but its orientation and landscaping created a seclusion Mitch could only get around with a boat specifically positioned on the lake and a pair of binoculars.

He hit a dense patch of fog and another tremor gripped him bone deep. "Shit. I thought I knew fog, but this place is colder than San Francisco. What intel did you get? I'm going to confront her in the morning before she goes to work."

"She's a secretive little thing," Kai said.

"No shit," Mitch muttered.

"From what I've found, she's not using her real name for anything. She's completely dropped it. The alias Heather Raiden goes back seven years, and I still think her using your middle name for her last name is . . . odd. Kinda creepy, actually. I mean, it's almost like there's a message there or something."

Mitch got that feeling, too, though he kept vacillating over the possible meaning. "Like, 'Fuck you, Foster. You're too stupid to find me even when I'm using your name?' That kind of message?"

But even as he said the words, he didn't believe them. Not at gut level. When she'd walked out on him, she hadn't been cruel. She'd been . . . withdrawn. She'd been . . . resolute. Keeping her husband a secret from Mitch—yes, that had been cruel. But when she'd admitted it, when she'd broken off her relationship with Mitch to go back to the husband, she hadn't done it in a careless or vicious way.

Even now, seven years later, his gut told him that if the man hadn't been there with her, silently standing sentinel when she'd confessed and broken it off, she wouldn't have been able to do it. Wouldn't have been able to resist his pleas for an explanation. For a chance to talk to her—in private.

God, he'd been such a fool for her. And remembering still both hurt and angered him.

Kai made an indecisive sound in his throat. "I don't get that."

Hope percolated to the surface. "You're picking up emotions from her?"

Kai was only one of seven firefighters exposed to radioactive chemicals in a military warehouse fire six years before. The way the chemicals had warped their DNA gave each member of the team paranormal abilities. Kai was empathic, but generally only picked up on emotions from those close by or those endangering the team. And at the moment, Kai was eight hundred miles away.

"No," Kai said, but he didn't sound convincing. "I think this is more intuition."

"Screw intuition." If Mitch clenched his teeth any harder, they'd crack. "Either use your powers or get me hard intel. I don't want to hear any shit in between."

"Damn, you're irritable. You're bringing me down, dude."

"Ice cubes generally aren't warm and fuzzy." Neither were men tracking down exes for explanations about conspiracies ruining their lives. He pulled into the slip designated for the rented boat and tied off. "And what the hell's up with your new attitude, Ryder? Did you get yourself a new lay or did you just finally get that stick out of your ass?"

"Someone sounds *jealous,*" Kai said, singing the last word. "I know where you can find a good stick . . ."

"Got that covered, thanks."

"Ah, good point. Back to said stick—her job at the university deals with vaccine research. She's evidently making headway in this new wave of DNA vaccines. She's well respected in the field. Travels, lectures, publishes in trade journals."

"How nice for her, but hardly scintillating." Although that remnant of her altruistic personality was just another annoying paradox. "Move on."

"She's low, low profile. No scandals. No legal disputes. No community work. No charity work. No family. No deep personal ties that I can find at all. I think Keira's abilities went askew here. I can't find anyone named Dex or Dexter in her life at all."

Keira O'Shay, another firefighter in the team, was clairaudient and had been trying to pick up thoughts from Halina by using a photograph Mitch had dug up from their time together.

He jumped to the dock and rain tapped his face as he jogged toward his rental. He couldn't understand why it wasn't snowing. It was sure as hell cold enough. He unlocked the car with a press of a button on the key fob and slid in.

"The more I need all your so-called powers, the more limits pop up," Mitch complained. "Talk about annoying."

"Dude, she's not working with an ideal candidate. Why don't you call me back when you warm up."

Mitch cranked the heater and revved the engine. "Tell me about her finances. Her house is small, but in a prime location. Comparable properties run well over a million bucks. She's driving a nearly new, fifty-thousand-dollar BMW."

"Don't bite my head off, okay?" Kai said, irritation deepening his voice with warning, "—but I don't know. She makes a little over a hundred grand a year at U of W. She rarely gets more than her expenses paid when she lectures. And we haven't been able to find any strange influx of cash. So, unless she's drug running on the side—"

"Or got a big payoff seven years ago . . ." Mitch muttered. That probability twisted the hot knife that had already plunged to the center of his body. As if she hadn't betrayed him enough in their relationship, the discovery of Halina's involvement in this conspiracy was beyond any sick plot he'd witnessed in his criminal law practice.

"Jessica has been combing through Schaeffer's financials," Kai said, referencing another team member. "She hasn't found evidence of a payoff."

"Yet." The car's heater melted the chill from the interior, but not from Mitch's soul. Halina's immersion in this conspiracy meant everyone who mattered to him was living in fear because of something that had involved him. "She will. I have no doubt."

"And I thought I was jaded," Kai said.

"So, basically, you've got nothing I can use."

"You're so welcome for giving up my week and researching this chick fifteen hours a day, dude. Though, I have to admit, the pictures were worth it. Where do you find these women? One is hotter than the next. This one, though . . . she may be my favorite. She's got a really exotic look—"

"Ryder."

"I'm tempted not to tell you what Ransom discovered about her trainer," Kai said, "and let her kick your ass tomorrow morning."

Mitch braked hard before turning out of the parking lot. He idled there, his mind suddenly consumed by this flash of information. "Ransom" was Luke Ransom, another team member and former firefighter who now worked as an ATF agent.

"What kind of pictures?" Mitch asked. "And what trainer? Why do you save all the good stuff for when I'm ready to hang up on you?"

"Just a few photos, really. Considering how long and deep I had to look to find them, I'd bet she doesn't even know they're on the Internet. A couple are from her lectures. A couple are of her with the U of W rowing team. She's given clinics there in the past.

"Luke says her trainer is a retired marine Special Forces guy with a company called Precision Tactical. He teaches everything from hand-to-hand combat to marksmanship. Gives classes out of Halina's gym. Runs clinics around the country for both military and civilian groups. Has a dojo in the back of his storefront where he sells the highest tech weapons and surveillance equipment between San Francisco and Seattle."

Mitch's brow fell. This was the strangest information of all. "That's . . . weird. Halina was so antiviolence she wouldn't let me kill a bug in the house."

"Hello," Kai said, his voice dripping sarcasm. "No one on the team but me had even held a gun before Schaeffer came into their lives. Now look at them—everyone but Seth is a near expert in every weapon from handguns to hand grenades, and even Seth carries when he feels the need. Schaeffer has a way of turning people violent."

That was very true. And Mitch didn't like the way this information was shaping up. He'd walked into this planned confrontation on solid ground: Halina was a traitor. And even while 80 percent of the information still pointed in that direction, he was getting undercurrents of something amiss.

Mitch joined light traffic on the main street, still alive with college students. "She hasn't gone to the store since I've been following her. But she's at the gym every day. What kind of classes does he teach there?"

"Krav Maga," Kai said. "Luke says her instructor is an expert. Learned the techniques directly from Israeli Defense Forces during his time in the military."

Mitch's mind flipped back to his last sighting of Halina in a sports bra and shorts before she'd disappeared into the bathroom, then emerged in a silk slip of nothing before turning off the light for the night. The memory of all those sleek lines, the hint of ab and arm muscles created by subtle shadow, the fullness of her breasts against that dark silk . . .

At a stoplight, he squeezed his eyes shut and shook the image from his head. Yes, she definitely had the toned body of someone training hard. But the radical nature of Krav Maga, an aggressive self-defense technique focused on brutal counterattacks and utilizing a myriad of fighting techniques from street-grappling to judo was extreme, to say the least.

"Ryder, are you just screwing with me again?"

"No, dude, what I'm telling you the woman Dubrovsky was before is very different from the one we're collecting information on now. This shit isn't adding up. Which is why I think I'm getting these bizarre vibes."

"Vibes." Mitch rubbed tired eyes. "Really? You can't give me something better than vibes?"

"She has two weapons registered in Heather's name."

Mitch swerved to the side of the road and stopped. He couldn't drive with all this shit flying. *"What?"*

"Twenty-first-century update," Kai said. "Chicks shoot guns. Even chicks who aren't freaking snipers like Keira. And, I have to say, it really turns me on."

"TMI. I don't want to know what twisted shit turns you on, Ryder." Mitch's fingers had gone white around the steering wheel. "And Halina wasn't any chick. I had *one* nine millimeter seven years ago and she hated that thing. When she found out I owned a gun, she got really weird for, like, days. Kept breaking dates with me. Refused to sleep with me until the damn thing was locked in a safe in the closet. *She* bought the freaking gun safe for me. Wouldn't look at the gun, let alone touch it."

"Aw," Kai said as if he were talking to Mitch's niece, Kat, about a skinned knee. "That really chinked your mojo, didn't it, dude?"

Mitch slammed his palm against the steering wheel—tired, frustrated, confused. "Are you hearing me?"

"What?"

Mitch's temper split. He opened his mouth to blast Ryder, but the guy burst out laughing first.

"God," Mitch said, "you are *such* an asshole."

"It's so much fun to watch you unravel, Foster. I can't wait to meet this chick."

That wasn't even funny. Mitch didn't like the fact that others could see how Halina's involvement in this mess and his impending confrontation with her unnerved him.

"Dude, you'd better be sleeping with one eye open when I get back."

Kai's laughter dimmed, but the humor remained in his voice when he said, "Both weapons are Heckler & Koch handguns. A forty and a forty-five."

Mitch put a hand to his forehead and rolled his eyes. Those weren't self-defense weapons. Those were killing weapons.

"You know how to pick the feisty ones, Foster. I've got to get back to work. Oh, but Luke told me to tell you to keep your smart-ass tongue in check when you talk to her. He said, and I quote, 'Foster can't afford to let her take his last ball.'"

Kai disconnected before Mitch could snipe back. He slammed the phone into the console between the seats with the same thought that had been rolling around his head for weeks. "Who the hell is this woman?"

Mitch passed a retail district near his hotel. He wanted to stop at one of the bars. Wanted to get just drunk enough to take some hot young thing back to the hotel and pound out this building stress. It was dulling his edge.

He glanced at the inviting neon as he passed, his body wound tight. This damn mess had kept him out of circulation for over two months. Way the hell too long for him to go without sex, which was contributing to his shitty mood. Only, he knew it wouldn't help this time. Or worse, after watching Halina for the last thirty hours, sex with a stranger would backfire and his mind would go where it absolutely could not go.

He turned into the Summit Hotel's parking lot, jogged to his suite, and headed to the shower. Turning it on hot, he stripped, set his gun on top of the pile, and stepped directly into the center of the spray. He groaned at the feel of pounding heat on his skin and angled the water so it poured over his neck and shoulders as he tried to stretch out the tension.

Krav Maga. Heckler & Koch handguns. Who the hell knew what else she was up to? Mitch tried to figure out this twist in the puzzle as he washed off. But by the time his temperature had risen to normal, and he'd compared the Halina he'd known to what he knew of this woman who now went by the name Heather, he was convinced he'd never known her at all. That he'd spent their almost-year together in a fantasy-laden fog. There was no other explanation for the drastic differences. At least none that added up to fit the evidence he'd collected.

Shit, he wasn't looking forward to this confrontation. He didn't want to see her. Didn't want to talk to her. Didn't want to fight with her. The more he learned, the more he wanted to stay as far the hell away from her as possible. Yet in the next instant he wanted to get in her face. God, just thinking about what he'd gone through after she'd walked out made him livid.

A sound tugged at his ear. A sound outside the shower.

Mitch's thoughts evaporated and the hair on his neck prickled into tiny needles. The skin across his shoulders rippled with gooseflesh.

He eyed the clothes piled on the floor through the gap between the curtain and the wall, and eased his hand through the space, reaching for his gun.

Gone.

Fuck.

The shower curtain whipped aside.

"Sonofabitch." A mixture of shock and fear zipped up his spine and he straightened, peering across the steamy room and through the water dripping in his eyes. "You don't even have the decency to wait until a guy is dressed? That's seriously chickenshit—"

His next word, "dude," melted in his mouth as his vision cleared and he focused.

On Halina.

Halina. Pointing one of those Heckler & Koch cannons at his chest.

Two

Heather was already breathing hard when she'd finally forced herself to enter the bathroom. Now, she could barely keep from hyperventilating. And her hands were shaking. Maybe she didn't have much cold-blooded killer running through her veins after all.

Or maybe it was just the sight of Mitch Foster, standing a few feet away. Completely naked. Dripping wet.

Holy . . .

Shit . . .

"Mitch?" Heather barely breathed the shocked word before darting another glance around the empty bathroom. *Reality check.*

She refocused on him with narrowed eyes. For some insane reason, her gaze darted to his right shoulder and searched his skin. The sight of that familiar tattoo—the Major League Baseball Association logo inked in red, white, and blue glory—confirmed that Mitch Foster was the man glaring back at her from the shower.

"What in the *fuck* are you doing here?" Her mind cleared and a million questions hit her at once, but she could only get out the most important one. "And *why* have you been *stalking me* for two days?"

"I wasn't *stalking* you, for God's sake." He slammed off the water controls.

Heather startled and realized she'd lowered her weapon. She took aim again, her heart skipping as she stepped back.

Mitch leaned down and swiped the towel off the floor. Before he swung it around his hips, her gaze swept over him again. Just a quick once-over, soaking in the sheer male beauty of his body. That's all it took for his raw sexuality to sink into her consciousness and take hold. Her breath eased out of her lungs with a low sigh of pained pleasure.

"I was watching you so I could find a time, an *appropriate* time, to talk to you, Halina. Unlike some people, who decide to jack a man in the middle of a shower, I have manners."

"You call watching me through my windows at night 'manners'? Have you forgotten how to use a *phone*?"

Hands on hips, he glared at her. *He* glared at *her*.

"And you would have returned my call, right? And we would have met at Starbucks like normal people, right? Had a regular, civil conversation, *right*?" He gestured between them, making a point to stare at the gun. "Because *normal* people always use *silencers* on their forty-fives during civil conversations."

"You're not pulling that lawyer shit with me. You've been watching my house for two damned days. *What* are you doing here? How did you . . . ?" Fear singed her nerve endings. "How did you find me? And *why*?"

One part of her mind scanned for her misstep even as another kicked up in alarm. He stepped out of the shower.

"Don't move, dammit."

"Or what, Halina? You'll shoot me?" A cynical grin cut across his face. Bright white. Gorgeous. He was simply gorgeous— a perfect blend of godly and devilish. "Give me a break. And stop waving that thing around before you shoot me by accident."

"If I shoot you, it won't be an accident." What an ass. "Are you working for him? Are you here to bring me back? Because I'm not going. And what I do next depends on your answer."

His gaze went hard and dark. All humor vanished, replaced by taut anger. "So you *were* working for Schaeffer. Then what,

Halina? It went bad? He turned on you? Like that would be a big surprise."

"I don't have time for this."

She stuffed the gun into her waistband and turned, exiting the bathroom and skirting the bed on her way toward the front door.

Mitch followed and grabbed her arm just before she reached the handle. He jerked her around hard. "Make time."

She moved automatically. A kick to his shin, a jerk of her arm, and she was free. Her stance instantly settled again, hands up and ready for a longer, harder fight. "Bring it on, Mitch, but make it fast."

A familiar edge of excitement lit his eyes. She'd looked into so many opponents' eyes over the years; she recognized the rush of adrenaline. But if she thought too much—about who this was, what was at stake—she might just cave.

His hands came up, palms out in partial surrender, with a half-assed grin of sardonic apology. "Whoa, whoa. Forgot I've got a little martial arts expert on my hands."

"*How* do you know that?" Her mind scattered as the implications of his presence sank in.

He dropped his head and raked all ten fingers through the too-long, deep black mass of his hair, pulling it off his face. The muscles of his biceps and pecs rolled with the movement, and her thoughts pinged in another direction. Damn, he was beautiful. So much more beautiful in person. The newspapers and magazines didn't begin to do his looks justice. High cheekbones and deep-set eyes from his Japanese mother. Straight nose, square jaw, olive-toned skin from his Italian-Irish father.

Her stomach squeezed as a flash of want seared her body.

"Halina"—he looked up, his gaze flat, serious—"Max Gorin and Andre Rostov are dead."

Panic trilled along her nerves, a violin off key. *I'm next.*

"Wh—? How do you know their names?" She couldn't think straight. Could barely think at all. "It doesn't matter. None of this matters."

She reached for the door again. Frantic for air. For space. Her vision doubled and she almost missed, but plunged the handle and jerked on the door. Mitch slammed a hand against the wood above her head and the door shut with a loud pop.

Heather gritted her teeth against rising panic. She hadn't been prepared for this. For *him*. She could fight anyone else. *Anyone.*

"But it *does* matter, Halina. It matters to *me*." He was breathing hard, his minty breath fluttering the hair that had fallen from her bun. "It matters to the people I care about. Because whatever you did seven years ago, whatever alliances, enemies, promises, or lies you made, are now messing with *my* life."

Confusion drained some of her fight. She turned her head and found his lips nearly touching her temple, outlined by a full day of dark whiskers. He smelled clean, a little spicy, all male, all Mitch.

She leaned her forehead against the door. For an instant, just an instant, her mind flashed back to his body, dripping water. Desire flashed through her system, so explosive and hot she groaned. Her eyes closed. She swallowed. That strong body was stretched the length of hers at her back, heat pouring off him.

"No," she said. "That's . . . not possible."

"Tell that to the dozen other people who've been suffering Schaeffer's wrath for the last five years."

Her eyes opened to the warm wood. "I don't know what you're talking about, but it can't have anything to do with me."

"I already know it does, Halina. *That's* why I'm here."

And *that* stunned her silent. Trapped her in a damned-if-she-did, damned-if-she-didn't scenario. But she'd been here before, and her past decisions had kept them both alive.

"I'm sorry, Mitch. I can't help you."

"You can and you will," he said. "You're not going anywhere until you answer my questions, Halina."

"Heather. It's *Heather*."

"I am *never* calling you Heather." His tone ground back into glass. "Fuck that. And *fuck you* while I'm at it. What the hell happened to going back to Russia with your *husband*, Halina? You're a little far from *home*."

Oh, hell.

He wasn't going to let this go. Wasn't going to let *her* go. Heather gritted her teeth. "Mitch . . . step back. Please. I don't want to hurt you, but I will."

She squeezed her eyes shut for just a moment. Long enough to envision one of her sparring partners standing behind her, pushing her to give it her all.

He gripped her arm and pain shot along her biceps. "Hali—"

"Sorry," she whispered, and threw her elbow into his ribs. He grunted and his air released against her shoulder.

She pushed up on her toes, squeezed her eyes closed on another whispered "Sorry, sorry," and slammed her head back, connecting with his forehead. Pain flashed in her skull, but as soon as he stumbled backward, she turned to face him. She waited half a second, hoping that hit would take him to the floor, but he lifted his head, his eyes dazed and hot with anger. Blood trickled down his forehead, making Heather's stomach pinch.

"Mitch, stop," she said. "You have to let me go. You have to stop looking for me."

He gripped the bed's footboard with one hand, pressed the other to his forehead. If she'd thought he was pissed when she'd surprised him in the shower, he was now homicidal. Nostrils flaring, eyes darker than Heather had ever seen them.

"I won't stop following you until I have all the answers to this clusterfuck, Ha—"

She stepped in and kicked out, aiming for his solar plexus. *Sorry, sorry, sorry.* But Mitch saw it coming and grabbed for her leg. Heather pulled the kick, trying to keep from breaking his ribs or—God forbid—stopping his heart, and escaped Mitch's hand. He grunted, flew back, and hit the wall.

Halina turned, hauled the door open, and raced down the stairs. She had to grip the handrail to keep from tripping herself. Her mind raced in every direction. She didn't start thinking in a straight line until she was halfway home.

She sped down the main boulevard, squealing around corners. "Okay, okay, it's okay." She strangled the steering wheel with both hands. "If he was followed, they'll know where I am. They'll come after me, not him. They want me. If he's not with me, he'll be fine."

On her street, she slammed the remote opening the garage, jumped the curb, and skidded to a stop in the driveway. She bolted from her car, door open, engine running. She just needed Dex. He was the one and only thing she'd never leave behind. Nothing else mattered.

She ducked under the garage door as it opened and rushed into the house. Dex was there to greet her as always. Halina didn't pause to snuggle like she always did, but raced past, using her momentum to ricochet off the far wall on the way to her bedroom.

Dex gave an excited bark and followed.

"No, baby, not playing," she said, breathless, as she jerked Dex's favorite blanket off the bed, grabbed a couple of chew toys nearby, and shoved her hand between her box spring and mattress. Her second Heckler & Koch touched her palm, cool and smooth, and she jerked it out and pushed it into her waistband—where the weight of three weapons now nearly took her pants to her knees. At her feet, Dex whined and pranced in place. His nails tapped on the floor and clicked against Heather's nerves.

"Okay, come on." She pivoted and nearly tripped over him in the tight space alongside her bed. "Shit, Dex, *out.*"

He danced out of her way, tail swaying, eyes bright. She rushed into the garage and ordered Dex to load up with a breathless "*Zagruzka.*"

He beat her to the car and jumped in the back. Heather slid into the front seat, slammed the door, dropped her three weapons into the center console, and jerked the transmission into reverse.

A dark car swept in from the street like a rabid raven, screeching to an angry stop and blocking Heather's driveway. She slammed on the brakes, Dex slid along the smooth leather backseat.

Her stomach plummeted. "No." She slammed her hand against the steering wheel. *"No!"*

A low growl vibrated in Dex's throat.

"Dammit." She pushed the gear into park and left the car running. If she had to, she'd smash that rental to get out of here without him. "Dammit, he doesn't understand."

And she couldn't make him fully understand without risking everything.

By the time she'd opened her door, Mitch was rounding the hood of his car. The combination of moonlight, streetlights, and headlight side beams turned the rage on his handsome face into shadows of menace. Skin taut, brows pulled low over fiery eyes, he advanced up her driveway. He'd pulled on a T-shirt, jeans, and running shoes, but hadn't bothered to fasten the jeans or tie the shoes.

"Don't pull any of your self-defense shit on me, Halina, because I won't hold back from hurting you this time." His voice was as threatening as Dex's growl. So much fury rasped through his tone, the hair on Heather's arms rose. "And don't even think about pointing a gun at—"

Dex launched into a ferocious barking fit. His attack bark, enraged and vicious, included glaring teeth and guttural snaps that made even Heather flinch.

Mitch froze midstep. His gaze darted past her and held on the car. She didn't have to look to know Dex was clawing and snapping at the windows. She'd trained him. Hours and hours of training, just like her fighting. And her shooting. She should have spent more time developing emotional barriers to Mitch. Would have if she'd thought this confrontation was ever a possibility.

"What the hell is *this,* Halina?" he demanded from several yards back.

"Stay away, Mitch, or I'll open the door." She kept a grasp on the handle, though she had no intension of releasing Dex.

"Who the hell are you?" He jammed his hands on his hips. "You're acting like a goddamned Russian spy."

The taunt created a dull, dirty ache in her chest, as if she'd been stabbed with a rusted knife. But even she was having a hard time not thinking of herself as Halina since he'd shown up. As the deceitful Russian who'd come from a murky past.

She held up a closed fist. Dex's bark ceased immediately. A few residual mewls rolled out of his throat before he went completely quiet and still. He remained sitting tall in the backseat, his gaze burning into Mitch through the slobber-smeared rear window.

"I don't know what to think about you anymore," Mitch said. "All the lies. The hiding. The secrets. Everything that happened back then. Everything that's happening now. I swear to God, Halina, I'm seriously reaching here. I've seen my share of crazy shit and I've discovered my mind can bend in ways I used to think would make it break, but you"—he tossed his hands in the air—"I don't get."

Heather glanced at the neighbor's windows. "Shh. You're going to wake the whole damn neighborhood."

"Your dog has already done that, or did you miss the whole Cujo scene?"

"You don't have to get me." She spoke slow and steady in hopes of holding herself together. "And I don't have time to explain myself to you."

She turned for the car. In her mind, she was already out the driveway, on the freeway, headed toward the storage unit. She'd have lots of time to get this mess straight in her head once she was on the road.

"Halina." The hard edge to Mitch's voice stopped her from pulling the door open. "I know you were a scientist for the Department of Defense when you told me you were working for Georgetown Medical Center. I know you worked under Gil Schaeffer at DARPA before he became a senator."

Regret stabbed her chest, but it was nothing compared to the fear taking over, making her shake. Overwhelming her like it had in that last month with Mitch, when she'd made all those drastic decisions. Memories she'd learned to suppress rose to the surface and she was suddenly reliving the nightmare of working at DARPA. The night closed in, pressing on her lungs, making it hard to breathe.

"Mitch. It's over. We can't go back. None of that matters now. You have to stay away from me."

"Staying away stopped working about a year ago. Whoever you're hiding from up here isn't just after you. They're after me and my sister and an entire group of firefighters who have become my friends. A group of firefighters who were exposed to classified chemicals in a government warehouse fire. Chemicals we've traced back to Schaeffer and DARPA during your time working there."

The chill air cut through Heather's clothes. Her brain worked crazily to put all this information into the framework of what she knew, which, up to this moment, she'd believed had been everything.

"I . . ." She was lost. Blind. Dropped into a black hole, feeling for an exit. "I don't understand."

"Neither do we. What we do know is that with Rostov and Gorin dead, Schaeffer will be coming for you. You're the last of the three scientists working on his project left alive now, Hali. You may have lived here peacefully for a while, but he needs you to finish it."

No, he needed her research—not *her*. And he wanted even more than that. He wanted the only leverage she had to keep Mitch safe. "I wasn't involved with their project, but I do need to leave."

"Don't give me that shit," Mitch yelled. "And you'd better not try serving it up to Schaeffer either. He's not a forgiving man."

"My lifestyle is a testament to Schaeffer's lack of mercy, Mitch."

"And I want more answers, Halina. For *me*. I want to know why you lied. I want to know why you walked away seven years ago. I want to finally be able to put you behind me."

A sound staggered from her throat. Her chest ached as if her trainer, Tommy, had suckered her with a roundhouse. Tears burned her eyes. Anger and pain and loss knotted into something explosive.

Don't. Don't. Don't. Don't lose it.

"Now, *that* I can help you with." She dragged in air. Pushed it out. "Good-bye, Mitch."

Halina turned away. A split second before she pulled the car's handle, a shadow moved in the corner of her eye. She turned her head, caught the reflection of something silver near the garage door. It flashed in her eyes then cleared, leaving the sight of a metal semiauto aimed at her head.

Instinctively, she pivoted toward it. Toward the man holding it. A stranger. Late forties, Caucasian, rugged facial features, dressed in all black including black gloves and black knit cap. His crisp, bright blue eyes had a cold calculating quality that made Halina's skin chill.

"Don't open that door, Beloi." His voice was low, commanding. But it was the use of her given last name, a name she'd run from for decades, that tugged her dark side forward. "Or the dog dies before he reaches the ground."

Dex's snarl rolled over her from behind, raising the hair on the back of her neck. Every one of her senses rose to the forefront. Every one of her skills crowded into her head, pushing and shoving for the lead.

"There are just too many players in this mess." Mitch's arrogant, condescending voice startled Halina. She'd completely forgotten he was standing only yards away. "I can't keep all you idiots straight. Now, *who* the fuck are *you*?"

"Don't move, Foster." The stranger's gaze never left Halina and an ironic smile twisted his mouth higher on one side. "What an asshole, huh? Comes here after years of screwing around and starts making accusations and issuing orders. Then, just to twist the knife, he tells you he wants to put you behind him?" The man tipped his head, narrowed his eyes, and softened his voice. "You want me to put a bullet in his brain for you, Beloi?"

The chill along Halina's skin turned icy and slid deeper. She darted a look to her left, found the stranger holding a second weapon on Mitch.

A double-fisted shooter? Tommy had never trained her to defend against this. Against every other freaking unearthly scenario—but no, not this.

Her mind shifted between the weapons, gauged their distance, the shooter's height, his aim. For a split second, she got into his head, considered his agenda, his goal, his focus.

She didn't want to do this. But she didn't have a choice, did she?

Dex had started barking again, scratching and biting at the window, trying to break free of the glass.

"Who are you?" she demanded.

"Just what I was going to ask," Mitch said. "Last I heard, Schaeffer was brain-dead. So who the fuck sent you?"

Halina's thoughts slipped off her attack strategy. Her gaze darted toward Mitch. "Brain-dead?"

The gunman laughed, his bright eyes sliding toward Mitch for less than a second. "You're so deep in the doghouse, dude. You probably want to shut your mouth now." Then to Halina, "He's had all this time to find you, but he shows up now, when you're the only one left. The key to a decade-long, multibillion-dollar project.

"Think about where he's been all this time, Beloi. Think about what he's been doing. And with whom. Then he shows up, *poof.* 'You'd better do this. You'd better not do that. And while I'm at it, I want to make sure I can forget about you for good.' What. A. Cocksucker.

"Who is he to treat you like this is your fault? He's fighting for himself, Beloi. Don't think he won't leave your ass in the dust when he gets what he wants, kid."

"Shut the fuck up." Mitch's raspy warning grated over Halina's skin. She cast an uncertain glance toward him. His face was pale, his eyes wide in distress. In *fear.* This mysterious attacker knew a hell of a lot of secrets—both hers and, evidently, Mitch's.

His gaze darted to her. "You *know* I thought you went back to Russia. You *know* I—"

"I'll just override you. He'll always listens to me over anyone else." Halina turned toward the suitcase he'd brought in for
her.

He grabbed her arm. "No time for that, *printcessa*. Didn't
you hear the man?"

"Mitch—"

"We'll be out there ten minutes and they'll call it clear." He
stuffed car keys and wallet into his jeans pockets, his gun into
the back of his waistband, pulled his shirt down, and tossed his
jacket over his arm as he opened the door.

"What about Dex?" she asked just as they faced a six-foot-
five man in a security guard's uniform.

"Sorry to wake—" His gaze dropped to Dex. "What's that
dog doing in here?"

"Disabled companion in training." Mitch said the first thing
that came to mind and gave the guy a look that dared him to
challenge.

The security guard returned a skeptical frown. "Go on. Follow the emergency exit signs and stay outside until the fire department clears the building."

He led Halina out by the arm, following the flow of people
as she fastened both the inside and outside ties of her robe.

This was good. A distraction to give him a chance to calm
down. He was on the border of losing it. If he focused on the
pain he'd suffered, the changes he'd made in his life because of
that pain, all he'd lost, missed out on, all because of a goddamned lie, all because she'd been too *chickenshit* to face him
with the truth . . . which he still didn't know . . .

Outside, the cold, wet fog hit them like a wall. Halina tightened her arms around herself and took tentative steps on the
concrete in her bare feet, pausing near the building.

People in robes, slippers, and pajamas clustered in the parking lot. A ladder truck, lights flashing, parked in front of the
hotel. Firefighters in yellow turnouts roamed in different directions.

"Fucking firefighters," Mitch muttered. "I swear I could go
the rest of my life without ever seeing one again."

Beneath his hand, Halina started to shiver. He tossed his jacket around her shoulders.

"Away from the building, people," one of the firefighters called, gesturing toward the parking lot. "Come this way."

"Stay at the back of the crowd," Mitch said. "Dex is dark and low. No one will notice him."

Once there, Halina pulled from Mitch's hold and dropped into a crouch, drawing Dex into a hug. With everyone watching the fire truck—which was doing nothing, along with the milling firefighters . . . fucking waste of taxpayer dollars—no one noticed they had a dog. Last thing Mitch needed was someone complaining about an animal in a non-animal-friendly hotel. Or bitching they hadn't gotten to bring *their* dog. Or, worse, wanting to pet the mutt. Any attention was unwanted attention.

Mitch crossed his arms and faced her. "Tell me, Halina. Why?"

She released Dex and pushed to her feet. Her eyes blazed with emotion, but the night had taken its toll, leaving only a ghostly trace of her beauty. Mitch forced himself to ignore the shadows beneath her eyes, the injury across her forehead, her nearly translucent skin. She'd brought this on herself.

"Maybe, if you were a good guy," she said, her anger showing only in the flare of heat in her gaze, "if you were genuine, if you cared, if you were *nice,* I'd tell you. But you know what, Mitch? You've been nothing but angry and mean. You came here with an agenda, one that was all about you. You don't give a shit what that agenda will cost me."

She took a breath so deep it raised her shoulders. Mitch's chest tightened with anger and regret and more of the self-disgust that was becoming far too familiar.

"So you can go to hell not knowing *why.* I know I hurt you. And you may not believe it, but it hurt me too. It was the hardest thing I've ever done and I've done a shitload of hard things in my life. I told you that night that I was sorry. There's nothing more I can say than I'm sorry. But that will never be enough for you. And it's clear nothing about me will ever be enough for you now. You don't believe anything I say anyway."

Tears spilled over her lashes and slid down her cheeks. She was shaking. And dammit, Mitch wanted to reach for her, hold her. At the same time he wanted to shake her until the words he needed to hear fell from her mouth.

"Fuck you, Mitch," she said, voice strong even pushing through a throat clogged with tears. "You don't deserve answers from me."

She didn't turn and walk away as he expected. She stood her ground and glared at him. Daring him to deny he'd been the worst kind of bastard. To deny he was risking her safety. Her sanity. Her life.

And he couldn't. She knew he couldn't. And she knew he'd hate himself because he couldn't.

Nor could he stand the sight of her tears, and reached out to wipe them. She knocked his hand away in one smooth, practiced move, then turned her back on him—nothing new there—and wandered farther into the darkness, Dex beside her.

Mitch heaved a breath and checked on the unfolding events at the front of the hotel, hands stuffed into his pockets. But there were no unfolding events. Nothing was happening. "What the hell are they doing?"

With Dex standing guard over Halina, Mitch approached one of the firefighters. "Sir," he said, "my wife's sick. Do you have an ETA of when we'll be able to go back in?"

"We're just doing a final check," he said. "Ten minutes."

Mitch slogged back through the crowd. Statements like "false alarm" and "someone pulled the box in the lobby" and "getting a lot of different stories" penetrated his troubled mind, escalating into a vague sense of alarm.

A small yelp sounded at the back of the crowd. The sheer wrongness of it sent dread skittering across his chest. He sidestepped a couple and peered through the darkness in the direction Halina had taken Dex.

She was crouched next to a dark shadow on the concrete and her worried voice cut through the night.

"Dex. *Dex.* God, *Dex.*"

Dread turned to fear.

"Halina." He called to her as he jostled through milling people, trying to get her attention off the dog and onto her surroundings. Her head came up and her light, frantic eyes met his, flooded with a plea for help just as another shadow moved.

"Behind you!" Fear burst at the center of his body and Mitch pushed into a sprint, drawing his gun. But she was too far away. The man behind her, dressed in a black jacket and black pants, slammed a fist to her arm.

Halina turned, grabbed his wrist, and pushed to her feet. She struggled for mere seconds before losing strength. Then she went limp and fell right into the man's arms. It was Abernathy, torn, scabbed lips and all.

Abernathy whipped Halina over his shoulder and threw her in the backseat of an SUV. A gray Chevy SUV. Mitch's mind snapped back to the freeway accident. To the car that had made that insane cut across traffic. "Sonofabitch."

Mitch passed the spot where Halina had been standing and chased the SUV as it fishtailed out of the parking lot. When the vehicle was well out of range, he came to a shaky stop and dragged in air.

He set his stance. "No way, you fucker." Aimed. "She's mine." Fired.

Ping-ping-pop!

The sound cracked the night. His third shot had hit a tire. The car squealed, weaved, but kept driving. Luckily, it moved slower.

Keeping his eyes on the car, Mitch pushed aside the crowd hovered around Dex and scooped . . . or rather hauled . . . the dog into his arms. Christ, he was heavier than Halina.

With his gaze on the SUV's taillights and the sparks jetting from the rim of the blown tire where it connected with asphalt, he shoved Dex into the backseat of the BMW. The SUV was nothing but a shadow and a few sparks by the time Mitch started after him.

Don't think, don't think.

He couldn't think about who had her. What Abernathy was or where he'd been. Mitch just had to get her back.

The streets of downtown Olympia were empty at nearly four a.m., the limping vehicle easy to locate. Mitch closed in on the SUV quickly, but when he was still half a mile behind, the Chevy jerked to a stop.

He gunned the BMW even while Abernathy climbed out of the vehicle, pulled Halina over his shoulder, and ran into a parking lot bordering the harbor.

"No, no, *no.*"

The BMW's wheels squealed into the turn and bumped over a curb on the way into the lot. Mitch scanned for Halina's white robe, the one thing giving him any hope of finding her.

He spotted Abernathy sprinting through a place called Port Park, Halina's limp form jerking on his shoulder. Mitch sped up, plowed over a grass separator in the lot, and nearly clipped the bastard. But he evaded with moves from an obstacle course and disappeared behind a building.

"That fucking Army Ranger's going *down,*" he growled through clenched teeth.

He jumped from the car, gun in hand, and stopped. Breath held, he listened for footsteps. The *plunk-plunk-plunk* of running feet on wood turned Mitch toward the dock.

Fear burned a streak down the middle of his body. If Abernathy got her on a boat, Mitch would lose her. And he *couldn't* lose her.

He sprinted toward the building, adrenaline making his head light. But he had the advantage. Abernathy was injured. Carrying a hundred and something pounds of deadweight. Mitch pushed himself, his strides eating up the planks.

He caught up with them just as Abernathy leaned toward a small aluminum fishing boat. Mitch couldn't shoot the guy without risking Halina, so he did the next best thing—he nailed the metal dinghy with half a dozen shots.

"You're not going anywhere, Abernathy," Mitch rasped between heavy breaths. "Put her down—*on the dock*—and I won't shoot you."

"You won't shoot me while I'm holding her. And you're not the only one with a gun." He moved into a pool of light from an overhead fixture to show Mitch the semiauto against Halina's head. "Back off."

"You won't shoot her," he said, praying the shake in his body didn't transfer to his voice. The sight of that gun at Halina's head flipped something rabid inside him. "She's the key to everything you want."

"I only want her research. I could get that without her; this is just the fastest way. But it's also becoming the most trouble."

"You don't have any other choice," Mitch said, slowly advancing as he spoke. "She destroyed it. She's the only person who can re-create the information. If you kill her, you kill any chance of getting that research. You start over at square one."

Halina moaned. Her arm made a languid arc toward Abernathy's head, but it didn't get anywhere near him before it fell away.

"If you believe she destroyed her research," Abernathy said, "you're a bigger sucker than I thought. Now, *move.*"

"Not going to happen. You're going to have to let her go and take a run at her another time."

Halina was waking up, or trying to. She wasn't a threat to the man holding her, but if she could just move out of the way enough . . . Mitch was a damn good shot, but the first two that had missed the SUV's tire kept him from pulling the trigger now.

Abernathy backed along the dock.

Mitch's heart accelerated. He squinted into the dark behind the guy. There was no freaking place for him to go. Information kept rolling through his head—Army Ranger, Military Intelligence, missions with Quaid . . .

A vision of Abernathy falling into the water, holding Halina like a rescue swimmer to block his body while dragging her to another shore flashed in Mitch's mind as just about the guy's only alternative play. And Mitch would be screwed. He couldn't shoot, couldn't go after them in a boat he didn't have. And going into the water after someone with Abernathy's training was a suicide mission.

"Stop or I'll shoot you," Mitch warned.

The bastard grinned at Mitch past Halina's legs. Then slid his hand up her thigh and beneath her robe. A spurt of fury raised Mitch's blood pressure.

"I'm going to empty my clip into you, bastard. And I'll enjoy every bullet. Halina," Mitch yelled. "Halina, *wake up.*"

"She's out, man. I gave her enough shit to keep her out for days."

But Halina flopped sideways, attempting to struggle.

"Halina, Dex needs you," Mitch called, closing fast and taking aim as far away from her body as possible. "Dex is hurt. He needs you."

A sound gurgled up from her throat and she thrashed in Abernathy's arms. He held on to her, but she threw him off balance just enough.

Mitch's stomach clenched. He squeezed the trigger.

Abernathy grunted. Blood immediately drenched a splotch on his jeans. He glanced down, muttered, "Sonofabitch," and stumbled.

Mitch sprinted for Halina. Grabbed a handful of her robe and jerked. She pulled from Abernathy's grasp and crumpled to the dock at the same time the other man tipped backward. He hit the water flat on his back, a glassy look in his blue eyes, the weapon still in his hand.

Mitch dropped to one knee beside Halina. He kept his gun aimed at the water while searching her body for injury with the other hand, praying his bullet hadn't grazed her. His heart was beating so hard it pushed the air from his lungs. But he found no liquid warmth, no stickiness, just lots of smooth, warm skin. *Thank God.* It was the most beautiful thing he'd ever felt.

"Hali." He gripped her face, darted a sweep over the dark

water's surface. Abernathy should have surfaced screaming by now. But he'd vanished. "Hali, wake up. Wake up for Dex. He needs you."

She didn't stir.

Mitch lifted her into his arms—definitely lighter than Dex—and cast one more suspicious glance across the water's surface before backing off the dock and rushing to the car, just yards away and still running. He dropped Halina in the passenger's seat and scanned the area again, sure they hadn't seen the last of Abernathy.

The drive out of town took longer than necessary as he executed a series of turns, switchbacks, and circles just in case Abernathy had called in help. But Mitch couldn't detect any tails. When the sirens started multiplying near the hotel, he hit the interstate.

He drove with one hand on Halina's wrist, her pulse beneath his fingers, calculating the rate by the dashboard clock. Sixty beats per minute—normal for someone in her physical condition. Her head was tilted toward him and he could feel her breath on his bicep, which also seemed normal. Still, it took a full five minutes before he could catch his own breath.

"That was too damn close," he whispered, his voice shaky.

He took an exit in Tumwater and parked in the dark space between two overhead lights in the lot of a Jack in the Box. Tugging out his phone, he dialed Alyssa.

"What's wrong?" she answered, voice worried but serious, capable, ready to handle anything.

"We were ambushed again." Shit, he still couldn't breathe right. "He got Halina and injected her with something. Some kind of sedative. He injected her dog too. He's a German shepherd, weighs as much as Halina and means everything to her. I have them both, but, shit, Lys . . ." He raked a hand through his hair, panic slicing along his nerves like a razor. "What do I *do*?"

"Are you close to an emergency room?"

"We can't go near a hospital." He didn't know how many were involved yet. Didn't know if Abernathy had called anyone else in. Didn't even know where Abernathy was for sure. "We'd be dead in the parking lot."

"Okay," she said, immediately detecting his frantic state and compensating with calm. "Her heart rate—"

"Sixty."

"Good. And she's breathing—"

"Easy, steady."

"Good. Okay. You can relax, Mitch. Do you know how long it took for the sedative to act?"

"Uh," he reached over and pushed hair off her forehead, resting the backs of his fingers there to feel her temperature. He didn't know why, he just did. "Fast. She fought for maybe thirty seconds before slowing down. Maybe another thirty before she was completely out."

"There are very few sedatives that work that fast. The good news is that I'm pretty sure what he used is relatively safe. If she hasn't had a reaction by now, she probably won't. It just needs to wear off, which should happen quickly. How quickly depends on how much she was given, but she'll be coming around in anywhere between ten and thirty minutes. If she's not, there's a problem and you'll have to reevaluate an emergency room."

"Are you sure? That's she's okay, I mean?"

"Based on what you're telling me, she sounds stable. Tell me about the dog."

"Oh shit." Another burst of panic burned through him. He got out of the car and opened the back door. "I don't know how to check his pulse, he's got so much damn fur . . ."

"His femoral artery, inside thigh."

Mitch felt along the dog's leg and found the pulse. "Damn, it's too fast. Way fast."

"A dog's pulse should be twice ours, so that's good. And his breathing?"

Mitch put his hand in front of the dog's nose. "Also fast."

"That's the way it should be. Enjoy the silence. When they wake up, they'll probably both feel like they've got hangovers. You might want to pick up some Excedrin for Halina. I know you can't get to a vet, so you can get some baby aspirin for the dog. *But* check with Halina before you give it to him, only give it to him if he's in *obvious* pain and only *one* baby aspirin. Got it?"

Mitch leaned on the roof and wiped the sweat from his brow. "Yeah."

"Mitch, are you all right? I don't think I've ever heard you so shaken. Not even when Dad had his heart attack."

No. He wasn't even close to all right. He'd almost lost Halina. *Really* lost her. And after what he'd discovered, he shouldn't give a damn, which made the whole range of emotions even more psychotic.

"Just freaking dandy," he told Alyssa.

"You don't sound dandy. Get your troublemaking butt down here with the rest of us. Your nephew wants to meet you."

Mitch disconnected with Alyssa and spent a long moment gazing at Halina. Damn, he was so twisted with fury and betrayal and desire and hope, he didn't know which way his head was spinning.

"I don't know what to do with you, *beda.*"

Trouble—she was definitely trouble. Always had been in one way or another. Trouble for his body. Trouble for his mind. Trouble for his heart.

Big motherfucking trouble in any language, English or Russian.

He turned his attention to his phone and found yet another hotel nearby. He didn't like the idea of stopping again, but he liked the idea of driving, unable to monitor Halina and Dex, even less. There was no doubt he'd hit Abernathy in the leg. Army Ranger or not, the bastard had to get that wound examined. And he wouldn't go to an emergency room—unless he had a way to get around the hospital reporting a gunshot wound. Like ties with law enforcement or leverage even higher.

Of course, with military intelligence in his background and Schaeffer's contacts at his fingertips, he had both and would be able to maneuver three hundred and sixty degrees.

Unless he was working alone during this blackout window

when he didn't have to account to Schaeffer. That would explain why Abernathy had come after them again instead of sending someone else. And why Abernathy hadn't had backup when he'd tried to take Halina.

Mitch's mind ping-ponged back and forth. He wanted to call someone and talk about it. Hash it out until the adrenaline ebbed and he could close his eyes. But everyone was sleeping—or should be. Instead of pissing more people off, he sent a text to Young, giving him Abernathy's identity and asking for deeper information.

At the hotel, Mitch parked directly in front of the lobby and locked Halina and Dex in the car when he went in to get a room. This time he requested one around back so he could get the car out of sight. And—just because he'd grown paranoid over the last year—he pulled a dime from his pocket and switched the BMW's license plates with those of another car around the side of the hotel before carrying both Halina and Dex into the room.

He laid Halina on the bed and stood there a moment, staring at her beautiful face. He brushed hair off her cheek and forehead and her skin felt like silk beneath his fingers.

"*Beda, beda, beda,*" he murmured, sliding his fingers across one high cheekbone.

She rolled to her side on the bed with a moan, and though the robe was big enough to wrap around Halina twice, the fabric gapped at her chest, exposing the supple curve of one full breast. She shifted her legs and the split in the robe parted to reveal the smooth, toned length of her inner thigh.

And Mitch realized not letting her grab clothes from her suitcase at the other hotel was the most asinine thing he'd ever done.

Six

Mitch stepped out of the bathroom followed by a trail of steam. The hot water had washed away the sweat, eased stress and aching muscles, but it hadn't relieved the tightness in his chest or cleared the memories running through his mind.

Halina and Dex were still asleep, but by the way Halina tossed, that wouldn't last much longer. Wearing his boxer briefs, Mitch picked up his jeans and frowned at them, wishing he had clean clothes. He held them up and smacked at the stains on the knees from kneeling on the pavement to pick up Dex.

Halina moaned and turned one way, then the other. She fisted her hands, turned her head. Sounds of distress ebbed from her throat. Mitch wanted to lie down beside her, gather her into his arms, and soothe her, but knew he couldn't. And just considering it made him want to take a sledgehammer to his head.

What was it going to take to get over her? She was beautiful, but he'd been with more stunning women. She was intelligent and clever, but he'd been with geniuses and Pulitzer prize winners. And although she wasn't showing it now, she could be painfully sweet, but Mitch had been with women who were sweeter than pure honey.

What he hadn't found was the perfect combination . . . at least not with anyone other than the woman lying in that bed. She was funny and fun-loving, adventurous, tough, compas-

sionate. Or at least she could be. She could have been everything. But she'd chosen lies and secrets over him.

"No . . ." she murmured, her voice tight with fear. "No, no,
no."

Mitch's gut twisted and he sighed. "I'm such a sucker, I deserved to get screwed."

He threw his jeans over a chair, sat on the edge of the bed,
and put a hand on her arm. "Everything's fine, Halina." When
she only continued to thrash, he took her other arm and added
pressure to hold her still. "You're safe. Everything's fine."

She quieted, but her breathing continued in hard, quick
bursts. The pulse in her throat throbbed beneath her skin and
all Mitch could think about was putting his mouth there.

Halina's lashes fluttered and she winced. "Mits . . ." She
slurred his name and sweet warmth curled in his gut.
"Mitch . . ."

"I'm right here." As soon as he spoke, she sat up and reached
for him. Her arms slid around his sides, wrapped his back, and
pulled him close. He breathed out, closed his eyes, and braced
her by the shoulders, touching as little of her body as possible.
"Halina, I'm right here, everything's fine."

She rested her cheek against his chest and Mitch stared at the
ceiling, forcing away the soft sensation trying to sneak in. Then
she suddenly pushed back, clutching his arms, panic filling her
beautiful blue eyes. "Dex, where's Dex?"

"Right next to you. He's sleeping. He's going to be fine too."

She turned her head in search of the dog and swayed. Mitch
tightened his grip on her shoulders.

"Are you sure he's okay?" she asked.

"Yes. I made sure."

"Positive?"

"He's just sleeping, Hali. He'll come out of it soon."

Her muscles relaxed. She slid her hands up Mitch's arms and
pressed her head against his chest again. A fine tremor shivered
through her body. Mitch kept his hands on her shoulders, fighting the urge to wrap her in his arms.

"God, I've never been so scared," she whispered. "Not since—"

Mitch waited, anticipating the unveiling of another secret, but she didn't go on. "Not since when?"

"I just remember Dex's weight falling against my leg. Looking down and seeing him collapsed on the ground. Then looking up and seeing you . . . I heard you yell to me, but I was so distracted by Dex. I was slow. I didn't get his hand before he . . ."

She held him tighter.

Her account brought on the same memories, which flooded into Mitch. Into his chest. He gave in to the need to feel her in his arms, and encircled her, holding her tight. He'd already almost lost her—permanently—three times, and after all he'd been through with the team, he'd learned to value every moment in life.

The sight of Abernathy tossing Halina over his shoulder like a doll, that sensation of coming up short when he'd raced for the car even when he'd pushed his body past its limits, had been as terrifying as being trapped in a dream.

"Shh." He stroked her hair. "It's over. You're both okay."

She nodded and turned her face into his neck. She breathed long and deep, the action instantly bringing back memories that flooded his groin with blood. She'd always loved to breathe him in, especially before and after sex. Before, it excited her; after, it soothed her.

And he so didn't need to be thinking about that with her naked beneath the robe, her hands stroking his back, her face warm against his throat. In fact, he didn't need to be holding her like this.

He put his hands on her upper arms, but before he pushed back, Halina kissed his throat. Her nails scored lightly across his back. Desire skittered over his skin in gooseflesh. Then her mouth started moving. Became more insistent and erotic with the stroke of her tongue, up his neck, across his jaw. Her hot breath caressed his skin. One of her hands lifted to his hair, and,

God help him, the only thing that filled his mind was taking her horizontal.

"Hali," he said, his voice husky, eyes closed as he soaked in the sensations he hadn't felt for so long, but that came back with searing clarity, along with the passion that had always accompanied them. "Jesus Christ, Hali, sto—"

She pressed a hand to his cheek and turned his face toward hers. Then her lips were on his. Soft and warm and full and . . . oh-hell-I'm-fucked delicious.

A sound came from his throat as her mouth slid against his and her eyes closed. Why did he even *try* to resist her? Why had he ever *thought* he wouldn't want her now?

Lord, yes, he remembered the feel of these lips. And he had one of those surreal this-can't-be-happening moments. Kissing Halina. Never in his most twisted fantasies had he ever believed he would ever feel her mouth again.

Which reminded him he *shouldn't* be feeling her mouth again.

He pulled back just enough to whisper, "Ah, fuck," against her lips before her hand tightened on his face and her mouth opened. Mitch didn't respond, but didn't pull away. Just groaned in tortured indecision.

Her tongue pushed between his lips, the feel of her penetrating his mouth to seek out pleasure so unspeakably erotic. He gripped her face and opened. Let her stroke his mouth. Oh, she tasted so good. Rich. Sweet. Hot. So hot. And he was so hungry.

Halina's tongue made a hard, savage roll against his, demanding the same in return. And that's when he finally lost it.

The instant he responded Halina was there, giving back as she always had, with double the passion and three times the heat. She pushed up on her knees and wrapped both arms around his shoulders. Her chest pressed against his as she grabbed his hair. The way she moved against him, the way she kissed him, the way she felt in his arms, it was all delectably familiar, tantalizingly unique. She was everything exciting, magical, sensual, and comforting all wrapped into one gorgeous human being.

One gorgeous human being who'd damaged him so deeply, he still hadn't recovered.

Halina sighed into his mouth, the sound so filled with desire and pleasure it pushed his panic button. He pulled away abruptly, fighting for focus.

"Halina, you're . . . you're not thinking straight."

He moved his hands to her arms and pushed her away. Instead of fighting him, she sat back and pulled the tie on her robe. The outside panel fell loose and the panic alarm inside Mitch's head screeched louder.

"You've had a really rough night," he said. "A horrible night."

She reached inside and tugged at the inner tie until the robe fell loose.

Mitch willed himself to keep his eyes on her face. "You almost died and your emotions are all—"

"Shh." She put her fingers to his lips, the touch gentle, but her eyes remained fiery.

When she leaned in and kissed him again, her mouth was insistent. This time, when she wrapped her arms around his neck and pressed her body close, skin met skin. The sensation wiped Mitch's mind completely clean. He couldn't form any thought but the way her nipples puckered against his chest or the way gooseflesh rose on her skin wherever he touched. And he thrived on affecting her, while knowing he shouldn't be close enough to affect her at all.

She pushed him back on the bed and sank onto him until their bellies pressed, her thighs spread across his hips, her sex separated from his only by a thin layer of cotton.

Nothing had ever felt so perfect.

His hands found their way under her robe and caressed the length of her body, shoulders to hips and back. She was slim, strong, soft. He wanted to feel her body moving, rocking and shuddering against his. Wanted to be inside her, claiming her. *Owning* her.

"So good," she whispered against his mouth, then kissed his jaw, his throat, his chest.

Desire burned hotter. It took on a razor-sharp edge. He couldn't think. With every other woman, Mitch had enough presence of mind during sex to recite the Declaration of Independence. Halina made it impossible for Mitch to even contemplate one immediate problem.

Her hands slid down his sides, tucked into the waistband of his briefs—

"Wait, Hali." He grabbed her wrists. His rib cage rocked with each beat of his heart. He was breathing hard, his eyes glazed, his cock engorged and shooting lust through his body. "What . . . why . . . ?"

He was so gone, he couldn't even form a question. Stellar defense attorney material right here. He raised his eyes to the ceiling. Swallowed. He couldn't do this. She wasn't a woman who would play by his rules. Hell, he couldn't even stick to his own damn rules with her.

He pulled her hands to his chest and sat up, carrying her with him. She straddled his lap, white robe parted to show creamy curves he wanted to sink into. Deep into.

He dragged in a breath through a throat so tight with regret, the air rasped. "We can't."

He started to push her off his lap, but she pulled her hands from his grasp, linking them around his neck again. The movement rocked her soft sex against his erection. He groaned, closed his eyes, and dropped his head back, gripping her arms hard. Damn, he wanted her so bad. *So* bad. Worse than any woman in so damn long.

"I know what I'm doing," she whispered. "I'm making a conscious choice." She framed his face with her hands. Mitch cracked his lids. She stared directly into his eyes and the heat there matched the hot pump of blood through his veins. "And *I want you.*"

Jesus, she'd always been impossible to resist. And seven years later, he was still completely helpless against her will. The thought turned something inside him, giving him the strength to grip her arms and push her away.

Abruptly, before he did something he'd regret—or at least more than he'd already done, more than he already regretted—he stood and stepped away from her. "I can't."

Hurt flashed across her face, and the sight tore at Mitch. She sank back on her heels, hands clenched, that damn robe still open . . .

"You *can't?*" Anger flushed her cheeks, but hurt darkened her eyes. "You can fuck a different woman *every week* in San Francisco, but you can't make love to me *once?*"

Shock hit him first but slid directly into anger. Every word held judgment and censure—neither of which he deserved. The anger he'd put on the back burner reheated.

"No, I *can't.*" He fought to hold back the confessions fighting to tumble forward—*because you meant everything to me, they meant nothing; because I loved you, not them.* And managed a lesser, "Because *you're* not *them.*"

She pulled in an audible breath and jerked back as if he'd slapped her. Mitch instantly heard his words in a completely different way, but it was too late to take them back. Too complicated to explain. Her eyes burned with a combination of fury and pain.

"Of course not." She stood from the bed, petulant, and faced him, the robe falling open carelessly at her sides. "I should have realized I'd never be enough for you anymore."

His frown deepened and confusion pushed questions to his lips. Halina had always been more than he'd ever hoped to find in one woman. There was nothing *enough* about Halina, only heavenly *excess.* But this belief was for the best. If she hated him, she wouldn't tempt him into a situation where he'd end up broken again.

His gaze strayed down her parted robe and stopped on her nearly bare sex, hidden by only a touch of darkness, and his mouth grew restless, hungry. Starved.

Why couldn't he just turn off and take her, the way he did with every other woman? Surely if he concentrated hard enough . . . Or why not imagine he was with someone else, the way he sometimes found himself imagining he was with her when he was with another woman?

"I'm not five-foot-nine," she said, growing angrier. "I'm not a double D. I haven't had any cosmetic surgery. I wasn't in the swimsuit edition of *Sports Illustrated*."

Mitch's gaze darted up, eyes narrowed. Knowing he'd had an active social life was one thing. With his high-profile dates, he often showed up in the social section of the paper. He'd occasionally had photos of himself and his date printed in magazines if the woman was remotely well known. But Halina wasn't quoting names; she had intimate details that would have required research.

"And just how do you know—" he started.

She swept past him, the robe flowing open as she walked. His mind took a U-turn and got lost.

Standing in front of the second suitcase Mitch had brought in from the car, Halina shrugged the robe from her shoulders. She met his gaze, her eyes bright with challenge as she let the white velour slide down her arms and drop to the floor.

The air whooshed from Mitch's lungs in a soft breath. His body grew heavy and the strength in his thighs ebbed long enough to make his knees shake. And while he had to use every ounce of brain matter to keep himself from drooling, she just stood, wordlessly taunting him.

She was so . . . gorgeous. She seemed almost ethereal with all that long dark hair flowing around her, all that smooth, perfect skin, those light aqua eyes. Even the bruised forehead couldn't detract from her beauty. Every curve of her body was honed, shaped with training and hours of strict exercise. He knew how much work it took to create each ridge he wanted to devour now.

"Halina . . ." His voice scraped from his throat, so thick with desire it hurt. "What . . . the hell . . . are you doing?"

"I was never up for an Emmy." She started back in on those stupid statistics as she bent to pull jeans and a T-shirt from the suitcase. Mitch found it difficult to swallow, watching her skin slide over sleek muscle. "I didn't earn a law degree from Vassar or a medical degree from Brown. I wasn't the daughter of a Silicon Valley mogul or a congressman or a major movie producer." She stood with clothes in one hand and flicked her wrist in a careless gesture. "I was always just me, no matter what name I used. Too stupid to realize the American dream was a myth for a second-class Russian orphan."

Exactly. I'm just Halina.

Her earlier comment came back to him. But it only blurred that already fuzzy image he'd developed of who she'd become. Halina's emotions had always taken a backseat to the scientist inside her. Rational. Logical. Practical. Sensible. Those had always been the ruling elements of her personality.

But as a criminal attorney, Mitch knew everyone reached a breaking point. And that personalities changed when compressed in the vise of fear and stress.

She turned and strode toward the bathroom with extra sway in her hips and every thought vanished from Mitch's mind. He had to reach for the bedpost just to stay upright.

"So you're right, Mitch. I was never one of *them*. I'll never be one of *them*. And since your tastes have clearly changed, I'll never be enough for *you*."

She stepped into the bathroom. Mitch's head was storming with thoughts, his body a mess of tumultuous emotions and sensations when the door started to close. He moved fast and without thought. His hand caught the door before it shut and he curled his fingers around the edge. Frustration whirled inside him as he shoved the door open. The force knocked her back and she dropped her clothes.

"Mitch, stop it." Her fast breaths blew strands of hair around her face. "You don't want me. Fine. I get it—"

"How *dare* you judge me? Or put words in my mouth? What the *fuck* do you know about my life, Halina?" He approached slowly, knowing he should stay back and yell at her from the door, but drawn like an addict to coke. "You don't know *shit* about who I am now. Or why I make the choices I make. You have absolutely no right to read a few articles in the paper and decide you know all about me. I can tell you right now, I am sure as hell *not* the puppy you whipped back then."

"No, that man had morals," she returned, not the least bit intimidated, which only angered him more. "That man didn't go around screwing women without regard. Or need high-priced toys or notoriety to feel important. It all presents a pretty shallow image from the outside. If I were another attorney or a client, I'd question your principles, your work ethic—"

"Maybe that's how I want it." His voice boomed off the bathroom's hard surfaces. He closed in on her, purposely towering over her because he knew she'd be too damn stubborn, too damn proud to step back from him. And he was right. She stood her ground, her chin tilted up so she could stare him down. "Maybe when other attorneys think I'm off screwing around, they don't work as hard on their case. Maybe that gives me an advantage."

He was too close. Way to close. Her body tossed off heat, daring him to touch. Her seductive scent, pure Halina, challenged him to ignore. Muscles tightened beneath her skin. Her nipples peaked hard just an inch from his chest. Her entire freaking body tested his control. And he wasn't anywhere near strong enough to resist this woman or this situation.

She pushed a hand against his chest and he grabbed her wrist—hard. Too hard. He was too close to his breaking point. No one pushed him like Halina did. No one.

"You've got to be kidding." Her sardonic half smile annoyed the hell out of him. "If you think you're going to tell me that you didn't sleep with those women, that they were all a ploy to get one over on the competition, you can just—"

He jerked on her arm and she fell into him, skin to skin. Lust sizzled through his body. Holding her against him, he walked her three steps backward until her ass pressed against the wall and his cock dug into the supple muscle of her lower belly.

Oh, yes. Delicious counterpressure expanded in his groin.

Knowing she could get away from him but didn't, didn't even *try,* kept pushing him. Pushing him to push her. And push her. And *push* her.

"Fuck no," he growled through clenched teeth. "I'm *not* going to tell you that." He gripped a handful of her silky hair, pulled her head back. "I *did* fuck them. I fucked every damn one because I was *fucking you out of my system.*"

He yelled the confession so loud, Halina winced. Still, she never made one move to get away. For a reason he didn't have the brain matter to figure out, that was *such* a turn-on. While at the same time he couldn't ever remember being this furious.

She stared up into his eyes, startled. And horrified? Or disgusted? He didn't know. His vision had blurred at the edges. His head was so turned around with the need to hurt her like he'd been hurt while hating himself for feeling that need. And all while wanting . . . *needing* to drive inside her, feel her around him, make her moan with pleasure, hear her call his name as she came.

"Really," she said with a strange inflection that read like indifference, but which seemed to cover something else. "Well . . . I don't think it worked."

Her hand pushed between them and slid along his erection. Mitch sucked air. His mind exploded with neon flashes of color. Sensation flooded his body, coiling and flexing muscles automatically.

"Because . . . what's this?" She curved her fingers around his length and stroked him with brutal friction. Mitch's mouth opened, but his throat closed around the sound that should have come. His head dropped back as pleasure burned through his lower body.

"You've been fucking the wrong people." Her dark whisper sounded just before her teeth clipped the skin at his throat. "You should be fucking the person you want out of your system."

By the time blood returned to his brain, she had his boxer briefs over his hips and on their way toward the floor. Mitch realized she'd just conned him not only into making a confession he'd never—ever—intended on making to anyone, let alone *her,* but she'd gotten him so worked up, fucking her until neither of them could think or breathe was all he could see anymore.

Other than his stupidity. And his gullibility. And his weakness. Those all glared.

She hooked one strong, smooth leg around his hip, a taut arm around his shoulders, and lifted herself up his body with ease. Mitch gripped her waist to balance them both. "Halina—"

Her lips brushed his as one hand returned to his cock with one long, slow stroke downward before pushing his head along her wet opening. Front to back. She bit his lower lip gently. Brushed his cock again. Back and forth, deeper and deeper, her hot lips hugging his head. Her wetness licking him like a tongue.

"Ah, Christ," he scraped out, completely absorbed in the way she touched him, handled him.

His mind veered toward the condoms in his wallet. Toward the uncomfortable thought of leaving her to get one. Of the possibility that this would all evaporate in the five seconds that would take.

Which his big brain knew damn well would be a good thing . . .

Another brush of his cock, even deeper. Her body closed around his head, snug and hot, wetting him, the way she used to tease him with her mouth.

Don't . . . Don't . . . Don't . . .

Don't blow it . . .

"*Goddammit,* Halina."

She centered him, then let go and tilted her pelvis, pressing his head fully into the lush heat between her thighs. Joined by her sweet voice going dark and dirty with, "Fuck *me* if you want *me* out of your system."

Mitch completely lost his mind, every thought disintegrating in the explosion of heat. His arm clasped hard around her hips and he thrust. The reluctant parting of her body mingled with a gasp from her throat and the arch of her back. And God, that was so hot. He would have said so but he could barely breathe. Speaking was out of the question.

Her body immediately clamped back down. A tug of frustrated confusion pulled a growl from his throat. He needed more. He needed to be buried. He needed to explode deep inside her. Mitch backed out and thrust again. The anticipation of her surrounding him . . . went unrealized. Again.

"Fuck." His brain resurfaced only long enough to figure out what the hell he didn't have right: the tight squeeze of Halina's eyes and the way her shoulders bunched and her breaths came in short, shallow pants of pain . . .

That's when the ultra-tight feel of her hit him in a totally new way and he realized the hot velvet fist of her body was two sizes too small for him. A streak of panic burned across his brain. "Ah, Jesus, Halina . . ."

He pulled back, regret thick in his throat.

"No." One hand dropped from his hair and rounded his back, pulling him in. "Don't stop. God, Mitch, please. Please, don't stop."

Holy fuck. Lust speared his groin, surged to his muscles and pushed his hips forward. Hard. His cock drove deeper. Her swollen, soft tissues squeezing him again. The unspeakable pleasure crashed through him like a storm wave.

Fuck, fuck, fuck. Don't come, dammit.

Padres suck. Zero-six loss against . . . against . . . who?

The high-pitched sound Halina choked back jerked him from the edge of climax far better than the thought of his beloved Padres' losing streak, because it wasn't a sound of pleasure.

He dropped his forehead to her shoulder, hating himself. Hating his lack of self-control where she was concerned. Hating the wild way he wanted . . . needed . . . *had* to have her, which had only ended up hurting her.

"Hali . . . fuck. Why . . . didn't you . . . tell me?" he asked between breaths. Confusion made him roll his forehead back and forth on her shoulder as if that would help him think clearer. "It wasn't . . . like this . . . before . . ."

"Yes." Her fingers loosened in his hair and her body slowly released tension. She wrapped her arms around his shoulders while Mitch helped keep them both upright by pressing her to the wall with his weight. "In the beginning."

His mind worked in fragments—a thought, gone, nothing, another thought. The realization that she hadn't been with another man in so long it had changed her body flooded him with thoughts he couldn't process, emotions that overwhelmed him, realizations that both answered and created questions.

Fix this, Foster. Goddammit. Turn it around.

Halina lowered her head, took his lips, slipped her tongue between them and found his. Mitch sank into the kiss on a greedy moan.

"Don't stop," she whispered between kisses, lips, bites. "I need it, Mitch. I need you. So badly I can't breathe. I need it the way only you give it."

"You . . . make me . . . *insane*, Hali."

"Come on, baby." Her urgent rasp, edged with such wild need, boiled his blood. "Give it to me."

Impatient, her thighs gripped his hips and pulled. His cock speared her body.

He broke their kiss with a curse and gritted his teeth around a growl. Halina pulled his head back and kissed him again, her hunger so fierce, his mind slipped into a euphoric haze. He melted into the sensations of loving her—the taste of her mouth, the sounds in her throat, the rock of her body.

He held her ass tight, thrusting carefully, each deeper than the last, urging her body to make room for him. Wished they were on a bed where his hands could touch her in ways that made her wet. Where his mouth could reach more places to taste her essence. Where he could stretch her thigh high to ease penetration.

He wanted her all, all at once. Wanted to breathe her, touch her, eat her, enter her all at the same time. Needed to be deep inside her. As deep as he could get. And, dammit, this wall was just not doing enough.

He stepped back, arched the base of her spine over his arm

and found her breast with his mouth. Swirled his tongue around and around her nipple, taking cues from the bite of her nails in his skin. Her body gradually relaxed into the movement instead of tensing against it. She grew hotter with each thrust. Wetter. Looser. Wilder. Until she was moving with him, lifting her hips, then driving them forward. Oh, fuck, yeah. It was coming back to her. And, God, it was good. So damn blessedly amazingly good.

He released her nipple from his mouth. Lifted his head to tell her he was moving them into the bedroom, but she met his gaze, those stunning eyes all smoky and edgy in a way he hadn't seen in so long that his voice caught in his throat.

She held his gaze, repositioned her shoulders square against the wall and made a languid, pushing roll with her body that made her rock, shoulders to hips. His cock pulled almost completely from her warmth, then slid back in with such excruciating languor, he couldn't resist his body's demand to thrust deep, embedding himself at her core.

Her eyes rolled back before they closed on a sound of exquisite pleasure. A sound that urged him toward that climax he'd been stalling. He slowly tested harder, deeper thrusts.

"God, yes," dripped from her mouth with so much pleasure Mitch could taste it.

He struggled back to the moment. He wanted to be looking into her eyes when the pleasure overflowed. But her expression of bliss gave way to something more . . . uncomfortable . . . was the only word he could come up with to describe it— emotionally uncomfortable.

Her eyes closed. "Purge me from your system, Mitch."

He pushed deep into her body and froze. The entire situation realigned in his mind as if someone had pressed a Reset button. They'd gone from the hottest first-step-toward-reunion lovemaking he could have ever imagined back to an angry get-it-out-of-your-system fuck.

Then he realized with cutting clarity that had never really changed. Only his perception had shifted . . . because . . . because when he'd realized she hadn't been screwing around all this time . . . he'd thought . . . *maybe* . . .

God, he was *still* such a damned fool for her.

Mitch channeled his anger and hurt and years of disappointment into his next thrust, holding her tight and driving deep. Halina gasped, bowed backward. Her hands slipped from his hair and clawed to hold on to his shoulders. Even angry, it was good. Even disappointed, it was good. She was so tight and hot and wet . . . and losing himself inside her was *always* so damned fucking good.

"Oh, God," she rasped, head lolling back, dark hair spilling into the air behind her, full breasts peaked and perfect.

"Is this what you want, Hali? All you want?"

"Yes. Perfect." Breathing heavily, she opened her eyes but didn't seem to have the strength to lift her head. "You . . . might finally . . . get rid of me, babe."

He didn't want to get rid of her now any more than he'd wanted to get rid of her then. Which was obviously going to become a real problem. But if a fuck was what she really wanted—a fuck was what she'd really get.

He moved to the vanity and set her ass on the edge. Slid his arms under her thighs and gripped her waist. She braced herself with bloodless fingertips tight over the lip of the counter and questioned him with those beautiful eyes.

"Hali," he said, meeting her gaze, irritation scraping both his heart and his pride. "Don't call me babe."

Surprise flitted through her eyes. She opened her mouth to speak.

But Mitch didn't want to hear it. He was done talking.

He pushed her legs wide with his forearms, purposely baring her. "Open up, baby," he rasped, letting his gaze blatantly rake her tight sex, letting her see him study the sight of his cock gliding from her, glistening. "Give me room to work."

"Mitch . . ."

The plea in her voice made his mouth turn, but all internal satisfaction had vanished. This was physical. And he was pretty damned sure the only thing keeping him hard was the erotic sight of her perfection, bare and swollen and slick as he slid slowly back in, pushing against the tightness until she had every last millimeter of him. Halina dropped her head back, eyes closed, lips parted, complete ecstasy washing her face.

Yes, that's all she'd wanted. His cock deep inside her. His cock driving her to orgasm. Not *him*.

Fine. He'd give her that. As good as he could. She'd never forget him, that was for sure. If he could leave her with a memory strong enough to bring him up in her mind once in a while when she was with someone else, maybe even make her push around a few melancholy what-ifs . . . he'd take it. He'd sure as hell done his share of both.

He shut off his damn mind and let his body go. With his hands gripping the sink, Mitch found a rhythm. A harsh, hammering rhythm that pulsed thrill after thrill through his cock, his balls, his belly, his legs, his chest. Halina struggled to hold the counter edge and Mitch gained almost as much pleasure from that tiny thread of helplessness as he did from the sex. Which was wrong. But this was a fuck, nothing more. So he let his dark side revel.

He leaned over her, sucked the tip of her breast into his mouth, bit down, and raked his teeth over the flesh.

"Oh my God." Halina's walls clenched around his cock, creating even more pressure, more friction. She dropped her head against the mirror and arched, offering her breasts.

They were too wickedly decadent to resist. Mitch lowered his head to the other, flicked his tongue against the tip again and again until Halina whimpered, "Please . . ."

SEVEN

The low, drawn-out plea shot a dark streak of lust to Mitch's cock and he drove into Halina harder. Grazed the flesh of her breast rougher, earning a cry from her open mouth, a deeper arch in her gorgeous body and a harder squeeze from her inner walls.

"Fuck, that's good," he murmured, licking at the red trail his teeth left behind before repeating the torture and thrusting deep to get the full effect of her grip on his cock.

"Ah . . ." Her cry filled him with triumph. Her need pumped power and victory into his blood. "Mitch . . . Mitch . . ." she said between pants. "Please . . . make me come. I need . . ."

Ah, shit. The words sent a blistering shock of lust to his cock and totally screwed up his rhythm. He wiped the sweat from his brow with his bicep.

"Fucking . . . does not mean fast . . . Hali." As if he could hold out. "But you've got me so twisted, I'll give you a hard ride to the finish."

He lifted her hips off the counter, took her hand from the edge, and closed her fingers around the towel bar on the wall beside her. Kissed her hard, sweeping his tongue through her mouth until they were both breathless, and whispered, "Hold on tight."

Gripping her ass with both hands, Mitch pulled her into him while driving forward.

"Oh . . ." Halina's head fell to the side. "Yes."

Oh fuck *hell* yes. She was beyond gorgeous, face flushed, muscles tight, body undulating and thrusting to the rhythm he set. So open, so sexual with one arm stretched above her head to the bar, the other hand digging into his forearm.

Mitch added a bend in his knees and used all the strength in his thighs and ass to drive harder, deeper, lifting Halina and letting her fall back onto his shaft, her body weight adding force to each thrust in the most intense, mind-bending slam Mitch had ever experienced.

"God," Halina cried, every muscle in her stunning body taut. "Mitch . . . God . . ."

Just another minute. He had to hold out just another—

She spasmed around him, gripping him so hard his throat closed. His control snapped. And the orgasm hit him like a tsunami—a wave that had appeared deceptively manageable until it crested into an uncontrollable monster and crashed. The first orgasm exploded at the center of his body and blasted through him.

Her walls continued to squeeze and suck at his cock, drawing him back into a vortex of repeat orgasms where he never quite came down from one before another built and peaked. Built and peaked. Built and peaked.

Until Halina's body had finally relaxed. Then Mitch found every muscle wrung out, every brain cell wiped clean, and every emotion but raw ecstasy shoved way into the recesses of his mind.

Just before his legs gave, he locked his knees and swayed there, using her hold on the towel bar to keep them up.

"Don't . . ." he rasped between breaths, "let go . . ."

Halina's face rested against her bicep, her chest rocking with her own pants. "'Kay."

The aftermath hit Mitch in continuous tingling ripples of contentment, relaxation, and pleasure. He couldn't think, his mind like a downed prizefighter, struggling and stumbling back to the mat with every attempt to get to his feet. The sensations were indescribable. Body-wide. Excruciating perfection.

"Baby," he barely slurred, "I think . . . that was a . . . multiple . . . record . . ."

He'd never had sex that good. In fact, he'd never had multiple orgasms with anyone other than Halina.

Too damn bad it was just a onetime fuck.

A shadow dimmed the sparkling aftermath. Disappointment, disillusionment, self-disgust. It all hovered, far too close. He needed to put space between them now that it was over. Before the emotions washed in. If he was close to her when that happened . . .

He forced the muscles in his legs to engage and hold him up, then gripped her waist to lift her from his half-hard erection. But she leaned forward, melting against him, draping her arms over his shoulders and pressing her face to his neck with a warm sigh across his skin.

The unexpected intimacy took a double-fisted grip on his heart. Soft, deep, intense emotions tightened his chest, and right on their tail, anxiety crawled in. He battled them all away. *Just enjoy the moment.* That's all he had to focus on. And when he gathered her close, she slid into his arms willingly.

As hard as he fought to smother that little light deep inside him, it continued to glow—brighter with each moment she lay sated and content against him. He continued to remind himself not to think. Not to hope. Not to open.

"Are we going to stay like this all night?" she murmured, with no sign of objecting to the idea.

A smile broke across his face. He gritted his teeth and forced it away. "Nice idea, but I wouldn't last more than a few minutes."

She lifted her head and met his eyes. Hers were that smoky, satiated aqua he remembered well from their time together. Despite all his good intentions, the sight pulled an array of memories from his mind—all better left buried. She pressed a soft, slow kiss to his lips, whispered, "Thank you," and dropped her head to his shoulder again.

Dual streams of hot and cold ran down his chest. *Thank you?*

What the fuck . . . ? Yes, exactly that . . . a fuck. Thank you for the great fuck.

Nice. Definitely time to untangle.

"Ready to move?" He didn't wait for her answer before lifting her. And then immediately froze as an unfamiliar sensation encompassed his shaft. A very wet, very warm, very . . . *real* sensation.

"Oh . . . *shit*." His gaze went distant. He'd forgotten. His stomach rolled with that hollow pre-puke ugliness. "Fuck, fuck, *fuck.*"

"What?" Her head came up, hand tightening on his shoulder as her gaze scanned the room then returned to his face, worried. "What's wrong?"

Mitch turned to rest his back against the wall. He was suddenly sweating again, and this time not from pleasure. A tremble started in his arms and not from muscle fatigue.

What the hell was wrong with him? He'd never made this mistake. Ever. *Ever.* Not even when the woman swore up and down she was on birth control, had every negative STD test known to man, and showed him a negative AIDS screening. He always, always, *always* wore a condom.

With every woman.

For seven goddamned years.

"Mitch." She pushed back and took his face in her hand, giving him a quirky little smile that made his heart fold. "Stop messing a—" She stopped when she saw his face. Her smile fell away, replaced by a deep frown. "What's . . . ? Are you okay?"

"Hali . . ." He'd sworn he'd never say this to any woman. But this wasn't any woman, this was Halina. Only, that didn't make it okay. It would have been better than okay seven years ago. It would have been everything he'd ever wanted. Now, it wasn't the least bit okay. Now, it was a catastrophe. And that killed him. Absolutely fucking killed him.

"What?" Halina said. "What is it?"

He licked his lips, hoped for a last-minute miracle, and looked her in the eye. "Hali, are you . . . using birth control?"

A fleeting second of confusion filled her eyes before the realization hit. And in that moment he knew the answer was no. Just as he'd thought. He'd known the answer before he'd even asked. But he'd had to ask.

"Fuck me." He closed his eyes and dropped his head back against the wall, but immediately lifted it again and met her gaze. "Hali, I'm so sorry. I don't know . . . I'm *always* careful. I always, always—"

"Mitch," she said softly. "Put me down."

She pushed off his shoulders, and Mitch lifted her then set her down. As soon as her feet touched the floor, she turned for the door.

"Hali, hey, Halina." He caught her by the waist and held on to her before she broke away and freaked out. He'd figured it out first, shouldn't he get the first freak-out rights? "Wait. Let's talk about this—"

"Mitch, I just need . . ." Her voice was breathy, unsteady. "Can I have just a minute to think? I need some space."

If they were in a better situation, he would have ribbed her about using classic letdown lines and suggesting she come up with something more original, like, say, *"Oh, by the way, this is my husband, and we're moving back to Russia . . ."*

Now that was original.

"Halina, this might not be as terrible as it seems." It took every ounce of second-rate Pollyanna in him to conjure this crap to keep her calm. And he loathed what was coming next. He never talked girl-stuff with women. The topic was off-limits. But he heard himself say, "Where are you in the month? I mean, when was your, you know, your period?"

Halina's fingers dug into his biceps, her body still straining toward the door. If he released her, she'd spin like a top. Her throat rocked as she swallowed and a small self-deprecating smile turned her mouth. But when she looked up at Mitch, she clearly wasn't happy or even relieved; the expression was ironic, cynical. "Exactly two weeks ago. And I'm as regular as a god-damned clock." She huffed a breath that was probably meant to be a laugh. "I can't even seem to handle something as simple as safe sex right." She glanced up, her light eyes sparkling through her lashes, her expression swamped with regret. "I'm sorry. I . . . was obviously . . . carried away. Please, Mitch, give me a minute."

She pushed back and out of his arms, disappearing into the bedroom.

Mitch stood there, his stomach a mix of fire and ice. He closed his eyes and clenched his teeth as anger pushed in to smother hurt.

Give her a minute. Just give her a minute . . .

A million thoughts floated in his head like bubbles, totally random and illogical.

How would they possibly handle the logistics of sharing a child? She had abilities; did that mean their child would have them? If she fled to Russia, how would Mitch ever get the child back? Worse, could her family claim the baby as theirs? Hide the child, and Halina, from him?

Christ, *him* with a *kid*? The absurdity of it had to be the reason his chest felt like it was filled with champagne.

He put both hands to his head. "Stop. Relax. Jumping way the hell ahead of yourself here."

He wandered to where his underwear lay on the floor and picked it up. He leaned against the sink and hung his head, trying to clear it. But visions of Halina filled his mind. Memories of that freaking mind-destructing sex made blood rush south.

What a damned idiot. He'd known fucking her wouldn't get her out of his system. It had done just the opposite. He'd relapsed with one taste. Now he either had to go cold turkey, satisfying the never-ending craving with cut-rate substitutes, knowing he'd never find satisfaction, or become an addict again and risk having his source cut him off without warning, as she was prone to do.

Whose grand idea had sex been, anyway? He couldn't remember now.

Not that it mattered. It was over. He needed to focus ahead. On disaster control.

He cleaned up and entered the bedroom. Halina lay on her side facing away from the bathroom, stroking Dex where he still slept beside her. She'd dressed in shorts and a T-shirt and her gorgeous legs drew Mitch's gaze.

Stop, shithead.

Reluctantly, he pulled his gaze from the smooth expanse of skin and stepped into his jeans. He tried to get a glimpse of her face to gauge her state of mind, but couldn't because she was turned away.

Resigning himself to the fallout, he rounded the bed and sat on the edge, facing her. She sure as hell didn't look like she'd just had deliriously great sex. She looked exhausted and worried, the way a woman on the run should look. And suddenly, it wasn't just Halina's life he had to worry about anymore, as if that wasn't enough. Now he had a seed of possibility lodged in the back of his mind.

She cleared her throat and stared at Dex's ear as she drew the fluffy thing between her fingers.

"I'm really sorry . . . I . . . that was really . . ." she said. "I don't know what the hell happened to me . . . I just kinda . . ."

"Lost yourself?" he offered.

The fact that he could still do that to her thrilled him far too much. And he still found the sight of her flustered too freaking adorable, too.

She let out a breath, pressed her lips together, and shook her head. "Listen, beyond chalking it up to a thoughtless mistake, there's really nothing to talk about yet. And we've got too much going on in today's reality to be worried about the what-ifs of several months down the line."

Mitch chuckled, relieved she hadn't flipped and started ranting about options that would have crushed him. "*There's* the logical, sensible Halina I remember. Reassuring to see signs of her."

Halina lowered a brow at him, but the quirk of irritation immediately dissipated and her expression softened. "I'm exhausted, Mitch." She closed her eyes. "Just give me a couple hours to sleep and I'll try to answer some of your questions about . . . before, okay?"

The sex may have been only physical—for her—but it still

seemed to have bridged some kind of gap between them if she was willing to talk to him. Which was good because there was something related to *today's reality* and their lack of birth control they needed to discuss.

"Fine, but before you go to sleep there's one thing . . ."

Her lids cracked and those light aqua eyes twinkled at him through black lashes. His gut twisted with resignation. He had to at least mention it, even if he didn't want her to utilize it.

He shut down his emotions, much the way he did when he walked into court. It was easier to do when she didn't have that body of hers plastered to him. "I'm agreeable to leaving the topic alone until you know for sure, but because this is a time-sensitive issue, I wanted to bring it up now."

A whisper of a smile tugged at one corner of her lips. "*There's* that negotiating, bargaining attorney I remember. Reassuring to know the bully hasn't taken complete control."

He laughed softly, but the topic on his mind killed any humor he might have felt. Better to just get it out and let it go.

"I don't know a lot about it, but I've heard there is a pill, one that has to be taken within—"

"Forty-eight hours after unsafe sex." She came fully awake and popped up on her elbow. Her eyes turned an ice-cold shade of blue and narrowed. "The morning-after pill. Is that what you want, Mitch? You want me to take a pill so you can forget this ever happened? Are you afraid a child would strap you to me? Or are you just horrified to have a child with someone like—?"

"Stop." He pressed his fingers to her lips, closed his eyes to gather patience and shook his head. "That is *not* what I said. And that is *not* what I'm implying. I don't know where the hell you got this shitty self-image, but those are your own sick projections, not mine."

She pushed his hand away, but didn't speak.

"No, I *don't* want you to take that pill," he said. "But I don't want you to feel trapped either. And as much as I would be willing to shoulder one hundred percent of the responsibility, it's impossible for me to imagine you giving it to me even if I offered. It's your life, too, Halina. I wanted to make sure you knew the choice existed before the window passed. That's all."

She scanned his face and her expression shifted to awkward discomfort. "I'm sorry."

"That's a solid no to the pill, then?"

"Yes."

Mitch released tension he hadn't realized cramped his shoulders and let out a breath. He took her hand and kissed the back. "Get a couple hours' sleep and we'll talk."

Halina cuddled her face back into the pillow, curved an arm over Dex's chest as if she were hugging a huge stuffed animal, and closed her eyes on a sigh.

Mitch, anything but settled, pushed from the bed and pulled a Heineken from the fridge. Dropping into the lounge chair, he picked up another pad of hotel paper, another hotel pencil, and turned his mind toward the uncomfortable subject of Schaeffer, Abernathy, and how the hell to get them both off the team's back.

Halina closed her eyes and pretended to sleep as a flurry of emotions hammered her. Man, she was making mess after mess after mess of this situation.

Everything was so controlled when she lived alone. She kept a rigid training schedule, ate well, slept well. She meditated, read, worked. For relaxation she sculled on the lake, rock climbed at a local gym, or took a day trip with a few other climbers to the state park nearby. And she spent a lot of time with Dex—training, walking, running.

Nothing ever went wrong. She never got sick or hurt. She never had conflicts with friends. She didn't have family or lovers to cause stress. Her work life was basically autonomous. A job she would have to call in to soon with an excuse for her absence. An absence she didn't know whether to qualify as temporary or permanent.

And after only hours with Mitch, she was falling apart.

She'd forgotten birth control, for God's sake! Okay, so it had been a really long time since she'd had sex. And okay, she'd really, *really* wanted . . . needed . . . Mitch. And, wow, okay, they'd gotten amazingly, beautifully, wildly out of hand. But . . . *still*.

Pushing him to keep the encounter physical had been . . . heart wrenching. She'd never expected him to slap his heart on his forehead. Couldn't fathom how he could have held on to those damn romantic notions after what she'd done. But the emotion she'd seen flash in his eyes had frightened her—on several levels. The final straw had been witnessing the wheels of his brain turning in that bright gold-green gaze as if he'd been trying to fit her into a mold he could understand.

She didn't want him to understand. The risk was too high. If she had to sacrifice his opinion of her to keep them both safe, so be it. She only had to get through the next few days without compromising the safety net she'd spent the last seven years protecting. Then he'd leave and life would go on—for both of them. End of story.

Unless . . . she got pregnant.

Halina blew out a breath and pressed her face further into the pillow. The irony of this situation ate at her. She just didn't have the capacity to appreciate the threat of unplanned pregnancy with the man she'd once hoped would father her children.

But this was not that man. And while Mitch's 100 percent responsibility offer was a sweet gesture—probably meant to keep her from going off the deep end—it was hardly realistic. As soon as he saw the crimp a child would put in his love life, his leisure time, his travel plans, that offer would be whittled way down.

And that assumed Halina could come out of hiding. Which she couldn't fathom.

She cracked her lids and watched him. He hadn't put his shirt back on and sat there with his jeans undone and all that smooth skin pulled tight over a trim, fit torso and muscular chest. Her gut expanded with renewed desire just thinking about how all that muscle and skin had felt against her. Hot and hard and . . . perfect. She couldn't hold back a moan at the memory and covered by shifting on the bed.

Mitch's bright eyes lifted from where they'd gone distant on some spot near the floor and watched her. His feet were propped up on another chair and crossed at the ankles. He held the end of a pencil between his lips with a pensive expression.

Just looking at him made her want to sigh. Made her want to crawl down to the end of the bed and right into his lap. She clenched the pillow in both fists and squeezed her eyes closed.

There, in the darkness, the sensations of her body took over. Her sex throbbed from the violent friction after so many years of disuse. Halina's gut burned with passion as she relived their frantic hunger for each other. And since that one time was the only time she'd have with him again—especially given the scare that had resulted—she let her mind drift back over every detail and smiled into the pillow.

That happiness or contentment or whatever it was seemed to allow her to relax into other memories. Memories from years ago she kept buried. The two of them cuddling on the couch beneath a blanket. Mitch playing keep-away with the remote. A popcorn fight in the kitchen. A weekend with his family getting teased by his brothers. So many smiles. So much happiness. Such deep love. A sense of completion. Of finally belonging.

As Halina relaxed into the delicious buzz of sexual satisfaction and her heart swelled with the love she'd never lost for the man across the room, images drifted through her languid mind.

By the time she recognized the color-washed tones over the scenes, or the scenes splitting into two distinct mini-movies playing side by side, she was already immersed in the visions.

She fought to escape. Her limbs struggled against unbreakable bonds and her muscles screamed with tension, burned with exertion, yet she didn't move. There was no escape. She knew this. She'd tried so many times before.

On the left side of her mind, the images shimmered in a red hue and played out a dark, tense scene. Mitch and several shadowy figures were present, the others there to capture Halina and kill Mitch. She couldn't detect any sign of herself in the vision, but knew for a fact she was there, somewhere. Outside the field of view or hidden among the shadows?

On the right side, the images took on a blue hue. Mitch was there again. He would be, of course—these were his futures. But Halina was absent—not just from the scene, but from Mitch's mind. From his heart. As if she'd never existed. He was over her. Finally, truly, completely over her.

Mitch mingled at some type of high-end party where all the men were dressed in tuxedos and the women in gowns. A young woman hung on his arm. A woman of such beauty, she drew every gaze in the room, men and women alike. Her deep honey-colored hair flowed over her shoulders in soft waves, and her burgundy gown reached the floor in a clinging, translucent slip of sparkles.

Mitch wound his arm around her petite shoulders, whispered in her ear, and kissed her neck, making her eyes close in pleasure and her hand fist in his jacket.

No!

Fear, frustration and pain mounted until she was boiling inside her skin.

Her gaze pulled toward the red scene where two, maybe three men surrounded Mitch. Halina's heart hammered against her breastbone and thudded in her ears. She couldn't hear Mitch speaking, but his mouth moved and he gestured wildly as if he were trying to make a desperate deal. The others continued to close in.

Impending doom crept through her body. *Run, run, run!*

One of the men raised his weapon and fear swamped Halina in one scalding wave. *No! No, no, no!*

She couldn't stand to watch. Couldn't bear to see him killed again. Couldn't live through the sight of his life draining from his body while he lay there helpless on the ground bleeding out.

Halina's attention shifted to the blue scene, where Mitch and his . . . woman . . . had drifted into a secluded hallway. Where they talked and laughed and kissed. The two were young and happy and carefree, both with so much life ahead of them.

The woman pulled him into a bedroom at the end of the hall with seductive, heavy-lidded eyes and a smile that promised ecstasy.

Hell, Halina could *not* go into that room. She simply could not watch him . . .

She tried to avert her gaze, but it stopped in the only other location available—the red scene. There, Mitch held up both hands, fear replacing grim hope. His mouth moved and Halina read the offers, bargains, deals, spilling off Mitch's lips in an effort to save her life.

Behind him, a battered and bloody version of herself crawled from one of the shadows, her hand pressed to her side, face tight in pain. The replica's mouth moved with pleas for Mitch's safety, for a trade—spare his life, take hers. In the vision, Mitch pivoted toward the battered version of herself . . . and Halina knew what was coming.

She glanced at the blue zone and found Mitch in the bedroom with the beauty who'd already stripped down to a bra and thong and was now dragging Mitch's shirt off while they kissed.

With agony ripping her apart, Halina returned her attention to the red zone just as a bullet exited a gun. It exploded in slow motion—the muzzle flash, the gunpowder cloud, the launching bullet. Halina's damaged clone, still crawling as if in too much pain to stand, screamed at Mitch. Too late. The bullet pounded Mitch in the back. He arched, head thrown back, mouth open in a scream.

Nooooo! Her own scream shattered the vision. Images exploded into millions of tiny colored shards of glass and shot through the darkness.

"Mitch! No. Mitch, *no!*" Her scream pierced her own ears and she sat straight up in bed. She couldn't breathe, couldn't see, couldn't hear anything but her own scream.

The hum of another voice faded in. Far, far away at first. Nothing more than a murmur underwater. She couldn't gather enough air to yell again, and the vision was gone now, but her whole body continued to shake. Halina pulled her arms tight to her chest, dropping her face into her hands.

She did what she always did when these came: She focused on her breath. One breath in, one out. One in, one out. But she hadn't had a vision like this in years; it was different from the one she'd had in the car with Mitch earlier. The ones after sex were always deeper, more detailed, and showed two sides of a future farther forward in time as opposed to one negative flash of the immediate future.

The terror from the most recent visions seemed to take forever to fade. When her hearing returned and her mind settled, she realized Mitch's arms were wrapped tightly around her, his body rocking her gently, murmuring at her ear.

"Just a dream." His voice was smooth and deep and delicious. "It's over."

But it wasn't a dream.

And it wasn't over.

The room phone rang and Halina jumped, her heart tearing out of her chest.

Mitch tightened his hold. "Shh, just the phone." He reached for it and Halina melted against him again. "Yes, we're fine," he said into the phone. "A bad dream. Yes, sir. Thank you."

Mitch hung up. "Just the front desk."

Halina wanted to dig a hole to China, learn a new language, and start a new life so dark Mitch would never find her. At least then she would forever be able to keep him safe. But with Mitch holding on like this, she was tempted to close her eyes, tighten her arms around him, and cling. It wouldn't be difficult to pretend her visions were meaningless dreams. Not when she was in his arms.

She drew a deep shuddering breath that scraped her sternum like broken glass. Which brought back images of shattering shards glittering at the end of her vision, and Halina knew she could never risk Mitch's life.

He brushed her hair back and cradled her face, so careful, as if she were precious. "Bad one, huh?"

This was classic Mitch—the Mitch she'd known all those years ago. He'd always seemed to own an endless well of patience and compassion and love inside him. It was one of the things she'd missed most. What she believed had made her so lonely after she'd left. If she hadn't been so deeply connected to him, she would have fared better on her own.

But that wouldn't change. Because those visions she'd seen had been the good and bad of his future. She knew from experience they were based on the decisions that were made now. Make the wrong choice, Mitch would die. Make the right one, he would live happily and, evidently, sexually fulfilled. They were both losing scenarios for Halina, but again, that wouldn't change either.

She might not know exactly when her visions were coming, she might not be able to control them, but she knew with absolute certainty they were accurate.

And that made her future impossibly agonizing. Unless . . .

"Is . . . is Schaeffer really brain-dead?" she asked.

Mitch's hands continued to travel over her, but she didn't need comforting anymore. He caressed the back of her neck. Slid a hand along her waist. His lips pressed against her temple and the breath he released carried the faintest moan of desire.

"He's in a coma," he said. "But everything about that man is a lie. I don't trust anything unless I see it with my own eyes, and his hospital room is off-limits, guarded by Secret Service."

Halina had a hard time paying attention to the answer with him kissing his way across her jaw, and down her neck, spreading tingles across her skin.

"I have condoms," he murmured, his hand sliding under her shirt and up her side. "If you want to . . ."

God, his touch felt *so* beauti—

His words clicked. She pulled back and gripped his wandering hand. *"What?"*

"Baby, you have to admit, us together—that was crazy-amazing." Lust created a dark gold haze over his eyes and his voice lowered. "I'm already hard again."

"No . . ." Her entire body tightened with a sudden renewal of desire. Panicked she'd have another logic lapse, Halina slid toward the edge of the bed to stand. "No, no, no, Mitch—"

He didn't let her get two inches before he hauled her back. "Is this about—?"

"Mitch."

She turned her gaze on him. He was looking at her with a

distant light of hope, making so many of her own dreams and beliefs rise from the shadows to taunt her.

He was the only man she'd ever wanted. Ever loved. The only man who'd ever believed in her, encouraged her, or treated her like an equal. The only man who'd made her feel worthy of everything she'd ever earned. And so much more.

For all those reasons, she scraped together her last ounce of strength and pushed her own needs and wants aside. "Look, it's not going to happen again, okay? Yes, it was amazing. But it always was. That's not what it was about. You came here wanting to put me behind you, remember?"

Keeping watch on him now would be so much more difficult. Halina had developed a certain numbness to his being with other women. Sometimes she'd even been able to dig deep and find sincere happiness for him. But now . . . she was certainly no saint. It would break her heart all over again.

But it was better than the alternative.

He was frowning at her, but in confusion, not anger. Which meant he was still trying to figure her out. Those knowing eyes, that sharp mind and all his experience in the courtroom gave him such an acute way of looking into people.

"Excuse me." She moved into the bathroom, shut the door, and pressed the lock. Then she slid to the floor, still holding the knob as tears burned her eyes. Her breaths came heavy and fast, everything hitting her at once now that she had a place to let down.

Exhausted, terrified, hurting, she couldn't keep it together anymore. She pressed her leaking eyes to her knees and took giant, gulping breaths to make sure Mitch didn't hear her cry.

She let out enough emotion only to get back under control. If she passed that delicate point of no return, he wouldn't have to hear her to know she'd been crying; her face would be ravaged with the signs.

Within sixty seconds, she had brought herself to that cold, icy place of resignation. So fast it scared her on some level. She'd taught herself to do it very young. A girl only had to get beaten so many times for letting tears spill to learn how to control them. But she hadn't realized how much of that girl was still inside her. She hadn't had to force herself to stop crying in years.

With hurt forming a shell, Halina pushed to her feet. At the sink, she splashed cold water on her face and tried to figure out what to do next. Getting away from Mitch would be best for them both. As far away as possible. But he was determined to get something out of her. And the thought of all those people Schaeffer had hurt because Halina hadn't come forward burrowed into her soul.

She wanted to help. She wanted him stopped. Wanted him to pay. Truthfully, she wanted him dead.

But she also realized giving up her evidence meant giving up the leverage that kept Mitch safe. Within hours of Schaeffer discovering he had her tapes and files, Mitch would be dead. She hadn't had any doubt of that before the visions. And now, with Abernathy willing to kill anyone who got in his way, and Mitch, so annoyingly and consistently *in his way* . . . the risk doubled.

But she could do this. She could handle this. She'd handled worse. For far longer.

And there was a good side to the visions, where Mitch survived and moved on to happiness. She just needed to continue to make the right decisions. Keep him making the right decisions. All without knowing exactly what those decisions were. But it didn't take a genius to figure out cause and effect, especially when it came to men like Schaeffer. At least not for Halina.

"What a mess." She took a deep breath before finger-combing her hair back into a bun.

When she opened the door, she found Mitch standing at the only window, feet spread, arms crossed. He turned as soon as he heard the door, holding his cell. He'd put his shirt back on— definitely a plus—and his face registered the same resignation that had taken over Halina.

She glanced through the room for the first time, a king suite—one bed, fireplace, sofa, big-screen TV, mini-fridge.

Pushing away the urge to lie down next to Dex, whose dazed golden eyes stared at her now, she crossed to the fridge and peeked inside. A sigh of relief drifted through her lips when she found it stocked. She grabbed a can of Coke and sat on the edge of the bed next to Dex, one leg curled under her.

She swept a hand over his thick fur and leaned down to look into his glassy eyes. Gratitude swamped her. "Hey baby."

The tip of his fuzzy tail wagged and his tongue slipped out to lick her nose. The love that sprang into her heart soothed a lot of the pain. Not all. Nothing could soothe it all. But it was a start.

With the side of her face pressed to Dex's shoulder, Halina met Mitch's eyes. "Thank you for saving him. I don't know what I would have done . . ."

Her voice choked off, but Mitch nodded in understanding.

She sat up, popped the top on the Coke, and decided to just rip off the Band-Aid. "Let's get this over with so we can go our own ways. What do you want to know?"

She took a long drink of the soda. Her mouth burst with flavored carbonation, and she swore she could feel the sugar passing directly into her veins. She drained half the can and let out a sigh. Then realized he hadn't asked her anything and met his gaze with one lowered brow.

"Halina"—his slow, smooth voice washed over her, making her chest ache—"we aren't going our own ways until we know if you're pregnant or not."

Dread slid around her shoulders like a blanket. She closed her eyes. "That could take a month."

"No," he said, calmly. "Seven days or sooner with a blood test. Ten days with a urine test."

She opened her eyes and met his gaze. His expression was tense, his eyes edged with impatience.

"Tell me you just looked that up on the Internet," she said, "because otherwise, I don't want to know how you know—"

"Alyssa." He tipped his head and sighed his sister's name. "You hang around with a doctor long enough, handle enough paternity suits for military guys who didn't father a kid by FedEx from Afghanistan, and you figure these things out."

"Well, I don't have a sister who's a doctor or handle paternity cases."

A grin turned his mouth, his eyes on that high-powered twinkle setting. *"You're* a doctor, Hali. And a woman."

"I'm a scientist, not a medical doctor. And neither makes me an expert on pregnancy-testing time limits." She pressed the Coke can to her forehead and rolled it side to side. "Can we change the subject before I hyperventilate?"

His smile faded, but his voice remained soft when he said, "Hali, I'm serious about taking the baby if you—"

"It's . . . not"—she laughed so she wouldn't cry—"a . . . baby . . . yet. Please, Mitch . . . Unless you want to be stuck with a psychotic melting pot of emotion, that's something I can't discuss until there *is* something to discuss."

He bit the inside of his cheek and looked at the wall. If he insinuated she didn't want their baby one more time . . .

Dammit, now he had *her* doing it. *There is no baby.* Yet.

His cell rang and he murmured, "This will only take a minute. Yes," he said into the cell, formal, clear. A business call. Probably someone overseas, considering the hour. "That's correct. No, just two of us."

Concern perked Halina's ears.

"I understand," Mitch said. "That's not a problem. I appreciate the last-minute accommodation. I'm not sure on that. Can I let you know tomorrow when we board?"

Halina's concern escalated to alarm.

"Great." Mitch picked up a pencil nearby and jotted notes. "Yes, ma'am, I've got it. Eight a.m. sharp. Thank you."

As soon as he disconnected, she asked, "Who and what was that?"

The set of his expression made her hands clench. Resolute, dominant, yet reconciled with the fact that he was about to catch some shit. Yes, she could read it all in one look. Seven years later.

"Our flight reservation—"

"Mitch, we can't fly—"

"Is on a private jet."

That killed her argument. "Well . . ." She crossed her arms tight to ease the sudden tingle across her shoulders. "You have made your mark, haven't you?"

"Honey, you live in a million-dollar house on a lake in the most sought-after neighborhood of Seattle, drive a brand-new fifty-thousand-dollar sports car with another one in storage, and you've got another twenty grand in guns and a cool hundred grand in cash. You don't have a lick of credit to your name-*s*." He emphasized the *s* as a *z* and dragged it out. "Don't *even* get me started on your finances."

Her mouth hung open. Anger coiled and coiled with no exit. "How—? What—? You—?"

"Yes, Halina," he answered her unspoken question, hands on hips. "I have a tendency to snoop in my spare time and I found it all in your storage unit. Don't worry, you'll get plenty of opportunity to explain all of that to me later."

"Explain my ass. I earned my money the same way you earned yours. I don't have to explain shit to you."

"Your finances don't add up. Not at a salary of a hundred grand a year."

"That is none of your damn business."

"It sure as hell is if you took a payoff from Schaeffer before you ran."

She pulled in a breath, mouth open in shock. Fury and indignation flushed her skin hot. Pushed her lungs against her ribs.

"You bastard," her voice scraped out of her throat, harsh with rage. "You get livid over me *judging* you, then throw that shit at me?" She pointed a rigid finger at his chest. "You'd better not say that again unless you've got proof of it, which I know you don't. Nor will you ever."

His mouth twisted in frustration, but he didn't argue. He leaned his ass against the arm of a chair and braced his hands alongside his hips. The muscles of his shoulders, chest, and biceps bunched, stretching his shirt and teasing Halina's gaze.

"You should get some sleep. We're flying out early to meet the team—"

"What?" In the speed of a finger snap, all her tension returned. "Wait. No. *What?*"

The lack of sleep was catching up with her.

Mitch relaxed his arms and straightened his spine. "That's what the jet is for, so we don't have to drive another twelve hours to reach them."

Them. All those people who'd suffered because of Halina. "Where?"

"Truckee, California, just outside—"

"Lake Tahoe. Why? What possible benefit can we gain by going there?"

He heaved a sigh and for the first time, shadows creased the inner corners of his eyes. "All the information we've collected is there. Two of the other couples on the team, Keira and Luke and Jessica and Quaid, live there too. Alyssa and Teague's home is huge, in the middle of ten acres and backs up to a national forest. Their property is surrounded by a military-grade security system and round-the-clock ex-military guards. We all fit there and we're all safe there."

She pressed the Coke to the side of her neck to cool the sudden heat flash and fanned her face with the other hand. She recognized the extreme measures and didn't have to ask why they were necessary. "No. You go, but not me."

"Hali, please don't start."

She barely heard him. A new sound rose in her ears, a hum or a buzz or something. She pushed to her feet, wobbled a little until her light-headedness eased, then shifted foot to foot with nowhere to go. No exit. No escape.

"What did you tell them about me?" She couldn't have heard the answer even if he'd given her one, but it didn't matter. She knew—he'd told them everything. She could tell how close they were by the way he talked about them.

"Not going." Her mind skidded sideways. Images of the terrors these people had suffered flashed in her head. They'd been threatened, kidnapped, imprisoned, killed. "Can't make me . . ." Her ribs had grown too tight, her throat too small. Suddenly, she couldn't get enough air. She fisted the shirt over her chest. "What, what . . . is this?"

She asked the question more to hear her own voice than for an answer. But suddenly, she was spinning. Her heart hammered so hard, she swore it beat outside her body.

"Hali . . . Hali . . ."

"Hali . . . Hali . . ."

Mitch's voice echoed and she squeezed her eyes shut to get rid of it, but when his arms came around her, she clung like she was drowning. He hauled her off her feet, pulled her into his lap, and surrounded her with his big body.

The buzz dimmed, replaced by the harsh rasp of her own breath.

Mitch's voice tried to soothe with, "You're fine, honey. You're safe."

But she wasn't safe. He wasn't safe. The others he wanted to drag her to see weren't safe. "Can't . . . go, Mitch." Her voice came muffled against his shirt, her mouth moving against the warm, pliant muscle of his chest beneath the cotton. "Not safe. I've hurt them enough."

His hand scraped through her hair, massaged the base of her neck. Emotion balled in her throat. "It's the safest place there is, Hali."

When she could breathe again, when the sky had stopped falling, Halina took a deep breath of Mitch before she said, "I'm okay now."

"No," he murmured, the rock of his body was almost imperceptible, but magically calming, "you're still shaking."

"I'm fine." This time she lifted her head. He tightened his fingers in her hair.

"Close your eyes," he whispered. "You were almost asleep."

Oh, hell, that was tempting. "Mitch . . ."

He rolled backward, taking her with him, and settled on his

side with Hali on her back, her legs draped over his, their fore-heads almost touching on one pillow.

"Shh." He closed his eyes. "I'm tired. We'll talk in the morning." He pushed his face deeper into the pillow, muttering something that sounded suspiciously like, "Someone wore me the hell out."

EIGHT

Owen stepped into visitors' reception at the Central Detention Center, unzipped his outer jacket. He jostled the fabric over his shoulders to shake off the light snow he'd collected on the walk in. A young female Hispanic officer, her dark hair coiled into a severe bun at the base of her neck, looked up from a computer screen at the counter with a resigned weariness in her gaze.

"Good morning, Officer," he greeted.

The woman's eyes met Owen's only for a split second before dropping to his chest and holding on the metal there. Her gaze jumped back to his expression freshened with respect, her body straightening to attention.

"Colonel, sir," she said with a serious nod. "I wasn't expecting you."

"I apologize for the lack of advance notice, but I need to see Mr. Abrute. I hope that won't be a problem."

"Of course not." She clicked through several screens on her computer and picked up a phone. "It's before regular visiting hours, so it might take an extra moment for me to round up another officer. Where would you like him, sir?"

"A private holding cell, please." When she met his eyes, he read her silent question: Did he want their meeting recorded? There was a certain amount of risk in taping their conversation, but Owen opted for the recording. "But . . . not too private."

"Yes, sir."

Owen went through the standard procedure for all visitors, emptying his pockets, surrendering his weapon, allowing his briefcase to be searched, clearing a metal detector. He could bypass protocol when needed, but he didn't like to pull rank unless absolutely necessary. The brass on his uniform was loud enough, and the only reason he'd worn it was for the psychological pressure on Abrute.

The man was waiting, hands in cuffs and clasped on the table, when a guard led Owen into the holding cell. Abrute looked like he'd been here two months, not just over two weeks. As the lab manager at the Castle, Abrute had worked with Cash O'Shay while he'd been imprisoned at the facility alongside Quaid Legend.

Abrute had been harboring 99 percent of O'Shay's finished project for Schaeffer—one Jocelyn had been hiding from Owen, among what seemed like a hundred other things. Owen had been lucky enough to swoop in and grab Abrute during the aftermath of the lab explosion and had been trying to get information out of him ever since. Information Owen could hold over Schaeffer as insurance, leverage . . . hell, he should really just come out and call it what it was—blackmail.

Unfortunately, Abrute was either deeply loyal, scared out of his mind, or really freaking stupid, because he'd been holding out. Abrute could provide both evidence and corroboration for O'Shay's and Legend's testimony about what had gone on at the Castle before it had been decimated, which would end Schaeffer. Only, Abrute wasn't talking.

The metal door clanged shut behind Owen.

"This is illegal," were the first words out of Abrute's mouth. "I'm an American citizen. You are violating my constitutional rights. I don't belong here. I did nothing wrong at the lab, only performed my job as I was instructed. I have served the American people faithfully for decades. *I don't belong here.*"

Owen approached the table slowly, hands clasped behind his back. Instead of sitting, he set his feet apart and stood tall, staring down at the man. Silently.

"I haven't been allowed to call anyone." Abrute's voice

gained strength, his belligerence replacing nerves. "I haven't been allowed to see my family. This is inhumane and against the Constitution."

Owen smirked. "I always find it interesting how people apply the law to benefit themselves, but ignore it all when it doesn't." He turned his smile into a severe line. "Holding Cash O'Shay and Quaid Legend at the Castle was illegal. O'Shay and Legend are both American citizens. Their constitutional rights were violated. They didn't belong there. They did nothing wrong, simply performed their jobs. They served the American people for decades. Not only were they not allowed to contact anyone or see their families, O'Shay's wife was murdered. Legend's memories stolen. Their families were taken forever, Abrute."

Abrute pushed out of his chair, but kept his cuffed hands flat on the table and glared up at Owen. "I did not have any part in that. All I did—"

"All you did," Owen cut him off, slamming his hands on the metal table. Abrute flinched and cast his eyes downward. "Was stand by and do nothing about it when you knew Cash O'Shay was imprisoned at the Castle *illegally*. When you knew Senator Schaeffer was using O'Shay to develop a military-grade protective device. A device you suspected would be sold independently through his own company, not offered to the U.S. military through the Department of Defense, which funded the project—whether knowingly or unknowingly.

"Crime, Mr. Abrute, is not only a matter of committing an act. Crime can also be manifested by the *failure* to act. Such as your failure to report Cash O'Shay's wrongful imprisonment and Schaeffer's fraudulent actions. And in the case of conspiracy, a coconspirator such as yourself need not know the full scope of crimes they've been involved in to be found guilty of that crime in its entirety and punished accordingly." He grinned at the man. "Ain't America great?"

"But that's not . . . I mean O'Shay wasn't . . . You're twisting everything around—"

"Looks like you'll be telling that to a jury." Owen gave the man a moment to consider the ramifications.

Abrute's gaze drifted toward the table again. His fingers curled into his palms, leaving his hands in fists against the gray metal.

"Well." Owen's voice was cool, but inside he boiled. He wanted to choke Abrute with those damned cuffs. "Since the deal I've offered you doesn't seem to sway you either way, I'll be rescinding—"

Abrute's head popped up, his black eyes wide, mouth open in shock. "What? What do you mean?" He straightened. "I've been working night and day on that damn formula. You can't—"

"I can do anything I want, Abrute." Owen straightened slowly, put his hands on his hips, and stretched to his full height, a solid five inches taller than the other man. "The way you did anything you wanted while O'Shay worked night and day on that formula for you. The way you let Schaeffer run rampant. Not much fun to be on the other side of the razor wire, is it?"

"O'Shay wasn't working on that formula for me! He was working on it for Schaeffer!"

The echo of Abrute's yell was still bouncing off the cement walls of the cell when the realization of what he'd just said reflected as terror in his gaze. A thrill of accomplishment traveled through Owen's gut in the sudden, cold silence that followed.

That statement was the first solid confession Abrute had made directly implicating Schaeffer in both the imprisonment of O'Shay and his work on a private project utilizing DoD facilities and resources. And he had it on record with both the voice recorder in his briefcase and the facility's video.

Foster would probably tell him it was inadmissible because of how Owen had obtained it, but Abrute didn't know that. And Owen would definitely use it to manipulate the man to the stand. A few more weeks in here and Abrute would probably drop to Owen's feet when he entered, begging him to tell every last secret he held on Schaeffer, which was all he really needed. But Owen didn't have weeks. And Abrute might not either. Prisoners like Abrute with men like Schaeffer gunning for them had a way of ending up dead even in solitary confinement.

"You have the ability to help yourself, Abrute. All you have to do is exercise it."

The other man pushed off the table and lifted his hands to gesture, forgetting the cuffs. They clinked loud, jerking at his hands. Rage and fear mixed and blasted across Abrute's face. "I told you before, if I say anything against that man, I will be dead within twenty-four hours of leaving this place."

Owen lifted his brows and shrugged. "Your other option is to plead out or go to trial. You'd be sentenced to prison and moved into the general population—"

"You can't do that." Abrute's gaze grew frantic. "Schaeffer would get someone in here to kill me just as fast."

Sweat trickled down Abrute's temple and Owen decided this was the perfect time to leave the man with a parting thought.

"I'll help you out here, Mr. Abrute. We're in a time crunch, so I'm going to put an expiration date on that deal I offered you a few weeks ago. It goes away in exactly forty-eight hours."

"B-b-but—"

Owen turned and pounded on the door. It immediately swung open, handled by a beefy middle-aged male officer. "Work fast," Owen said on his way out. "Or pray, Mr. Abrute. Pray hard."

Mitch followed Halina up the steps of the jet, carefully keeping his gaze down, averted from her ass. Harder to do than it sounded when he'd awoken with a steel erection pressed into that softness. And his entire body pressed to the back of Halina's. His face tucked into her hair. His arm draped over her waist. His fingers entwined with hers.

The way they used to sleep together.

He was such an idiot.

In his own defense, he didn't remember shifting into that position after sleep had grabbed him and dragged him under. Maybe she'd done it. Though, if she had, she was regretting it as much as she was regretting having sex with him, because she hadn't yet looked him in the eye this morning.

Halina stopped short just inside the plane and Mitch almost ran into her. He put a hand to the wall to halt his forward movement, doing his damnedest not to touch her.

At her side, Dex glanced up, his metal tags clicking.

"New fear of flying?" he asked, not bothering to hide his irritation. Without waiting for an answer, he said, "Pick a seat."

She glanced through the cabin with all the empty, wide, luxury leather chairs. "Aren't we assigned seats?"

"Nope. It's all ours."

"This is awfully big for two people."

"I think Dex qualifies as a third considering he weighs as much as you do. And it's the only size they had available on such short notice." Mitch stepped past her and walked down the aisle. Pausing in the center of the plane, he turned, held his arms out, indicating the seats around him.

Her gaze made a quick, hot slide down his body before she surveyed the plane again. Mitch gritted his teeth against the desire climbing inside him.

When she shrugged, Mitch dropped into the nearest captain's chair and called Dex. The dog didn't even look at Halina before he abandoned her to perch beside Mitch's chair. He let a vengeful smile lift his mouth as he scratched Dex's ears with one hand and pulled a laptop from a nearby compartment with the other. While the hourglass spun on the computer screen, Mitch scrolled through messages on his phone.

A text from Seth Masters, the only team member who remained a firefighter, said: *Call me when you can.*

Halina approached, assessing the seating arrangement—two chairs on either side of a small table. Before she decided to get as far away from him as possible—even though the idea had merit—Mitch grabbed her hand and swiveled toward the aisle.

When Halina halted in front of him without pulling her hand from his, he looked up. Her hair was a mess, finger combed into an untidy bun. The lump on her forehead at her hairline, developing a horrible green rim around the purple center, could never be completely hidden. She didn't have a shadow of makeup on her face.

And she was so beautiful she made his chest ache.

There was something so sexy about a woman who didn't mind being messy. Who cared less about how she looked and more about how she felt. About life, fun, pleasure. Halina had introduced him to that kind of woman, which was why he didn't date them now. And after watching her in sexual abandon the night before, he had an overwhelming urge to lift her by the waist, part her legs with his knees, and pull her over his lap. To press against her and make sure she realized just how hot she made him.

He patted the arm of the chair beside him instead. The flash of disappointment in her eyes was more likely irritation. She glanced at the seat, saw the way it would trap her between him and the window, and hesitated.

"Sit," he said. "We have a lot to talk about."

But he'd wait to start that until they were settled in.

She stepped past his chair and lowered herself into the seat. Looking out the window, she asked, "How did you pay for this? How did you pay for the hotels?" She turned those light eyes back on him. "They'll know where we are. They'll follow your financial—"

"I know, Hali. I used cash and an alternate alias credit card for the hotels and I put the charter on my account, which won't be billed for a month. This flight won't show up anywhere. The records are confidential. I've used this company for years and they know how important that is to me."

"I've been so . . . freaked, I didn't think . . ." She glanced around the plane. "How much does it cost to charter a jet like this?"

Mitch kept his eyes on his phone and whisked through his other messages. "The price is worth the convenience and security when it's necessary, which has definitely taken a hike in the last year."

"I developed and sold an invention to a large pharmaceutical company." Her sudden change of subject drew Mitch's gaze.

She met his eyes, matter-of-fact, nonconfrontational. "That's how I made the money I used to buy the house and the car. The money I use for any large purchases. I live off my salary."

Mitch stared a moment. Not sure how to take this voluntary share of information.

Halina licked her lips. Took a small breath. "I invested the rest under an individual corporation so my taxes are lower. And I actually chose to take a lot of the payment in company stock, which was, evidently, a good gamble. The pharmaceutical company is bursting at the seams, and in the last five years since I've owned the stock, it has split seven times.

"That's why you couldn't find it when you looked at my finances."

"I . . . see." When she didn't go on, but didn't avert her gaze either, he asked, "What did you invent?"

She glanced out the window. "A micro-sheath for needles that target hard-stick patients—the chronically ill, the elderly, children, those with various medical conditions that make drawing blood difficult. The sheath allows smooth insertion. There's less roll-away, fewer misses and resticks. The tip of the sheath also has both gripping and cutting properties. It adheres to the skin and punctures both the skin and the wall of the vessel like a hot knife through butter. The result is efficiency and accuracy for labs, comfort for patients."

She rested her head against the seat. "Not near as sexy as a secret payoff by a shadow government agent," she said with sarcasm and a shrug of her shoulders, "but there you have it."

He may have told Kai he didn't find her work interesting, but they used to talk for hours on end about scientific advances, their applications in medicine, the ethical and financial implications. She'd fascinated him. Everything about her had captivated him, challenged him. Even now, he could think of a hundred questions to ask her about her invention.

Instead, he said, "Thanks for telling me."

"Hey, Mitch." The friendly female voice sounded down the aisle and Mitch looked up.

Christy, their flight attendant, walked toward them.

Mitch smiled. "Hey, beau—" The word "beautiful," an endearment he used with most women because it was easy, natural, rarely caused anyone to bristle, and because it never failed to make them melt, caught on his tongue.

Though Halina had been completely still and quiet and Mitch had forgotten she was there for a moment, she instantly filled his mind.

"Christy," he said, blundering the change.

At least she pretended not to notice. Mitch didn't look at Halina to see her reaction, reminding himself it didn't matter. She'd made her desires crystal clear.

Christy put a hand on the back of the seat opposite Mitch and turned her beaming smile on Dex. "Who is this handsome devil?"

Mitch grinned down at Dex, sliding a hand over his silky head. "This is Dex." He gestured toward Halina. "And this is Dex's . . . um," he frowned, strangely unsure how to phrase that relationship. "Owner?"

"Noooo," Christy said, leaning toward Dex with a big grin. "She's his *mama*." She said it with a southern twang that made Mitch laugh, then glanced at Halina. "He's gorgeous. Can I pet him?"

Halina nodded, smiled. "Sure."

Mitch glanced toward Halina. Her eyes were already on him, assessing. He turned away, seeing Christy from a whole different perspective this morning. She was a stunning, funny, intelligent woman. The very kind Halina had obviously noticed he chose to date—her knowledge of which was something he needed to get around to asking her about.

Christy crouched in front of Dex. Her straight, deep purple skirt stretching tight over smooth thighs and tight butt. And when she leaned over to take Dex's face in both hands, her cream silk blouse draped at the neckline, giving a soft-porn-worthy view of perfect breasts.

If Mitch had to guess, he'd bet Halina's mood would be sour when Christy left their seats.

"Oh, what a sweetheart," Christy purred.

"Yeah, he's great, isn't he?" Mitch agreed, then asked, "How's Tyler?"

Christy grinned up at him. He didn't have nearly as difficult a time keeping his eyes off her breasts as he did keeping them off Halina's.

"Good," she chirped. "Just started with a private security firm as an explosives expert. Your recommendation went a long way. And, God help us all, he's started taking law classes."

Mitch chuckled, a sense of purpose smoothing his rough edges. At least his clients needed him. "Fantastic. Tell him to come see me when he's ready for an internship."

"Are you kidding? Just try to keep him away. You're his hero."

Mitch snorted a laugh. "He's the hero."

Christy straightened. "What can I get you two before we take off?"

Mitch glanced at Halina. "You still like grapefruit juice?"

Surprise flashed in her eyes. "Yes."

Mitch placed an order with Christy, waited a moment, took a deep breath, and faced Halina again. Her gaze had turned cool.

"Who's Tyler?" she asked. "Her husband?"

"Brother."

Halina glanced toward the front of the plane again, her gaze drifting down Christy's long legs. He knew damn well what she was visualizing, but he wasn't going to volunteer any information. If she wanted to know, she could ask directly.

"Is she married?"

"No, why?"

"How do you know her brother?"

"He's a previous client. Explosives expert, former military."

Halina's gaze returned to Mitch's face, one brow lifted, but he couldn't read her expression. "You have a lot of military clients."

"I've found the government likes to screw everyone, even their own. Which is a great segue to what we need to discuss, don't you think?" He pulled a pad of paper and pen from a slot in the side of his chair. He hadn't exactly *planned* on putting off this talk, at least not consciously. But he had to admit, the thought of it now had his stomach wound tighter than his first freaking day in court as a damn kid.

He slid into the same persona he used with clients—detached, competent, straightforward—and angled his chair toward Halina. "Let's just start with why you passed Saveli off as your husband and get it out of the way."

Her mouth turned up at the corners in a bitter smile. "You don't waste any time, counselor."

"And, Halina, let me just tell you that I know Saveli risked his entire political career by helping you. So give me a good reason for the man to do that."

She pressed her hands together, linked her fingers, and squeezed them. A stress-relieving gesture he remembered from long ago. "How would you know that?"

"Because I know about your family. Your uncle and his business. And I know if anyone had found out that Saveli was helping you with whatever you were doing at DoD—"

"He wasn't helping me with anything at the DoD. How do you know about my family?"

"Friend."

"What kind of friend? Who are you trusting to get this kind of information for you? How do you know it's accurate?"

"This person has deep government sources—"

"*Government* sources? Why would you trust someone in the government? You just said the government likes to screw everyone."

Her tone got under his skin. "You say that like I haven't already *been* screwed. And as a former government employee, you'd know all about doing that well, wouldn't you?"

Her mouth tightened. Chin dipped in a signal of thinning patience. "I told you I'd try to answer your questions. But I'm not going to take your attitude. If you can't be civil, I'll move and we'll talk when you can treat me at least as well as you treat your clients."

Her cool tone infuriated him. "My clients don't *fuck me.*"

Hurt streaked through her eyes and she surged to her feet. Dex immediately followed, jumping up from where he'd lain beside Mitch's chair. "Don't you—"

Christy approached with a drink tray and a scowl for Mitch. "We're not even off the ground and you've pissed her off already?"

Self-disgust made his chest heavy and tight. His anger and hurt lost its edge. "It is my specialty."

"Not on this flight, Mr. Foster," Christy said, distributing glasses and drinks. "Don't make me kick you out at thirty thousand feet."

Christy opened the top of a black box and presented three lines of miniature liquor bottles to Halina. "Some spark for your grapefruit juice? You might need it. Lord knows he and I have spent a few hours disagreeing on flights in the past—"

"Hold on," Mitch said, taking the opportunity for a distraction. "When have we ever disagreed?"

Halina sat, but her gaze cut between them again. Dex relaxed only after Halina did. Christy tapped the Belvedere vodka, her brows raised at Halina, who hesitated, then said, "No, thanks. Just the juice is fine."

Mitch relaxed. He didn't like being a watchdog, but he found himself already protective over the health of a *possible* pregnancy. He'd driven Alyssa crazy during her pregnancy. She'd gone so far as to have Teague run interference at times.

Christy ticked off the number of things she and Mitch had argued about on her fingers. "World hunger, arms trading, globalization, global warming, immigration . . ."—she paused for a dramatic deep breath and dove right back in—"offshore drilling, gay marriage, education, racism, poverty, taxes, social media—"

"Stop right there." Mitch pointed at her, grinning at her quick mind. "We *totally* agreed on social media marketing."

Christy rolled those big blue eyes toward the ceiling again, thought about it. "Ah." She gave him a smart nod. "You're right."

Grinning, Christy relayed takeoff instructions and turned

to leave them in privacy. "Oh, Mitch." She glanced back and pointed toward the rear of the plane. "Change of clothes and toiletries in the bathroom." Then she grinned at Halina. "Yell if he gets out of hand."

"Hey." Mitch reached out and gave her arm a squeeze. "Thanks for picking up the clothes."

"Anytime." She laid her hand over his. "You know that."

Christy strolled toward the front of the plane and Halina watched her go.

Mitch remained quiet until Halina's gaze returned to his, and she lifted her brow in question. "What?"

"Why don't you just ask? I know you want to know if I'm sleeping with her."

"That's . . . arrogant," she said. "And no. I absolutely *do not* want to know that you're sleeping with her—"

"That's not what I said—"

"And I'm sorry I mentioned the other women last night. I was . . . frustrated. It won't happen again." She sighed heavily, crossed her arms, looked out the window. "In answer to your earlier question about Savili, I didn't question his motives for helping me."

Up front, Christy took her seat, belted in, and pulled out a book. The airport slid past outside the windows as they taxied to the runway.

Mitch grabbed on to the subject. At least he could legitimately direct his frustration there. "He was taking great risks to help you here in the States and could have faced even harsher consequences back in Russia after he returned. It was selfish of you to ask a man with so much to lose to come to the aid of a second cousin whom he barely knew and to whom he owed nothing."

She paused in the act of lifting her juice glass and gave him a cold stare. The engines revved and Halina paused before answering as they lifted into the sky.

Once the engine noise had dimmed, she set her glass on the table without drinking and crossed her arms. "I was desperate, I asked, he agreed. After Schaeffer threatened me, it was clear I had two choices—give him what he wanted or run. I knew if I just dropped everything and ran you would have searched for me. And I knew if you found me, they'd find me." Frustration edged into her eyes. "I was trying to avoid *this*."

That stab hit its mark, but he tried not to react. Her confession was too clean. Too simple. The extremes she'd gone to in an effort to hide, too drastic. Mitch had heard hundreds of schemes, from the painfully simple to the ridiculously insane. This didn't add up.

"Schaeffer already had your research," Mitch said. "Even if you refused to give it to him, he could have gone to court. By virtue of your employment with DoD, the government owned it all. That wouldn't have changed if you'd quit or were fired. The courts would have forced you to turn it over or put you in jail until you did."

He settled back in his chair, pressed his elbows to the arms, and threaded his fingers. "So give me the rest, Hali. Give me the *inside* story."

NINE

Halina was baking inside her clothes. She could feel every beat of her heart at her throat, hear it in her temple near her ear. Heat burned across her chest, up her neck, and over her cheeks.

She'd never felt claustrophobic, but right now, she felt trapped. She pushed from the chair, squeezed past Mitch, and paced in the aisle. Beside his chair, Dex sat up and whined. Mitch petted his head.

At the front of the plane, Christy looked up from a book and raised her voice to be heard over the engine. "Do you need something?"

"No, thanks." She gave the sweet flight attendant a brittle smile. "Just stretching."

The other woman nodded and returned to her book, swiveling her chair just enough to give Halina and Mitch more privacy. Halina forcefully blocked thoughts of the woman and Mitch from her mind. Even if they'd never been together, Christy was too close to the hundreds of other women Mitch favored and reminded Halina of all she wasn't, all she'd never be.

His furious confession of sleeping with them to get over Halina crossed her mind. She didn't know what to make of that. The passionate, heat-of-the-moment way in which it had been made led her to believe its truth. And at first, that behavior made complete sense. But it didn't explain his continued playboy lifestyle.

Doesn't matter.

Doesn't. Matter.

She just wanted to get this info dump over with. There was a lot he already knew, a lot she could simply elaborate on. A few things she could give him. Some she even hoped would ease the pain she'd caused him in the past.

But there were things she'd never expose. Not unless all the fail-safes she'd created crashed and someone was holding a gun at Mitch's head.

"When I started with the program," Halina said, "I was told we were all working to improve the human gene pool. The theory was that by strengthening the human genetic structure, future generations would experience a higher quality of life.

"And before you ask," she held up a hand, "yes, I realized I was working for the Department of Defense, not the United Nations. And yes, the short-term goal for this project was to enhance the genetic makeup of American soldiers. But the long-term goal was to make the enhancements available to *all* Americans. My dream was always that someday it would be available to all *humans* worldwide, which wasn't unrealistic. DARPA research has benefited the American public for decades.

"The anthrax vaccine, penicillin refinement and distribution, wound-stasis foam, revolutionized prosthetics, and too many defenses against infectious diseases to name. Of course there's GPS, the Internet, biofuel, voice-recognition software, radar, nuclear power. I believed—I *still* believe—my work has a place among those amazing discoveries. My research, God, it was fascinating."

She closed her eyes as the remembered thrill of her discoveries expanded inside her like a hot ball of energy. She'd known with her entire soul that she'd found her life's work. Had been over the moon when it had become all that she'd hoped for and more. Had been devastated when she'd had to break it down and run.

"I found safe ways to alter genetic structure that would have brought fabulous advancements to humankind," she continued, her gaze going distant as she remembered the thrill of each breakthrough. "The enhancement of almost every essential function in the body, creating stronger, smarter, more compassionate human beings. The eradication of horrendous diseases—AIDS, hepatitis C, diabetes, dozens of cancers.

"The benefits this type of change could have brought to society were endless. Increased quality and longevity of life, prevalence of an efficient, productive workforce, advanced intelligence, unlimited innovations in science, engineering, medicine, the arts, elimination of virtually all birth defects, decreased pain and suffering.

"Financially, there would be drastic reductions in medical care, enabling a healthcare system that could offer coverage to everyone without burdening the public. Huge boosts to the economy would ensure unemployment's extinction. Federal and state governments would have a steady flow of income, schools would have funding from private and public sources, education would be available to everyone, not just the most intelligent or the wealthiest—"

She stopped herself, breathless. She'd whipped herself into a light-headed frenzy simply recalling the *possibilities*. She'd discovered a method of life-altering science that would better the lives of nearly every human being on the planet.

What more could one person do for humanity? What better purpose could one person hold in life?

She'd been complete.

Mitch's love had been the sprinkle of twenty-four-carat stardust over everything she'd ever dreamed for in life.

"I can see how it thrilled you."

Mitch's voice dragged her right back to earth. His expression confirmed the tone she'd suspected. He was struggling to remain neutral, but beneath the mask, he was hurt. It shone in his eyes, in the flecks of gold sparkling among the green. In the tightness of his mouth. In the deeper shadows beneath his eyes. Hurt, sadness, loss.

Regret swelled in her throat and tightened her chest. He'd given her everything. He'd given her 150 percent of himself . . . and she'd held back, lied, given him nothing but a shell of the real her, then abandoned him.

"I'm sorry you couldn't share it with me back then," he said, his voice soft, pain radiating in his serious tone. "Disappointed I missed out on that part of you."

Halina turned her gaze out the window to the pale blue sky, but closed her eyes on the sudden, sweeping pain. "Me too," she whispered. "I know you probably don't believe me, but it was so hard—"

She choked, unable to finish. Which was just as well. She would never be able to do the emotions justice with simple words. The pain had been too deep, the loneliness too all-consuming, the loss too overwhelming.

"I can imagine," he said, his earlier anger still at bay. "One lie turns into two, which turns into—"

"Four, then sixteen . . ." She squeezed her eyes shut, the weight of all the lies making her feel heavy in her seat. She shook her head in frustration, then looked out at the sky. "And working for DoD—at least in the capacity I did, with the clearances I had—was a lot like working for the CIA. Nobody can know what you do, where you work, whom you really work for. I know it was the same for the others in the lab—at least to some degree. Though in hindsight, I also know that I believed Schaeffer when he put the fear of God into me about letting even the slightest information leak.

"Changing my name at the beginning was a condition of my employment, standard procedure, he'd said. One for work, one for personal, different from my given name. But I never verified that with others. It just wasn't something we talked about.

"And in the beginning, with you and me"—her stomach clenched hard, regret thick and hot as she glanced at him, then away—"I didn't think it was a big deal. I thought there would be time, you know, once we got to know each other better, to explain. But we . . ."

She sighed, dropped her head, and rubbed at the sting of

tears in her eyes. She wasn't going to be able to hold them back for long. She could feel them building deep in her chest. The guilt had eaten away at her for so long in silence, it pounded at her now to be freed, expressed, his loss grieved.

She cleared her throat. "We got so close, so fast. And before I knew it, I was a thousand lies deep with you and terrified of what would happen if . . ."

She couldn't finish.

Mitch did it for her. "If you told me the truth."

She pulled her lip between her teeth and bit down to keep herself together. The shame of it overwhelmed her. God, she wished she could have avoided all this. Wished she could have just shaken him off earlier and gotten away.

The white noise from the plane's engines filled the cabin for a moment, and when Mitch didn't say anything, Halina chanced a sidelong glance at him. He was staring blankly at the table as if dazed by a blow to the head, his brow drawn in deep, confusing thought, a few fingers sliding back and forth over his mouth.

She needed to redirect to the facts and veer away from the emotions. Halina rested her shoulder against a wall separating seating sections and continued.

"Schaeffer lied to me about the purpose of the project—but I only found out after I'd discovered a dependable, repeatable way of successfully altering DNA sequences to include all the benefits."

Halina's stomach clenched in preparation for giving him the deepest information she planned on offering. This was the line in the sand. When he glanced up, she took a breath, let it out, and met his gaze.

"He wanted me to *clone* my little genetic miracles."

Mitch tipped his head, two fingers pressed against his lower lip, a frown creasing his forehead. "Isn't cloning one of those things you do in labs? I mean, it's common in all genetic research, isn't it?"

Frustration burned in the pit of her stomach. "Not this type of cloning," she said. "He wanted me to take all my amazing

genetic research, combine the mutations into one human being, and *clone* that creation. He wanted to clone it and *clone it*
and *clone it* until he had an army of perfect little genetic *people.*"

That seemed to strike some sort of understanding. Mitch
jerked back, dropped his hand. His gaze sharpened on hers.
"What?"

Halina pushed off the wall and dropped her arms. "He
wanted to *grow people.* In labs. Like bugs in giant glass jars. No
parents. No siblings. No communities. He just wanted me to
clone them so he could grow them like plants, train them to
kill, and send them to *war.* Do you *realize* the extreme ramifications of that scenario?"

She held her breath as she watched his brain cells fire and
connect. His eyes darted back and forth as he thought. Then
they came back to hers.

"You knew what he wanted to do with those clones,
Halina," he said. "You *were* working on the project."

Her mouth dropped open. *"That's* what you pulled from
what I just told you?" She bent and waved her hands in font of
his face. "Hello. Are you listening to me *at all*? I'm in this mess
because I *wouldn't* work on that project."

Dex whined as if to say, "Don't fight."

Mitch ruffled the fur at his ears. "I hear you telling me
Schaeffer had, evidently still has, plans to turn your Nobel Peace
Prize–worthy research into an automated, mass-murdering
army." He frowned at her. "Do you really expect me to be surprised?"

The sudden pain of a deeply personal stab to the heart
flooded her vision with tears. She threw her hands in the air.
"You've just reduced my entire life's work to the complexity of
making muffins."

The tears spilled over and she swore. Rubbed them away
with quick sweeps of her fingers.

"You knew, you were involved and you lied about that just
hours ago when you thought I'd let you go if you knew nothing. I'm sorry if I don't get overly excited about everything you
tell me, Halina. I'd like to know it's true first."

"I knew about it—at the end. And I've already made it very clear *I . . . was . . . not . . . involved.* Knowing about something and being involved in something are as different as knowing how to drive a car and being a mechanic. And, yes, I lied, for the same reason I lied seven years ago. I don't want what I know in the hands of the wrong people."

And that was another line of information she wouldn't cross. If she told Mitch that she'd done what she'd done back then to save his life, not her own, she'd never get away from him. Whether he'd stay with her out of gratitude or guilt didn't matter. The fact remained that if he stayed with her, if he pried too deep into this mess, Schaeffer would kill him.

She hadn't given him up, hadn't given up the last seven years of her life just to let him walk into Schaeffer's crosshairs now.

"And just like you said," she said, "if I had quit, all my research would have remained with Schaeffer, and it wouldn't have taken him long to find another scientist to take all the discoveries I'd made and implement the science. I saw two choices and cloning wasn't one of them."

"Rat him out to someone high up," Mitch said, filling in her options in a smooth, cool tone, "hope they weren't tight with Schaeffer, and wait for one of two results—exoneration or execution. Or steal the research and run."

She nodded and turned her gaze out the window. Shadows from her past crept in, but she didn't need to hide those anymore. Mitch already knew about them, too. Still, the disappointment and shame of how those ties had followed her here hurt.

"Remember how proud I was that I'd been picked for the job above the other candidates?"

In her peripheral vision, she saw Mitch nod. She remembered telling him about it when they'd first met.

"Schaeffer chose me because of my family, not just my work or my achievements." She laughed, a disgusted laugh filled with irony and bitterness. "And he chose well. I feared his authority the way I feared my uncle and the men who worked for my uncle. I respected the value of secrecy for its power to keep a person alive. I understood how every choice brought a consequence, and I had experienced or witnessed punishment at every level. I knew a threat when I heard one. And I knew—and still know—men like my uncle, men like Schaeffer, follow through on their threats. Even men in comas have others who will follow through for them."

Another long moment of silence fell between them. She could feel their mingling pain filling the space as if it were physically tangible.

"You're wrong," he finally said, his voice emerging flat, but still soft. "If he'd chosen correctly, you'd be dead and he'd have your research." He lifted his gaze from the table. "You proved him wrong, Halina. Dead wrong. But you also paid one hell of a price to do it. And you made me pay a hell of a high price too, without ever giving me a choice."

Her chest took that hit, directly beneath her breastbone. She winced. Lowered her gaze to the table. "You're right. I can't deny that. But you also say that like I made the decision lightly, which I didn't."

"And how would I know that, Hali? You made all the decisions without me. You didn't even give me a *chance* to choose."

His hurt was beginning to fade in rising anger again. Halina tried to brace for it even knowing it was useless. This was going to get dicey.

"Instead of coming to me for help," he said, "someone who knew the ins and outs of law enough to be considered for appointment to the attorney general's office and the presidential advisers list, you went to a distant relative who you didn't even truly know you could trust. And you cut all ties—and when I say cut, Halina, I mean with a fucking axe—with the one person who cared about you the most, and who had the most influence to help you."

She put up her hands, mostly as a reminder to hold her own frustration in check. "You have a very selective memory. You're obviously forgetting that at the time you had already been *fired* from the attorney general's office. Fired because you had mishandled a case involving a major—*major*—player in the chemical industry—"

"You damn well know I didn't mishandle anything—"

Dex gave a half bark, as if to remind them their conversation was growing too heated for his taste. Mitch lowered his hand to Dex's head.

"That's not what everyone who created *influence* around the Hill believed," Halina said. "They were made to believe that you were on a mission to railroad that chemical company. You had no pull with anyone who could have helped either of us at that time.

"And, really, Mitch, to expect me to come to you after all those months of me lying—about where I worked, who I worked for, what I did, why I came to this country, basically, who the hell I *was*—then asking you to bail me out for my own stupidity? And to risk your life doing it? I know you think I'm selfish, but even I'm not that callous."

Halina thought back to her turmoil over wanting to confide in him yet knowing if she did, she risked his life because he didn't have the power to protect himself. "You were so amazing to me all those months we were together, treated me better than anyone in my entire life. Loved me more than anyone has *ever* loved me. Honest with me at every turn. Took me on trips, bought me presents, introduced me to your friends, your family, even your work colleagues, like you were *proud* of me . . ."

Halina suddenly choked on the memories and stopped short.

Her appreciation of how well he'd treated her evidently didn't move anything inside Mitch. His eyes narrowed and his face tightened in anger.

"So . . . what?" he asked. "You felt *obligated* to let me down easy? Thought the way you handled it was more . . . humane?" He laughed at the absurdity of the idea, but then cut it short abruptly as something ignited in his eyes. "Wait. You *knew*? You knew all those months, while I was killing myself to shut that company down, that it wouldn't happen?"

Halina tensed her muscles. Clenched her teeth. This was

what she'd been afraid of—unintended information spilling over. He was so damned smart. He had the most amazing way of piecing puzzles together. Now her mind was pinging around Classified Chemical searching for damage-control scenarios.

"You just let me fight for it and stress over it," he said, his voice rising again. "Just watched as it ate away at me. As I fought myself right out of that job."

"Don't put that on me," she said. "I tried to get you to back off the case. I tried everything to get your mind on something else—I made love to you, tried to take you on vacation, tried to talk you into moving to the west coast, hid your home files. I crashed your computer, for God's sake. But you *wouldn't* give up."

Mitch pushed from his chair, his eyes both shocked and angry. "That was *you?*"

Halina's breath froze in her chest. What had she said? Where had she gone wrong? He was too clever. Too perceptive. She should never have tried to explain anything, never given him any information.

He advanced on her, nearly a foot taller and staring down with so much fury burning in his eyes, she knew whatever misstep she'd taken, it had been huge.

Dex put himself between them, looked up, and barked.

"*You* destroyed my office and took those files? The files that connected *Classified Chemical* with *Schaeffer?*"

Oh. Fuck.

Her stomach iced over and dropped.

She didn't have to worry about that family blood becoming a problem for her—she sucked at this spy business.

God, she felt so stupid. So . . . inept. She crossed her arms defensively. "I didn't hurt anything in your office."

He lifted a hand toward Halina. Her mind sharpened. Her arms dropped to her sides. Dex growled. Mitch's gaze was shining bright green and laser sharp as he put a rigid index finger to her chest. "If you lied about that needle invention, I'll find out. If you took a payoff from Schaeffer, I'll find out. And I swear to God, Halina—"

Something moved in her peripheral vision, but Halina didn't remove her gaze from Mitch. The amount of anger he was emitting had an unnerving sizzle sliding over her skin.

Mitch looked toward the movement, immediately dropped his hand, straightened, and curbed his anger. And Halina knew Christy stood nearby.

"Everything . . ." the attendant started hesitantly, "all right back here? You've even got poor Dex riled."

Halina dropped into a seat next to the window and across the table from where Mitch had been sitting. Dex perched faithfully at her side and rested his head on her thigh.

Christy offered two fresh beers to Mitch even though he hadn't touched the others. He took them with an absent gesture toward Halina. "We're just . . . hashing out some issues."

"Halina?" Christy looked past Mitch. "I'm not kidding about tossing him out. The copilot's my little brother, but he's a big guy, and he'll do anything I tell him to do."

Halina huffed a laugh and glanced from the corner of her eye toward Christy. "Could he throw me out? I'm ready to go."

Christy turned those bright blue eyes on Mitch. "Come on, Mitch."

"Okay. Okay." He set the beers on the table and raked his fingers through his hair. "I'll take it down a notch."

Christy leaned in and lowered her voice, but Halina still heard the woman murmur, "Better take it down a couple or I'll have something to say about our family accepting your charter again. We've only got twenty minutes left on the flight. Behave yourself."

Halina didn't feel worthy of Christy's loyalty. It didn't matter that she'd made the best decisions she could have made at the time. It didn't matter that her decisions had kept Mitch alive and safe. It didn't matter that her decisions had kept a psychopath power monger from creating an army of super killers. Halina still saw herself as Mitch did—a deceitful, selfish, manipulative liar willing to do anything to keep herself safe, including fuck him. An evil-minded scientist who'd contributed to Schaeffer's sick scheme and let him run free to harm others, which, no doubt made Halina just as guilty of the man's crimes in Mitch's mind.

Christy returned to the front.

Mitch rubbed the back of his neck. "Why did you do that? With the files and my computer? Why were you trying to get me off the case?"

Halina took a deep drink of her juice and winced at the tangy sweetness. Her taste buds twanged and tingles spread through the pivot points on her jaw. She set down the glass.

"Schaeffer knew we were dating. I don't know how, I never told him. But he came to me one day and very simply stated that if you didn't get off the Classified case, you were going to lose your job. Then insinuated that I might want to help you out if I didn't want to see that happen to you."

Halina stared at the table and concentrated on plugging this little leak in Pandora's box without either creating more or breaking the damn lid off. And she tried to do it without any more lies. If she had to remember one more lie, she might as well just check herself into an asylum.

"I shrugged it off. But then you came home talking about the problems. And then the problems got worse. And worse. And worse. And I'd find myself in an elevator with Schaeffer or pass him in the hall or see him in a meeting and get, 'How's Mitch's job going, Halina?' or 'I hear those high-stress jobs can really put a lot of pressure on relationships,' or 'One black mark on an attorney's reputation can kill his chances to advance.' I knew if I didn't try to do something . . .'"

Halina downed the rest of her juice, forced it past her throat, tight with the half-truth forming there.

"It doesn't seem so monumental now, but at the time, your losing a job you loved so much seemed like the end of the world to me."

Before he plugged in the time line to those facts and realized they were several months askew—but very true and an important piece to a bigger crack in Pandora's box—Halina lightened the subject.

"So this is a family deal, this charter service?"

"Yeah." He turned to stare out at the clouds. "The brothers are all pilots. Christy flies too, but prefers not to. Tyler flew for the air force. I represented him and that's how I found out about this charter service."

He turned away from the window and stood without looking at Halina. "I need a break. I'm going to call Seth."

Mitch walked toward the front of the plane and Halina stared at the cream leather seat he'd vacated. She knew he didn't believe her. But it sure would have been nice to hear even a couple words of support or understanding . . . even just acknowledgment of the stress she'd gone through.

She certainly didn't expect, need, or even want gratitude. Just . . . understanding. But it didn't look as if that would be coming. And she ached with the punch of his dismissal and rejection all rolled into one.

TEN

Schaeffer slammed down the newspaper and stabbed at the nurse's call button. "Peggy!"

She didn't answer. The bitch was ignoring him on purpose. He was her only goddamned patient. She was probably flirting with one of those pompous Secret Service agents again.

He held the button down. He had no idea if that made it buzz any longer out at the nurses' station or wherever the hell the nurses got the signal, but he hoped it did. When he released it, he yelled, "Peggy, get in here and deal with this damned beeping, for God's sake."

The door opened and the crotchety bitch swept in. "How difficult is it to keep your arm straight, Senator?"

"How difficult is it to shut your mouth and do your job, *nurse?*" He shook the paper out and glanced through the door where one of the agents stood. "Where the hell is Colonel Young?"

"No sign of him yet, sir."

"That's not what I asked." Gil scanned the columns for the article he'd been reading when that damned IV pump had started beeping for the millionth time that morning. He was so ready to get out of this godforsaken place, and if shit like this article kept popping up, he'd never be able to leave.

Peggy snapped the door to the IV pump closed and rounded the bottom of the bed.

"What?" Gil said, still half waiting for the *don't bend your arm* mantra. "No warning from the warden?"

With her hand on the doorknob, she faced him. He didn't take his gaze off the paper. "I'm done wasting my breath on you. I'm saving it for patients who actually care about their treatment."

"Hallelujah."

"And you are not a prisoner, Senator. Please, use this door at your earliest convenience. It's big enough for even you to get through."

The fat dig burned. Gil flashed a glance her way with a threat on his tongue, but she slammed the door so hard the blinds over the glass rattled. Gil winced at the noise and muttered, "Fucking bitch."

He started reading where he'd lost his place, but the door opened again. He didn't bother to look up. "I'm not going to choke down any more of this hospital crap you call food. If you can't get the kitchen to provide something decent to eat, then get your ass out to Bistro Bis and pick up two orders of eggs Benedict."

"Thanks for thinking of me, but I've already eaten."

The deep male voice, filled with too much confidence and attitude to be one of the Secret Service agents', filled the room. Gil looked up just before the door closed again. He took in the sight of Owen Young in uniform, his chest weighted down by medals, and snapped the paper before returning his gaze to it, even though he wasn't reading anymore.

"Don't you fall face-first into your food with all that weight on your chest, Young?"

"You should be nicer to the people here, Senator," he said, approaching the bedside. "They hold your life in their hands."

"They do a job, same as you, nothing more. And they do a shitty job of it too. You all have a lot in common." Gil slapped a backhand against the article and glared at Young. "This has become a problem, Owen. You need to handle it, and you need to handle it better than you're handling Foster and those menaces he calls a team."

Young's sharp green eyes darted to the paper, scanned the headline, *Syria's Chemical Weapons Linked to American Chemical Mogul,* and returned to Gil's face. "It'll blow over."

"No, it won't." He snapped the paper again—he just loved the sound—and folded it. "The FBI has been trying to contact me for a week."

Young's lids lowered and his jaw clenched. "And you're just telling me about it now. We had a discussion about communication, Senator. The last time you delayed informing me, you lost Quaid Legend."

"I've been a little under the weather—"

"You've been *hiding out.* The doctors said you could have left the hospital last week if it weren't for the new ailments you come up with daily. Now I know why, especially given your dislike of the staff and—God forbid—the food."

"You know what you need, Owen?" Gil narrowed his eyes. "You need to get yourself some pussy. Why don't you go on over to the Alibi Club tonight? I'll call and let them know you're there as my guest."

"What I need, Senator, is information and in a timely manner."

"Have you forgotten who you're talking to?" Gil demanded.

Owen angled his head, the move calculated and menacing. "Have you?"

He held Gil's gaze too steadily and with too much authority. Gil was sweating beneath his pajama top, one the Secret Service had brought him from home. The sweat would start pouring off him any moment, and Owen would mistake that for weakness.

"No, Owen. I'm talking to the man who should have found and captured Legend, O'Shay, and the lousy team of firefighters who broke them out of a top-security federal—"

"Prison?" Owen interrupted.

"Lab," Gil countered. "What progress have you made since you came in yesterday?"

"I've discovered that you failed to mention you involved

Abernathy in this train wreck of a scheme, Senator. And I've discovered Abernathy is running the wrecked car down a hill at three hundred miles per hour to inevitable catastrophe."

Anger surged. "Abernathy's balls had better be in Pakistan."

"If they are, he's not attached to them. He's here, Senator. He confronted Halina *Beloi* and Mitch Foster outside *Beloi's* home in Washington State last night. And it might have helped me find them earlier, *before* Abernathy, had I known her *real* name."

"That wicked bitch," Gil muttered, heat and pressure swelling inside his body. Sweat trickled from his forehead and into his eyes. Gil grabbed a washcloth and wiped his face. "I didn't think she'd ever have the balls to use her real name again."

"You're missing the point—"

"No, I'm not. The point now is that Abernathy's trying to get her research and take over while he thinks I'm incapacitated."

Gil tossed the covers back and swung his legs over the side of the bed. The momentum sat him halfway up, but without the strength to pull his body forward, Gil fell back, struggling to retain some dignity with the use of the bed's handrails. By the time he'd righted himself, Gil was struggling to breathe and every damn machine made some kind of outrageous noise.

Gil sat with his back to Owen, but he could sense the other man's smirk. He shot a glare over his shoulder, but didn't catch Owen grinning to himself. The man was still frowning.

"Why didn't you tell me Abernathy was in this up to his balls?" Owen paced slowly toward the windows, his hands clasped and fisted behind his back.

"Because he's not supposed to be," Schaeffer bit out. His face had to be glowing candy-apple red by now. His eyes had to be bulging out of his head. The damn heart rate, blood pressure, and oxygen monitors were dinging and beeping as if warning of an imminent nuclear explosion. "Like I said, he's supposed to be in Pakistan, handling the acquisition of smart weapons. You have to *stop* him. You *have* to find Beloi before Abernathy does.

"He doesn't give a fuck about anything but that project. And he's got strong connections in Indonesia. That's where he wanted us to grow this in the first place. He won't take the time or go to the trouble to kill the whole damn team like he should. They don't pose any significant threat to him. He'll just grab Beloi and drag her under. Which will turn Foster and the others into a pack of rabid hyenas against me."

Peggy rushed in, took one look at Young, and turned from Mr. Hyde to Dr. Jekyll. "Oh." She gave Owen a grin, one that made her look far less crotchety and a hell of a lot younger. "No wonder he's trying to launch these things through the roof. But, then, you kinda have that effect on me too, Colonel."

Owen grinned. "Good morning, Peggy."

"Yes. Yes, it is." She slid her blue gaze up one side of Owen and down the other on her way toward the monitors. "Thanks for turning it around for me. Mmm-mmm. Definitely something about a man in uniform."

"That is the worst display of unprofessional behavior—" Gil started.

"If you can't keep yourself calm, Senator, we'll damn well do it for you." The wench turned right back into Mr. Hyde, fur, fangs, and foul mouth. She silenced some monitors, messed with others. "I've had it with you and your temper. If you want to die, I'll call over to Bethesda Naval Base and ask Trina to pay you a visit. She's been begging me to let her come spike your IV since you got in. Seems you've made your share of enemies in the nursing population."

"I knew you weren't very smart." Gil spoke to Peggy, but shook his finger at Owen. "Now I have a witness to your murder conspiracy."

Peggy slammed the door of the IV pump again and gave Owen a long-suffering look. Owen just chuckled and Peggy slid past him with a hand on his bicep and a murmured, "Don't leave without saying good-bye, Colonel."

When the door closed behind him, Owen's smile vanished. "What does the FBI want?"

"I'm the one suffering here, not that bitch."

"Senator," Owen said, drawing his attention away from the door. "What does the FBI—?"

"They're asking about my relationship with Classified Chemical. My name must have come up during their investigation into *this*." He rattled the paper.

Owen's gaze narrowed. "What the hell aren't you telling me now?"

"Nothing! There is nothing to tell. There is no connection between me, Classified, and that chemical bomb in Syria. You've got to be asinine to think I'd jeopardize my position in the Senate or on the Armed Forces Committee by getting involved with something like this." One monitor started beeping again and Gil growled, about ready to rip off every wire, every tube. "That's why you need to get them off my ass. There's nothing to sniff. Make it happen, Owen."

"You want me to control an FBI investigation. Why not just ask me to bring you every Taliban head on a silver platter, Senator? I think staying here for a while is the best idea, because your head still isn't on quite right."

"Owen—"

"And because Abernathy is among the many who are starting to believe you're not going to come out of this *coma*. They're all starting to feel safe. Starting to make moves. If you show yourself now, they'll all go underground like rats in the light. The last few weeks will be a complete waste. The guys I have on Foster and Beloi's trail will be screwed, and Abernathy will be working underground. They'll all be as impossible to stop as that FBI investigation.

"And we both know that if Foster doesn't want to be found, he won't be found. His resources in the military community are endless. His finances, thanks to you and Classified, and that damn chemical leak at Lejeune, are deep. Every member of the team that supports him has powerful abilities your sick games gave them."

Gil's jaw had clenched, his fingers curled into fists. "Watch your step, Owen," he said, his voice breathless with the increase of his heart rate and breathing. "You're making me see black."

"Welcome to my world, Senator." He lowered his voice and never broke eye contact. His warrior instincts were in full swing, and putting Gil even more on edge. "*You* created this problem. *You* dragged me into it. *You* threatened my future and my life. So you'll just have to deal with my way of repairing *your* fuck-ups."

Arrogant, condescending sonofabitch. Gil reached over to a bedside table and picked up a folder of information he'd printed out from the mini-office set up in a corner of his hospital room.

"I don't care how you make it happen, Owen, just make . . . it . . . happen." Gil slapped the file against Owen's decorated chest. "Here's a file on the agent who's got her fangs out for me. A Special Agent Sofia Seville."

That name made Owen's gaze dart back to Gil's and remain. Made him reach for the folder and hold on to it.

Gil let go, triumph sliding through him. "I see you recognize her name."

"We served together in Afghanistan," Owen said, guarding his expression again. "I knew she'd retired from the army and gone to the FBI, but last I'd heard, she was working out of Virginia."

"Well, she's here now and obviously trying to come down hard on me to make a name for herself. Use your past relationship with her, Owen. Create a new relationship with her. I don't give a fuck how you do it, but pull her fangs out of me."

"Senator, Seville and I only have a distant professional—"

"Don't give me that shit, Owen. I've seen her picture. Don't tell me you weren't doing her while on tour together in Afghanistan. A man can't even get a decent whore in that place without the fear of getting his cock blown off by a suicide pussy bomber."

"You're mistaken, sir—"

"Don't argue with me, Colonel. Just make it happen *now* so I can get the hell out of here without having to worry about them ambushing me at home."

★ ★ ★

Mitch pressed his elbow into the leather armrest and rubbed his eyes as Seth's cell rang in his ear. He had a hundred more questions for Halina, but he needed to get ahold of his emotions and gather his temper before he continued. This was too important to blow over a seven-year-old hurt.

"Chief Masters," Seth answered, all business.

"That sounds like a porn name," Mitch said. "You make the ladies call you that?"

"I might . . . if my divorce was final."

"Shit." Mitch scraped a hand through his hair. "Is that still hung up? Those papers should have arrived two weeks ago. Did you call my office?"

"I'm on a first-name basis with Megan. She says they're sitting on Tara's attorney's desk."

Mitch's secretary was the best in the business at follow-up. But it was Mitch who would need to call to light a fire under the attorney who was pulling a new trick from under the carpet every other week to stall the divorce—at the direction of his client, Tara Masters. A woman who'd committed murder to send Teague to prison in an effort to hold on to custody of Kat Creek. Of course, Schaeffer had been the one to manipulate Tara's already twisted mind.

"Sorry about that, Seth," Mitch said. He felt for the guy. "I'll call today."

"Hey, it's not like I'm exactly eager to get back on that playing field again. When I am, I'll be on your doorstep. Right now, this is more important. Keep your focus right where it is."

Mitch had one hell of a lot of respect for the guy. He hadn't cheated on Tara during their marriage, even though she'd stopped sleeping with him a year before he initiated the divorce. Remained faithful even after Tara had been found guilty of murder and kidnapping, declared mentally unstable, and sent to the state mental hospital.

"Are you on duty? I thought you were—"

"No, I've got another two weeks of vacation and it's weird

going from twenty-four-seven for months at a time to nothing. Habit," Seth said. "Listen, something bad is going down here."

Mitch refocused. Seth had diverted his search for information on the electronic chips used in the testing of both Cash's son, Mateo, and Quaid to gather information from the employees of the Castle who hadn't died in the explosion. "Where are you now?"

"Bishop, California," he said. "A few of the people on my list have homes here. Neighbors tell me they commuted into Nevada to work, stayed there for weeks at a time before coming back again. But that's not the weird part."

"Can't wait to hear this." Mitch crossed one arm over his chest in preparation for more bizarre news. He could tell by the tone of Seth's voice the guy was unnerved.

"The people," Seth said. "They're all gone. Not just the ones who worked at the Castle, but their families too. Spouses, kids, they're all gone. Their homes are abandoned. The neighbors said they were there one day and gone the next."

Mitch's hand closed around his bicep, his mind going dark with the implications.

"Most of the houses are locked up, blinds drawn," Seth continued. "But I found one with . . . a door ajar."

"Right." Mitch scoffed. "Dude, don't go getting yourself in any more trouble than we've already made."

"The houses are still mostly intact," Seth went on with an uneasy urgency in his voice. "Like the people living there made a grab for essentials and bolted. It's fucking eerie, man. And what's even freakier—"

"Seth"—foreboding weighted Mitch's gut—"you said *one* door was ajar—"

"Most of the houses have some kind of bloodstains." Seth's voice dropped, filled with fear and insinuation. "And I'm talking streaks, pools, dude, not a few drops. I've been to my share of accident scenes and suicides, have hauled dozens of gunshot and knifing victims to the hospital, and the amount of blood in these places . . . People don't survive that kind of blood loss, man."

Nothing but Seth's breathing filled the line for a moment. Mitch's shoulders were cold. He rubbed the back of his neck and found all the hair prickled on end.

"Any similarities between the employees missing? Did they all work in the same department? Did they all perform a certain job?"

"I've been focused on the lab employees. I figured the guards and those with military background would be less willing to talk."

"*Fuck.*" Mitch closed his eyes. "Get the hell out of there, Seth. Go back to Alyssa and Teague's. Whoever's doing this will be watching for us. If they suspect you've figured out that much, you could be in a really nasty spot."

"I've already checked out everyone who lived in Bishop. I'm on my way out of town. There's one more guy I need to check out. A Chuck Torrent. His home here was one of the few undisturbed and without blood. But he's got two other homes."

"Seth," Mitch argued. "You're obviously not the only guy who's going to be looking for him. I don't need anything happening to you—"

"This Torrent guy was Abrute's lab assistant. They own homes in the same place. Their wives are friends. If I find Torrent, I might find Abrute."

Mitch hissed out a breath. If Seth could find Abrute, the man could be an absolute gold mine of information. "Promise me, Seth, you'll get out at the first hint of trouble."

"You don't realize how much fun I'm having, do you?"

"You don't realize how hellish the rest of my life would be if something happened to you, do you?"

Seth laughed, but the sound didn't hold any of his natural, deep good humor. The others would tear him to pieces if something happened to Seth because Mitch sent him on a mission. "True. I wouldn't wish their wrath on even you, buddy."

"Where are you headed?"

"Las Vegas," Seth said, "then Palm Springs."

"Joe's flying you?" Joe Marquez, a former Air Force pilot and client, had become a trusted friend.

"Marquez is the bomb, man. Can I keep him?"

"No, he's mine."

Seth laughed again. Lighter. "He'll get a big head if he knew we were fighting over him."

"He's good, Seth, with things other than planes. Like weapons. And tactical shit. Smart, savvy. Make sure he backs you up."

"Oh, man," Seth whined like a kid who'd been called away from his friends for dinner. "He's not the backup kind of guy. He's going to take all my fun."

"Not as fast as Ryder would," Mitch said. "I mean it, Seth. I don't like you being alone out there."

"Heh," he huffed a laugh. "I'll take Marquez over Ryder any day."

Mitch got a couple of promises out of Seth before they disconnected, but his mind remained steeped in trouble.

And he still had to face some very dark corners with Halina.

Mitch stood, stretched, and returned to his seat. Halina's eyes were closed, but her hand moved on Dex's head where the dog still had it settled on her thigh.

He sat, twisted the top off a beer, and drank half the bottle before he took a breath. Hopefully that would kick in soon. He'd wait until the alcohol took his edge off before he tackled Schaeffer's tie with Classified in more depth.

"Tell me how your ability works." This would be far easier to start with. "It would be nice to be able to use it to get ahead of Abernathy instead of reacting to him. And if you can see the future, why didn't you know I was coming to Washington?"

Her eyes opened, and she looked as exhausted as he felt. "It doesn't work like that," she said with irritation tightening her voice. "I can't just *see* the future. I get flashes of the futures of others, but only people I'm close to and never my own.

"Everyone thinks it would be great to be able to see the future, but it's not. I'm tortured with things I don't want to see, things I don't want to know. Like a girl at work who's got a cheating boyfriend, or the child of a neighbor having a terrible accident, or a lover contracting cancer—" She stopped and her eyes widened at the same time the words sank into Mitch's brain. Fear sizzled along his spine as she clarified, "Not you."

Relief trickled in. "Good to know."

"I don't know how or why they come and I don't have any control over them. If I did, I'd make them stop."

"Why did you separate friends from lovers? Do you see their futures differently?"

She leaned her elbow against the arm of the chair and rested her temple against her fingers. "I don't like talking about this with you, and I don't see how that matters."

"It's not a freaking day in the park for me, either, Hali, but we won't know if or how it matters until we put it with all the other pieces of the puzzle."

She hesitated. "With friends, the visions come after spending a great day together, or after bonding over something, like a shared experience. With lovers, they come after sex."

Mitch's gut clenched, like he'd been hit. Stupid. He knew she'd had sex. With other guys. Probably great guys. Probably guys who treated her a hell of a lot better than he had over the last fifteen hours. Probably guys who didn't slam her up against the wall and fuck her until she begged them to make her come.

His body ignited. Mitch poured the rest of the beer down his throat to keep himself from catching fire. But that didn't help a million questions from bombarding him.

"And I have two different kinds of visions," she said. "I have the kind I had in the car last night—quick flashes of danger involving someone"—she looked away—"someone I care about, and longer complex visions I have with lovers after sex."

"How did you handle the boyfriend with cancer?" he asked. "Did you tell him about your ability?"

"No," she said with an inflection that insinuated he was ridiculous. "I just found a different way to get him to see the doctor, where I knew he'd be diagnosed."

"Well, you're obviously not together anymore. Why? Did you leave him too?"

And as soon as it was out of his mouth, he knew he'd lost control again.

She sat straight and looked him directly in the eye. "No, I didn't *leave* him. I went to every doctor's appointment with him, every chemo appointment, stayed with him while he puked all night; then I got up and worked all day, went grocery shopping, and cooked for him when he was too weak. When he finally found remission, our relationship had changed so drastically we both agreed to just stay friends."

Okay, he was an ass. He was worse than an ass. He rubbed his eyes.

"Another man I was seeing was a bicyclist," she said, rage burning in her words, "and I saw an accident on a bridge he always crossed with his team that crippled him. Instead of letting him go on the ride, I made love to him so he'd be late and miss their meeting point. He took a different route that day and stayed safe. Two of his buddies died on that ride."

Like you made love to me all those years ago to keep me in the dark?

Oh, the words were so close to slipping out. He twisted the top off another beer and took a long drink to drown them.

His mind turned to the freeway accident. "Did you see the gray SUV last night? The one that caused the accident?"

"I just saw the accident. I saw—" Her gaze went dark and dropped away.

"Saw what?"

She picked up her empty juice glass and rolled it between her palms. "I saw us in the accident."

"I thought you didn't see your own future."

"Essentially, it was *your* future. I just happened to be there."

His stomach went cold with the sudden realization of how horrifying that had to be. "What . . . happened?"

"I don't want to talk about it," her voice softened.

"Did we die?"

"It didn't happen," she murmured, "there's no point—"

"*Did we die?*"

She set the glass down with a hard *click* and met his eyes.

"*You* died. Okay?"

The horror in her bright eyes, the glaze of tears filling them halfway, made Mitch's throat close. His mind grew curious about exactly what she'd seen, but he doubted he could stomach the answer. Wasn't so sure she could handle giving it.

He let a moment of silence pass. Let her wipe the tears out of her eyes and her breathing settle before he asked, "So what about this bicyclist guy? How did you stop seeing his future?"

"I stopped seeing *him*."

"You must have found some way of dealing with these visions, Hali." His frustration came to a boiling point. "Or, what? Did you just go through a series of short relationships? Sleep with a guy, realize you saw his future like the others, and then break up? And what about friends? Do your friendships end this way too? Is it different with different guys, different friends? Does it happen with some guys and not others? I mean . . . how does your power *work?*"

She was shaking her head before he even stopped talking. His frustration finally boiled over. He pushed to his feet, pacing toward the back of the plane, hands laced behind his head.

"I don't know how my visions work because I don't get close enough to anyone to figure it out. It's less painful to live alone than it is to see the futures of the people I care about, then feel responsible for keeping them safe or worrying that the great break or happiness that was coming their way could be changed by some decision they made in the meantime.

"I don't have friends, Mitch. Not like your friends. I don't have boyfriends. Or lovers. I tried it twice. That was enough to know I couldn't do it."

Mitch stopped walking. He stared at the wall, absorbing her words. But he couldn't. He couldn't fathom such an isolated existence. Yet, he didn't doubt her words. The research confirmed that information. Making love to her—correction, fucking her . . . he ground his teeth . . . had confirmed her sexual inactivity, but . . .

He didn't understand. His mind simply couldn't work that puzzle. It went against human nature, even for someone on the run. She had the means to be comfortable. She could have sought out help for her powers, at least enough to find a way to allow a relationship and friends.

Mitch sensed more secrets. More lies.

That's when something staring him in the face suddenly came into sharp focus—something he'd been looking right past all this time. "That bad dream last night . . ." An eerie crawl worked its way through his body. "That wasn't a dream. It was a *vision,* wasn't it?" He turned and dropped his arms. "You saw *my* future again."

Her face slowly drained of color. She heaved a breath, but didn't answer.

Mitch opened his mouth to ask what she'd seen, then remembered her fear as she'd woken, and wasn't sure he wanted to know. Of course, given the situation, he *had* to know.

"Tell me, Halina. Was it the accident again?"

"No." She returned her gaze to his, her eyes challenging, but the color in her face still absent. "It was a good glimpse of your future."

Good? How good could it have been? "What was in it?"

Her lips pursed. A veil shielded the emotions in her eyes, making her seem impassive at best, annoyed at worst. "You have a nice future awaiting you, Mitch. Not much different from the life I imagine you've been living."

"You mean the one you've been watching me live. Why would you do that?"

"I don't stalk you, Mitch." She laughed softly, but without humor. "Your handsome face is always popping up in the society pages. You're a little hard to miss."

"My face does not come up in a Washington—"

"My coworker has a subscription to the *San Francisco Examiner,*" she said, her whole disposition changing as if the exhaustion had finally hit her. "I'm lucky enough to get the paper delivered to work every . . . single . . . morning."

No wonder she knew so much about his life. Not a particularly pretty picture when he thought about it viewed from her perspective.

"What did you see?" he asked. "In the vision last night?"

A dry smile lifted the edges of her mouth and she leaned back in the chair, her gaze distant, her mood subdued. "Just you, at some highbrow event, looking every bit San Francisco's most eligible bachelor in your designer tuxedo as you were seduced by one of your gorgeous women."

His brows fell.

"And you were so . . . happy." Her gaze had gone distant, like she was remembering. "Just . . . top-of-the-world *happy* . . ." She almost whispered the last word as if in pain. But she pushed her lips into a smile.

Mitch took another drink of beer, realizing he should have started the morning with something harder from the case Christy had shown Halina.

"So no worries about where your future will lead," she said. "No matter what the outcome of last night between us, your life will stay as sparkly, magical, and sex-filled as ever."

He jerked the bottle from his mouth, spilling some of the beer. He wiped it off his chin with the back of his hand, glaring at her. His life wasn't remotely sparkly or magical. And that's all he had—sex. Never anything more. The life had always left a frustrating, painful hollow inside him. And now, after being with Halina, it felt like a fucking chasm.

He didn't want to go back to that existence. But he wasn't interested in a life of deception, either.

She had no fucking clue how empty his future looked to him right now.

"And you *believe* these visions?" he asked, incredulous. "You, the hard-core scientist. You've created a life of isolation based on these *visions*?"

Her gaze cleared and her eyes were like blue ice. "I believe these visions because every single one of them has come true. Every one for seven years, no matter who I have them of or what they show, it's happened.

"I believe them because they're *accurate*."

Mitch opened his mouth to argue, then thought about how Halina had described them. She saw the *events* of a person's possible future. She wasn't empathic, like Kai, so she didn't know how people felt. She wasn't clairaudient, like Keira, so she didn't know how people thought. She only knew what showed on the outside. And Mitch knew he was a great showman—mainly because he didn't give a shit what anyone else thought of him. He went into a situation for a specific outcome and became whoever, whatever was necessary to achieve the goal.

Of course she thought his life was sex-filled, magical, and happy. That was exactly how he'd meant to project it—to everyone, including himself.

He finished off the beer and changed the subject. "When and how were you exposed to the chemical?"

She pulled her knees into the chair and wrapped her arms around her legs. With her chin on her knees, she stared blankly at the table. "An accident at the lab. About a month before I left."

The second jab hit his gut and forced him to refocus. "You had these powers *before* you left me?"

"Yes, but I didn't know what they were. I thought I was going insane from the stress."

He lifted his hands to his face and rubbed again. "Halina, you *had* to be involved in the project if you were exposed."

Her light eyes swung up and held on his face. "Your belief in me is refreshing, Mitch. But you're wrong." She held up a hand, eyes closed. "Hold on a second, I'm savoring the words . . . *Mitch, you're wrong.*" A blissful smile lit her face. "Man, that really has a ring to it."

"Ha-ha," Mitch said.

When Halina opened her eyes, the humor was gone. "I was looking into Rostov's work after hours and I dropped a tray of slides. I wasn't wearing my lab jacket and I had on a top with spaghetti straps. The chemical splashed all over my chest and arms."

"You told me you weren't working with Rostov," Mitch countered, "but now you're saying you were checking on his work."

"He was my competition. I wanted to see how far he'd come. I had to re-create the slides I'd destroyed or he would have known either Gorin or I had broken into his secured area."

"Competition?"

"He was trying to alter chromosomes with chemicals. I was trying to alter the chromosomes with natural processes. I didn't believe in using chemicals. Knew there would be serious side effects."

This just got deeper and deeper. She knew so much more than she was telling him. "How do you know that?"

"Because I know the chemical. It originated in the area of uranium mines in Kazakhstan, on the southern border of Russia. I grew up hearing stories about what happened to the men working in those mines—exposure to the raw chemical causing disintegration of limbs, blindness, fatal deformities, mental illness, death. At least once a year some horrific accident would kill thousands.

"And the chemical had to go through a radical stabilization process before Rostov could use it in the lab. Nothing that needs to be altered that severely should be used in genetic engineering—at least not in my opinion."

There were those damn morals again.

He just wasn't buying this bullshit story she was trying to sell. Mitch had yet to meet someone who could compartmentalize their values and core personality characteristics so completely to only certain areas—or certain people—in their life.

"Classified supplied the chemical for Schaeffer," he said as if he knew, but was guessing.

She paused, bit the inside of her lip. "No. They performed the stabilization."

"And if I had exposed Classified with my case in the DA's office, Schaeffer couldn't have used the chemical in its raw form. I'd have cut off the supply of chemicals to the project."

She nodded, then murmured, "And thanks for not calling it *my* project."

She'd tried to save his job. She'd suffered through that torment with Schaeffer so Mitch could hold on to the job he loved. The job that could have led him to bigger, better opportunities.

That was the Halina he'd known and loved. Not the one who'd broken his heart with a fake husband and lies upon lies.

His gut, the one that gave him all his solid hunches and insightful intuition, told him the prior was the real Halina. And that the woman she now presented was only a façade she wanted him to buy into. He had no idea why. But he knew enough to know he still had a lot to uncover.

"If you have visions with sex, and you had your powers before you left me . . ." Mitch said, and took another drink of beer, wondering if he really even wanted to know, but unable not to ask. "You must have had visions of my future."

She didn't respond, just stared at her hands where she picked at her cuticles.

"And?" he prodded.

She sighed. "And you're just one example of how I know my visions are accurate. You're living the grand life I saw you living before I left, filled with success, money, travel, friends, a family who loves you." She paused. Her jaw jumped. "And of course, lots and lots of women who can't get enough of you."

"All right, you two." Christy came sauntering down the aisle in all her long-legged glory and Mitch sat back, gripping the arms of the chair to hold his frustration in check. "We'll be landing in a little bit. If you want to use the showers, it's going to have to be fast and now. Mitch, your things are at the back of the plane. Halina, yours are in the front. Given the trouble signals I'm getting from you two and the lack of time, you're staying in different bathrooms."

Mitch pushed to his feet. "I feel like I'm at sixth-grade camp."

"No, Mitch." Christy turned him toward the back of the plane. "Here you won't be sneaking into the girl's bathroom." She pointed. "March."

Mitch wandered toward the bathroom and glanced back as Christy guided Halina toward the other bathroom, then sat nearby and rained attention on Dex.

In the shower, Mitch thought over all the surprises Halina had delivered this morning.

The way she'd stayed and cared for her sick lover made Mitch feel like he'd never mattered to her. Her visions of him with other women made him feel like a bottom-feeder and gave him a little more insight into why she might have run without him. There was no incentive to stay if she'd believed they'd only end up apart. Mitch couldn't fault her for being scared or taking care of herself. Even her reasons for not coming to him with the problem were on target.

But being fired hadn't taken away his knowledge of the law. Having a black X next to his name on Capitol Hill didn't mean he couldn't have reached out to other sources for help. He hadn't been rendered useless. And after all that shit had come down on him, he'd needed her emotional support. She'd stayed and supported the other guy through his cancer. Yet, even knowing how much she'd been hurting Mitch at the time, she'd abandoned him anyway.

Wasn't the heart of a solid relationship believing in someone even when all the chips were down? The way Alyssa had believed in Teague when he'd been convicted of murder. The way Keira had taken a chance on Luke even when she knew their fundamental differences wouldn't change. The way Jessica had changed her whole life to start over with Quaid, a man who didn't even remember her as his wife.

But a few hard knocks and Halina had turned away. She hadn't trusted him enough to lay her deepest troubles at his feet. In fact, she hadn't even trusted him enough to have a sit-down, heart-to-heart about Classified Chemical. There were so many reasonable ways for her to have asked him to back off the case other than stealing his files . . .

His mind caught. The image of that cardboard file box housing the Classified files filled his mind. He pictured it in his office by his desk.

He shut off the water, toweled off, and dressed quickly. He emerged from the bathroom with a knot of anxiety burning beneath his sternum. This was a ridiculous long shot. Halina walked toward him from the opposite end of the plane and made his stomach do a twisted roll at the same time his chest tightened up.

She paused beside their seats, a thoughtful frown on her face, then took a slow look down his white button-down and khakis. Not exactly his style, but they fit well and they were comfortable. When her gaze returned to his, she was smiling in approval, a hot little simmering grin. "You clean up nice, Foster."

"Ah, yeah . . ." he breathed. "Was thinking the same . . ." He had no idea what he was trying to say.

She wore light jeans cut low on her hips and fitted to those sleek legs. A top that could have been considered lingerie. Really just sheer fabric a shade darker than her eyes that hugged her torso like a second skin. A second skin with tiny straps over her shoulders and a bodice that cupped her breasts into sweet mounds that made Mitch's mouth water. And sexy, strappy heels that made his mind go completely haywire.

His hands clenched and flexed at his sides, remembering how he'd had them on all that beauty last night. All that and more. But he hadn't appreciated it near as much as he should have. Especially given the realization that he'd probably never get another chance.

Regret created swampland out of his gut. He swallowed past a tight throat.

"Took my mouth right out of the words . . ." he murmured, then realized what he'd said and laughed. "You know what I meant."

"Yeah," she said softly, the first real smile he'd seen on her face in seven years, her Caribbean gaze sparkling with happiness. "But I like what you said better."

She'd left her hair down, in a loose braid that she'd pulled forward over her shoulder and swooped low enough on her forehead to cover most of the colorful bruise. She still didn't wear a speck of makeup, and that alone would have filled Mitch's groin with blood. But when she turned to slide past the aisle seat before lowering into the one by the window, Mitch caressed a look over her shoulders and the crisscross straps that created a ladder over the upper half of her back. She wasn't wearing a bra. His whole body had gone weak by the time his gaze paused on her ass and thighs, perfectly fitted into that soft denim.

He gripped the top of his chair to get himself to the target and not fall on his ass in the middle of the aisle. Christ, she looked edible. Completely, scrumptiously, *edible*.

He dropped into the chair and Dex nudged his nose under Mitch's hand to be petted. He scratched the dog's ears absently. Wasn't he mad at her? Didn't he want to ask her something important? Couldn't he just forgo all that and pull her into his lap?

"Buckle up," Christy called. "We'll be in Reno in five."

Reno. Thirty miles from Alyssa's house. And the team. And meeting his new nephew for the first time.

Mitch's mind came back online. "Halina."

She looked up, her gaze distant and exhausted.

"The files on Classified Chemical that were in my office," he said. "In a brown—"

"File box," she finished. "What about them?"

Mitch licked his lips, tightened his gut and asked, "What did you do with them?"

Her brow tightened. Her crystal gaze went distant again. "I . . ."

He waited as long as he could stand, probably not more than a few milliseconds. "Did you destroy them? Throw them away? Shred them?"

"No. I just . . . hid them." Her confused eyes focused on his face. "I hid them in your apartment."

Mitch leaned on the table, his mind envisioning the apartment, every crevice, every closet, and he shook his head.

"They weren't there. When I moved out, I cleaned that place top to bottom myself. They weren't there and they weren't with the things I moved."

"That's because I hid them underneath the sink."

Again he shook his head. "No, I cleaned—"

"Beneath the loose floorboards under the sink."

Mitch's spine tingled. "What loose floorboards? I didn't know there were any loose floorboards."

A tiny smile lifted a corner of her mouth. "That's because you hardly ever did the dishes and you never fixed them like I suggested."

A soft spot opened in his belly regardless of his attempt to keep it closed off. "That's because someone always dragged me into the bedroom right after dinner and never gave me time . . ." He stopped his thoughts. Redirected his brain. "That was a big box, Halina. There's no way it could have fit—"

"As I said, you never looked under the sink. That old landmark building had charm, but it was falling apart."

His stomach leapt with hope. "You didn't take them when you left? Why not?"

"No. I'd completely forgotten about them by that time. Hiding them hadn't worked. They didn't matter anymore."

Mitch stared past Halina, his mind turning as he scraped his lip between his teeth.

"Mitch, the chances that they're still there—"

"Is that something you can see?" His gaze darted back to her, hopeful.

"No, I see the futures of people, not things. What about the others on your firefighting team? Could one of them see if they're still there?"

Quaid. He could see the papers. Maybe. If they used Cash's son, Mateo's, ability to pinpoint items on a map and combined it with Quaid's ability to see clearly . . .

The plane's tires touched the runway, bounced, and set down again for a smooth landing. He and Halina unbuckled and Christy came toward them with a smile. "You two look rested after your showers. And in better moods."

He gave her a half smile. "You mean I passed behavior modification."

"For now."

He glanced at Halina's heels and sighed with longing, then returned his gaze to Christy. "Have you looked outside?" She grinned. "What? You mean all that snow?" Shrugged. "I couldn't resist. I have boots for her too. Brian would like to know if you'll be needing us again or if we're released."

Mitch nodded. "I'll be needing you again. I'm not sure what time—later this afternoon or this evening, I'm guessing. If it's going to be tomorrow, I'll call you, but go ahead and get rooms anyway, just in case."

Halina cuddled close to Dex in the backseat of the Suburban, waiting for Mitch on his umpteenth stop in the town of Truckee before heading up the hill to Teague and Alyssa's house. Nelson, one of the security guards, had picked them up at the airport. With someone else in the car, Halina's plan to argue with Mitch over his idea to fly to Washington for those papers was out. So was asking the million questions about the people she was going to meet.

"What could he need at all these places?" Halina muttered.

Nelson, a good-looking dirty blond with deep brown eyes, grinned over his shoulder from the driver's seat. "Toys."

She lifted her brow. "Like he doesn't have enough."

"For the kids." His smile widened and a crescent dented his cheek. "If he walked in that house without something for them, they wouldn't give a damn, but he'd feel like hell."

Mitch had told her on the short walk from the jet to the SUV only that Nelson was an ex-marine he'd represented three years ago against the corps. He was dressed in black jeans, a heavy brown hunting jacket, and boots. Gloves, a knit cap, and a Smith & Wesson .45 semiautomatic rested on the console.

"Really," she said in interest. She and Mitch hadn't had the opportunity to be around children when they were together. Halina hadn't believed she'd ever have a family until she'd met Mitch. Had always believed her own upbringing had messed her up too much to be a parent. But he'd made her see herself so differently. He'd made her believe in herself.

She thought of her possible pregnancy, and even though, logically, she knew it was wrong to consider bringing a child into this dangerous, stressful existence she called a life, she desperately wanted to be pregnant with his baby.

"He's good with them?" she asked.

"He's awesome with them. They idolize him."

"Have you and Mitch been friends a long time?"

"Few years. We didn't start out that way, but when a guy saves your freaking ass against the Marine Corps, you kinda bond, you know?" He grinned, but there was a humble edge to it. "I owe him. But I'd like to think we've grown beyond that into friends."

Halina had always been able to see the exterior of Mitch's life, the activities he allowed in the public eye, but knew very little about his work.

"I'd like to hear more about that, about the work Mitch did for you—I mean, if you don't mind talking about it."

Nelson shifted in his seat to be able to look back at her without twisting. "I'll talk about the work Mitch does all day to anyone who will listen. The man is a damn god in my eyes."

Considering the hell she'd been going through with Mitch, that statement hit her funny. Plus, she was a little punchy from exhaustion and when she started laughing, she had a hard time stopping. She laughed so hard she snorted, which made Nelson laugh and Halina laugh harder. When she finally brought herself under control, she had to wipe tears from her eyes.

"Oh my God," she breathed through residual laughter, "did he make you drink the Kool-Aid?"

Another rolling laugh from Nelson filled the small space with warmth. "I'll try to make a long story short here." He gazed past Halina and out the side window. "I joined the marines straight out of high school. Grew up poor and planned on using the corps as a way to get to college. But they had other ideas for me and set me up on the fast track for MARSOC—that's the Special Forces of the Marine Corps. I was totally on board.

Loving life. Reached MARSOC in record time. Seemed I had a knack for intense situations and working under pressure. Probably from being beat up at school as a kid for being the runt."

Halina chuckled, gesturing to his significant bulk. "You must have had a growth spurt."

"Sixteen."

She nodded and sat on the edge of the seat, resting her elbows on her knees and her chin in her hands, enjoying this nonconfrontational talk with a pleasant man.

"After six years with MARSOC, working missions in every third world country on the damn planet, my CO retired—my commanding officer," he clarified. "The new CO came in with tight political ties, a huge chip on his shoulder, and several grudges to settle. Again, to shorten this up, let me just tell you that he took horribly unethical—sometimes inhumane—actions on certain missions to move political agendas and stick it to superiors. Revenge at that level is very convoluted and manipulative.

"I got caught in the middle when I refused his orders on a mission in Afghanistan. I was the captain of the team and he ordered us to open fire on a village without any intel or proof they harbored the Taliban members he claimed. There were women and children in this village and I told my men to stand down. My CO was livid—not because we didn't desecrate the village, but because I was insubordinate in front of the others. And I was court-martialed."

Halina's muscles tightened in defense of this man. She didn't know him, didn't know whether he was lying or telling the truth, only knew how manipulative and vicious those in power could be and how trapped a person could feel when that wrath fell.

"My CO was hell-bent on making an example out of me, to send a message throughout the corps that no one crossed him. Unfortunately, he also had powerful allies. And they set out to bury me. They charged me with so many offenses I lost track.

They fabricated evidence, bribed and threatened my own men to swear to things that didn't happen. I was in military prison, looking at losing everything—my career, my pension, and my freedom for the rest of my life—when I found Mitch.

"He'd just nailed the corps big-time for a chemical spill into the water supply near Camp Lejeune. They'd known about the contamination for months but did nothing about it. A lot of men got sick. A couple died. Mitch took on a class action suit that no one else would touch. He filed against the corps and the chemical company and won. Got lost pay and lifelong medical care for the guys affected. Got multimillion-dollar settlements for the families of the men who'd died. The chemical company paid up, but had to file for bankruptcy afterward. Though I heard they're up and running again now.

"Anyway, I figured he was probably the only person who would even touch my case. My JAG attorney was a piece of sh—" Nelson cut himself off, grinned. "Piece of crap. He basically told me to plead to whatever they offered. That I was screwed. I called Mitch, asked him to take my case. Actually, I begged like a man at the guillotine.

"I'm not exaggerating when I say Mitch saved my life. He got every charge dropped. He got me back pay from the time they arrested me and cut off my salary to the time I chose to take an honorable discharge instead of reinstating to my former command. He even got me a lump-sum settlement for emotional pain and suffering. He saved my pension, saved my future, gave me something to live for."

Pride swelled inside Halina. Tears stung her eyes. To know her sacrifice hadn't been wasted, to know Mitch had been out here, doing work like this, meant everything to her. "He's an amazing attorney," she murmured. "No doubt about that."

"He's an amazing *man*. One of those people who restores faith in the human race." Nelson said, thoughtful. "And, yes, a brilliant attorney." Then he grinned, and added, "But I keep that to myself because he eats it up.

"After he had everything with my case settled and he knew

I was solid—physically, mentally, financially—he went after my CO. He went after the superior officers who cooperated with my CO. He even attacked politicians."

Halina sat back, frowning, part confusion, part shock. "Why? He wasn't going to get anything out of that."

"He didn't get anything out of my case either. Wouldn't let me pay him. I had to make a *huge* stink about it. Had to go to his office and physically back him into a corner with the threat of damaging his GQ face to get him to agree that I could pay him fifty bucks a month if I really had to." Nelson chuckled. "Asshole. I pay him five hundred a month, but I could pay for the rest of my life and never pay him enough.

"He has that kind of arrangement with a lot of military guys. Knows we make shit. Knows we work hard. Respects what we do and why we do it. He has a financial adviser in his firm now who assesses what a guy makes and works out some kind of acceptable payment, puts them on a plan if they need it. That way Mitch can avoid threats like mine. But from what I've heard— and I've heard a lot—he gets paid pennies for what he does. At least for military guys. I don't know how he handles his other clients."

Halina's heart ached with this new window into Mitch. "What happened with the others he went after?"

Nelson's grin was vengefully satisfied. "My CO was stripped of his command and demoted several levels where he has no authority. His wages were garnished so severely he's living in a cardboard box. The superiors lost years of service and also had wages garnished—all big hits to their future since their retirement pay is based off their highest year's salary. Everyone has letters in their files, which will make people think twice about hiring them for contract work after they retire. A few politicians got so much negative press, they resigned from their seats in the House and Senate. Mitch made sure they'd all feel the repercussions of their actions for the rest of their life."

That last statement struck her heart like a fist. Mitch's seething anger toward her based on his perceived betrayal seven years ago now made more sense. Maybe he wasn't consciously seeking revenge on Halina, maybe he truly did simply need her to help him put Schaeffer away, but she was starting to see a theme in his past. She couldn't help but wonder if revenge hadn't been hardwired into Mitch. And whether the scars she'd left on his psyche hadn't instigated that burning need to punish.

Halina knew everyone had black marks on their souls. She'd spent a lot of time thinking about how they got there. But she'd never considered how, or if, they could be removed. Like a scuff on the floor, polished away with time and repetitive behavior. In her own experience, she believed those dark grooves embedded in her childhood would stay forever. She also believed she was more easily scarred because of them. But removal?

Movement outside drew her gaze. Mitch opened the passenger's door with a mischievous grin and kicked his shoes on the running board to shake off the loose snow before climbing in. An icy blast of air made Halina curl closer to Dex.

"You must have found something good," Nelson said. "You look like you drew blood."

"Yeah." He shut the door sounding a little breathless. As he shrugged out of his jacket and buckled his belt, he said, "You know those creepy little figurines Kat's into with the bug eyes? Dogs, cats, fish . . ."

Nelson made a sound and cringed as he pulled back out onto the road. "Those things freak me out. I told her I'd rather teach her Barbies to shoot than play with those things."

Mitch barked a laugh. "Bet Teague loved that."

Nelson made another sound, this one more noncommittal.

"I got the brand-new one." Mitch reached in the bag and pulled out a small package. He pushed it into Nelson's line of sight. "A raccoon."

Nelson put up an arm as if to protect himself. "Ah! The burn! Get that thing away from me. I'm going to have nightmares."

Laughing, Mitch turned it around and inspected the package. "It's not that bad."

"Dude." Nelson looked at Mitch like he'd told him he was going to have a sex change. "You've been working too hard."

He held it up for Halina to see and gave her a pained, questioning, is-it-that-bad look. It was the most congenial, most spectacularly ordinary thing he'd done yet. Almost as if they were . . . friends. The thought filled her with melancholy warmth.

She scrunched one side of her face at the deranged little creature. "Hmm," she murmured, letting her smile relax as she looked at him. "I think they were going for the so-ugly-it's-cute design."

A grin spread across his face. "Exactly!" He jabbed a fist into Nelson's shoulder. "See. So ugly it's cute."

"Ow." Nelson laughed, rubbing his shoulder. "Fine. Whatever. *I'm* not playing with it." He mocked a full body shiver. "But I wouldn't mention that theory to Kat. And you might want to wear earplugs when you give it to her. What did you get for Mateo?"

"What else?"

"Crayons," the two men said in unison.

Their playfulness gave Halina insight into a different side of Mitch. One she'd thought had been stamped out of him since they'd parted. Seeing it again was bittersweet.

Mitch turned to Halina again. "You've got to see this kid's talent. He's like a Crayola van Gogh. I've got his pictures framed all over my office."

Halina's heart felt too big for her body. God, how she loved seeing him happy. Loved knowing how much he'd given back to others. Loved seeing what a rich, loving life he'd built for himself.

Loved knowing that doing the right thing made her life and all she'd given up . . . bearable.

"Listen," Mitch said to her, his voice serious again, "just to prepare you, everyone is here. These people are like the most bizarre, dysfunctional extended family you'll ever meet. Stems from some stupid kumbaya firefighter thing."

Nelson laughed.

"As I explained, they all have powers," Mitch continued. "But they all hold them in check around the rest of us—most of the time. Kai is empathic, Keira is clairaudient, Teague has thermokinetic abilities, uses them mostly for healing, though he's learned a few new tricks recently."

"He's melting every piece of metal he can get his hands on," Nelson said. "When he started welding kitchen utensils together, oh my God, I thought Alyssa was going to stab him with one of his new-fangled sporks."

Mitch laughed, then rested his head against the seat with a smile that just wouldn't quit. "Hell, I've been missing all the good stuff." He spoke over his shoulder to Halina. "Quaid, I told you, is a remote viewer and can teleport. His wife, Jessica, is a scryer, but her abilities seem to have improved as well and she shares some of her husband's abilities. The boy, Mateo, is also a remote viewer, though he uses his skills a little differently from Quaid. And Luke, Keira's fiancé, is Teflon Man and a supreme pain in the ass."

Nelson laughed again. "Come on, you're throwing a lot at her at once." He glanced in the rearview mirror and met Halina's gaze, which was probably glazed over with the complicated emotions arising with the information overload. "If he gives you a test, I'll kick his ass."

Halina's mind was clogged with the onslaught of unbelievable information. "Teflon Man?"

"Bulletproof," Nelson said. "Fireproof. Explosion proof. Et cetera."

"Though we haven't tried acid on him yet," Mitch said, his sarcasm thick. "And I've been trying to get Keira to let me go at him with a freshly sharpened set of Henckels. But maybe I can chuck a few of Teague's sporks at him while I'm here."

"Such a wet blanket, that Keira," Nelson muttered. "I liked your nuclear explosive idea."

"I know, right?" Mitch said.

Nelson laughed. "*Meltdown.*"

"Seriously."

They were like two mischievous little boys planning to tie fireworks to the cat's tail.

"But he did forget to mention," Nelson said, "that Keira and

Luke's powers combine to create new and stronger powers and that the whole team is learning how to work together to create hybrid abilities." He glanced at Mitch. "When are they going to learn to transfer those to us?"

Mitch's smile twisted. "I'm not so sure I want them."

"Enough," Halina said, dropping her head and rubbing her temples. "Way too much information."

Her stomach twisted tighter with every mile along the road. Her decision seven years ago had touched every one of these people in a negative way. Some in horrendous ways. She didn't know what to expect and felt the tension all the way up her spine. All she could do was grit her teeth until they finally turned in to a long driveway lined with pines, and paused at a metal split-rail gate.

Out of the woods, three men emerged, each wearing the same clothes as Nelson—black jeans, brown hunting jacket, boots. But these men wore their gloves, and knit caps, and each had a semiauto machine gun over his shoulder and a handgun strapped to his thigh.

ELEVEN

O wen planted both elbows on his desk and rubbed his face. His laptop played the video surveillance tapes from the lab where Halina had worked seven years before, prior to leaving DARPA.

Working from the distant past forward to the day Halina disappeared, he'd already viewed four months of monotonous tapes. Now, two months prior to her disappearance, the activity had become far more interesting.

The same four sections were displayed on his screen—one corner visualizing a wide-angle shot of Halina's lab, one of Gorin's lab, one of Rostov's lab, and one of a refrigerated storage area they shared. No audio accompanied the files, but Owen didn't need any. After working with Schaeffer at DARPA before he'd become a senator, and now after watching the man work the Hill, Owen knew Schaeffer's body language, his facial expressions. He knew his voice cues too, and although those weren't relevant here, their addition in his head helped Owen understand the intensity of what Rostov, Gorin, and Beloi had gone through.

On the screen, Schaeffer duckwalked into Gorin's lab. The two men immediately began to argue—Owen believed they were really finishing an argument they'd started the day before. And that's where the power of the footage lay—being able to watch the progressing tangle of relationships and Schaeffer's escalating manipulation and abuse.

The frequency with which Schaeffer visited all three labs increased over time. In addition to that common thread, the confrontations between Schaeffer and all three scientists intensified. The only difference he could detect was that the man's confrontations with Halina took longer to develop—probably because she was far more congenial than the men. Far more eager to please. Definitely the hardest worker and the most brilliant of the three.

Schaeffer had tried befriending Halina first. Mentoring her. When that didn't get the results he wanted, he'd moved on to seduction—which wasn't just a joke, it was a sadistic joke. As time moved on, his tactics deteriorated to the same heavy-handed methods he'd used to control Rostov and Gorin. And while Rostov and Gorin had fought back—both verbally and physically—Halina had endured. When it had become too much, she'd escaped.

Owen found the footage increasingly difficult to watch. Day in and day out, Schaeffer's demands, his rants, he threats continued. He'd become physically abusive with both Rostov and Gorin. Threatened Halina with physical abuse.

The varied responses to Schaeffer's abuse fascinated Owen. Rostov battled back, full tilt. He and Schaeffer had the most volatile relationship. Rostov's independence showed in the way he stood up to his so-called boss with both physical and verbal tactics. Gorin, far more interested in the research than people, tried to avoid Schaeffer by ducking out when he knew the other man was coming. By ignoring him when he came in. And when it all became too much, Gorin snapped. Went on destructive rampages through the lab, ransacking the place. Once Schaeffer tossed up his hands and walked out, Gorin would often dissolve into sobs and sit in the corner for hours. Talk about dysfunctional.

But Halina was different. She was strong, but silent. When she argued with Schaeffer, it was controlled, logical, reasonable. She would point out her reports, gesture to her experiments, speak calmly. Halina held it together even as Schaeffer's anger rose.

Her composure only faltered when Schaeffer lost his temper and threatened violence. And even then, she held herself together until he left the lab. Only then did she break down.

She was a strong woman and Owen had one hell of a lot of respect for her. Considering what she'd been through as a kid, where she'd come from, what she'd accomplished . . . she might have been the strongest woman he'd ever known.

That thought made his gaze drift toward Sofia's file on the edge of his desk.

No. Sophia was the very strongest woman Owen had ever met. Strong, yet soft. Compassionate. Funny. Smart.

Damn. Why did she have to be involved in this?

Owen paused the lab footage, took a breath, and opened Sofia's file. Her official FBI photo stared up at him. His breath caught in his chest, and Owen held it as his gaze skimmed the image. She was even more beautiful now. Soft olive complexion, deep whiskey-brown eyes, long, almost black hair that shone with cinnamon highlights in the sun. That last part he didn't see in the image. That last part he remembered.

And he remembered so much more. Their friendship. Their bond. Their mutual respect. Their shared goals and values. Their similar sense of humor.

She'd been his best friend for so long. He still thought of her often. Wished they could have stayed in touch. But the sexual tension had become too strong. They knew they either had to act on it or let go.

Since he'd been her CO, since he'd been an officer and she enlisted, since she'd been a gold nugget, ripe for promotion and success, he'd let go.

She hadn't been happy, but she'd understood.

And he'd missed her. Had never been as close to any other woman in his life. Including . . . maybe especially . . . his almost ex-wife, Libby. He'd thought he'd been in love with Jocelyn for a long time before her recent death. But the woman he'd loved hadn't been real. She'd been nothing but an illusion. It had only taken him an hour of looking through the files she'd created to set him up to take all the blame in this fiasco to realize she hadn't been the woman he'd thought.

Owen could only hope Sofia had turned out better than Jocelyn.

Schaeffer had come so close to a beating when he'd accused Owen of screwing Sofia in Afghanistan, he still vibrated with the need to punch something.

The intercom on his phone buzzed and Owen startled. He pulled his gaze from Sofia's photo and closed the file.

"Yes, Stephanie," he said then cleared his throat when his voice came out raspy.

"The FBI is here to see you, sir."

Alarm swirled in Owen's gut. His gaze darted to Sofia's file, then back to the phone.

Owen closed his eyes and covered his face. Her smile appeared on his closed lids and excitement, longing . . . desire . . . heated his body. When he opened his eyes, his gaze took in the frozen images of the lab and Schaeffer yelling at Halina.

All his emotions spiraled into a knot and lodged beneath his ribs in regret. He knew exactly how this would look to her. Just the way Schaeffer and Jocelyn had planned to make it look—like Owen was as corrupt as they were.

"Uh . . . sir?" Stephanie said. "Special Agent Seville—"

"Yes, Steph, sorry. I'll . . . be right out."

Halina gasped at the sight of the armed men skulking out of the snow-dappled forest. Mitch laid a hand on her knee from the front seat. She jumped and gripped the armrest, her gaze darting from the men closing in on the gate to Mitch's face. Dex craned his neck and growled at the men.

"*Tikhiy*," Mitch murmured, then said to Halina. "It's just the guards."

Jesus Christ. She released her breath as they drove through the gate and Mitch and Nelson waved at the others, who waved back. Behind them, the men closed the gate and dispersed back into the forest.

A shiver traveled across Halina's shoulders and into her chest. "Okay, that was just . . . creepy."

When she turned to face the front again, she realized Mitch's hand was still on her knee, and she was holding it there. But his focus was out the windshield, and Halina followed his gaze as she released his hand.

The sight filling the wide windshield melted the last remnants of fear. A log-style home lay at the end of a curved drive. The wraparound porch was protected by Plexiglas and held two different sitting areas marked by rattan chairs with fluffy pads clustered around low coffee tables. A layer of foot-thick snow blanketed the high-peaked roof and icicles stretched from the eaves. A curl of smoke rose from a chimney near the back, warm light glowed from the windows, and everything was so . . . still.

She stared for a moment, soaking in the same sense of tranquility she often found on the lake in the bitter early morning hours, or when she went for a five a.m. row on the weekends when everyone else was still warm in bed.

Cravings stirred deep within her. She recognized the achy sensation of longing for a different kind of life. For companionship, friendship, love. Yes, she wanted passion too. The kind of passion she'd never found with anyone but Mitch. But having passion without the rest was like having icing without the cake.

A door closed and the car shook. Halina's gaze came into sharp focus and she found herself alone with Mitch; Nelson was strolling toward two of the other guys.

She avoided looking at Mitch. He'd want to get out of the car in a few seconds. Want to go inside with the others. Her shoulder muscles tightened. Her heart rate sped.

"I have no idea what to expect in there." She had to pull harder to get air. Sweat filmed her face and neck. "I know one person out of how many? Twelve?"

"Counting the kids," he said, "yeah, twelve."

"How much have you told them?" Halina asked, pressing a hand to her suddenly dizzy head.

"Most."

She swore under her breath. "They're going to hate me. How long are we staying?"

Mitch's hand squeezed her knee again. "Hali, they are not going to hate you."

"They should."

"For them, this is about Schaeffer, not you. Teague escaped prison and took Alyssa hostage. Dragged her around the state, put her life at risk several times. Yes, Teague did those things himself, but we all know Schaeffer drove him to it."

Hope sparked in the shadows of her heart. If he could see Teague's actions as justified . . . maybe he could expand that view to include hers. "Even you?"

He held her gaze. Silence grew.

A smile lifted his lips—a dry, forced smile. "Extenuating circumstances, right?"

His hand left her knee and he turned to exit the car. The slam of the door felt like a fist to her heart. He could forgive Teague. But not her.

He pulled open her door and stood aside as Dex hesitated. Her dog glanced down at the snow, back up at Halina, down at the snow, and whined.

"Come on, boy," Mitch said and Dex jumped down and sniffed the snow.

Halina climbed out and breathed deep. The air was sharp, crisp. Knowing what waited inside took the fairy-tale feel away from the beautiful home. She crossed her arms tight and just stood. Her feet seemed stuck.

Dex stood next to her, lifting his paws and setting them back down, looking at the snow with another whine.

"I don't think he likes it," Mitch said.

"He doesn't know what it is."

"Come on, Dex." Mitch started for the house and gestured to the dog. "Inside."

Dex bounded ahead and Mitch grinned. When he looked beside him and Halina wasn't there, he turned and started back.

"You're in good company here, Hali." He put an arm around

her shoulders and urged her forward. "These are people who understand you. Who've been through the same hardships—or worse."

They climbed the stairs and he paused in front of the heavy wood and glass doors. He turned her toward him and took the collar of the faux-fur-lined parka Christy had picked up for her. His expression was serious, confident.

He'd relaxed since they'd deplaned, and while Halina had grown more tense as they'd approached this new confrontation, Mitch had grown almost peaceful. She didn't know if anything she'd said on the plane had made a positive difference in his opinion of her. If anything, it had seemed to anger him more. Hurt him more. She'd hoped the truth—or partial truth— would have alleviated some of the pain she'd caused him.

"Together, we're strong," he said, conviction in his voice. "Together we cleared Teague of murder, took Mateo away from Rostov, and rescued Cash and Quaid from the Castle. Now that I've found you, we've got everyone back. We're so close. Focus on making Schaeffer pay, Hali."

There was that need for revenge again. She'd been a fool to think he could forgive her—even for only what he knew, which wasn't the worst of it.

"You're going to close the circle," he whispered urgently, begging her to jump on board. "I'm sure of it."

She lowered her gaze, unable to hold his when she knew she wouldn't be the link he was hoping for. The link he thought he needed. That they all thought they needed.

A baby's fussy complaints sounded through the doors. Halina tensed, glancing toward the glass, then back at Mitch. All the seriousness had vanished from his face, replaced by a huge grin as he turned toward the entry.

"God, I can't wait to get ahold of that kid," he murmured, more to himself than to Halina as he bent to pet Dex. "*Tikhiy,* boy."

When Mitch opened the door, a soft ding sounded deeper in the house. Halina had a similar security system to signal an open door or window. She stepped into the house after Mitch, immediately focusing on the voices and laughter coming from somewhere to the left. The scents of burning wood and lavender would have made any normal guest feel instantly at home. Halina stayed by the door while Mitch walked deeper into the foyer.

The joyous—and loud—scream of a little girl immediately filled the halls, echoing off the slate floors and making Halina wince.

"Uncle Miiitch . . ." She drew out his name as she ran down the hall toward him. She looked big for six, but Halina didn't know much about kids. Her dark curls flew out behind her and a grin cut across her face.

Mitch leaned down to catch her just as she flung herself at him. Kat locked her arms around his neck, and Mitch closed his eyes in a look of complete joy.

"This is my favorite part of coming here," he murmured, rocking her side to side. "I swear I leave just to come back for this."

Unexpected memories slammed Halina. Memories of the way Mitch used to greet her at the airport after coming home from a business trip. The way his face lit up the moment his eyes met hers. The way he'd drop his bags, wrap her in his arms, and pull her off her feet. The way he'd kiss her like he hadn't seen her in two months instead of two days. So much love . . . so much happiness . . .

The memories rattled her weakened barriers. Tears prickled Halina's nose and rose to her eyes. She looked away, blinked fast, and focused on controlling her breathing.

Just as Mitch straightened with Kat's arms still circled around his shoulders, his name echoed down the hall again. This voice was younger, less polished, "Uncle Miiitch . . ."

He dropped back to one knee to catch another child. Smaller than Kat. With a head of wild brown curls. It had to be Mateo. The momentum behind the child's slight weight tipped Mitch backward. He caught himself with one hand, while both kids clung to him like chimpanzees. Mitch's laugh echoed off the walls.

Halina smiled as she watched the cluster of joy at her feet. Mitch had enough happiness in his life for both of them. That was good. That was what she'd wanted. What she still wanted when she went deep, past all the superficial issues this situation brought up between them.

"What took you so long?" Kat asked.

"I picked up a friend." He tipped his head toward Halina.

Halina tensed again as two sets of big brown eyes turned on her. She was going to say hello, but Kat gasped and pushed off Mitch like he no longer existed.

"*Doggie,*" she said in such a high pitch, Mitch and Halina winced in unison. "Ooooh, he's so *ceuuuute.*"

Mitch stuck a finger in his ear. "Kat, honey. Hold that squeal down."

But Kat was on her knees, her arms around Dex's neck, and Dex was licking her face, making her giggle.

Mitch glanced at Halina nervously, but she smiled. "She's fine. He loves kids."

His smile returned as he looked down at the boy who had one hand fisted in the back of Mitch's jacket, the other in the front of his shirt. Even with a sudden frown marring his perfection, the kid had a flawless cherub's face that moved something deep inside Halina.

"This is Mateo." Mitch reached up and tousled his long golden curls. "Hasn't Keira given you a haircut yet?"

The boy's deep, rich brown eyes darted up to Mitch's face, then back at the dog.

"What's wrong, little man?" Mitch pushed to his feet and wandered toward Dex. "Do you want to pet the puppy?"

Mateo recoiled, turning his face against Mitch's shoulder. "No."

Discomfort flared inside Halina. She looked at Mitch for guidance, but he had narrowed his eyes on Mateo, trying to coax him out of the sudden antisocial plunge.

"Maybe I should take Dex to the car," Halina said softly.

"Nooooo." The pleading whine came from Kat. "Please don't."

Mitch still watched Mateo with a curious expression. "I think he's just got to warm up to Dex." To Mateo he said, "How about a present?"

The boy turned his head enough to meet Mitch's eyes. Mitch pulled a thick box of crayons from his jacket pocket and held them in front of Mateo. The boy's brown eyes softened and the sweetest smile turned his mouth as his hand curled around the box.

"Thank you," he murmured, pulling the box into his chest and sandwiching them between his body and Mitch's as he leaned back into him. "Three of my others are broke."

Mitch rubbed his back. "Three of your others are brok*en*."

"Yeah." Mateo completely missed the correction.

Mitch chuckled and glanced at Kat. "Doesn't look like my other gift is going to get much attention now. Think that one can wait."

Halina took a breath to release the tension in her stomach and smiled, watching Kat try to press her nose to Dex's without getting licked. Halina tried like hell to keep her mind averted from this insanely sweet scenario—her, Mitch, two beautiful kids, a loving dog, a serene home, safety, happiness . . . but . . . those old dreams kept pressing in on her reality.

"He no like snow." Mateo's voice was soft. Timid. And when Halina looked at the boy again, he was already staring at her. He met and held her gaze with clear, intelligent eyes. Something eerie slid over the back of Halina's neck. "He no want to go outside."

The instinct to reassure Mateo came first, but Halina's mouth had gone so dry, it was hard to open. And that strange sensation headed down her spine.

"Mitch, what . . . ?" She lifted her gaze from the boy to Mitch's face just as someone walked in behind him.

"What's going on in here?" Alyssa stepped out from behind her brother with a smile that washed everything in the foyer with light. She carried a bundle wrapped in blankets in one arm. Brady. Just shy of two weeks old according to Mitch.

Halina smiled easily, instantly. Her instincts pushed her forward to hug Lys, but fear held her back and awkwardness filled her belly. "Hi, Lys. I'm sorry to come here like this. I tried to tell him—"

"Let me guess—he didn't listen." Alyssa came straight to her, leaned in, and wrapped one arm around her shoulders in an awkward hug around the fussing baby. "You're always welcome."

Relief released her insides like a Slinky falling downstairs. Her emotions tumbled out and cluttered her chest. Familiar emotions—but not safe. They were the beautiful kind. The sweet, gentle, loving kind. The kind Halina felt toward a true, longtime friend. The kind that brought unwanted flashes of the future.

She immediately brought down an emotional wall between them and eased back from the hug. She wasn't even sure how she created the barriers anymore. It had become so automatic over the years. Keeping people out was reflexive. When she became too friendly with someone—a coworker, a member of her rowing club, even her trainer—she found ways to pull back from the attachment.

Halina searched for Brady in the blankets, but he wiggled and squirmed, drawing the baby blue fleece around himself in a wad of frustration.

More people filtered into the foyer behind Alyssa and pulled at Halina's attention. Four men and one woman, all wearing complex, curious expressions. Some darker than others. Halina's emotions bounced until she was all knotted up again.

"Oh." Alyssa glanced past Halina and her smile put sparkles in her beautiful eyes. Eyes identical to her brother's. "*That's* why Kat was squealing with rapture."

"This is Dex." Halina turned toward Kat and Dex. "Is he okay? I can take him out—"

"Are you kidding?" Alyssa said. "With this little guy wailing all day, Kat could use something a little extra special."

Halina smiled. At least Alyssa hadn't held a grudge.

"Dude," Mitch said to a tall, dark-haired man with the deepest, most vibrant blue eyes she'd ever seen. "Hate to tell you this right after you found out Mateo's empathic, too, but I think he's talking to animals now."

Halina frowned, unsure if this was another one of Mitch's jokes or something she was completely missing. Then that funky sensation she'd had played back in her mind and she didn't know what to think.

Everyone looked at the dog, then at Mateo, then at Mitch, as if choreographed.

Mitch burst out laughing. "Oh, God, you should see your faces." He kissed Mateo's cheek and handed him off to the man, who must have been Cash, Mateo's father. "But he doesn't seem too thrilled about the dog even though he can talk to him."

Mitch pivoted toward Alyssa, rubbing his hands together like a miser. She was jostling the fussy, squirming ball lost in blankets. "Where's my Brady?"

Alyssa smiled, extending her arms, offering the baby. "He's all yours. Has been inconsolable all day." Mitch reached for the bundle as Brady's tiny fists found an exit and pounded the air, punctuating his cries. Alyssa pulled him back at the last second and gave Mitch a warning look. "No swearing."

His grin widened. "Never."

As Mitch cradled the infant, something shifted in his expression. Something fundamental, rich, and warm. Halina couldn't define it, couldn't explain it. Could only melt inside as she watched him soften and open in ways she could never have imagined witnessing.

He swayed with the baby and shushed him. "What's wrong, buddy?" he asked, his voice unbearably soothing. "Is there too much action around here? You should be used to that by now."

Holding Brady in one arm, Mitch nudged the blanket off his face. "Let's get a look at you, kid."

Mitch's audible indrawn breath made Halina step closer. Without taking his gaze from Brady's face, Mitch tipped the baby in his arms so Halina could see him. And it was obvious why the baby had taken his breath. He was stunning. He was perfection. He had Alyssa's creamy skin and dark hair. But, the other features, clearly from the Fosters' mixed ancestry, also reminded Halina that Alyssa and Mitch were twins. The sprinkle of dark hair, full lips, and shape of his eyes may have been contributed by Alyssa, but they were clearly Mitch's as well. Only the color of the baby's eyes was different—bright blue.

"Oh, thank God," Mitch breathed with extra drama as he sliced a glance at one of the men who had drifted to Alyssa's side and wound an arm around her shoulders. This had to be Teague. She'd have known by the blue eyes he'd obviously passed on to Brady. "He looks like us, Lys."

Everyone burst out laughing, including Alyssa's husband, who said, "Did you miss those eyes?"

"They're all born with blue eyes," Mitch said. "They rarely take."

"Not that blue," Alyssa said, leaning into her husband while staring at Brady with a perplexed look. "How'd you do that?"

"What?" Mitch asked.

"Get him to stop fussing? He's been miserable all day."

Sure enough, Brady had quieted, his unfocused gaze fixed on Mitch's face. And when he smiled down at the baby, the resemblance between the two hit Halina with a fist of longing so strong, it closed her throat and pushed tears to her eyes.

"It must be an uncle thing," Mitch said.

"Great." Alyssa rubbed her eyes. "Want to move in?"

"Lys," her husband hissed with a half smile, "bite your tongue."

Laughter filled the space.

One of the men standing toward the back of the group stepped forward. "Since Brady has claimed the shark's balls and Foster probably can't even remember to take a leak on his own now," he offered his hand to Alyssa, "I'm Kai, the one Mitch talks shit about all the time."

Halina took his offered hand in a shake. He had green eyes, messy brown hair, and an angled, unshaven jaw. He also wore a very attractive—even a little wicked—grin. Another mischievous one. He, Nelson, and Mitch would be a handful to have around.

"You're the empath," she said, releasing his hand.

"Knew he was talking about me." Kai's grin widened. Eyes sparkled. "Don't believe *anything*."

Halina laughed. Unless this was a façade, he didn't seem to be holding a shitload of animosity toward her. Maybe Mitch had been right about her fitting in here better than she'd expected.

"Twenty bucks," Alyssa said to Kai. "In the jar."

Kai's gaze swung to Alyssa, his mouth hanging open. "What? What did I say?"

"You said," the tall blond man next to him muttered, "the *s-h* word."

"Aw, man." Kai made a disgusted sound and pulled out his wallet, shaking his head. "I lose more fu—"—he froze, darted a look at Alyssa, then pulled out a twenty—"darn money at this place."

"Why do you think we want you to stay?" Teague said then lifted the hand on his wife's shoulder in a wave to Halina. He wasn't quite as friendly, but he wasn't cold or rude either. "I'm Teague, her lesser half."

Alyssa frowned at him with a teasing, "Shut up."

Teague kissed her head. "Come on, people." He turned his wife down the hall in the direction they'd come. "Let's take this into the living room."

The group slowly followed Teague and Alyssa toward what Halina could see was an open living area beyond. She glanced at Mitch. He'd wandered to a corner of the foyer and stood with his shoulder propped against the wall. He held the baby in front of him, perpendicular to his body, but still cuddled up close, and just . . . stared.

Brady must have fallen asleep, because he was silent and still. She couldn't quite figure out that look on Mitch's face. Contemplative, deep, but soft and so very peaceful in a way that made her belly float. Made her wish. Dream. Hope. Imagine.

All the things she couldn't do. He was so lost in his thoughts he didn't even seem to notice the others leave.

Kat was the last one out. Pausing at the hallway, she swung around, bent at the waist, and slapped her knees. "Come here, boy. Come here, Dexy."

Hearing her attack dog called Dexy put a smile back on Halina's face. "He's trained in Russian," she told Kat and nearly laughed at the scrunched up face the little girl gave her. "Say, *prik-ho-dit.*"

When Kat repeated the phrase, Dex trotted to her and followed Kat into the living room. And for a moment, a flickering, blissful moment, everything was right. Halina felt content, uncoiled, like she could breathe.

She turned back to Mitch, reluctant to enter the living room without him. And just what the hell was that about? She'd been dying to get away from him since they'd collided.

"Come here," he said softly without looking at her.

Halina wandered toward him. When she stopped at his side and glanced at Brady, he was indeed asleep.

She sighed. Smiled. "He's . . . heavenly. Sheer perfection."

Mitch's grin lit up like the flare of a candle, as if he were surprised and thrilled she would think so. "If you think that's heavenly, smell him."

She scrunched her nose. "What?"

"Trust me." Mitch lifted the baby toward her. "Put your nose beside his head and breathe deep."

With her brow drawn, she gave him a skeptical look, but, curious, did as he directed. Brady was warm and soft against her cheek, and she closed her eyes at the yummy feel of him, at the way her belly went liquid. Then she pulled in his baby scent. So . . . unique. She didn't even know how to describe it. He smelled warm and new and clean. Sweet and innocent and . . . she straightened and breathed out on a sigh. "Oh . . . he's just so . . ."

Mitch's eyes twinkled with a kind of joy she hadn't seen in him . . . maybe ever. "Yeah."

They both simply stood there and stared at Brady again in silence. Emotion and anticipation hung heavily between them, unspoken. They could have had this if she hadn't run. They could have this now, at the worst possible time.

She let out a long, anxious breath. "Mitch, I can't go to Washington." She spoke soft and low. Her earlier anger over his assumptions and manipulation were gone and she didn't want to upset him. She wanted him to understand. "I have a long road ahead of me to build a new identity."

His eyes went dark, his mouth stern, and her panic started to slip out.

"You've never done it," she said. "You've never lived it. You don't know what it entails. A complete and total change of habits. I'll have to change what I eat and where I shop. I'll have to retrain Dex to respond to a new name and language. I can't practice Krav Maga anymore. I'll have to get rid of my Heckler & Kochs and buy another type of weapon.

"When I go to gun ranges, I'll have to start out looking like an idiot and build up to my current ability. I'll have to find another job, now not only outside genetics, but outside vaccine research. I'll have to build a new background. It takes *months*. Over *a year* to know the cover is solid. Everything I do, everything I say, everywhere I go could potentially give me away. It's *exhausting*. And what you're putting me through is draining me."

"Halina—"

"You have them, Mitch." She gestured toward the hall. "You have a million contacts, people who are indebted to you, friends, family. I have no one. *No one*. The longer you draw this out, the worse my chances are of building an impenetrable wall."

He repositioned Brady in the bend of his arm, the joy gone, replaced by frustration. "First of all, you're the one who hid those files. You know exactly where they are. Second of all, you're not safe on your own, Halina. They'll find you. If not Abernathy, someone else. Maybe Schaeffer's guys, maybe another Abernathy, trying to take over. But they *will* find you.

And they *will* kill you. When these guys want you, they get you. It doesn't matter what kind of face you put on, what kind of wall you build. That's why you're here, Halina. Not only because you can help, but because you're safer here. And if you'd give it a little more time, you'd see we're going to get rid of Schaeffer's threat and there will be no need for you to hide anymore.

"Isn't that what you want, Halina? To live a normal life again? To be *you*? Do what you want, go where you want, eat and shop and play the way you want? What's the point of living if you can't enjoy your life?"

"You probably never heard the words 'you don't always get what you want' growing up, did you?"

"Sure. Heard 'em all the time." A smile broke over his face. "And I lived to prove them wrong."

She dropped her head and rubbed her temple. "God. Your poor parents."

Mitch took her chin in his fingers and lifted her face until she was looking into his eyes again. "Together we're strong."

"Together, I'm putting the rest of you at a much higher risk." She crossed her arms, shook her head. "One loss versus a dozen, Mitch. I shouldn't be here. I shouldn't be near you or any of these people."

He gripped her bicep in an aggressive move so totally at odds with the innocence he held gently in the other arm that Halina startled.

"Halina." Her name was a harsh reprimand. "You are not dispensable. Your life is not worth any less than anyone else's, and I don't ever want to hear that come out of your mouth again."

He clenched his teeth and when he spoke again, his tone leveled. "Seven years ago, you should have trusted me. You should have told me what was happening so we could have dealt with it *together*. You didn't give me the chance to prove I wouldn't let you down. *I want*—" He stopped, took a breath. "I'm *asking* . . . for that chance now."

* * *

Bruce Abernathy wound the beaten truck over the fire-breaks of Tahoe National Forest along the east border of Teague and Alyssa Creek's property in Truckee, California. His leg ached like a sonofabitch. Every dip in the road shot so much pain through his pelvis and up his back, he was sweating and panting. Working alone, he wasn't set up for all this confrontation or chase. He should have gone in for the hard kill right away. Hit with shock and awe and pulled Beloi out. He'd underestimated both Foster and Beloi, but he was done screwing around.

Nearing the heavily wooded spot he'd chosen after scouting via satellite and referring to weather maps, he focused in on the snowflakes as they hit the windshield and melted, then whisked away by the wipers. Damn, this was beautiful country. Maybe he'd get a place here when this all finally paid off. Once he had Beloi, everything would snap into place. He'd have those crazy-ass smart soldiers on the ground within a year. Good-bye Taliban. Good-bye North Korea. Good-bye Anonymous for that matter. Americans would be safe from threats both outside and inside the nation. And he would finally reap a financial reward equal to his sacrifices for this country. He'd sure as hell left that in Schaeffer's hands too long.

He parked at the rear of the thickly wooded ledge and unpacked his gear. Before he found his way to the edge of the cliff, open to the opposite end of the meadow facing Creek's home, he climbed into the ghillie suit he'd thrown together specifically for this location. With white ski pants and jacket layered with brown netting, heavily taped with local pine and manzanita branches, once he took position, he'd blend right into the forest floor. For now, his ghillie provided camouflage for setup.

The canopy went up first—an expanse of burlap spray-painted white and forest green to blend with the snow-coated trees and hung in the branches above. Couldn't make a good shot with snow blocking a lens. Once cover was in place, he tossed down a dirt-brown plastic tarp and broke out the rifle.

Within twenty minutes, he lay belly down on the edge of a two-hundred-foot ledge looking over a snow-filled mountain meadow. Across that meadow, the Creek home nestled among the trees. Its A-line face with those amazing floor-to-ceiling windows gazed out over a view that had to be as stunningly picturesque as the one he stared at now. He pulled in a breath of the icy air and it scraped his lungs.

A stillness filled his chest. Migrated to his head. His hands. Pristine. Peace. Perfection.

Damn, that felt . . . unbelievably *right*. More right than anywhere on earth he'd ever been—and he'd been to every godforsaken corner of this planet.

Yeah. He definitely needed a place here. The sooner, the better.

To get a clear view of the target, without so much as a pine needle between his barrel and the house, he edged forward from the manzanita thicket beneath the towering pines. He found a position and slid the rifle out in front, across an exposed section of flat river rock. Squinting at the house across the frozen meadow, he reached forward and released the bipod, giving the rifle legs and stabilizing his aim.

Something rustled the brush behind him. Flash fire burned in the pit of his stomach. He tensed, waited. When the sound faded, he trained his breathing back into a shallow, measured rhythm. He swiped snow off the rock face, lay a swatch of fleece down, and pressed his cheek against it, gazing through the scope.

After sweeping the area with his rifle scope, he homed in on the vast expanse of glass and flipped down a magnifier. And suddenly, he was in the living room with them. A ghost floating among them. Whispering at their ear with the barrel of a rifle. And they were oblivious.

Adrenaline swirled and eddied in his veins. He'd almost forgotten the force of these emotions. How moving control and power could be. How intoxicating.

He slowly panned the living room and kitchen beyond, pausing to center each face in the crosshairs of his scope. The wooden beams between windowpanes created blind spots, but he waited for the perfect shot, and when he had it, just for the satisfaction, he punctuated each satisfactory aim with, "*Click, dead.*"

Luke Ransom, Keira O'Shay-soon-to-be-Ransom, Kai Ryder, Cash O'Shay, and Alyssa and Teague Creek. And even though he hated killing kids, that talented Mateo would have to go too. He knew as much as the rest of them, and, with time, would probably more dangerous than all the current adults combined. But the man he wanted to kill most, Mitch Foster, wasn't in the room. And Beloi was missing too. As were Q and his wife, Jessica.

He'd only get one shot at sending Foster's brains across the room. Only one chance for Beloi to witness the event that would give her the incentive to cooperate. The next time he confronted her, he didn't want an ounce of resistance. Honestly, in his condition, he doubted being able to win. And he never went into a fight at a disadvantage—not if he could help it.

Discipline. Patience. He could wait.

TWELVE

All she wanted to do was run. But at least Mitch had gotten her mind to bend in another direction. If she could open up, if she could trust him, and if he could forgive . . .

There were a lot of ifs in there, but for another shot with Halina, ifs were better than nos.

He led her into the living area where all the rooms were open to each other. Kai mixed drinks in the kitchen on the left, Keira and Luke sat at the dining room table straight ahead, each with a computer and a notepad, Cash beside them furiously scribbling on another pad, his fingers pulling absently at his hair. To the right, a huge sectional sofa and several club chairs delineated the living room, but the entire space flowed together without any walls.

Mitch tried not to let the sour note between him and Halina darken the joy of holding Brady. For a moment, a crystal-clear, painfully sharp moment, he could have sworn he and Halina had connected on a level nearly as deep as they had all those years ago. Looking at Brady with the very real possibility of having a child of their own . . .

Every time he thought of it, a bolt of lightning shot through his belly. He wasn't sure if it was more fear or more excitement, but both were definitely present.

Mitch hovered over Cash's shoulder, but couldn't read anything on the paper. "You close to figuring that out yet?"

Cash made a frustrated sound and continued to write.

Mitch's gaze shifted to a pile of shards on the table where some type of stone had been shattered with a hammer. "What's that?"

"Something Quaid's been messing with," Keira said. "Something having to do with energy something-or-other. You know how Quaid is."

Yes, he did. Quaid was still a little . . . off . . . from his time in captivity. His mind seemed to drift on tangents. He went deep into himself when he delved into some newly discovered aspect of his powers. The shards of something glass or ceramic on the table was only one in a long line of projects he'd vanish into.

"What's he working on?" Halina murmured by Mitch's side, but she was looking at Cash, not the table.

"Halina?" Kat came up to them with Dex beside her. "Can we take Dex in our room to play?"

"Of course." She glanced at Alyssa. "If it's okay."

Alyssa nodded and Kat and Mateo scurried off to the back of the house, both of them calling some warped form of *prikhodit* that made everyone chuckle. Dex trotted behind them and sent Halina one last glance before he disappeared.

"When Cash was imprisoned at the Castle," Mitch said, "Schaeffer had him developing a superskin for the military. Think Gore-Tex meets neoprene with ten times the strength of body armor."

Her gaze turned on Cash, though he didn't notice. "Did you do it?"

He turned his head to glance at her, then returned his frown to the pad. His jaw shifted sideways. Knee bounced and he didn't answer.

That was a strange reaction. Mitch was just going to ask if he was okay when Cash tossed his pencil down and rubbed his eyes.

"Yeah," he said with an irritable edge, "but I ate the final notes to get rid of them so Schaeffer wouldn't get the formula. I'm trying to re-create them now."

Cash rested his chin in his hand, but didn't meet Halina's eyes. Something was definitely up with him. Out of the group, Cash was one of the nicest, despite his years isolated in prison. Since the team had rescued him and the man had been with them every day, he'd been polite, congenial, considerate, easygoing.

Halina definitely put a burr under Cash's skin. And Mitch realized he might just have to eat the promise he'd made Halina before coming into the house. He hadn't imagined anyone in the team holding a grudge after they all knew how manipulative Schaeffer could be.

But Cash's wife had been murdered by Schaeffer's men. Cash had lost three years of Mateo's life when Schaeffer had put him in prison. Out of everyone, Cash had lost the most.

"And now," Cash said, the edge in his voice growing toward anger, "after getting my brains banged around my skull during the escape, I can't remember what I did."

Mitch put a hand on his shoulder and squeezed.

Cash looked up. When their gazes met, Mitch saw both realization and understanding pass through Cash's blue eyes.

His voice leveled when he told Halina, "But I'm getting closer."

"You . . . ?" Halina started, confusion clear on her face. "*Ate* them? What does that mean?"

"I, you know," Cash picked up the pencil and pulled the notebook back in front of him. "Ate the paper the notes were on. I didn't have any other means of disposal."

Halina's eyes rounded in shock.

"*Mission: Impossible* style," Luke said, grinning at his soon-to-be brother-in-law, drawing a lopsided smile from Cash.

"If we try hard enough," Kai said from the kitchen, "we can fit every part of this mess into a television series. *Mission: Impossible, The Pretender*—"

"Let's not try," Mitch said.

"Are you in another bad mood?" Kai asked. "Let me make you one of my smoothies—"

"No smoothies," Teague said from the sofa. "Brady is finally happy. If you turn on that blender, I'm going to stuff your head in it."

"Good point," Kai said.

"The formula will be powerful leverage against Schaeffer," Mitch told Halina.

"How?" she asked.

"We can sell it back to him," Mitch said. "Tape the exchange and get his confession. Pull in the FBI for a sting if we can arrange it." Mitch turned his attention back to Brady and lifted the baby's tiny fingers with his pinkie until they encircled it. "He'd expose himself as participating in Millennium's business while acting as a senator and sitting on the Armed Forces Committee."

"Though we're not even a hundred percent sure we'd get backing from the FBI because not all interactions with a politician's business are illegal while he's in office. We'd have to prove a few things along with his offer to buy it, and his confession of holding Cash against his will."

"It's all such a long shot," Halina murmured, gaze going distant. "The formula, the papers, collecting this foggy evidence . . ."

"But it's better than nothing," Cash said. "And it's better than life in a cell."

Halina's eyes clouded with guilt. They turned the color of smoke against the ocean and Mitch was caught between wishing he could help her and thinking he should be relishing a sense of vengeance. But he couldn't find a desire for revenge anymore. All he wanted now was to shine light on all the shadows and move forward without any monsters in the closet.

"Kai's right," Alyssa said, coming up beside them and sliding her arm through the bend of Halina's elbow. "Mitch has lost all his manners. This is Keira, Luke, and Cash, Keira's brother." Alyssa turned toward Teague, who was sitting on the sofa. "You've met Teague and our daughter, Kat, and Cash's son, Mateo."

"I didn't forget my manners," Mitch said. "I was going to let her enjoy that view," he gestured toward the floor-to-ceiling windows overlooking a frosted mountain meadow from the living room, "for a minute before throwing you all at her."

Kai set a couple drinks on the dining room table for Keira, Luke, and Cash, then dropped into a chair. He stretched out his long legs, crossed them at the ankles, and folded his arms over his chest. "So, tell us how your power works . . . this precognition."

"That right there," Mitch pointed at Kai, "is what no manners looks like. Let the woman relax for a few minutes, Ryder."

Mitch wandered toward the windows, appreciating the view as he ran the back of one finger over Brady's petal-soft cheek. He loved the feeling of peace he had here. Especially now, holding his nephew. He gave up on the scenery to stare at Brady. His mind drifted to the thought of his and Halina's possible child. What their baby would look like. If he or she would resemble Brady. Thought of how the cousins would play together the way Mitch and his cousins had when they'd been kids.

He'd had such a great life. Fantastic parents, great brothers, best twin he could have hoped for, loving supportive extended family. More friends than he'd ever imagined.

He wanted to share it all with a child.

He wanted to share it all with Halina.

He'd adored bringing her to his family's house in San Diego for holidays. She'd endured his brothers' teasing, his mother's third degree, his father's endless chats. And she'd fit in like she'd already been part of the family.

Those had been some of the happiest days of his life.

"It would be helpful to be able to know what's coming next," Kai said, breaking into Mitch's thoughts, his voice moving back toward the kitchen. "Especially when I can feel Abernathy close."

Mitch pivoted toward Kai. "*What?* How close? Why didn't you tell us before?"

Before all his questions were out, Mitch was already calculating scenarios and travel times. If Abernathy had somehow gotten his leg wound patched up and driven all night . . . this was one relentless bastard.

"What do you mean you can feel him?" Halina asked Kai.

"I don't know how to explain it other than a sixth sense," Kai said. "Like when you hear something in your house at night that triggers an internal alarm. I feel that anxiety or dread or whatever you want to call it when someone is targeting our team."

He turned to look at Mitch. "And I didn't tell you because I'm just now picking it up loud and clear. You know I don't know anything about—"

"Distances or time frames," Mitch said, disgusted. In his arms, the warm bundle squirmed and squeaked unhappily. "All of you and your limitations." He looked down at Brady, shook his head as he gently bounced the boy, which wasn't working for the kid a second time around. "They're killing me, Brady. *Killing* me."

"You're not going to be able to fix this problem, bro." Alyssa came over and took Brady from Mitch. "He's hungry."

Mitch wasn't ready to let Brady go and felt a little lost without his nephew in his arms. He stuffed his hands in his pockets and watched Alyssa cuddle beneath Teague's arm on the sofa and toss a baby blanket over her shoulder to take the baby to her breast discreetly.

Teague murmured something in Alyssa's ear and she glanced up, grinning with a ridiculous amount of love. A mix of joy for his sister and jealousy for the bond she and Teague shared twined in Mitch's chest.

I want that.

The sentiment was more a feeling than a thought. One that echoed through him. And he found himself hoping Halina was pregnant even though he clearly saw the trouble that would cause down the road.

"Abernathy must have gotten discharged," Keira said.

"Discharged from where?" Halina asked.

"I started calling the emergency rooms in the Olympia area, said the FBI was looking for a fugitive who'd come in with a gunshot wound to the leg. When nothing came up, I fanned out and finally found the jerk going by the name Steve Carpenter at the emergency room of a community hospital outside Portland."

"Portland?" Halina said. "Are you sure it was him?"

"The slug he took out of the guy's leg matched the caliber of Mitch's gun. The patient matched Abernathy's description. He had Abernathy's tattoos."

"Tattoos." She turned to Mitch with an accusatory tone. "How did you know about his tattoos? You said you didn't know who he was."

Annoyance rippled across Mitch's shoulders, but he smoothed it down. "Quaid knew about Abernathy's tattoos—" A soft ding echoed through the house. Everyone's attention shifted toward the foyer and the new voices coming from that direction—Jessica's smooth and soft, Quaid's much deeper.

"Speak of the dual devils," Kai said, coming out from behind the counter and walking into the foyer.

Halina looked at Mitch again and a spark of panic burned in her eyes.

Kai returned through the hallway, followed by Jessica, her deep red hair up in a sleek ponytail. The new color in her face and life in her eyes reminded Mitch of the importance of this work. Of the significant changes their successes thus far had created in everyone's life. That he wasn't torturing Halina for the hell of it, but to set things right.

Kai, Jessica, and Quaid paused a few feet from Halina. She drew herself up and shot one angry look at Mitch before Jessica held out her hand in greeting. Mitch noticed the tension in Jessica's face, the tightness of her shoulders, the rigid line of her arm extending the hand toward Halina. And the way she edged protectively in front of Quaid as if Halina would take him.

"I'm Jessica," she said. "Quaid's wife."

Just as much tension radiated through Halina, only hers was defensive. She reluctantly shook their extended hands, Jessica's first, then Quaid's as they were introduced.

In that moment, when Quaid took Halina's hand, the atmosphere in the room shifted. A sensation as intangible as mood, but far more serious. Quaid held on to Halina's hand too long, his expression growing serious. Dark.

Halina's jaw tightened, her eyes grew both scared and fierce, the combination oddly intimidating. With one small shift of her body, alarm kicked to life inside Mitch as visions of her striking out pushed him forward. He put a hand on Quaid's arm and squeezed. "Ease up on that grip, man. You're killing her blood supply."

Halina shot Mitch an irritated, uneasy look as if she weren't sure whether to plead for help or kick him in the balls. The room had gone quiet. Quaid's gaze was deeply intent on Halina, who continued to look between Quaid and Mitch.

With the unspoken choreography of people who'd worked together in tenuous situations before, Mitch eased closer to Halina's side while Jessica came in behind him, replacing Mitch's hand on Quaid's arm.

"Quaid," Jessica murmured, looking up at her husband while sliding her hand down his arm. "I think Halina needs some space."

Mitch slipped his arm around Halina's waist and her unsure gaze flickered toward him for an instant. "You're okay. He's harmless."

Her gaze returned to Quaid's and locked. "Bullshit."

Kai stepped up to them from the side, hands on hips, glaring at Quaid. "I thought Jessica had you house-trained." He backhanded Quaid's bicep. "Stop acting like a jackass and let go of her hand."

"You said she was precognizant, but not . . . like this . . ." Quaid spoke to no one in particular, his gaze still on Halina. Then his head tilted as if he'd heard something in the distance. "Do you . . . travel?"

Halina's muscles were so tense, she quivered against Mitch where he stood behind her.

"Let go"—she paused to take a breath—"of my hand."

When Quaid still didn't read the warning in Halina's voice, Kai put both hands on Quaid's and tried to pry it from Halina's.

Quaid jerked his elbow and clipped Kai in the ribs.

Kai released Quaid's hand and bent, holding his side, "You motherfucker—" He pointed a finger at Alyssa, "If you charge me, he's paying for it. And if he's paying for it, that's two curses, mother and fucker." He turned back to Quaid, straightening. "What the hell is wrong—?"

"What's your power?" Quaid demanded of Halina, his focus so complete it was as if no one else existed. "What can you do with all this energy?"

"Mitch," she rasped, pushing at him with her free hand, "get away from me. I can't fight like this."

"Quaid, honey, it's Jessie," Jessica continued to try and draw his attention. "Let go—"

"Do you move among time when you travel?" Quaid asked. "Can you materialize on alternate universes? How long does your power last before you have to recharge?"

"Stop!" Halina said through clenched teeth and set her feet in a scissor stance.

"You're not going to fight him, Hali," Mitch said.

"If he doesn't let go of my hand," Halina said, "I sure as hell am."

"Jessica," Luke called from where he was sitting at the dining room table, "call off your man."

"Are you hard of hearing?" Jessica shot back. "He's not exactly listening."

"Hey, Quaid," Luke called, "does Keira have to threaten to shoot your ear off again?"

Mitch glanced over his shoulder and found Cash leaning back in his own chair, squinting as he watched the situation escalate. "Hey, asshole."

Cash's blue eyes flicked to Mitch.

"Suck it up, get over it, and get off your ass. Since you're the only one he listens to when he's wigged, get him to back off or I'm going to let her go—and no one will like the way she'll rearrange Quaid's face. Abernathy looks like hell."

Cash's expression tightened with anger, but he stood with a heavy sigh and strode straight to Quaid.

"Quaid, it's Cash," he said just before he smacked one flat hand hard against the side of Quaid's head, the other immediately to his solar plexus. That loosened Quaid's grip. Cash fisted Quaid's shirt at the shoulders and shoved him back three feet.

Jessica immediately took Cash's place.

Mitch knew the quick announcement Cash had given was so Quaid wouldn't fight back when his mind unsnagged from wherever it had gotten hung up and processed who was pushing him around.

Cash turned, striding back to his seat with a curt "Happy?" on his way past Mitch.

Mitch turned Halina toward him and rubbed his hands over her back. Her fingers clutched at his T-shirt over his belly, scraping his muscles. He flinched with pleasure. His attention refocused on the feel of her against him and the thrilling rip of electricity through his body everywhere she touched.

Jessica pulled Quaid to the sofa by the arm and Mitch held on to Halina. More because she felt so damn good than because she needed him. He knew damn well she didn't.

The others moved back into the open living area behind them, sitting at the dining table or on the sofa with Jessica and Quaid. Kai returned to the kitchen, scowling and rubbing his ribs.

A quick, hot release of breath exited Halina's mouth and tingled over Mitch's chest. With his back to the others, Mitch closed his eyes in pleasure and gritted his teeth. She felt so damn good. And he needed her again so damn badly. Badly enough to throw every ounce of good sense he owned—which had dwindled considerably over the last thirty hours—into the icy waters of the Truckee River.

"What were you saying about Abernathy's tattoos?" Quaid asked.

Halina lifted her head and pulled out of Mitch's arms. She looked around him to address Quaid, but she stayed close, her hand on one side of his waist.

"Mitch shot him near Portland," she said, her voice hard, confrontational, "but now Kai feels him here. I said that's a long way to go with a bullet in his leg, but Keira said they identified him at the emergency room through your description of his tattoos."

Quaid was still looking at Halina like he'd seen the second coming of Christ—mystified and awed. "I worked with Abernathy over the last few years on military ops in different parts of the world. I know his tattoos. And one bullet in the leg isn't going to stop this man."

Halina's shoulders slid lower. Her gaze fell to the carpet and she whispered, "Shit."

"Once, in Islamabad," Quaid said, leaning forward, resting his elbows on his knees, "Abernathy's Jeep hit an IED and flipped. Broke his arm in two places, his collarbone, jaw, ribs. Then an army of Taliban fighters descended on us with AK-47s and Abernathy was shot three times, collapsed a lung. He still saved two other guys and crawled to the rescue chopper. The guy has nineteen lives."

"God," she murmured, dropping her head and rubbing her eyes. "I'm glad I didn't know that last night."

Halina sagged sideways against Mitch. Her waist felt so small beneath his hand. Her hip so firm against his crotch. He wanted to drop his mouth to her neck, slide his hands down her taut belly and slip them inside the front of her jeans. He wanted to feel her, all soft and hot and wet.

"You can see why it's important to get ahead of this guy." Kai wandered toward the sofa with various concoctions trapped in a group between his two big hands. "We might be able to do that if you could see the future. So how does it work?"

She lifted her head again, crossed her arms. Mitch expected her to pull away, but she continued to lean against him, as if in a silent request for security. He didn't know if she was doing it consciously or unconsciously, but he didn't care. He shifted to pull her back against his chest. Then he put his hands on her waist and held her firmly against him.

"What do you mean, how does it work?" she asked.

"I mean, what triggers them? What do you see in these visions? How far in the future? How accurate?"

She hesitated. "They're . . . different. The visions are related to people I'm close with, but they come at different times. They're not reliable . . . exactly. Some are flashes of the immediate future. Some are more detailed, but I have no idea how far in the future they are." She paused, shot a half glance over her shoulder as if thinking of Mitch, but didn't meet his gaze. "But I do know they're pinpoint accurate. I've seen them come true time after time."

Her words slammed his stomach. His mind vaulted back to the memory of her writhing in a nightmare, crying his name only to wake and tell him she'd seen him with another woman. *On-top-of-the-world happy.* No, her visions were not pinpoint accurate. Or . . . she'd lied.

Again.

"Other than that," she said, refocusing on Kai, "I know next to nothing about them. I have to keep myself from getting too close to anyone so I can avoid having them."

One of Kai's brows fell. "Why would you do that?"

"That is a *really* stupid question."

Her patience for all this was thinning, and she was probably ready to blow, but the you–can't-be-that-dense bewilderment in her voice almost made Mitch laugh.

"You're empathic, right?" she asked.

"Yeah," he said with a so–what tone.

"Can you *sense* exactly how I'm feeling right now?" Halina asked, her body quivering with tension against his.

Keira eased back from the table, and Mitch met her gaze. Her expression signaled a warning, and he slid the hand at Halina's waist across her belly so he'd have an arm around her if she lunged for Kai.

"Whoa. Whoa." Kai put his hands up, palms out. "Hold on. Relax—"

"I can't relax when you're *pushing* me." She leaned forward, her fingers digging into Mitch's forearm, prying it away from her belly. When he didn't relent, she shot an angry glance over her shoulder.

"We're in this together, Hali," he murmured.

An unexpected softness appeared in her beautiful light aqua eyes before she looked away. The tension melted from her fingers. Her body relaxed back into his. An irrational amount of accomplishment and happiness and hope rushed through his head and filtered into his heart.

"Hey, look," Kai said. "We're all one big ugly family here. We're all battling the same dragon. Which reminds me, where's your phoenix?"

Her phoenix. Mitch hadn't thought of that. He pictured her naked body the night before as she'd let the robe slide down her sleek form. Then again as she'd turned and walked away. His cock pushed at the dense fabric of his jeans and the supple curve of her ass. The way she met his pressure had to be his imagination. Had to be because of the way his mind slid right into the memory of lifting her and letting her fall back on his shaft, slamming into her at the same time.

All his blood screamed south. He had a sudden rush of dizziness. Just as he had then. Only he was still throbbing in his jeans—not inside her. He whispered a curse.

"You know," Kai went on, "your scar. The one that looks like a phoenix. We all have them—from exposure to the chemicals."

Kai leaned down, pulled off one sock, and hiked up the leg of his jeans to reveal a reddish-purple mark starting on the top of his foot and traveling up the side of his leg.

"That's just the tail. You can't see mine in full unless I'm naked." He lifted a hot green gaze and a grin to Halina. "I'm happy to drop my—"

"Ryder." Mitch released Halina's waist and stepped back, unable to hold contact without doing something about it. "Don't make me kick your ass." He touched Halina's arm and she looked at him. "Where is yours?"

Halina hesitated, then slid her hand beneath her hair, lifting it off her neck. The scar was pale pink, barely darker than her skin, which was probably why Mitch hadn't noticed it. The phoenix was an abstract, stylish sweep that disappeared into her hairline. Its tail flared across the base of her neck. And Mitch had a sudden, insane need to trace it with his tongue.

Kai passed on his way to the kitchen with an empty glass and paused to glance at her scar. "Mmm, sexy." He flashed a smile at Halina. "I'll show you mine later."

"Not if you're dead," Mitch muttered, earning another grin from Kai.

"So," Kai said, continuing to the kitchen and setting the glass on the counter before wandering back toward the massive windows. "*Do* you travel? Like Quaid does?"

Halina tossed her hands in the air. "I have *no idea* what you're talking about."

"Teleporting." Quaid pinned his gaze on Halina again. "Your energy is . . . *spilling* . . . out of you."

"My . . . what?"

"Your energy. You've got electromagnetic current screaming through your body."

"Electromagne—*what?*"

"Electromagnetic current. It's—"

"I know what electromagnetic currents are. And of course they're in me. They're in everyone. They're found everywhere on earth. They come from the sun, radiation, heat, light, every living creature. We all have electromagnetic currents inside us."

"But you have an extreme amount. The way it flowed into me when I shook your hand is the way I feel after I teleport, but times a hundred. A rush. A high. I don't know how to explain it exactly, but the amount of energy inside you is on par with what I get crossing all the alternate planes of reality in the universe when I travel, *combined.*"

Everyone's gaze turned from Quaid to Halina, like a tennis match. She closed her eyes and rubbed her forehead.

Mitch closed a hand over her shoulder. "Come sit down, Hali."

"I don't want to sit down." She dropped her arm and turned to Mitch, but she looked exhausted, her emotions raw and exposed in every expression now.

"Quaid and Mateo have already located the papers in Mitch's old apartment," Kai said, now standing sideways, splitting his attention between the windows and Halina. The new look on his face made Mitch's gut tense. He was serious now. With an edgy concern darkening his eyes. "If you see the future, isn't there a way you can see how this is going to work out? See if you get them without trouble?"

She crossed her arms and shook her head. "It doesn't work like that. I can't just call up the future anytime I want. I can't control when the flashes come to me or what I see."

"Everyone here has some control over their powers even if it's small," Kai said. "We've all developed our original abilities by taking that small amount of control and building on it. You can't think of *any way* you can instigate the visions?"

Mitch fisted his hands to keep them from rubbing his own tired eyes. Halina's face flashed with color and she slid a don't-you-dare look his way.

Which, of course, taunted him into asking, "What if she did?"

"Then I'd say she needs to try and focus on what she wants answers to," Kai said, "then instigate her powers and see what kind of visions come. It'll probably take some practice."

Mitch could practically feel Halina's heat. It matched his own—only hers came from anger; Mitch's came from sexual need.

"Intention," Quaid said. "With all that electromagnetic power rolling around inside you, Halina, you need to be focusing your mind on your intention. If your intention is to see the outcome of your trip to Washington with Mitch, that's where your focus should be while you're calling up your power."

She rubbed her face with both hands. "I need some air."

Mitch caught her arm. "Halina, it's twenty degrees outside and it's *snowing*."

She glanced out the window, where a light sprinkle of flakes dusted the sky. "That's why jackets were invented."

"No." The command in Kai's voice caught Mitch off guard. "No one's going outside." He pulled his phone from his back pocket, hit one button, and said, "Send a few guys to check the tree line on the west side of the meadow."

Halina stepped closer to Mitch. He loved the way her fingers tightened around his arm. He slid it further around her waist, pulling her close.

"What is it?" Mitch asked.

The room had gone quiet and tense. Everyone serious. Keira and Luke both held weapons in their hands now. Cash got up from the floor and moved into the kitchen, unlocking a cabinet over the refrigerator. He pulled out two more weapons, handed one to Kai.

"Don't know exactly." Kai shot a look at Halina and all signs of his earlier teasing were gone. "Get with Quaid and figure this out, Halina. You may not have another chance."

Owen checked the tuck of his uniform shirt in the window's reflection, then ran his hands through his hair, which was too long and probably a freaking mess.

"Why didn't I wear a suit today?" he muttered before taking a breath and opening his office door.

He started down the short hall toward his secretary's desk and stopped in three steps. Seville was standing directly in his line of sight, hands clasped behind her back, face tilted up as she studied the photographs Stephanie had framed and used to decorate the office.

Seville wore a long, straight navy blue skirt with a slit up the side, a long-sleeved translucent cream blouse that showed a lace camisole beneath, and sexy navy heels, one of which was tilted on its spike, her foot twisting back and forth as she smiled at the images on the wall.

The way she held her arms pushed her breasts against the fabric of her top. In profile, her skirt showed off a flat belly and trim backside. And with her head tipped back like that, her long, thick dark hair fell past the middle of her spine.

"Are you going to stand there and stare?" she asked, never looking away from the photos, her familiar smoky voice rich with a smile. "Or are you going to say hello?"

Heat cascaded through his chest and pooled between his legs. He'd forgotten how much he loved that voice. "Uh . . . staring works for me . . ."

She turned her head, grinned at full throttle, dark eyes twinkling with mischief. That he'd forgotten too.

Slowly, she let her body follow, turning toward him. And, oh, holy hell . . .

"You look . . ." He scanned her, head to painted toe and back, delighting in the glimpse of those white teeth in her smile. He put his hands on his hips, knew he was grinning like a complete idiot, but couldn't stop. "Wow."

She twisted to grab a briefcase and a blazer on a chair and started toward him. And, whoa, he didn't remember that walk either. She paused within six inches, grinning up at him. A dazzlingly white grin against warm Mediterranean skin. So many long-repressed wants churned up inside him. Wants that had developed in those years after the end of his very early relationship with Jocelyn decades ago and before he'd met Libby. Long-ago wants never acted upon because of all those damned military rules.

"Am I drooling?" he asked.

She laughed. The sound was so . . . happy. Almost like a kid in the joy, but there was definitely a full-fledged woman in its edge of heat. "Am I? How do you manage to get sexier every time I see you?"

Then she dropped her briefcase and her jacket at her feet, careless where they landed, pushed up on her toes, and wrapped her arms around his neck. He hadn't been prepared for a full-body hug, but he got right into the swing of it. Hard not to when a woman this gorgeous offered to press herself up against him.

He leaned down and wrapped his arms tightly around her. That warmth in his chest radiated outward and filled his whole body. Her scent, a barely there, wildly seductive spice, stirred the air. He closed his eyes, memorized the feel of her against him, knowing he had to release her in another second. "The bureau looks good on you, Lieutenant."

"If I'd known I'd get a greeting like this," she murmured near his ear, "I'd have come a long time ago." Her hand brushed the back of his hair. "I hadn't realized how much I've missed you 'til now."

"Sir, can I—" Stephanie's voice sounded in the hallway, jerking Owen—painfully—back to reality. "Oh. I'm sorry."

His secretary turned toward her desk, and Owen released Seville. "It's all right, Steph. What did you need?"

"Um, I was just going to offer you both something to drink . . . ?"

"I'd love water." He glanced at Seville, once again struck by the beauty of her narrow face and dark hair falling in loose waves over her shoulders. Long, dark lashes. Fine, straight nose. Full, deep-rose lips in a stunning smile. He wanted to sigh. "Seville?"

"Nothing for me, thank you."

Stephanie disappeared and Owen bent to pick up the blazer Seville had dropped. "You've just ruined my reputation." He straightened and grinned at her. "You know that, right?"

"A little scandal never hurt anyone in this town."

Owen cupped her jaw. Ran his thumb over her cheek. Her skin was soft and warm. Her smile bright. "I wish you were here for a whole different reason."

Her brows dipped, smile dimmed. "I'm . . . sorry."

He dropped his hand, turned toward his office, and sighed. "Come on in."

Owen closed the door after her and watched her wander around his office, her steps slow as she scanned the diplomas and certificates on the wall. Owen sat on the corner of his desk and crossed his arms. Let himself soak her in. Let himself wish he could turn back the clock, make different decisions . . .

She paused at the watercolor his daughter, Jennifer, had given him about five years back. Owen had framed the typical grassy field of stick figures under a rainbow and smiling sunshine.

"How are Jenny and Zane?" she asked.

He was impressed she remembered their names. "They're . . . good, I guess."

She turned toward him with a questioning frown.

"Things are a little strained right now with the . . . uh . . . divorce."

Her shoulders lowered and sincere sympathy tugged her eyes at the corners. "So the rumors are true. You and Libby . . . ?"

Owen nodded.

Her head tilted and concern floated in her dark eyes. "I'm sorry, Owen."

"It's okay. A good thing. Long time in coming. I just wish . . ."

"Easier for the kids?"

He chuckled. "I love the way you finish my thoughts." He forced himself to create some distance. "What about you? Married? Kids?"

She laughed, the sound less pleased, and gave him a you've-got-to-be-kidding look. "A life outside the bureau is highly discouraged."

"So I've heard."

A moment of silence stretched.

"Look," Owen said, "I'd really like to flip the bureau the bird and talk for hours, hear all about your life over the last ten years . . . but I don't want that time with you tainted with this crap."

"Agreed." She nodded, smiled. "I'm so relieved you understand."

Okay. Back to business. They were on solid ground again. But the disappointment covering his brief burst of pleasure felt like a storm cloud.

He pushed off the desk and instead of sitting behind it, dropped into one of the two seats across from the massive piece of furniture. He patted the arm of the other chair. "Come. Sit."

She eased to the edge of the chair and crossed her legs.

Owen chuckled. "The Seville I knew would have plopped her butt into that chair and planted her elbows on her knees."

A sly little smile tilted her lips. "Don't like the new Seville?"

"Plenty to like about both."

Surprise lit her eyes and she glanced away, pulling her lower lip between her teeth.

Which of course drew his gaze to her mouth.

"Seville, let me—"

"Sofia," she said. "Call me Sofia, Owen. We're not serving together anymore."

Sofia. His insides did warm, decadent things. His mind tried to read between the lines of her *"We're not serving together anymore."*

In the end, he just nodded. "Let me help you out here. I'm sure you understand that all my work for Schaeffer is classified. I couldn't talk to you about it even if I wanted to."

Her eyes lost their sparkle. She nodded. "I know."

A knock on the door broke into the conversation.

"Come in," Owen said.

Stephanie walked in, handed him the water. "Would you like me to . . . ?"

"Yes, hold my calls. Thank you."

When the door closed behind Stephanie, Sofia said, "I'm not here to try and get answers out of you," she said, voice low. "We have all the answers we need. I'm here because I'm worried about you. I'm sure you've read the papers, Owen. And you were expecting me, so you know the FBI is investigating."

Owen nodded.

"I've been working on this case against Schaeffer for three years, since it was handed over to me by a retiring agent. When your name popped up on the radar last month . . ." She put a hand to her chest. "Scared the hell out of me."

Owen sat back, frowning. *Three* years?

"I can't discuss any details," she said, "just as you can't. What I want you to know is that it's big, it's close to breaking, and, as my friend, as someone I respect and admire, I don't want you anywhere near it when it does. I know very little about this arrangement you have with Schaeffer. But I know you, Owen. I know what kind of man you are. And I believe in that man." She reached out, curled her fingers around his hand, and squeezed. "And I don't want to see Schaeffer ruin another good man."

THIRTEEN

Mitch released Halina. She turned and looked at him as if she wanted to say something or ask something, but didn't know how. Reluctantly, she disappeared into the office off the living room, keeping a notable distance from Quaid. Alyssa and Jessica were right behind.

Mitch was about to grab Alyssa's arm to pull her aside before she went in, but they both paused beside him instead of following the others into the office.

"Tell me about Halina's power," Alyssa said, her don't-even-think-about-bullshitting-me glare making her eyes spark green.

He didn't want to bullshit anyone. He wanted this whole freaking mess over. "I can only tell you what she's told me, which isn't much." He gave her the quick and dirty details of Halina's visions.

Jessica crossed her arms and turned a serious gaze on Alyssa. "They could be triggered by dopamine."

Mitch frowned. "Excuse me?"

Alyssa smirked at him. "Dopamine is a chemical in the brain. A feel-good chemical that is released under different circumstances, the interactions you're describing being some of the highest. Orgasm is the highest that I know of."

"Oh-kay." Mitch drew out the word, a weird sensation tightening his stomach. "This is . . ."

"Awk-ward," Kai sang from where he stood beside the dining room table, listening. "Talking to your sister about orgasms. Definitely awk-ward."

"Grow up already," Alyssa shot at Kai.

"Why would I want to? You and Teague take such good care of us kids."

"Quaid senses heavy electromagnetic energy in her," Alyssa said to Jessica, ignoring Kai. Then explained to Mitch, "When a person has a lot of dopamine in their system, their aura shifts. Auras are simply extensions of our inner electromagnetic fields and take on different frequencies based on the source of the energy."

"Good Lord." Mitch pointed dramatically toward his face. "Look at the glaze over my eyes. Come on, ladies, speak English. So, this dope makes her happy and creates a certain electrical charge in her body. How does that relate to the visions?"

Alyssa shook her head. "That I don't know. It might be a shared frequency with the other person. It might be something in the universe connecting with her frequency when her dopamine reaches a certain level. I don't think knowing how it works really matters, only how to utilize it. We don't know how Keira hears others' thoughts through a photograph. Or how Luke becomes fireproof. Or how Kai feels emotions. But they know how to make it happen, and by making it happen, they learn to control it."

The room went silent. Too silent. Kat's laugh drifted down the hall.

Mitch's body temperature spiked at the implications. But fear tempered the excitement. "You're not suggesting what it sounds like you're suggesting . . . right?"

Alyssa's eyes lost the excited haze she always got when some new way of looking at medicine or the human body tripped in her head. She focused on Mitch again and he could see the moment his insinuation hit. Her eyes widened, her mouth dropped open. "Oh, no, I . . . I mean, it's . . ." Her brows dipped together in a confused pout. "I didn't mean to suggest that, but . . ."

"Jesus Christ," Kai grumbled, "you always get the best end of every situation. How the hell do you do that?"

Mitch stood there for a moment, stunned into silence. Have sex with Halina for the purpose of inducing orgasms—repeatedly—so she could learn how to wield her power to envision the future? A duel stream of hot and cold ripped down his torso.

He covered his discomfort with a laugh. "Uh, no. That's *not* going to happen." He wiped his hand down his face, fighting the confusing combination of need and fear rising like a tidal wave inside him. "And I want to see her beat the sh—crap out of the person who suggests it."

"Actually, I think Alyssa's on to something," Jessica said. "I happen to know a little about the dopamine effect. I learned about it in rehab, then went on to study it on my own."

Jessica reached behind Mitch and picked up an apple from the bowl. After unsuccessfully struggling with Quaid's death in the warehouse fire, the grief had dragged her under, and she'd become addicted to drugs, alcohol, and sex. She'd been clean now over a year with no signs of relapse. And with Quaid back, their relationship strengthening and growing every day, no one would ever guess her harrowing history by looking at her.

Mitch crossed his arms and set his stance, preparing to take Jessica's points and throw out a rebuttal to every one, just as he did in court.

She eased back on a stool and tucked a few loose strands of her deep copper hair behind her ear. "Basically, dopamine is released in the brain in response to a rewarding experience. Generally food, sex, and drugs have the highest incidence of dopamine release. I also read that recent studies have shown aggression may also stimulate the release of dopamine. You and Halina may have a head start there."

"Ain't that the truth?" he muttered.

"While this is really only a hypothesis on Alyssa's part, the details describing the when and why of her visions confirm the probability—"

Alyssa hissed in a breath, drawing Jessica's attention, and whispered, "Don't use that word around him. It's too big. Scares him and scatters brain cells."

Mitch gave his sister a look, then turned back to Jessica. "Continue, before all my brain cells scatter the hell out of here."

"Dopamine functions as a neurotransmitter," Jessica said. "A chemical released by nerve cells to send signals to other nerve cells, so there is electromagnetic energy involved. Considering the high levels of this energy Quaid felt in Halina and the high levels he knows to exist in the universe from teleporting, I think Alyssa's hypothesis is a pretty damned solid one."

Mitch spread his arms wide. "There *have* to be ways to increase dopamine in the brain other than sex."

He'd already broken the seal on his heart by trying to fuck her and failing. Every time he touched her, he was drawn deeper into those feelings he'd buried. Emotions he'd been sure he'd never feel again—for anyone, including Halina.

"Sounds to me—" Kai started.

Mitch waved him off. "We don't care what you think."

"Like," Kai continued anyway, "unless you want to stuff her with triple chocolate cake or set her up with a few lines of coke, you're going to have to step up to the plate, brother."

"Ryder . . ." Mitch warned.

"Heh," Kai chuckled, "never thought I'd see you step back from a strike straight down the middle. Hey—this dopamine thing can happen with anyone. You said she'd had it happen with other guys." Kai turned fully away from the windows for the first time since he'd started acting strange. "I'll take care of it. Don't worry, dude, I've got your back."

"Ryder," Mitch growled, "I swear—"

"Shit or get off the pot, Foster." Kai's grin was filled with clear challenge.

"Kai," Alyssa scolded.

"It's me or Cash."

"Don't bring me into this," Cash said with a what-the-fuck look.

Kai looked back at Mitch with that grin he was ready to slam off his face. "And I'm pretty sure I'm the more aggressive of the two of us."

Mitch knew Kai was only pushing his buttons. Knew he'd never touch Halina. But it was still that straw. Before he knew what happened, he was across the room, separated from Kai's amused expression only by Ransom's hand against his chest.

"He's fucking with you, dude." Luke pushed him back, smiling. "Just the way you fucked with me by coming on to Keira before we were back together. Payback's a bitch."

"Fucking assholes," Mitch muttered, turning away.

"Teague, honey," Alyssa called into the office. "Would you just pass the jar around to the guys?"

Mitch pulled out his wallet and Frisbeed it into the office before Teague could step out, hitting his brother-in-law in the chest. Teague caught it effortlessly, laughing.

"Just take whatever's in there," Mitch grumbled.

Alyssa frowned and crossed her arms. "I think I'm going to have to come up with another form of punishment. Money doesn't seem to be much of a deterrent anymore."

"Wait 'til we get the money for Kat's wedding, babe," Teague said, sliding Mitch's wallet into his back pocket.

"Can we get back to this issue, please?" Mitch turned to Jessica, who was sitting in a chair across from Keira chewing a bite of apple, her pretty face alight with amusement.

How could they all be so laid-back when his world was falling apart?

Keira sauntered up to the kitchen bar, picked up a baby carrot from the vegetable tray, and grinned. "Like my better half said, payback's a bitch."

He frowned at her in confusion for a second until he'd realized she'd read his mind.

He pointed a stern finger her way. "We made a deal. You're supposed to stay out of my head."

Luke wrapped his arm around Keira's shoulders. "You must have been—"

"Projecting." Everyone said at the same time.

Mitch rubbed his face with both hands. "Jesus fucking Christ."

"Teague?" Alyssa said. "I think I've hit my cursing limit. How about a dopamine hit?"

Teague came over and took the baby from her arms. "It's a tough job, sugar, but *I'll* never step back from a strike straight down the middle. You'll get that hit right after we talk to Halina."

Teague used his free arm to pull Alyssa up and into him, kissing her.

"You can't do that shit," Mitch said. "He's only a couple weeks old."

Alyssa grinned as she took Teague's hand and followed him through the office doors. "You're reading the *old* baby books. And I'm a doctor. I cleared myself."

"At least leave Brady with me," he called after them. "You're going to warp the kid."

Teague's laugh drifted clearly to Mitch. "Wait 'til you're a parent, dude. You'll get it whenever and wherever you can. Besides, Brady's got to be a little warped to fit in with this crowd."

Jessica stood and followed Teague and Alyssa into the office, where Mitch could already hear Quaid talking about physics and energy waves and probabilities that made Mitch's head swim.

He leaned toward the door. "Lys."

Alyssa turned and met Mitch's gaze. All he had to do was dart a look at Jessica, then Quaid and meet her gaze again, and he knew she understood he was asking her to buffer Halina from them.

She nodded and before Teague closed the door, Mitch saw Alyssa position herself on the sofa beside Halina.

Mitch leaned against the kitchen counter, an apple in one hand, a knife in the other. He sliced off a section and used the knife to put it in his mouth as he stared through the living room and out the picture windows. Of course he saw nothing but the stunning, picturesque scene beyond. But he trusted

Kai's instincts, and the man was pacing like a caged panther. Whatever he was feeling had Keira and Luke on edge too. They both had their holsters at their hips. Cash had started scribbling in the notebook again, but seemed distracted. Agitated.

Mitch sat down next to Cash and leaned his forearms on the table. That's all he had to do to have the man spilling his guts.

"Look, I'm sorry," he said, his gaze holding on the paper, gesturing with both hands, his fingers spread wide. "I just . . ." He dug his hands into his hair and rested his head there. "If she'd just told someone about Schaeffer, even if he wasn't put away, he could have been fired or demoted or *something*. He wouldn't have been able to continue that program. Rostov wouldn't have gone off on that tangent. Zoya—"

He stopped. Heaved a breath.

"It might have happened that way," Mitch said, letting his mind wind around other scenarios for the purpose of relieving Cash's pain. But it also opened up a lot of windows Mitch had never considered looking through before. "But think about Schaeffer's nature, Cash. Do you really think a few lousy uncorroborated charges from some foreign worker would have damaged him that severely? Do you think he would have *let* a measly immigrant hurt him? He'd have killed her first. Even if she had gotten as far as ratting him out, we both know she would never have lived to see trial. She knew that too."

Cash lifted his head and glanced at his sister, who sat across the table with so much guilt in her eyes Mitch had to look away. Keira had to live with the knowledge that Rostov had stolen Mateo because he was trying to reproduce her powers through a genetic connection and the knowledge that Cash's wife had been killed trying to protect their son.

Cash dropped a hand on the table and reached for Keira. She took it in both of hers and lifted it to her mouth for a kiss, eyes closed. Tears slid down her cheeks as Luke massaged her neck beneath her hair.

"And even in the best-case scenario, say Halina had successfully gotten Schaeffer out and the project had been canned. Rostov had already made strides. The seed for his crazy-assed plan of creating paranormal abilities through some genetic connection had already been planted. Without Schaeffer's threat, Rostov would have been free to do whatever he wanted. There's no telling what he might have tried. You might not even have your son now."

"Mitch," Keira said softly.

"Look, Cash," Mitch said, "I'm not defending what Halina did. Believe me, she and I have been at each other's throats about this very subject, and I'm with you two hundred percent. I didn't lose my wife. And the pain I've suffered is nothing compared to yours. But in my own pathetic life, it's enough to motivate me to see that Schaeffer pays.

"She wants that too. But she's scared. She's trying, within her own limited capacity, to help."

Cash pulled his hand from Keira's and nodded. "I'll . . . try to . . . be civil."

Mitch slapped him on the back, picked up his apple and knife, and rose. His body felt heavy, his chest as dense as granite. He wanted to wind his limbs around Halina, sink into a soft bed, and sleep holding her for . . . days. He wanted to wake up and realize this had all been a nightmare.

Mitch glanced at the room where Halina was getting grilled and sliced another piece of apple, feeling as if his guts were being sliced the same way.

No longer hungry, he turned toward the sink, set the apple down, and rinsed his hands. Kat's chirp, Dex's excited bark, and the patter of Mateo's little feet created a joy-infused chorus coming down the hallway.

"Uncle Mitch, look. Dex can shake."

He stood there while Kat proceeded to demonstrate the new trick, and Mateo, obviously intrigued by the dog, remained standoffish and hung back.

Mitch couldn't drum up his usual enthusiasm, but still gained as much relaxation and enjoyment from watching Kat play with

Dex as he did from an entire bottle of wine. No, on second thought, he got a lot more from being with the kids.

"Good boy," Kat praised in her sugar-sweet high pitch.

"That's pretty cool, Kat. You'll have to show Halina when—"

The office door jerked open on the other side of the dining room, and Mitch looked over, surprised they were done so soon. But Halina stood there, her hands gripping the jamb, her eyes wide and sharp with what Mitch could only describe as sheer panic.

His stomach went cold. "What's wrong?"

Her gaze swept the open space, while her chest heaved with quick breaths. "Mitch . . ."

He took a step toward her and she nearly lunged out the door with her hands up. "No! Don't move." Panic choked her voice. "Just . . ." Those light, bright, wild eyes took one more sweep toward the windows, then her gaze jerked back toward Mitch, her fear now stark terror. "Down! Dex, *okhrana detey!*" She sprinted toward Mitch. "Get down!"

Mitch didn't have a chance to get anywhere. Halina hit him at a full run, shoving him down. Before they even hit the floor, an explosion detonated in the living room, shattering the picture windows.

Mitch turned, throwing his body—already partially tangled with Halina's—across the mound made up of Kat, Mateo, and Dex. Glass sliced through the air. Crashed against tile, furniture, and appliances. And cut into Mitch's back. He tried to cover Halina as Halina tried to cover the kids and Dex. Kat's screams were muffled. But Mateo didn't make a sound.

Within seconds, the glass explosion had cleared, and icy cold cut through the house. Mitch's ears vibrated with an incessant buzz. He pushed up and glass sliced into his hands. Dex still lay sprawled across Kat, licking tears off Kat's face and watching Halina for instruction.

Mitch's gaze searched for Mateo. He was there, but so damn small with his knees pulled into his chest and his head ducked, hiding beneath Dex's big body like a pup. His dark eyes gazed stoically out from beneath a fringe of golden curls while his tiny hand remained fisted in Dex's collar.

Halina's dazed eyes wandered haphazardly before finding Mitch's. She instantly focused. "Are you okay?" When he nodded, she righted herself and brushed glass off Dex's fur, feeling over his body while her gaze searched Kat. "Honey, are you—?"

One of the guards, Dillon, swept in, reaching for Kat. Another one stood behind, ready to grab Mateo.

Dex shifted his body to cover Kat's again. With his lips peeled back, ears flat against his head, he snarled and snapped.

Dillon yanked his hands back, shaking one out with a "Holy shit."

"*Tikhiy*, Dex," Halina said, sounding breathless, and Dex transitioned into a whimpering, worried pup again. "Go ahead. Take her."

Dillon pulled Kat into his arms just as Nelson came out of the office carrying Brady, whom he'd taken from Teague.

Cash appeared beside the second guard and pulled Mateo in to his arm, crouched to check Halina. More snarls rolled from Dex's peeled lips.

"*Tikhiy*, Dex," Halina repeated.

A mournful whine ebbed from Dex's chest. The dog lowered his head, nuzzled Mateo's hair from his face, and licked him. Mateo in turn wrapped his arms around the dog's neck and whispered, "Thank you," with the same simplistic inflection he had for the gift of his crayons earlier.

"Basement," Teague ordered. "Full security."

Cash exchanged a look with Mitch. He sent a glance toward Halina before meeting Mitch's gaze again. "Do you . . . need anything?"

"No. Go."

He disappeared with Mateo. Dex danced in place impatiently, his gaze darting between the door the kids had disappeared behind and Halina, whining.

"Hold still," Halina said, breathless, her shaking hands working at his collar.

Mitch's heart hammered. Keira was already at the windows with a high-powered rifle, scoping out the shooter. Luke, Kai, and Quaid had disappeared into the other half of the house. Teague crouched beside them. The house was now freezing, even with adrenaline filling Mitch's veins.

"Baby, his collar is fine . . ." Mitch covered Halina's hands with one of his. Glass sliced into his skin and he swore, pulling back. He yanked the shard from his palm and sent a questioning glance between Halina and Teague.

Teague read his concern and bent to look into Halina's eyes. "Halina, are you hurt?"

"No. Help me with his collar . . . my hands . . . won't work," she panted between breaths.

Teague unfastened the collar.

Halina released a breath, then murmured, "Go."

Dex sprinted to the door leading into the basement and pawed at it. When it didn't open, he jumped, hit the handle with his paw, and when the latch freed up, pushed it open with his muzzle.

"That's pretty slick," Teague said.

Halina swept the collar from Teague's hand and held it tight to her chest. She shivered and her teeth chattered. "Thank you."

Mitch lowered a questioning brow at Teague and murmured, "Shock?"

"Single white male," Keira said, voice cool as steel. Mitch turned to find her speaking into a radio. "In a ghillie. Across the meadow on a ridge. Retreating in a dark green Ford F-150."

Teague turned toward the others reentering the room.

"All clear," Luke said.

Mitch rolled to a seat, wincing, and helped Halina do the same. He checked her eyes and found them still dazed. Pupils as tight as a pin.

"Halina, let's get you warm." He put a hand to her jaw, avoiding the cuts oozing blood down her face. "Can you stand?"

Her eyes, so light they looked almost colorless, made incremental jumps over the destruction and finally landed on his face again. "His working collar. Shouldn't have it on in the house."

Only, that's not what he'd asked. And Dex had been wearing the collar since Mitch had met the dog. He'd had the collar on in both hotels. He'd had it on here since they'd arrived.

Mitch brushed her hair back from her face. "You're okay. Dex is okay. Does anything hurt bad?"

Her gaze focused and moved over him. And the panic in her eyes rose. "It was him. Abernathy. He was . . . he was . . ." Her gaze jerked down, over Mitch's chest. Without releasing Dex's collar, her bloody, shaking fingers started yanking at the buttons. "Take it off. Take this damn thing *off.*"

He looked down. Took hold of her wrists. "Why? What's wrong?"

"No more." She violently pulled out of his grasp and ripped two buttons off. She ground out her words. "No more . . . white shirts. I don't ever . . . want to see you wear . . . a white shirt again."

More Jerks. More buttons ticked to the floor. The icy air bit into the skin of Mitch's chest. Tears streamed down her face and mixed with blood.

Mitch fought to get a solid hold on her wrists, every touch ripping at his skin. Finally, he grabbed hold and pulled hard to bring her back from the edge of wherever she'd gone.

"Halina. What's wrong with white shirts?"

"You're . . . always . . . in a white shirt . . . when you . . . die."

"When I . . . what are you talking . . . ?" But then he remembered the car accident. He'd been wearing white then too.

He looked to his right, where bullets had pierced the kitchen island. If Halina hadn't seen it coming, he and Kat and Mateo would be dead. Already drained of blood on Alyssa's kitchen floor.

Jesus. The icy reality cut at his belly.

She'd saved his life. Again.

And she'd risked hers doing it. The way she'd risked Schaeffer's abuse to try and save his job.

He gathered her into his arms as gently as he could, and she held on tight. Still shivering, teeth clicking together. Her touch shot electric shocks of pain through his body, but he didn't let go.

"My fault." She pressed her warm mouth to his bare chest. "All my fault. I told you . . . I can't be here."

"Our guys are after them," Keira said. "Someone else is up on the ridge, but they're not pursuing. Looks like Fish and Game."

"I'll . . . g-go." She pulled away and met his eyes. The terror was still there, but the daze had cleared. "I'll go g-get the papers from the apartment. You st-stay with the others."

"No—"

"I won't run, I p-promise. I'll get the box and bring it b-back." She hiccupped and her beautiful eyes pleaded with him. "I have to get away from here. He wants me and I'm putting everyone else in d-danger. We need to separate."

He wrapped his hands around Halina's head and lifted her face until she looked him in the eye. "You're right, we should go somewhere—"

"No. Not we. *Me.* Just me. He was trying to kill you to make me cave. But he won't kill me. He can't. Not until he gets what he wants." She curled her fingers around his shoulders. "You're not safe with me. You never have been. I need to go alone."

Never have been . . .

The words swirled in his head for a second, needing attention, but he couldn't focus on that. "Not happening, Halina. I'm not letting you go it alone again." He put his forehead to hers and whispered. "Together, we're strong, remember?"

"No." Something shifted in her eyes. Something edged with resignation and hopelessness. And pain. "Together, we're dead."

Halina pulled from him, struggled to her feet, and turned.

"Halina, don't—"

Mitch reached for her, but she stepped away and by the time he got to his feet, Alyssa stood in his path, her gaze intent.

"Give her some breathing room, Mitch."

The sight of lingering terror in his sister's eyes added layers of guilt and stopped him. He pulled the blanket she already held around her shoulders tighter at the neck. "Are you okay?"

"Yeah," she breathed the word, creating a puff of mist. "Thanks for watching out for Kat and Mateo."

"That credit belongs to Halina and Dex." Mitch gave her another squeeze before pulling away. "Go. Get warm with the kids."

She lifted a hand to touch his face but winced when she couldn't find anywhere to put it. "Take it easy on Halina. And let Teague take care of these cuts. Otherwise I'll be coming at you with a needle and thread."

Mitch winced, which made a smile twitch at her lips and eased his concern. Alyssa disappeared into the basement. Halina had long since disappeared into the bathroom down the hall. Mitch stared down the dark stretch, not sure what to do.

"I won't get cut, you will." Luke's irritable voice drew Mitch's gaze to the living room, where Luke had grabbed Keira's hands in the act of picking up a large piece of glass. "Go make sure all the glass is out of your skin. Then check the others."

Luke released her and carelessly scooped pile after pile of razor-sharp glass into a corner with his bare hands, never receiving a nick. Mitch hadn't expected Luke to be harmed because of his ability, but Keira and Kai looked pretty good too, only minor abrasions bloodying their arms and faces. They'd been shielded at the dining room table by the angle of the shots and direction of shattering glass. He glanced back at the window, then at the destruction around him.

He was trying to kill you to make me cave.

Mitch couldn't deny he'd been the target. It certainly hadn't been Kat or Mateo.

He grabbed jackets from the hall tree and returned to toss them to Luke, who distributed them to Teague, Kai, and Keira. Mitch couldn't throw one on with all the glass still stabbing his skin, but he pulled out a space heater from the office, faced it toward the dining room table, and turned it on.

Quaid, along with a couple of the security guards, had already set up ladders against the house and created a pulley system with ropes from the eaves. They raised and covered the gaping openings with sheets of plywood. The cold wouldn't be rushing in for long. But Mitch moved to the fireplace and stuffed it with three more chunks of oak anyway. The skin of his arms and back pulled and he swore. A headache pressed behind his eyes and pain nudged at the back of his skull, making him realize for the first time that he'd probably hit his head sometime during that fiasco.

"Let me work on your back." Teague's voice brought Mitch's gaze around from the fireplace. His brother-in-law stood there in his thick parka, his face pinched with barely contained fury. "It's pretty bad."

"Dude, go downstairs with Alyssa and the kids."

Cash opened the door leading up from the basement. "No, don't go downstairs. Alyssa just kicked me out. Said I was *hovering*."

Teague made a told-you face and gestured to Cash, who took a seat at the table where Teague had set a large first-aid kit. Cash watched Keira wiggle a piece of glass from Kai's bicep.

"I'm getting sick and fucking tired of these assholes," Kai muttered, grimacing. "The whole lot of them."

With the adrenaline wearing off, every inch of Mitch's skin burned. He looked down at his arms and found his white shirt covered in blood. Had that been the reason for Halina's frantic response to his white shirts?

The memory sent a shiver through his body.

Mitch wandered over to the table and dropped into a chair. He pulled his arm slowly out of his shirt. The action tugged glass from his skin and made it feel as if he were being ripped apart. He swore and paused a few times to breathe through the pain. And to thank God over and over that he'd gotten the brunt of the glass, not Kat. Not Mateo. Not Dex. Not Halina.

Luke sat in front of Keira, cleaning a cut on her temple, while Keira complained over his fussing, but never moved away. Mitch wished Halina had let him fuss over her. At the other end of the table, Teague started on Mitch's remaining projectiles with long-handled tweezers.

Mitch's mind and heart needed relief. Just a few moments of relief. He tried to let his mind go while Teague tugged and tore at his skin. Tried to keep it bent away from the life-altering moment they'd all just shared. Keep it from drifting toward what everyone could have lost. It wasn't easy. Especially with Teague reminding him.

"Thanks for covering Kat, man," Teague said. "I . . . don't know . . ." He shook his head, his normally bright blue eyes deep gray with the almost-terror of what could have happened to his daughter.

"That was all Halina," he murmured, letting the thought swirl in his mind until it found a place to land. "Halina and Dex."

Quaid came in the front door, shaking off snow in the foyer, but kept his parka on. "Where's Jess?"

His presence made Mitch realize how fucking cold he was in the house.

"Downstairs with the kids," Teague said.

"Oh, sure." Cash swabbed at Kai's cuts with hydrogen peroxide. "She lets Jess stay, but I *hover*."

Quaid's mouth turned up in a half grin as he sat at the table in front of his project. A small knife, leather cord, and other supplies were laid out, and Quaid picked up a round piece that had been carved of material the same deep russet and bone color as the rest. But this had been honed into a circle, with another circle removed from the center so it was basically a flat ring.

"The guys split up," Quaid said. "A few went to search the sniper's location for evidence. The others are reinforcing and securing the plywood and checking the perimeter. They called in another half dozen for duty. With dogs."

"Thanks, bud," Teague said, tone flat, exhausted.

Mitch pointed at the shattered mess in front of Quaid. "What's—?"

He flinched, cutting off his words, and darted a scowl over his shoulder at Teague. "Perfect opportunity to get back at me for all those jailbird comments, huh?"

Teague lifted his brows. "Hadn't thought of that, but now that you mention it . . ."

He tugged another shard of glass from Mitch's shoulder blade and pain sliced down Mitch's spine. He swore and turned his gaze back to the ring-shaped thing Quaid was messing with. "What's that?"

"I'm hoping," Quaid said, wrapping copper wire around one third of the piece, "this will become a haven for Halina."

"How?"

"This," Quaid said, touching the material of the ring, then gesturing toward the mess of pieces beside it, "is part of that ferrite bead. It's one of those ceramic things you see on top of telephone poles that wires run through."

Teague worked at a particular deep piece of glass in the back of Mitch's arm and Mitch kept flinching every time it hit a nerve. "Where'd you get that?"

"He climbed up the damn pole with that fucking hammer," Kai said. "Dumbshit. I had visions of that metal head hitting those charged lines. I told him to let Ransom do it. Was hoping we could finally find a way to tap out a few of his snarky brain cells. But noooo," he sang toward Quaid. "You never did listen to me."

Quaid grinned, tying a black leather cord to the ring, and looked at Mitch. "The ceramic material acts as a damper or a choke for electromagnetic signals, absorbing them to some degree, which is why they use them on the telephone lines, to limit interference. This wire," he pointed to the copper, "is a conduit. A way for her—when she develops the skill—to direct the stored energy, to either dissipate the heat or send it."

"Send it?"

"Yeah, as in shoot it, move it, transfer it, whatever. Or she could also use it to give the energy somewhere to travel where it can dissipate as heat."

Mitch rested his forehead on his hand. "And how is that supposed to help?"

One of Quaid's dark brows lowered. His mouth quirked.
Definitely a *use-your-brain* look. "It should absorb at least some
of the electromagnetic energy that's tormenting her with
glimpses into alternate universes."

Mitch sat back and got poked with tweezers. "Sonofa—"

"Hold still," Teague said. "I can't even think about healing
you when you've got glass in there."

"Alternate *what*?" Mitch looked back at Quaid. "What the
hell are you talking about?"

"I don't think Halina's seeing the future—as in the concrete
future. The ultimate future. Whatever you want to call it. From
what she describes, from what I feel in her, and from what I
know, I think she's seeing possibilities of the future. I think she's
seeing into alternate universes which are serving up the most
probable positive outcome based on the most probable choices
available and the most probable negative outcome based on the
most probable choices available." Quaid grinned. "I know how
much you love the topic of probability. Want me to explain
how that works in the universe and alternate planes of reality?"

"Hell no." A shiver slid down Mitch's spine. "You're saying
she told you that when she has these visions, there are two
sides, a good and a bad?"

"That's how she explains it. They play side by side like mini-
movies. That's straight out of the alternate universe playbook."

"Like there is such a thing," Mitch grumbled.

"And hopefully," Quaid said, ignoring him and holding up
the ceramic ring, "until she can control her power better, this
little gem is going to control it for her. Or at least help. Small
alterations in the amount of material used, possibly even the
placement on her body, could allow her an incredible amount
of control over what information she receives. Who knows,
maybe she can even send information. Hell, Jessica didn't know
she could transport until she found me. Imagine how information like Halina's could be utilized."

And manipulated.

It was the first thought that came to Mitch's mind. The second was whether or not Schaeffer knew about her powers.

The ring came flying at Mitch while he was deep in thought. He barely caught it before it knocked him in the forehead.

"Have her try it." Quaid started cleaning up the mess in front of him.

Across the table Luke made a derogatory sound in his throat and shot Mitch a narrow-eyed scowl.

"You might want to think about starting out with one O, dude," Luke said, his voice lowered to a fake confidential level. "Don't try to live up to me in this situation. Who knows what multiples would do to her. Just relax and embrace your ordinary place among humans. We can't all be above average."

Keira snorted a laugh.

"The day you're above average, Ransom—" Mitch started.

His cell rang. He looked at the display, which read GI JOE, and shot one more glare at Luke. "Oh, look. Someone I want to talk to even more than I want to talk to you. It's the IRS."

He stood from the table and jabbed at the phone to answer. "Young," he bit out, walking toward the foyer for some privacy—something that was impossible to get within five hundred miles of these people. "What the hell are you doing, sitting on your hands? Abernathy just shot the hell out of Creek's house and nearly blew my brains out the back of my skull."

A second of silence followed and a trickle of fear slid down Mitch's spine. "Owen?"

"He's either desperate . . . or off his meds."

"Off his *what*?"

"Conjecture on my part. I think the guy's bipolar or manic or something."

Mitch slapped a hand against his forehead, then winced. "And you didn't think I'd want to know this?"

"It's not a diagnosis," Owen said, "it's just my . . . feelings about him."

"I'm so sick of *feelings* and *intuition* and *vibes*."

"You sound like you need a vacation as bad as I do."

Mitch rubbed his eyes. When he dropped his hand, everyone at the dining room table was staring at him. He turned and
wandered across the foyer and into Teague's office. Mitch
pulled at his hair and turned to stare down the hall where
Halina had disappeared.

The sound of the shower drifted to him, making him ache
in the pit of his stomach and throb all through his pelvis. She
was naked. Wet. Her hair dark. Her skin shiny. And, God, he
not only wanted her, he needed her.

But when he thought of her face, he couldn't envision her
eyes hot and heavy-lidded. They still appeared wide with icy
fear, and he longed to pull her into him and hold her.

"So what's up?" Mitch asked.

"I've been watching more of the videos."

Innuendo lay heavy in Owen's voice, painting a thick line of
dread down Mitch's spine. "And?"

"And Halina has a hell of a lot more information than she's
admitting to. She's the one who stole the tapes I told you were
missing from the labs—"

"How can you know that?" Mitch's protective response was
immediate, fierce, and completely uncontrollable.

"That *backup footage* I was watching . . ." Young said. "You
know, it's called backup because the ones in front of it, usually
called the originals, were stolen. Besides that . . . the backups
recorded her *stealing the originals*. Are we clear there?"

"Got you're an asshole."

"Thanks. It's always nice to have hard work acknowledged,"
he said cheerfully, before his voice dipped back to serious. "And
tapes aren't the only thing she stole. About two weeks before
she left, she began gathering information. To what end, I
couldn't tell you, though I could guess. I've been tossing blackmail and evidence back and forth. Haven't decided which I like
better yet. But she has *everything*."

Mitch's stomach squeezed with excitement and sickness.
"What do you mean *everything*?"

"I mean she took digital images of every page of every file
in Rostov's lab. Then moved on to Gorin's lab. Then did the

same in her own lab. One night, she went into the refrigeration room they shared and pulled out a tray of test tubes. Started working with them. I couldn't tell what she was trying to do—sabotage or investigate or what—but her hands were shaking so bad when she tried to put them away, she dropped a few.

"Whatever was inside them—which we know now was the chemical that your team was exposed to—hit the floor and splashed all over her. And right before my eyes, she burned. I watched as her skin bubbled and boiled on her body."

Mitch's stomach sank and he backed against a wall. His knees went out. He slid to the floor, his hand on his forehead.

"It was horrible," Young said softly, true sympathy in his voice. "I'll spare you the details and just tell you that she did her best to give herself first aid and eventually passed out on the sofa in her office. In the morning, every burn, every mark created by the chemicals was gone."

He paused. The line went quiet. Ninety percent of Mitch's mind was seven years behind him, pulling out nuances of Halina's behavior he'd considered erratic at the time, but which he'd chalked up to stress or overlooked because of his own stress. He'd always told himself it would get better. That it was only temporary. He'd always believed they loved each other enough to weather anything.

But he hadn't even known what the hell had been going on. Now he couldn't understand how he'd missed it all.

"Are you going to tell me?" Young asked.

Mitch's mind returned to the foyer. To the heavy, carved entry doors. To the chill coating his skin with gooseflesh. "What?"

"Her power," he said, irritation stretching his voice. "What's her power?"

Mitch blew out a breath, the shock in his belly slowly transforming to anger. She'd had all this information all this time and she'd held it back. Kept it secret. Risking everything that was important to him. Risking his *family*.

"We're not clear on that yet." His voice sounded cool, like it did in court when he was detached. "She seems to see pieces of the future, but when and how is sketchy. Quaid thinks she's seeing alternate realities, not concrete futures. All these brainiacs keep talking quantum physics and probability schematics and electromagnetic energy gradients and shit. It's all just . . . guesstimates at this point."

"Don't tell me, after taking down dozens of military top brass, cutting through the most secretive levels of espionage and conspiracy for the little enlisted guy, that you can't figure out one fucking woman. One goddamned paranormal power when you're surrounded by them."

Young's cut-through-the-bullshit approach stunned Mitch right back to stark reality.

"Get on your game, Foster. I've given you a hell of a lot to work with here. Maybe even everything you need to tie a big bow around Schaeffer's fat neck and walk him into the AG's office. All you have to do is get Beloi to cooperate."

Young's voice was the darkest, the most serious Mitch had ever heard it.

"What's going on, Owen? You're tweaked beyond capacity tonight."

"I'm sick of this shit. I want my life back. I'm not getting any younger and I'm only living once. The longer this goes on, the less life I have to reclaim. Get me something solid on Schaeffer so I can take down both him and Abernathy before they do any more damage. Then we can *all* move on."

The phone went dead in Mitch's ear. He stayed there, ass on the tile foyer floor, elbows on knees, and let the cell fall away from his head. He didn't want to believe Halina had held all this knowledge back. Didn't want to acknowledge she could have been allowing both him and his family to suffer unnecessarily by harboring evidence of Schaeffer's compulsive manipulation. Didn't want to believe she'd walked out on him when she'd had the evidence to free herself and stay.

But . . .

"They should hate me."

Now he understood just why she believed that.

The depth of hurt that lunged up from the shadows of his

soul overtook him as he imagined a demon would. Pulling him into the dark. Drawing out all his bad—anger, viciousness, malice. Every painful thing she'd ever done filled his mind. And with the hurt of her betrayal and abandonment threading through seven years of his life, he had plenty to think about on his way to the bathroom where her shower ran.

FOURTEEN

Halina rested her head against her arm on the shower's tile wall and let the hot water pour over the cuts on her shoulders. They were sparse and shallow thanks to the way Mitch twisted at the last minute, shielding her, Dex, Kat and Mateo from most of the glass. She should be out there with him now. Taking care of him. Wished she could be—the way Alyssa and Teague, Keira and Luke, Jessica and Quaid took care of each other. The way she and Mitch used to take care of each other. She hadn't recognized that element of their relationship as something she'd missed until she'd come here, met these people.

But in light of what had just happened, that was so minor. What she lacked in her life was worth giving up to keep them safe.

Her fingers tightened around Dex's collar. She opened her eyes and glanced sideways at it. She fingered the deep brown studs. Tears of pride burned her eyes when she remembered how he'd reacted in the chaos and protected Kat and Mateo. That one incident was worth every hour of training over the last four years.

The bathroom door opened. Halina didn't hear it. Only knew from the shift in the steam. Her delayed alarm sensors kicked on just as she heard, "Halina."

Mitch. His deep voice husky with frustration.

The tension drained from her shoulders. The burn of alarm

melted from her belly. Resignation welled into some emotion she couldn't describe or explain. Inside, a combination of failure and fear coiled deep in her gut. She wasn't ready to do this. To give up everything that had kept him safe for so long.

But it wasn't keeping him safe anymore.

He pulled the curtain aside. The rake of metal rings against the rod made her flinch. One look at the darkness of his eyes, the pull to his face, the tightness of his mouth, and she closed her eyes and rolled her head back toward the wall.

"Just . . . let me finish my—"

Mitch stepped over the edge of the tub—still in his khakis—and grabbed her biceps. "You have all the evidence we need to put Schaeffer away, don't you? You've had it all this time and you've hidden it."

The trained, strong part of her wanted to knock his hands away and hit back. But another part of her felt guilty and ashamed and mortified over what had happened to these good people. And that part of her wanted him to shake her and shake her until her brain rattled in her skull.

"No. I mean, yes, I have had some, but—"

"You've put my family at risk—"

"I know, Mitch. I . . ."

"—all these years just to save yourself," he spoke over her.

"No." She couldn't gather any anger, only desperation. "No, I didn't know . . . I didn't understand the risks until—"

"Until I found you. You've had a hundred opportunities to help over the last twenty-four hours."

She closed her eyes as shame ravaged her. "I . . . I didn't realize . . . I was trying to—"

"Kat and Mateo were almost *killed*, Halina."

The torture in his voice stabbed at her. Guilt overwhelmed her until she wanted to cave under its weight. "I know. I *know*." She choked on a sob. "I didn't want to come here. I tried to tell you . . ."

She pulled out of his grasp to shut off the water. Trembling with the grief and pain of her guilt, she pulled the towel off the shower curtain rod and buried her face.

She had to accept that she'd hit a wall. There was nothing she could do to help him anymore. She'd successfully kept Schaeffer away when she'd had control over her research and her cover. But Mitch wouldn't stop. She couldn't protect any of them with him interfering like this.

When she lifted her eyes to his, there was so much hurt, so much anger there, she wanted to crumple. She stepped from the tub and wrapped the towel around her body.

A swamping sense of failure made her reach for the sink to help her stand.

She pushed Dex's collar into his hand. "Here's everything. Everything I have. All my research, all Rostov's and Gorin's. And more. Lots more. It's in there. Alone it's not enough to destroy Schaeffer. But maybe with what you have now . . . maybe . . ."

She turned away, reached for the doorknob, and paused. With her back toward him she took a deep breath. "The moment Schaeffer discovers I've given you these files," she swallowed past the terror and tears in her throat, "you're as good as dead. He knew I had the incentive to keep them hidden. And he knows you don't. Like you told me, Mitch, when he sends men after you, there's no escaping. Your only chance now is to do something with them before he—or one of his men—finds you."

And to get as far away from me as possible.

Halina exited the bathroom and entered the guest bedroom across the hall. Closing the door at her back, she leaned against it, dropped her head back, and closed her eyes. Failure swamped her body. Ultimate failure. But also a twisted relief. Carrying the responsibility for Mitch's safety had weighed on her every day of the last seven years. Making sure he was alive and well without him discovering she was watching, continuing to remind Schaeffer she held the evidence and was prepared to use it without leaving any hint of her location, living in constant fear that she'd make a mistake along the way and it would cost Mitch his life—it was exhausting.

Now, she only had to concentrate on getting away from him

and hiding. With his band of followers and their paranormal abilities, that would be difficult. But now that Mitch knew everything—or would after he absorbed the information from the discs she'd just given him—now that he believed she'd completely betrayed him and his family, he might stay away.

Unless she was pregnant.

But she couldn't do anything about that now.

What she could do—the very last thing she could do—was attempt to buy Mitch time.

Halina opened her eyes and glanced around the room. Her gaze halted on a phone beside the nightstand. She went directly to it and dialed information. With the credit card numbers for her unused alias, which she'd memorized—just in case—she placed the call.

"Yes, I need to get flowers urgently to one of your patients," she told the gift shop clerk who answered, speaking quickly and keeping her voice low. Her gaze held on the door, ready to cut the call if Mitch walked in. "Can you do that?"

"Of course, ma'am."

"They're for my uncle," she said, rubbing her aching forehead. "He's a senator and always uses an alias when he's in the hospital. I know you can't give me his alias," she said before the clerk objected. It wasn't her first time using this tactic. "I'm only asking that you get these flowers and a message to him. He's critically ill and I'm in Arizona. I may not make it to see him before he passes and I really want him to know I'm thinking of him."

"Oh, dear," the older woman said. "I can send the flowers to his room, I just can't guarantee—"

"I understand," Halina said, in the back of her mind chanting *please, please, please.* "Even knowing I was able to attempt will ease my guilt. The earliest flight I could get is tomorrow morning and I just don't know if he . . ." She purposely trailed off, but didn't have to try to sound desperate.

"I'd be happy to do what I can to get the flowers and your message to him."

"Oh, thank you." Halina's relief sounded in her voice. "If he is too sick to receive them, if someone can just whisper the message in his ear and give it to the others who are there with him, I'd be forever grateful."

Mitch stood dripping on the tile floor for a long moment after Halina had exited, staring at the rich brown rhinestones on Dex's collar. He drew in thick breaths of steam-filled air. His heart assaulted his ribs as his mind spun and spun, trying to put everything into a place.

She *had* told him she'd feared putting others in danger here. She *hadn't* understood the extreme effects of Schaeffer's rampage until she'd arrived. And she'd hardly had time to assimilate everything and make such a monumental decision as to whether or not to give up the information saving her own life in order to save others.

Mitch turned the collar over and slid his fingers along the black canvas. A stiff area in the center made his heart trip again. Three stiff squares lived at the center of the collar—squares the size and shape of micro discs.

Air whooshed from his lungs. God, she was clever. He couldn't think of a safer place for them than on her attack-trained shepherd's neck.

When it counted, she'd come through. He hadn't told her how he knew she had the information. Didn't tell her what information he thought she'd had. Yet, she'd turned over—what at least looked like—everything, as she'd claimed.

It was a huge sacrifice. One that moved Mitch and gave him the strength to make that leap of faith that terrified his heart, but one he knew he had to make.

He exited the bathroom and paused in front of the guest bedroom door. The house was quiet and cold. Everyone had descended into the basement and only plywood covered the gaping windows. But the heat was on full blast, beginning to warm the house again.

He turned the knob and pushed the bedroom door open.

Halina, still in her towel, crouched in front of the suitcase one of the guards had brought in, collecting clothes.

"Please don't yell at me anymore." Her voice was quiet and flat. "Just let me get dressed and I'll leave."

Mitch closed the door at his back and stood there a long moment. With its intact windows and the heat pouring from a vent nearby, this room was warm. "Is that what you want?"

"It's what you need. What everyone needs."

The fact that she hadn't jumped to a *hell yes* was a good sign. But they had a long way to go to rebuild the bridges they'd burned. And Mitch didn't even know where to start.

"I shouldn't have . . . judged you," he said. "I'm sorry."

She didn't respond, just threw a pair of jeans on the bed. Then a long-sleeved shirt.

He crossed his arms and approached her, stopping a few feet away. "Halina, what did you say to Dex? I recognized *protect,* but not the other word."

"Children," she said, her voice weak, distracted as she tossed underwear, socks, and a bra onto the pile. "We did search and rescue for a while. Had to stop because when Dex located a body instead of a live person, he went into weeks of depression. Something about the smell . . . affected levels of neurotransmitting . . ." She paused. Sighed. Shook her head. "Never mind. I taught him search—*poisk,* find—*nakhodit',* hunt—*okhota*—"

"Hunt?"

"It means the same as attack, but signals the dog he has to find the target first."

That comment made Mitch think back to when he'd first found her, less than two full days ago, and all the security measures she'd had in place. An attack-trained shepherd, Krav Maga training, weapons training. He thought about how long she'd lived in fear. How much she'd given up to stay safe.

How much time . . . investment . . . security . . . power . . . she'd just handed over to him in Dex's collar. She hadn't needed to. She could have stood her ground. Continued to deny. Mitch would never have found it.

"Halina, tell me about the visions."

She crossed her arms. "You know about the visions. There's nothing else to tell."

"You didn't tell me there were two sides. A good side and a bad side."

"It doesn't—"

"It *does* matter. Were your visions of me with other women the good vision or the bad?"

Her brow pulled in a frown. "What kind of question is—"

"Tell me, Halina," he said, growing frustrated. "I want to know both sides of the futures you saw for me."

She pressed her lips together and tightened her arms. "The women were the good side of your future, Mitch. As I said, you have a happy life ahead of you."

"And the bad side?"

She hesitated. A mixture of anger and resignation shone in her eyes. "The truth is that in the bad side of your future, you're dead. Murdered. Can you leave now, so I can get dressed? I'd like to get out of here before Abernathy decides to come back."

"Murdered?" he said, stunned. "I mean, everyone dies. It's the ultimate bad future, right? But *murdered*?"

"Actually, dying isn't the worst future, Mitch. Difficult as it may be to believe, there are worse fates than death."

He didn't like that little reminder. "Come on, Halina. Give me a little more than that."

"I don't know the details," she said. "All I know is that in all of my visions, your life splits and goes one of two ways. The details of each vision are slightly different—a different woman, a different location, a different manner of death—but they're all similar enough to know your fate. You'll either live a life of bliss with your harem or die by murder."

Frustrated, Mitch ran a hand over his face. "Why don't you ever see yourself in my future?"

She closed her eyes. "I'm always in your future, Mitch. I'm the reason you die, *every time*."

"For Christ's sake, Halina—"

"Did you not almost die in a car accident yesterday?" she asked, her anger and incredulity growing. "Did you not just almost die in the living room? How many times have you come that close to death in the last seven years? When I've been out of your life?"

He thought back. "Actually . . . quite a few."

"*Un*related to Schaeffer."

Okay, none. She had him there.

"Are you really going to tell me I don't know what I'm seeing? That I don't know what I'm talking about?"

He rubbed his eyes and pinched the bridge of his nose, searching for patience.

"I don't care whether you believe or not." She turned toward the bed, picked up her panties, and pulled them on without removing her towel. "And I'm not going to argue with you. If you continue to insist what I've told you is nothing but fiction, you're going to end up getting yourself and everyone you love killed. I'm not going to be here to witness it. And I'm sure as hell not going to stay here and be the cause of it."

He grabbed her arm and turned her toward him, shaking his head in disbelief. "You're a *scientist*, Hali. How can you believe that these visions you don't even understand are stronger than our own free will to choose?"

"Because they're *ac-cur-ate*. If *that*—" She gestured toward the door. "Wasn't that enough to convince you that I shouldn't be near you?"

He shook her out of sheer frustration. "I have to be near you, Hali. *You* are my good future. I don't give a fuck what your visions show. *They aren't reality*. I am reality. You are reality. Me wanting you—that's reality."

Pain filled her eyes and they glistened with tears. "Mitch—"

"I don't believe futures are predestined. We have the power to choose, and every choice changes that future." He gripped her jaw with his free hand, willing her to hear him, believe him. "And I choose *you*. Let Fate suck on that for a while."

A laugh huffed from Halina's chest. Her eyes closed and her head fell forward, resting on his chest.

"You leaving isn't what I need, Hali." He slipped one hand beneath her hair, the other arm around her waist, and pulled her close. "I want you to stay. I need you to stay."

She pressed warm palms to his stomach, but didn't push him away. Mitch tilted her head back and looked into her heavy-lidded eyes. Her gaze was so exhausted, so discouraged, it broke his heart. And he wanted so desperately to mend that break.

He lowered his mouth to hers. When she softened beneath him, when she kissed him back with so much desire he could taste it, he pulled away.

"No more talk about predestined futures, Hali. This is reality, baby. No one can make the choice to change that but you or me." He stroked her cheek with his thumb. "Do you want to change this reality, Hali? Because I don't."

"I've always wanted you," she whispered. "Only you."

Mitch lowered his hand to the knot in her towel and pulled. The terry fell away, leaving them skin to skin from the waist up. He let out a moan on a long breath.

"Let's give fate a kick in the ass, baby." He slid his hand to her breast and squeezed until she moaned. "Make love to me, Hali," he begged with a shake in his voice. "It's been so fucking long."

She pushed up and covered his mouth with hers. Open and wet. Her tongue searched for his and when they joined in a languid roll, heat rushed to his groin. He walked her backward until they reached the bed, then gripped her waist and lifted her. She wrapped her thighs around his hips, dug her fingers into his hair, and dropped her mouth against his neck, sucking.

"Ah, Hali . . ." The feel of her wanting him was a fantasy. And so different from the lust they'd shared last night. This was hotter and deeper. This was real.

Mitch slid his hands to her ass and pulled her against him. She broke the suction on his neck to groan and arch. Her hands fisted in his hair. And, oh, heaven. She felt like heaven.

He laid her back on the bed, bent to press a kiss to her belly, and trailed kisses upward, cherishing her beautiful body. Holding her head with both hands, he looked directly into her heavy-lidded eyes. "I've never wanted anyone the way I want you, Hali. I didn't say it very well last night, but it was still true. The other women were nothing but survival. I played the part for the press, for the women, for myself—to get through the night. But I always ended up empty. Alone. Without you."

As she searched his eyes, Mitch pulled her arms from around his neck and raised them over her head, threading their fingers. Then lowered his mouth to one of her breasts.

She arched her lower back and pulled their hips together with the strength of her legs around his ass.

Mitch groaned her name against the breast he savored, more gently than he had last night. Smoothed his tongue over the still-visible teeth marks.

Her hands tried to slip from beneath his, but he held them.

"Let me touch you," she whispered.

"I got here first," he murmured, then closed his mouth over the nipple and sucked hard. Halina moaned.

That long-lost but familiar sensation of sensual power flooded his body as she whimpered. He growled and moved his torment to the other breast. He released one of her hands and caressed his way to her stomach. Used his knee to push one of her legs to the side. Edged his fingers beneath the band of her panties and slid his hand over the heat between her thighs.

He released a long, heavy breath of pleasure against her breast. "Oh, Hali."

She was soft. Smooth. Hot. Wet.

Perfect.

She lifted her hips into his hand with a deep sound of need in her throat. "God, the feel of you touching me . . ."

The pleasure overflowing in her voice made him think of all the years she'd gone without sex. Without intimacy. Without release. If she was going to have to suffer through visions when this was over, he was going to do his damnedest to make the pleasure worth the pain.

"Magic," he whispered. "We are magic together, baby. Always have been."

He slid his fingers over her swollen soft outer lips and squeezed them together while making small, gentle circles to massage her hidden clitoris. Her indrawn breath, the way she rocked her hips to the motion, shot adrenaline into his blood. One of her hands dropped to the bed and fisted the comforter as she arched her back and closed her eyes.

"Mi-itch . . ." she whispered in a broken voice, revealing her rise to the edge of orgasm.

"Quaid made you a necklace," he murmured against her skin. "Thinks it will help stop the visions. Do you want to try it?"

"No," she breathed. "I want to learn . . . to use them."

Mitch grinned. "I'm at your beck and call to help with that."

His heart took up too much room in his chest as he watched pleasure twist through her body, tighten her nipples, and wash over her face. He wanted this to last. He wanted to watch her like this for hours. And even though they didn't have hours, he slowed his hand, stroked his fingers along the slick strip leading to her heat, and basked in her sounds of growing pleasure. Then slipped a finger inside her, drew the wetness out, and gently, so gently, stroked the warmth over her clit.

She strangled a cry of pleasure. Mitch repeated the motion as he leaned back to watch the erotic sight of his sun-darkened hand moving between her creamy, pale thighs, his big fingers disappearing into her, then drawing out, her hips rocking against his hand.

"Christ, you're beautiful," he murmured, following the motion of her hips with his hand, letting her lead herself to orgasm using his touch.

And when she reached that peak, Mitch took over with quick strokes that stiffened her body just before the sensation broke with hard spasms of an intense release.

A new surge of warmth coated his fingers and a voracious hunger hit him low in the gut. Halina's dark lashes lifted in a languid sweep, but couldn't stay open. It made him smile. Made his heart flood. He leaned down and kissed her. The looseness of her mouth, the lazy, languid, sexual way she stroked his tongue with her own set him on fire.

"When do the visions come, love?" he whispered against her mouth, then laid a trail of kisses down her neck.

"About five minutes into relaxing," she murmured, her voice thick.

Mitch smiled against the curve of her breast on his travels lower. "Then you won't be relaxing just yet."

Her fingers combed through his hair on a sigh and a barely audible, "God, I've missed you."

Emotion slammed his chest so hard he couldn't breathe. His heart sizzled with a burning, painful pleasure. He moved lower, slid his hands beneath her ass and lifted her sweet spot to his mouth.

"Oh . . ." Her stomach muscles bunched and she made a half curl, grabbing his head with both hands. Mitch stroked her with his tongue, pulled the sensitive swell between his lips, and sucked. Her unique and sweet taste filled his mouth, and he swore they were in an equal state of pleasure when Halina's eyes closed and her head fell back on a whispered, "Mitch . . . you're *so* good . . ."

There were about seven steps between good and mind-blowing, and Mitch intended to explore every damn one.

Halina shuddered again as Mitch moved up her body. She was limp after her second orgasm, her mind completely warped in the most delicious way. He'd ditched his pants, rolled on a condom, and lay half on top of her, half on the bed, all that warm muscle stretched against her body.

She stroked her hand along the arm stretched across her waist. Turned into his kisses along her jaw and took his mouth with hers. His lips were full, soft, and perfectly shaped. And had the most sensual ways of moving. But she was ready to feel him inside her, filling her.

Lowering her hand from his arm, she circled his erection with her fingers and smiled at his groan of pleasure.

"Careful, baby. It's loaded."

"Hope so." She rolled him backward, opened her thighs, and straddled his lap.

"Can't wait, Hali," he rasped, his expression tight with a mix of pleasure and pain. "Need you."

She pushed up on her hands and rocked her hips, placing his head at her entrance. Mitch clasped her face in both hands. "Look at me while I fill you."

His eyes were so hot. So filled with emotion. Fierce emotions she couldn't read beyond lust and affection. But she didn't need any more than that.

She lowered her hips, sinking onto him, even as he lifted to meet her. He pressed tightly into her body, his size stretching her and exciting every nerve. With her bottom lip between her teeth, she took him deep. The level of excitement on Mitch's face was its own thrill. Watching him on the edge of control was pure ecstasy and she rocked and moved just to see it intensify.

He lowered, pulling out of her, the sensation a delicious drag until he thrust upward again. Something deep inside her shot sparks of pleasure through her pelvis like a mini-explosion. Halina sucked air against the burn of the pleasure now and pain lingering from the night before.

She squeezed her muscles, gripping his length. Rocked into him, wanting more. Bit the side of his neck on a groan.

"Fuck, Hali," he rasped, lust tight in his voice, but sweet emotion flooded his eyes. "Nothing has ever felt this right."

Her mind and heart were so tangled, she only knew this overwhelming bond developing with him. Stronger and even more rock solid than it had been when everything between them had been so right.

His cock hit that place again and pleasure exploded through her.

"Yes," she breathed. Eyes falling closed, head dropping back.

They moved together as if they'd never been apart, their rhythm erotic, sensual perfection. Mouths and hands taking in every part of each other. Communicating more through their eyes and their touch than they ever could through speech. The passion peaked within minutes. Their bodies damp with sweat, thrusts growing intense.

Mitch whispered, "Ready to come, love?"

"Yes. Please, yes."

He put one hand on her jaw, bringing her gaze back to his. "Focus, Hali. The papers, Washington."

A stream of darkness cut through her pleasure. Reality encroaching on this rare moment of bliss. But she nodded.

Mitch slid his hand down her neck, over her breast, dipped his head, and took the nipple into his mouth, sucking, licking, finally biting down, shooting the sting of lust straight between her legs.

"Come for me, Halina."

His words gave her that final erotic push. The orgasm broke hard, a crash of exquisite pleasure smashing through her body. Her mouth opened on a scream, but her throat closed around it. The muscles along her spine contracted and she arched. Fingers and toes curled until they cramped.

"Oh, fuck yeah." Mitch's throaty murmur rippled across her skin just before he lunged deep, his muscles going rock hard beneath her hands. That guttural sound of supreme pleasure and satisfaction rolled deep in his chest and pushed more ripples of excitement through Halina.

Her lungs finally released and she gasped for air, but the pleasure hadn't finished ravaging her yet. A backlash of delicious spasms shook her exhausted muscles and they contracted and flexed and continued to rocket sparks of ecstasy everywhere.

In the long moments afterward, Halina lay against his chest as Mitch's hands caressed her back, his nails scraping softly, shoulders to hips, as he pressed kisses to the top of her shoulder.

Halina wished time would stop. But it didn't. And eventually, Mitch pulled back, took her chin between his fingers, and tilted her head so she was looking directly into his eyes. His fiery, intense, dangerous eyes.

"God . . . Hali." He was still breathing heavily. "Hasn't . . . been that good . . . in seven . . . years."

Words of love, of apology, of regret . . . pleas for forgiveness . . . they all rode high in her chest as the desire to hold this perfect moment overwhelmed her. She wrapped her arms around his shoulders, her hands combing through his thick soft hair, willing herself to hold them in.

She managed to keep them all back . . . except . . . "I've missed you so *damn* much."

Hearing the words aloud, barely even a whisper, words that didn't begin to describe her years of aching loneliness, words describing a reality she knew she'd have to live again, tore her open and tears spilled over her lashes.

She lowered her head, but Mitch took her face in both hands and wiped her tears with his thumbs. "You don't have to worry about that anymore."

He kissed her lips and ran a hand over her hair before gripping her waist and lifting her. He settled her on the bed beside him. "I'll be right back. Don't move."

She curled onto her side and murmured, "Like I could."

His grin hit her dead center in the chest. A flash of those beautiful teeth. Light in his eyes. Color electrifying his skin. He looked so refreshed, so alive. So real. And in that instant she realized how stiff and plastic he'd appeared in the photos in the papers and magazines and interviews. Remembered his words to her before they'd made love. And her heart burst open.

He stood, braced his hands on the bed, and lowered himself in a push-up to kiss the tear tracks from one cheek. Then kissed her lips so sweetly, the tears almost started up again.

She watched him walk to the door with a small smile lifting her lips. "Still have the best ass, Foster."

He paused in the doorway, twisted to look at her, and the way the light drifted over him showed off every muscle in that sleek body. He smiled. Slow, hot, with so much love in his eyes Halina's heart swelled painfully.

He disappeared through the door and Halina was left wondering . . . could they make this work? There was so much for them to overcome. But he loved her. She believed that. And she loved him. So very much. If he could forgive her, they had a chance. The question was if.

Mitch moved through the room quietly, laying a blanket over her. Then climbed behind her on the bed and curved his naked body to hers. He pulled her into his arms, pressed his face to the back of her neck, and kissed her.

Halina's heart compressed. She squeezed her eyes closed. His hand slid gently down her arm, scraping his nails lightly back up. His lips dropped kisses along her neck, then her shoulder. He let out a long sigh, threaded their fingers, and brought her hand up to his for a series of kisses.

She let herself fall back into him, his body warm and strong behind her. Let herself drift into the pleasure buzzing through her body. Let her mind float and play with images as they came. Visualized the apartment in that old Victorian in DC and the space beneath the sink. Remembered the panic as she'd jammed the box into the dark hole.

Tension built in her chest. In her limbs. She squirmed against the growing restriction, but found herself as frozen as if she were stuck in concrete. Panic crawled over her skin and tightened her chest, making it hard to breathe. She tried to pull in air, tried to call out, yell for help, but could only wheeze out a thin throaty whine.

Breathe. The thought caressed her mind. *Direct your focus.*

Halina slowed her spinning brain, and concentrated on the images coming into view—transparent layers atop each other, like two movies playing together on the same screen.

The screens slowly separated. Color softly filled each side. For Halina that told her which was the positive future, which was the negative. She watched the positive screen first, chest less constricted with a new sensation of control. There, Mitch was in a comfortable-looking room of a house Halina didn't recognize with the team gathered around. The space was opulent with rich finishes, fine furniture, and windows looking out over a river. Everyone was spread out through the room, much the way they'd been tonight at Alyssa's, files and papers spread out before them, the team skimming the contents and talking. The atmosphere was serious, but hopeful.

Those images started to fade before Halina had a chance to really study them for more clues. But even before this image fully disappeared, another showed up, then another, and another, in quick succession, like a slide show. These images seemed to be from even further into the future and showed the other members of the team and the kids. In the short clips everyone looked happy and healthy. Then Mitch appeared, with another stunning woman, at another private party. Nothing had changed from Halina's prior vision except the woman's identity, but no one Halina had seen him with in the past. Mitch still knew everyone, dressed to the nines, and took the woman's invitation to the bedroom with pleasure.

Just the thought of moving her attention to the other outcome started the turbulent swirl of terror. Her throat ached with the need to call out for help. Her limbs burned from straining against their restrictions.

You're safe. You're not alone. Together we're strong.

The reassurance gave her the strength to redirect her attention to the other side. Her vision filled with the sight of Mitch, handcuffed, blood covering his face. Her whole body reacted, but with the cement holding her in place, she only jerked against the restraint. He stood with his shoulder against a cinder block wall, his hair falling across one eye and an *I'll-kill-you-the-second-I-get-the-chance* look beaming from the other. A dark figure, similar to the figures from the previous vision, stepped in and slammed Mitch across the face.

In slow motion, Halina watched his head jerk sideways. Watched pain rip across his handsome features. Watched blood spill from his mouth. Watched him stumble and drop to one knee. She tried again to scream. Again, her mouth served as nothing more than an empty cavern.

The dark figure closed in on Mitch while he was still down. The shadow pulled a weapon from his jacket, pressed it against Mitch's head.

No, no, no!

Halina thrashed against the muck holding her down, sucking at her limbs. Forced her voice from her lungs. "No!"

"Halina!" Her body shook hard. "Halina, wake up. Come out of it." Another hard shake. Pain shot through her jaw. "Halina!"

The explosion of a gunshot burst inside her head. She sucked air as she broke the surface of reality, a sheet of glass shattering in a million shiny shards. Glittering so bright, they blinded her. Halina cringed against the light.

"Jesus Christ." The rasp sounded in her ear, but came from far away. She had the sensation of someone's arms around her but not holding tight enough, and she was sure she'd simply slip through the embrace. "Hali, shh, you're all right."

Within ten seconds, the vision had cleared and Halina was enveloped in Mitch's arms, his warm body infusing her cold flesh. A headache double the size of her head exploded through her brain.

"Shh, shh," he murmured, pulling the blanket around her shoulders with one hand, stroking her hair with the other. "You're safe. You're safe. I'm here. It's over."

Halina shivered uncontrollably. She had no strength to cling to Mitch the way she wanted to as the violence against him played over and over in her memory. She curled into his protective embrace, fighting to think past the pain.

"You . . . get the papers," she said, her teeth chattering, chest burning. "Everyone . . . is safe. You . . . you . . ." She hiccupped in agony as she thought of him with the other woman. She'd hoped this vision would be different. That *she* would have been the woman he was with in his positive future. But this was just another of the same. Mitch dying in a white shirt. Or Mitch living happily without Halina.

"I what, baby?" he murmured.

"You have another woman . . . a different woman . . ."

"Halina," he crooned. "That's not—"

"Or you die. Beaten . . ." She had to draw air to go on. "Then sh-shot . . . in the head. Because you were trying to h-help me."

Mitch took her face in his hands and tipped her gaze up to his. "Halina, that's not reality."

"It's m-my reality. Nothing's changed. Every time you die, it's b-because of me." She pulled out of his hold and curled into a ball, huddling into the blanket. "Your death is always m-my fault."

FIFTEEN

Mitch slowly shifted out from under Halina's deliciously warm, soft body where she slept cradled between his legs, her cheek to his belly. When she laid her head on the bed without even fluttering her lashes, he paused to stare down at her. He stroked the hair away from her cheek and she licked her lips in sleep and sighed.

He was relieved she could at least find peace in sleep. It seemed to be the only time she was at peace. And with the vision she'd had—correction, the visions she'd been having for days, not to mention the months before she'd left him—it was no wonder. If Mitch had to watch Halina either enjoy other men or take a bullet to the head in visions he believed would eventually come true, he'd have gone insane by now.

But each moment of pure rightness with Halina, like this one, gave him the determination to hold on to the belief that they would make this work. They had to. He'd move heaven and earth to keep her, which was good, because he was anticipating that's exactly what he'd have to do.

So he'd better damn well get started. Before she woke and that wicked determination of hers took over. Keeping her with him after that vision was going to be an arm wrestle.

Mitch reached down and pulled his phone from the pocket of his pants. He took a quick photo of Halina and pulled on the still-damp khakis, wondering where Alyssa would have put the clothes she'd had one of the guys pick up for him.

He opened the bedroom door quietly, watching Halina for any signs of waking, and almost tripped over the pile of neatly folded clothes in the hallway at his feet. He grinned. "Godsend, that girl."

He'd realized this sometime around their fifth birthday. Alyssa had taken the battery out of his brand-new remote control airplane after he'd slammed it into their neighbor Jimmy's head at the party. That's when he knew God had made her his twin for some ulterior motive. Not until he'd reached his teens did he realize that motive had to do with keeping him alive, functioning, sane, and out of jail.

He glanced down the hall, but it was empty. The house still quiet, but not as cold as it had been earlier. He dressed in the bathroom, and thought he was prepared for the devastation when he turned the corner into the living room—after all, he'd lived through it. Barely. But the sight still hit him hard, and his jaw tightened as he stared at the disarray.

They'd done a decent job getting the room back in order, but dust glittering with glass slivers clung to every surface. Sheets of plywood blocked the serene view, reminding Mitch of the extremity of their situation. He glanced at the kitchen island as he passed and the bullet holes that could have so easily ended his life. Kat's life. Mateo's life. And his stomach iced over.

Mitch paused at the front door and glanced through the sidelight. Nelson stood on the porch leaning against a pillar. Mitch opened the door and Nelson glanced over his shoulder.

"Come in for second?" Mitch asked.

Nelson turned and entered the foyer. "What's up?"

"Halina's sleeping in the guest room. I'm going into the basement with everyone else. She's been known to . . . slip away, if you know what I mean. And she's pretty freaked at the moment."

"Understandable," Nelson said. "I'll have Dillon move to her window and make sure we all watch for her."

Mitch nodded. "Thanks. Do me a favor and take the keys out of all the cars, will you? She's ex-DoD."

One of Nelson's brows rose. "Okay."

Mitch locked the door behind Nelson and watched the other man jog toward the driveway where half a dozen cars were parked. He didn't need to know she'd been a *scientist* at DoD, and Mitch wasn't in the mood to explain all the details.

He opened the door to the lower stairway and was greeted by Kat's giggles, the sound particularly sweet to his soul.

In the basement, the mood was subdued—all except for Kat. The kid was amazingly resilient.

"Look, Uncle Mitch," she called as if this was just like any other day, "look what Dex can do."

Everyone was still there, scattered across the space much as they'd been upstairs. Alyssa lay curled on her side, head on Teague's thigh, eyes closed. Brady lay beside her, head at her breast, barely visible above a blanket. They'd never looked more tightly bonded—and all that after the worst incident of their lives.

Teague glanced up at Mitch's arrival, then gazed back down at his wife and child, gently twirling a strand of Alyssa's hair around his finger. The three of them were a picture of comfort, peace, fulfillment, purpose.

I need that.

After making love to Halina again, his want had turned into a fierce, overwhelming need that hit him so hard, it stunned him for a moment. So . . . foreign, yet, when he imagined the scenario with Halina, so . . . right. Still, seven years and a shattered heart later, still so . . . *right*.

He refocused on the others. Cash sat on the other side of the sofa, feet kicked up on the ottoman, sketching some crazy-ass formulas in a notepad. Jessica was curled into Quaid's side in the middle section. Kai, Keira, and Luke sat around a table covered with paper and computers. At the center, the swearing jar overflowed with cash. On a side table, chips, vegetables, nuts, and dips covered the surface. Beneath, a red and white Igloo cooler surely contained half a dozen different drinks.

With the mess upstairs, this would be their living space for a while. Luckily, the bedrooms hadn't been damaged, and half of the team had other places to sleep.

"Dance, Dexy," Kat said, holding up some kind of treat in her hand. Dex eased up on his hind legs, following Kat as she popped around in a circle giggling at Dex's accomplishment, then gave him the treat.

Mateo sat on the floor nearby, his cherub face compressed into a comically stoic expression, those deep brown eyes intensely concentrating on Dex. Mitch wandered toward him and crouched beside the boy, but spoke to Kat.

"Nice, Kat. What are you feeding him?"

"A treat."

"Yeah, I got that." Mitch looked at Teague.

"The guys brought in dogs and set up a wider perimeter," Teague said. "One of them had treats he carries in his truck for his nonworking dog. Don't worry, Kat's not peeling grapes for him. Yet."

Alyssa laughed softly. She looked more tired than usual and concern nagged at Mitch, but he knew better than to say anything. "I sure hope Halina will let Dex sleep in Kat's bed."

"Amen," Teague muttered, then glanced at Mitch. "Is Halina sleeping?"

Quaid tipped his head and looked over his shoulder at Mitch. He didn't need to ask the question Mitch knew he wanted the answer to. Knew everyone wanted an answer to.

"For God's sake," Kai said, dropping a stack of paper and standing. "Just ask him, Quaid. It's not like we gave you and Jessica any privacy."

"And I remember," Luke muttered with a glance at Keira, "he wasn't particularly *sensitive* when it came to us, either."

Kai sauntered to the snack table and tossed a handful of cashews into his mouth. "So how'd it go, golden boy? Did you manage to keep from scrambling her brain with too many—"

"Kai Joseph Ryder." Alyssa's stern reprimand cut him off.

Kai stopped chewing and froze with his hand in the cashews. After half a second, he looked up and over at Alyssa. "Ransom started it."

She let out a breath and dropped her head back to Teague's

thigh. "God, you're exhausting." She rolled her head toward Teague. "He's like a third child."

Mitch burst out laughing, along with everyone else. Lord, he felt good. Loose and relaxed and energetic and hopeful. And it wasn't just because of the sex. It was because of the *who* and the *how*. And—he hoped—because of the meaning behind the act.

"We've been talking," Kai said.

Mitch winced and took a survey of the faces in the room. "That cannot be good news for me."

"Why don't you get Young to grab the documents in your old place?" Kai asked. "He's already in DC, has more flexibility on when he could go in to get them. It will save us time. If he grabs them before we get there, he can look through them and see what's what."

Mitch hadn't thought of that. It seemed like a good idea on the surface, yet something held him back.

"What?" Kai asked. "Do you trust him or not?"

Mitch hesitated, then shrugged. "Mostly."

"I could flash there," Quaid started, then glanced at Jessica. When she nodded, he continued, "and meet Young. Go in for the papers with him. Stick to him until you get there."

Now Mitch nodded. "I'm better with that."

"Which works great," Teague said, "because we've all decided to come with you to DC anyway. So we can all meet up with Quaid and Young at the same time."

Mitch turned a frown on his brother-in-law. "Your wife had a baby a little over a week ago, numb nuts."

"And she deserves some peace and quiet with said baby," Teague countered. "Getting out of here will give a crew time to repair the windows and clean up the glass without us underfoot. We're all too wiped out to handle that. Plus, I'd like to have Alyssa and the kids somewhere . . . bunker-like . . . if you know what I mean."

Mitch totally knew what Teague meant. His mouth kicked up into a smirk as he met his twin's gaze and raised his brows. "What, no argument?"

She smiled and sat up, holding Brady over her shoulder and

leaning into Teague. "Guess I'm getting used to your buddies' five-star bunkers."

More like she realized her children weren't safe in their own home anymore. Guilt pinched Mitch's conscience. He pulled out his phone. "Guess I need to call the pilot, tell him to gas up for the flight."

One quick phone call was all it took. He disconnected and said, "Two hours and we're good to go."

Alyssa groaned and rolled her head toward Teague. "Two hours to pack up three kids and nine adults?"

He kissed her forehead. "You worry about nothing, baby. I've got it."

"What's up with Dex's collar?" Kai asked, moving to the sofa with a laptop. "Why'd she need to get it off him?"

"Hopefully this is the beginning of the end." Mitch strode to a desk in the corner. "Anyone got scissors, a knife . . . ?"

"There's a butt-load of glass shards upstairs," Kai said with a tired grin. "But try this." He pulled a switchblade from his pocket and held it out.

Mitch took the knife and started in on the nylon threads. His mind tried to stray toward Halina. Toward all she'd said. All she hadn't said. All it could mean. To making love to her. To the bond they'd developed between the time he'd walked into that room and the time he'd walked out. But no one in the room would let him think, everyone demanding to know what he was doing and why.

"Come on, Foster," Kai nagged after the second round of bitching had circled through the room.

The point of the knife slipped off the tight stitching and dug into Mitch's thumb. "Jesus eff-ing Christ," he muttered and shoved the wound into his mouth, griping around his finger, "can't you see I'm working here?"

After a few more rips, he worked the collar open enough to get the bulk of the blade between the heavy folds. He separated the material to uncover three micro-disks preserved in tiny ziplock pouches.

Kai sat forward. "Now, *that* looks promising."

Mitch handed the chips to Kai and finished opening the collar to make sure it was empty. He explained his phone call from Owen and his confrontation with Halina.

"She believes she's the cause of my death in the visions," Mitch said. "And she's devastated at the harm she's brought here, which is my fault. She told me she shouldn't come."

Kai slid one of the disks into a slot on his computer and everyone gathered around to watch, including a sleepy Alyssa holding a sated Brady. Electricity seemed to crackle, anticipation seemed to hum. Mitch didn't know if that was from all the paranormal power buzzing around him or his imagination. But nor did he care as he texted Owen, *Got the footage. Where should we look?*

Owen replied, *You work fast.* And added dates and time stamps to the text. Mitch read the first off; Kai fast-forwarded to the coordinates and hit play.

For the next half hour, they all watched in stunned silence as Halina suffered verbal and physical abuse from Schaeffer by day, then moved through the various labs, photographing files by night. Mitch's hatred for Schaeffer had grown to mammoth proportions. His mission to grind him into dust an absolute in his soul.

"I've seen enough." His voice rasped through a throat thick with sickness and guilt. He held out another disk to Kai. "Look at this one."

Kai popped it into the computer and maneuvered to the drive. "If that was the surveillance, what's this?"

"Not sure," Mitch muttered, and he was more than a little apprehensive to find out. "I'm guessing documents."

Hoping documents. Hoping this was going to be what they needed to do exactly what Owen had promised—tie a bow around Schaeffer's neck and walk him into the AG's office. Only Mitch's idea of a bow would be chain and it would be tight enough to cut off air supply.

Kai pulled up the directory. "Bingo."

Kai opened the first five files and clicked through. Mitch held his breath as he scanned the pages, but released it, frustrated when he found them filled with chemical formulas, words as long as his arm that looked more like Greek than English, and handwriting as bad as his own.

Kai whistled softly through his teeth. "This looks like a job for the brains in the room."

"I'll take that one," Cash said from where he stood behind them. "I recognize a few of those formulas."

"Hallelujah." Kai popped the disk and handed it over his shoulder. "Pays to hang with the geniuses."

"I'm interested in links to Schaeffer running this mess," Mitch told Cash. "Anything we can use against him. The formulaic details can come later."

"Got it." Cash retreated to a recliner in the corner, propped a laptop on his thighs, and got to work.

Mitch gave the last disk to Kai and met his gaze. They exchanged a *this-is-it* look and Kai pushed the disk into the slot.

"More video," Kai said, looking at the file types. "Is there more surveillance?"

"Young said she only took the tapes from four weeks before she left."

"Those were on the other disk."

Mitch clenched his teeth. His stomach twisted with a sickening mixture of hope and dread.

"Where do you want me to start?" Kai asked.

"Skip to the middle. The earlier surveillance snippets were weak."

Kai clicked on the sixth of the twelve video clips in the file. Mitch sat back, crossed his arms, and fisted his hands against his body. He had no idea what to expect.

When the image first came on-screen, he was disoriented. It took him a moment to realize the video was taken from eye level. Or rather, below eye level. Maybe shoulder level. Movement displayed the inside of a scientific lab. The camera had been tilted down, toward a dark gray countertop covered in instruments, chemicals, supplies, beakers, test tubes. A notepad and pencil sat off to one side, a laptop off to the other.

Jerky movements jiggled the camera. Muffled taps and scrapes made Mitch's heart jump.

"There's audio," he said, excited. "Turn up the sound."

Kai tapped the sound controls and the quick rasp of breathing filtered through the speakers. Then hands appeared in the image. Female hands. Halina's hands—Mitch knew those long, graceful fingers. She had beautiful hands. She was wearing the tennis bracelet he'd bought her on a weekend trip to Vermont early in their relationship. The weekend, he remembered, he'd fallen deeply in love with her.

But the memories dissipated with the frantic movement of her hands on the video. The way her shaking fingers yanked open a drawer and slid the notepad in, then jerked open another and, with a sweep of her arm, dropped all the chemicals on the counter out of sight.

Just as the drawer slammed shut, a voice blasted, "I told you to handle it, Halina."

The camera jerked up from the counter and their computer screen filled with Schaeffer's image as he approached from across the room. Halina backed down the counter away from him.

"It's like a helmet cam," Keira said softly from the side of the group.

"She must have worn something in her hair," Mitch said. "She always put it up for work. In a twist or a ponytail."

"You said you could do that." Schaeffer stood only a few feet away. With the camera tilting along with Halina's head, Mitch had the sensation of literally standing in Halina's shoes. He saw the menacing look in Schaeffer's gray-brown eyes. The snide curl of his thin lips. The disgusting shake of his double chin when he spoke sharply. And he heard the threat in Schaeffer's voice. The innuendo thick in his undertone.

He instantly knew a jury would salivate over the chance to punish Schaeffer for his harassment and intimidation. But also knew that kind of charge wasn't enough to end his sick games. Wasn't enough to keep the team safe.

"No, I didn't," she countered, a shake in her voice. "I've

been telling you I have *no* control over him, but you don't listen."

Him. Mitch's mind twisted, contemplating all the possible players this *him* could be—Rostov, Gorin, Saveli. Hell, even Abernathy and Young popped into his mind.

Schaeffer's hands jetted toward the camera, then disappeared from view while the whole image shook violently. The fucker had obviously put hands on Halina. Schaeffer was so close to Halina now, his bared teeth appeared crisply in the image, in all their imperfect, brown-edged glory.

"Don't talk back to me," Schaeffer rasped, low and threatening, spittle clinging to the sides of his lips as he spoke. "Just *do* what I told you to do."

"I . . . I . . ." The high-pitched panic in Halina's voice tore at Mitch. "I'm trying. I—"

"Trying isn't good enough, Halina." Schaeffer leaned closer. The whites of his eyes carried fine red lines. The area around his mouth was tightly wrinkled. "Get your boyfriend off Classified's ass. And I mean *now.*"

Mitch's gut fisted. This was what Halina had told him on the plane. No, not told him as much as confessed after he'd uncovered it.

"You've already had him fired from his job," she said, clearly through gritted teeth, though there were tears of desperation in her voice now. "I've done everything I can think of. But he's . . . he's so . . . *driven.* I've gotten rid of his home files, but he's still got some on his comput—"

Already fired him? She'd told him she'd been trying to *prevent* him from getting fired.

"Then crash it," Schaeffer yelled on the screen. "For Christ's sake, you're a fucking genetic scientist, Halina. Use your brain." He shook her hard again and she whimpered. "I don't care how you do it, but do it. Classified is getting spooked. As long as Foster is on their ass, they won't process our chemicals, which means we can't continue this project. They're losing millions. We're losing billions. America is losing lives."

Schaeffer pushed her back with a jerk. The camera shook

hard and Mitch clenched his fists, found himself wanting to reach for Halina to steady her—that's how real this video was. And when her fast, harsh breaths filled the computer speakers, Mitch's matched them.

"We're not going to let one man stand in the way of all that." Schaeffer dipped his chin, gave her a heavy-lidded glare and pointed at her. "You get him off Classified, Halina. If we have to do it, you'll never see him again. You've got forty-eight hours."

Mitch pulled in a sharp breath. Time seemed to freeze for a long moment while his mind *click-click-click*ed pieces into place. "Holy. Shit."

"Please," Halina begged on-screen. "I need more time. I need—"

"You need to do what you need to do to end this. Or we will. Permanently."

Schaeffer turned, stalked across the lab, and exited.

Around Mitch, several long, heavy breaths exited his teammates. But he continued to watch as the camera shook with Halina's muffled sobs. Watch as the camera panned down the cabinets with Halina's slow slide to the floor. Watch as the camera tilted toward the floor, then her feet, then went dark when she pressed her head to her knees.

And listened as her wrenching, hopeless sobs hammered from the speakers.

She hadn't been trying to save his fucking job. She'd been trying to save his goddamned *life*.

His mind tried to scatter in half a dozen different directions, scrutinizing the new connections that suddenly made sense. All the inconsistencies in her background. All the paradoxes between who she'd been and who she'd become. All the resistance to Mitch's interference. All the jealousy over other women when she'd been the one to leave him.

"Oh my *God*," he murmured.

Kai stopped the video. The room was silent—even Kat had stopped chattering, which left an eerie emptiness to the space.

Mitch's gaze blurred over the screen, his abdominal muscles rigid in protection against the punch after punch he'd taken watching those videos. Sitting forward, leaning on his elbows, his pressed his thumbs to his lips. Inside, chaos reigned. He couldn't imagine the fear she'd suffered. The confusion. The stress.

He was sliced up the middle with pain. One side dying over the abuse she'd taken to protect him. The other twisted over her keeping it all secret.

"He wasn't after Halina," Quaid said. "He was after you. He just used Halina to get to you."

"That doesn't make sense," Luke said. "She might have lied about why she ran back then, but Abernathy is after her research now. And we know she was the third scientist. Let's watch some more—"

Mitch waved the idea away and rubbed both hands down his face. "Do it somewhere else. I can't see any more of that."

Kai picked up the laptop and moved to the table. He put earphones in and watched more video.

Mitch sighed and pressed his fingers to his eyes, trying to reconcile his emotions and thoughts. But it wasn't working. He pushed off the sofa to pace and stared down at the carpet, hands on hips.

"What is your issue?" Alyssa asked in that you're-being-an-idiot-again, big-sister tone. "She not only saved your life—more than once—she's given up hers to keep you safe."

"Which is completely selfless, I agree," Mitch said, turning toward her. "And I'm beyond humbled anyone would sacrifice to that degree for me—"

"I'm beyond shocked," Ransom muttered.

Teague held up his hand and added, "Beyond scandalized."

Kai took one earplug out and said, "Beyond disgusted."

Mitch sighed, looked at Cash. "Would you like to throw yours in before I go on?"

Cash's eyes, usually sharp and bright, had a dull haze over them this morning. He shrugged. "Beyond . . . envious? You should start looking at what you have instead of what you fear you don't have."

Mitch set his stance and pushed his hands into his hips. "Well, someone's tune has certainly changed."

Cash had already dropped his head back into that damned notebook again. But he lifted it to pin Mitch with a suddenly clear gaze. "That's what happens when someone risks their own life to save my kid's. She didn't have to think about ordering Dex to protect the kids. Didn't have to pull Mateo into that huddle when she went down. Doing that added an extreme amount of risk to her own life."

Cash gestured with the hand holding the pencil. "You can measure people's sincerity, integrity, and character in a million different ways, and maybe it's because of my military background, maybe it's because of what I went through at the Castle, but when someone is willing to risk their life to save someone else's, they get an A plus in my book. That's the kind of character that comes from the soul. You can't teach—or fake—that shit."

Mitch's shoulders slumped. He lifted his hands out to the side. No point in debating the point of whether the means justifies the end. Because in this case, of course it would have been justified. Mitch just had to suck it up.

"Well." He let his hands fall against his thighs. "This is all moot, isn't it? That leaves me with one question." He pulled out his phone, opened the picture of Halina he'd just taken, and handed the phone to Keira. "Is she going to leave me?"

Keira glanced at Luke, who met her gaze for a moment, then shrugged. Keira took the phone and put her fingers to the glass, tracing the image. Mitch waited a moment, but finally turned his back and rubbed his forehead.

He tried to realign his mind with the case and turned to Kai. "Anything different on the other footage?"

"No," Kai said, expression solemn. "Just a lot of threats to kill you if you exposed Classified. And to kill her if she failed to stop you."

He dropped his head back and let his gaze blur over the ceiling for a moment. Then drew a breath and turned his gaze to Keira.

The moment her eyes met his, he had his answer, and his stomach ached from the hit. "She's going to run again," he said, his voice rough. "I can see it on your face."

Keira nodded. "She is . . . possessed . . . by the need to get away."

Gil flipped news channels to try and catch every angle of what the media was calling "the chemical conspiracy of the decade." Whoever had released that bomb in Syria had killed over a hundred people and left another couple hundred with radiation burns over most of their bodies. They would soon be added to the casualty list.

"Dumb fucks," Gil swore at the screen.

A knock sounded on the door, but it didn't open.

"Go away," Gil yelled and flipped to another news channel.

The door creaked open an inch and the face of a young girl peeked in. Behind her one of the Secret Service agents pushed the door open.

The girl was about sixteen, wore bright blue scrubs, and carried a bouquet of flowers.

"What the fuck is this?" Gil asked, making the girl's smile fall. She glanced over her shoulder at the agent.

"Flowers, sir," the agent said with a use-your-eyes tone. "I've checked them for explosives and bugs. They're clean."

"I don't want any fucking flowers. Where's Peggy? She shouldn't have let this come through."

"Peggy's on her dinner break, sir," the agent said. "The other nurse is in another patient's room."

"It's o-okay." The girl's face had gone white and she backed out of the room, right into the agent. "I'll . . . j-just bring them to the children's ward—"

"Get the card, Agent," Gil said.

The girl pulled out a clear plastic stick holding the card and the agent took it from her shaking fingers. She scurried away as the agent walked to Gil's bedside and handed him the card.

"Great security in this place. Who the hell knows my alias?" He didn't wait for an answer. "Go find out how this happened." The agent left the room and closed the door behind him. Gil looked at the front of the card—the gift shop downstairs. He knew who it was from. She'd done this a couple times before. Fury burned beneath his skin as he pulled the card from the envelope and read:

> *My dearest Gil,*
> *You are constantly in my thoughts.*
> *Never doubt my commitment to our prior arrangement.*
>
> *Forever, Halina*

Gil tossed the card aside and swiped his phone from the side table. He speed-dialed Young and listened to it ring, his gaze still on the television. The call rolled into voice mail.

Gil barked, "Call me." He disconnected and stared out the window for a long moment. He thought of Abernathy, of what would happen to the program if Abernathy got Beloi's research. Of what would happen if he got Beloi's other files. Of what would happen if Abernathy were caught and talked.

Sweat trickled down his temple.

He made another call.

"Yes, sir?" the man answered in a low, cool voice.

"Your new target is Bruce Abernathy," Gil said. "Major Bruce Abernathy."

"I'm still working on—"

"Change of plans," Gil said. "This is more important."

"I'm close to Torrent," the man said, his voice deep and slow. "If I find Torrent, I'll find Abrute."

"I understand," Gil said. "And, as I said, this is more important."

"You're the boss." He disconnected.

A weight fell instantly from Gil's shoulders. A smile turned his mouth. He was powerful enough to order a kill even from a hospital bed.

He pushed the nurse's call button and after a moment a harried, "Yes, Senator, this is Carla. Peggy's still on her dinner break. What can I help you with?"

"Cake, Carla. I want chocolate cake."

SIXTEEN

The mood on the plane was light—at least with everyone other than Mitch. If she didn't know him as well as she did, she would have fallen for the cool veneer he'd been using to cover complex emotions he wasn't sure what to do with.

He wanted to talk, she could tell by the occasional thoughtful looks her way, by his restless fidgeting. But he obviously wasn't ready, because he hadn't spoken a word to her in the hour since he'd herded her into the private space in the front of the plane, gestured for her to sit beside the window, then trapped her there by sitting in the aisle seat next to her.

He'd played with Kat, read to Mateo, talked strategy with the team, and was now talking on the phone to Owen Young, whom Halina had known in passing when she'd worked at DARPA all those years ago. But Mitch hadn't said a word to her. Nor had he looked her in the eye. And though they used to be able to sit in comfortable silence forever, this wasn't comfortable. She loved the feel of him close. Hated the turmoil bubbling just beneath the surface. Loathed the millions of miles of distance between them.

But Halina stared out at the clouds and reminded herself it was better to have the distance, because unless something drastically changed soon, she'd have to leave.

Mitch disconnected and put his phone into the pocket of his jeans. "Owen and Quaid are going to pick us up at the airport."

Halina recognized the opening to a conversation for what it was. But she wasn't anxious to take it and remained silent.

"Are you going to tell me when you're leaving me," he asked, staring blankly across the seating section at the faux-wood wall. "Or are you just going to leave?"

Alarm burned in her belly. "What are you talking about?"

He finally looked at her. His eyes held so much pain and disappointment, she felt it in the pit of her stomach. "You're leaving me again, right? Are you going to warn me, like you did last time, or am I just going to wake up one day and find you gone? Will I ever know if I have a child? If *we* have a child?"

Her throat closed with all the pain of her past, joined with the very real possibility of the horribly unfair scenario he presented.

She shook her head, at a loss for any better alternative. "Would you rather I stay just long enough to cause your death? Just long enough to watch you die?"

The hurt in his gaze flared into anger with the speed of a match strike. "Is there more? Am I going to keep turning around to find a new lie as long as you're here?"

"No." When her voice shook, she swallowed. "I told you, I've given you everything. There are no more lies."

His gaze radiated pain as it drifted away. After several moments of silence, he gave a small shake of his head. "Halina . . . I just don't *understand*."

Here it comes. She tightened her threaded fingers to ease the ache created by building stress.

He let out the breath he'd been holding, his brow pulled into a deep frown. "I don't get why you couldn't confide in me. You went on and on and on for weeks, months, enduring that stress, that treatment. Never once did you talk to me about it. Like you never needed me. Like you didn't trust me. Like you didn't believe in me. What the hell was our relationship about, Hali?"

"Mitch, no . . . I . . . ." She shook her head, her answer evaporating into a mist.

The visible torment tightening his face and shining in his eyes made her wish she'd never met him. Made her wish she'd never been born. Made her wish—for the first time ever—she could erase those ten months of bliss they'd spent together, the only truly bright spot in all her life, and wipe that pain from his soul.

She scraped in air and forced words out. "I'd . . . seen your future. So many times. And I realized that I could try to hold on to you and watch you die . . . or I could let you go and live happily without me." Her voice caught. She paused. Looked down at her hands, unable to meet his eyes for fear of breaking down. "Deep down, Mitch, I've always just wanted you to be happy and safe."

It felt like forever before he asked, "Is that why you read the papers?" His voice was low and rough, filled with emotion. "To make sure I was safe?"

She nodded, squeezing and releasing her fingers. "If I didn't see you in the papers for a week or two, I'd Google you. If that didn't turn up a court case or a magazine article, I'd call your office. If I went to San Francisco to speak or meet with colleagues, I'd watch for you outside your—"

He pushed to his feet and she startled. She leaned back and glanced up, but wasn't prepared for the amount of hurt and anger in his eyes. "You were *in* San Francisco? You saw me. *Physically saw me,* and you didn't say a word?"

Her heart pounded in her chest, and she gripped the arms of the chair. She was really screwing this up. And just when she didn't think she could make it any worse.

"I . . . just needed to know you were okay. That Schaeffer hadn't questioned my commitment to your safety, that my threat wasn't valid. I didn't want to hurt you by contacting you—"

"*Hurt me?*" he almost yelled, growing furious. "For Christ's sake."

Mitch gripped the back of the chair. She glanced toward another section of seating where Kai and Cash sat side by side, their expressions serious, their watchful gazes on Mitch. Quaid appeared in the aisle, standing tall, arms at his sides, supremely quiet, but just as intense.

Mitch didn't notice anyone. All his fury remained focused on Halina, his fingers deeply indenting the leather, his nail beds white. His eyes sparkled with raw emotion, deep green and glittering gold.

"It took me years to . . ." He stopped. "You have no idea how many nights I . . ." He stopped again. To watch such an accomplished speaker struggle so hard for words ripped at Halina. "You were *everything.*"

"As were you." She raised her own voice now. "And I didn't want to find you hanging from your apartment ceiling by a rope, or on the sofa with a bullet in your head. I didn't want to get a call telling me you'd been in a fatal car accident. Shit—" she threw her hands out in frustration. "Call me selfish."

"You . . ." His expression compressed in horror. "You *saw* all that happen to me?"

"Worse. I saw them *do* all that to you. And more. And yes, I could have gone to you and told you, but we've already been over how well that would have gone. And to repeat your own words, when these guys want you, they get you. It doesn't matter what kind of face you put on, what kind of wall you build. I knew that all too well. And I was powerless to help you— with one exception.

"I had something Schaeffer wanted. And I had something that could expose and shut down his entire project if not send him to prison. I didn't lie to you about the research. I only mixed up the order it happened. He came to me for the cloning after I'd broken off our relationship and—"

"After?" Near rage filled his expression. "You mean you didn't leave Washington after you left me? You were still *there*?"

"I stayed until I was sure you'd gotten out of DC and back to California safely."

Cash pushed from his seat, stepped in front of Quaid and up beside Mitch. The gaze he turned on Mitch was one of the most fierce looks Halina had ever seen. "I thought you might need to see my face. I'm hoping it will remind you that you're missing . . . The. Big. *Fucking.* Picture."

Mitch's eyes slid closed. He dropped his head and rubbed his eyes. Scraped his hand through his hair. With his fingers deep in the black strands, he said, "I need a drink." He turned toward the back of the plane and disappeared.

Halina stroked Dex's thick fur as she stared at the house through the back window of one of the SUVs Owen had dropped off for them at the airport. It looked like a freaking castle, with turrets and six different types of gray stone. Huge paned and arched windows broke up the stone façades on at least two levels.

"When he does it," Alyssa said from the seat beside Halina, "he does it right."

In the front seat, Mitch and Nelson had been talking logistics and security since they'd landed. Square footage of river frontage, exit routes, basement details. Nelson pulled up to the entrance in the circular drive and the heavy, hand-carved wooden door with matching sidelights. The warm blond color of the wood and mottled bronze oxidized metal fixtures softened the harshness of the cold gray stone.

"Where'd you dig this up?" Alyssa asked during a lull in the men's conversation.

"I can't take credit for this one." Mitch didn't look back when he spoke. Probably because he knew he'd have to look at Halina if he looked at his sister—she was sitting in his line of sight—and he hadn't looked at her or spoken to her since he'd walked away from her on the plane after Cash's scolding.

She'd hoped he'd be able to forgive her, but that had just been a fantasy. She'd crushed his most basic trust. That was something no one forgot. Something Halina didn't believe could be forgiven. At least not forgiven in a way that could mend the tear she'd created between them. Trust, she knew from experience, was fragile. Easily broken and poorly healed.

"Owen found it," Mitch said. "It's secure and off the map,

not connected in any way to anyone in this mess. It's going on the market in two weeks and the Realtor is a friend of a friend of a friend. The owners moved to Europe, so they won't be an issue, and the place has a state-of-the-art security system, which gives us a head start on locking it down."

He climbed from the car and shut the door. Hurt throbbed beneath Halina's ribs as she helped Alyssa unbuckle Brady's car seat and lift it out of the car, then helped Kat down to the ground. Mitch met Nelson and the three other guards from the other SUV at the driver's door and they pointed around the property, thickly covered in deciduous trees bare after dropping their leaves over the fall months.

Dex jumped to the ground beside Halina. She looked at Teague and asked, "How is Owen Young involved in this?"

"Young was working under Jocelyn Dargan at DARPA before she was killed," Teague said. "Jocelyn was Schaeffer's right hand and tagged Young to do some of her dirty work. When Jocelyn died, Schaeffer blackmailed Young into her position. He's not happy about it. Knows we're out to shut Schaeffer down, so he helps where he can."

Halina grabbed three duffel bags as they were unloaded from the vehicles and carried them toward the front door.

It opened before she reached it and Quaid stepped out. He'd driven the other SUV back from the airport. When they'd met them at the plane, he'd mentioned they'd found and taken the box without any problem, but nothing more.

"Hey," she greeted him. "Have you looked in the box?"

"Just glanced in to make sure there were files. I've been doing other important stuff, like grocery shopping. It's in the family room at the back of the house."

She nodded and started past him.

"Hey," he said, "where did you live in Russia when you were a kid?"

Discomfort niggled along the back of her neck. "I . . . was born in St. Petersburg, but moved to Chechnya to live with my uncle when I was nine. Why?"

"Just curious. I've spent some time in different parts of Russia. I thought it might help my memory if we talked about different locations."

Not on her preferred list of things to do, but . . . "Sure."

The house was so massive it was overwhelming. Like a monster waiting to swallow her. She'd never been in a house this big. This grand. And it didn't appeal to her. The ceilings went on forever. Dark marble floors gleamed in the light streaming through the windows.

Halina continued slowly down the hall, Dex's nails clicking on the marble beside her and echoing off the hard surfaces. A formal dining room sat to the right, complete with chandelier that probably cost five, maybe six figures. A formal living room followed, with fireplace and furniture that looked far too uncomfortable to sit in. Large, historical paintings covered walls painted in rich, dark colors. She passed an office, a lounge, a library.

Her shoulders were nearly up around her ears by the time she reached the kitchen. There she relaxed. Even took a breath of amazement. The space was huge and open. Wood cabinets stained with a light country wash. Polished granite counters in a contrasting dark caramel and black, covered in the groceries Quaid had bought. A wall of windows that looked out on a sculpted yard and the Potomac beyond.

In an area across from the kitchen a large whitewashed country table filled a bay window with eight matching chairs. Halina recognized the setting immediately—the one she'd seen in her last vision. The good side in her last glimpse of Mitch's future. A relieved smile turned her lips. She was still making the right decisions—even if they were killing her.

Halina turned away from the windows toward a huge family room that sat off the kitchen. The windows continued into this room, giving it a nice view. It held plush furnishings and another fireplace.

The box sat alongside the hearth, and the sight made a sharp pulsing pain beat beneath her ribs. She dropped the duffels in a corner and stared at the smashed top, bent sides, and dusty, aged cardboard. A cold wave of memories crashed over her. Vivid images filled her mind—down on her knees in the kitchen, the loose planks scattered around her as she forced the box into that space. Sweating, shaking, heart pounding.

Such a mistake.

Or had it been? If she could turn back time, pull the box out, meet Mitch at the door, shake him and insist he listen . . . would she?

Her gaze blurred over the cardboard. Fist lifted to her chest where her heart hammered as hard now as it had then.

She didn't have an answer. She couldn't think. Couldn't feel anything but this blinding, splitting failure. And loss. God, she couldn't bear it anymore.

She knelt in front of the box. The shredded top looked like it had spent too much time with rodents. The thought made shivers crawl over her arms. She closed her eyes until they passed and rubbed at the gooseflesh left behind.

"If I find something dead in here," she barely whispered, "I'm going to scream."

As she lifted the box top, the front door opened and voices flooded the house. Followed by Kat and Mateo's little running feet. Halina closed her eyes and moaned. She couldn't face anyone now. She needed to be alone.

While everyone was milling through the front rooms, Halina flicked through the folder tabs. She'd only glanced inside the box that one night to make sure it held the Classified files and didn't really know what it contained. When nothing jumped out at her, she grabbed two handfuls of files and pulled them from the box. A soft thud drew her gaze back to the empty space. Something small and blue tumbled around the bottom. Not a mouse—thank God. She reached in and picked it up. As soon as she drew it into the light, her stomach dropped to her feet.

It was a box. A signature Caribbean blue Tiffany's box. The air whooshed out of Halina's lungs and a flood of tears rushed her eyes from nowhere.

"Shit," she whispered, wiping the streaks away, too aware of the others so close. "Not now."

She sniffled and looked out the windows, holding the box tight. When Mitch had bought her jewelry, it had always been from Tiffany's. And he used to come home with something new for her at least twice a month. Bracelets, earrings, necklaces, charms, watches. The way his eyes glittered as he watched her open gifts, it was as if he was the one getting a present. He'd loved to give. Especially to Halina. The man had the biggest heart of anyone she'd ever known.

She huffed a humorless laugh. "At least he used to."

She looked back at the box, turning it end over end in her fingers. He must have hidden this gift in the file box, planning to give it to her at the right moment. Her heart sank.

Throw it back in, one voice said.

Open it, another argued.

She slowly lifted the blue top and peeked inside. Instead of something shiny laid out on a bed of shimmering satin, a black velvet jeweler's box filled the Tiffany's cardboard square.

Her chest squeezed. Her breath caught. She darted glances at the doorway and around the kitchen as if she expected someone to be watching her.

The box was the size and shape of a ring box. She couldn't pretend she didn't know that. But nor could she pretend that only meant one kind of ring. Or that it had been meant for her. It could have been a gift for Alyssa.

This was stupid. She had to know. No matter what it turned out to be, it wouldn't change anything about the present.

With one more glance at the door, she reached in and pulled the hinged top back.

The shock of sparkle made her gasp. A strangled sound came from her throat and she stopped breathing, unable to tear her gaze away.

It wasn't a gift for Alyssa.

It was an engagement ring.

An amazing combination of diamonds, one large and centered, several others reducing in size as they flared down the band in a simple but stunning and elegant design.

A dagger stabbed her heart. Twisted. Hot tears trailed out of her eyes but her whole torso had gone icy cold.

"Oh my God." The whisper shook coming out of her numb lips. The sparkles turned into blurry, five-pointed stars. Halina's breaths were ragged as she covered her mouth with her free hand.

She suddenly understood—everything. His fury, his deep hurt, his smoldering desire, his sense of complete betrayal. Mitch hadn't just cared about her. He hadn't just loved her. He'd planned his future with her. He'd committed his heart and soul to her.

Staring down at the gems, still sparkling happily after all this time hidden in that dismal box, something inside Halina broke— a physical snap at the center of her body.

Owen grabbed a bottle of water from the small refrigerator hidden beneath Stephanie's desk. His secretary was long gone for the evening and Owen was glad to be alone. He entered his office with a sick, dull ache in his belly and fell into his desk chair. An hour of grilling by the head of DARPA, Carter Cox, was not a pleasant experience. Owen had known it was coming. Sofia had warned him she'd gone to Cox first to get permission to talk to Owen. Not that she'd needed it, but she was playing nice.

Owen smiled at the thought of Sofia. And the pleasure of seeing her earlier took away some of the discomfort in his gut. He'd been impatient to get the divorce papers before he'd seen her. After he'd seen her, he'd made a call to the divorce lawyer and asked him where the hell they were. His attorney was looking into it.

Owen turned on his computer and flipped through the messages his secretary had left him while he'd been in with Cox. A couple from his team. A few last-minute meeting changes. And one from . . . Jennifer? His daughter, Jennifer? He couldn't remember the last time she'd called him. Not in months. And not in over a year at the office.

His brow pulled. Head tilted. He reached for his cell and tapped into the recent calls. One missed call . . . from Libby. But no message. The burn of alarm slid along his nerves. "What the hell?"

He dropped the messages and called Libby back on her cell. The call rolled into voice mail.

"Shit." Owen disconnected and called Jennifer at home.

She picked up on the second ring with a blustering, "Oh, Daddy, he's the cutest thing *ever*. I *love* him. Thank you, thank you, *thank you!*"

The enthusiasm and pure love in her voice created a flurry of emotions he wasn't ready for. Longing and loneliness blind-sided him with a direct hit. But it didn't take long for anxiety to creep in, because Jen's voice dropped and she went on.

"Mom's pissed, but she's always with Philip," Jenny said, referencing Libby's lover of nearly a year, "and now that Josh has his license, he's always with his friends. I'm always alone and . . . and . . . this is the best present ever. I really *needed* him."

Her voice rose with emotion, the way it always did before she started to cry. And now that she was having her period regularly, those tears came a lot more often. But they still stabbed at Owen's chest. He rubbed a hand over his mouth, aching at the thought of telling Jen he hadn't done whatever she was so thankful for. Owen hadn't forgotten her birthday, it was still four months away—she'd be fourteen. There was no special occasion coming up, nothing he'd missed. And he was doubly twisted over the fact that all this love was going to end up going to—probably—Philip.

"I miss you, Dad," Jen said, her voice soft, but still brimming with pain. "Thanks for coming to my recital the other day. I saw you in the back."

"I miss you, too, baby." A sad smile lifted his mouth. At least he'd done something right. "I was going to come up after," he said, then cleared the roughness from his voice, "I brought flowers—"

"I saw them."

"But . . . it was so crowded, and you were busy . . ."

"And Philip was there."

Owen smiled. "I don't want to cause any more . . . issues. Baby, I just want you to be happy."

"Well," she suddenly bubbled to life again. "This little guy sure makes me happy. Where did you get him? He's *perfect*."

"Honey,"—the uneasy sensation grew—"get what? What are you talking about?"

"The *puppy*. You don't have to pretend it wasn't you. Mom already knows."

Puppy? "How does your mom know it was me?"

"The man who brought him told me and she overheard."

Owen stood so fast, his chair banged the wall. Every muscle in his body tensed. Hands and jaw clenched. "A man"—he could barely get the words out—"brought a puppy to the house and told you it was a gift from *me*?"

"Yeah," Jen said, apology and resignation in her voice. "Sorry, Dad. If I had known I could have made up a story to cover for you. You know, I found the puppy or a friend couldn't keep him or something. But I didn't know. I hope she doesn't give you a bad time."

Sweat broke out over the back of Owen's neck and shoulders, down his spine. "Babe, what did the man look like?"

"Um, I don't know. Kind of like you, but not as handsome. Wait . . . that's weird to say, right?" She laughed. Owen wanted to absorb the sound, but couldn't. "Anyway, he had short blond hair and his face was all cut up. He said he'd been in a car accident. Kinda looked like Frankenstein."

Owen bent at the waist and planted his free hand on his desk. He was breathing hard. Seeing crimson. "How long did he stay, honey?"

"Just a little while. Came, dropped off the puppy . . . I think I'm going to name him Roscoe. Do you like it?"

Owen closed his eyes, searching for patience. "Yeah. Great name, Jen."

"Then he left. He was really nice. Hey, Dad?"

"Yes, honey?"

"Can I see you soon? I know you're, like, really busy . . . but . . ."

"Yes. Absolutely." He dropped back into his chair, covered his eyes with a surge of sickness rolling in his belly. "How about next week? Want to stay here for the weekend? We can go house hunting for a new place for me."

"Um . . . can I have Roscoe at your apartment?" she asked timidly. "Because no way will Mom take care of him for me and I wouldn't trust Josh."

"Abso"—*fucking*—"lutely, baby. Bring Roscoe."

Owen said good-bye to Jen, then reconnected and dialed the cell number he'd gotten for Abernathy from his file.

"Colonel Young," Abernathy answered on the second ring, his voice distracted, but with an air of knowing. "I've been waiting for your call."

"What's this about?" Owen said, he voice low and cold and controlled.

"I'm assuming you mean the dog? Damn, your daughter is the cutest little thing—"

"*What . . . is . . . this . . . about?*" One hand was clenched around the phone, the other in a fist. Every muscle in his body was rigid.

"Just a demonstration of how quickly I can get close to your family."

Owen clenched his teeth. "Why?"

"Well, see, I'm going to need your help, Young. I understand you met Foster and his crew at the airport today. The whole chauffeur gig doesn't really suit you, but, to each his own."

"What do you want?" He enunciated every word clearly.

"For starters, I want you to show me where you put them up. We can go from there."

"I don't know what you're—"

"Let's not play that game. I don't have time. If you want your daughter to stay safe, Young, you'll get your ass down to the parking garage in three minutes. I'm waiting in your car."

Abernathy paused, giving Owen just enough time to go a little insane. "If you can't make it, I could always check on the pup—"

"Tangi Valley," Owen said through gritted teeth, wishing he could forget what he'd done in that hell called Afghanistan. What had been done to him. But willing to use it if it would keep his kids safe from a psychotic predator like this.

Abernathy went silent a moment. Then, "An urban legend."

"The truth," Owen rasped. The scars on his back burned. "*My* truth. Soon to be *your* truth if you . . . *ever* . . . go . . . near . . . my . . . family . . . again."

Abernathy hesitated. "I'm . . . glad we understand each other. I'll see you in three."

SEVENTEEN

Mitch had wasted as much time outside as possible. But the sun was gone, he was shivering now, and he couldn't see anything but the reflection of city lights off the river and silhouettes of the two guys guarding the riverbank.

He and Halina had made a lot of memories walking alongside this stretch of water. He'd thought reliving them might help him find some kind of resolution. But he found himself thinking less of the past and a lot more of the future.

He kept coming back to Cash's words of advice—focus on the big fucking picture.

There was so much he loved and wanted about this new, improved version of Halina, his desire for her—as a lover, a friend, a partner . . . a wife—coiled and coiled inside him until he felt like a spring ready to pop.

Yet what kept him out here perched on a log near the shore instead of inside with Halina was fear from the past. Fear of that impending loss she'd all but admitted to today on the plane—running from him, pregnant or not.

He couldn't fault her reasons, even if he didn't fully believe in their source. She did. And she wasn't even leaving because she didn't love him. She was leaving because she loved him so much.

His brain just kept doing this—spinning and spinning and spinning. Yet he found no answer. No relief.

"Fuck," he groaned, dropping his head into his hands and rubbing his temples with his palms.

"Hey."

Mitch's head came up fast at the deep voice. Too fast. A rush of blood hit his brain and pain slid beneath his skull. "Ah, shit."

"Sorry," Quaid said. "I was waiting for you to come in, but . . ."

"Did you find something?" Mitch asked, squinting toward Quaid's dark silhouette. "A connection between Schaeffer and Classified? I know it was there when I last had the box."

"Haven't found anything in the box yet." Quaid tossed a jacket to him.

"Thanks." Mitch pulled it on. "Then what's up?"

"Couple things."

"Sit," Mitch invited, gesturing to the log.

Quaid took something from his back pocket and sat next to Mitch. He unfolded some papers and Mitch took them.

"What's this?" Mitch shone a flashlight over the pages. Scientific formulas lit up under the light. He flipped the flashlight off. "Shit, I already have a headache, dude. What is it?"

"A possible formula for the skin Cash has been trying to finish."

Mitch perked up. "He finally got it?"

"Not Cash," Quaid said. "I got this from Owen Young today when we were picking up the file box. He said he got it from Abrute."

"What? When?" Mitch straightened. "How?"

"He has the guy in custody. Illegal custody, actually." Quaid laughed. "Gotta love that, right?

"See, when Cash destroyed the Method pages at the Castle, Dargan sent Abrute home to get copies of Cash's experiments. Evidently, he'd taken them from the lab for 'safekeeping.' We think he was going to sell them, but whatever. Anyway, Abrute left the Castle just before the explosion. Young was informed during the investigation and questioned Abrute. When he realized Abrute's potential, he locked him up, put him in solitary, and had him working on finishing the formula."

"Why the fuck didn't he tell us this?"

"Young says Abrute would rather take his chances at a trial than risk Schaeffer's hit men. And he's not talking."

"Give me five minutes in a cell with him and he'll start talking," Mitch said into the night. He glanced at the notes again. "Has Cash seen this?"

"Sure. He's been studying it the whole time you've been out here."

"And?"

Quaid shook his head. "It's not right. Won't work."

"*Fuck.*" Mitch slammed the papers against his thigh.

"But it's closer than he'd been," Quaid said. "He says he'll use parts of it. Seems excited. That's got to mean something."

Mitch nodded and braced for the other half of the couple things Quaid had come out to talk about. "What else?"

"Halina."

The burn of panic cut through his gut. "You guys were supposed to watch her—"

"She's still here," Quaid said. "She took files up to one of the bedrooms to work on them. Dillon's standing guard outside her window. She's not going anywhere."

Mitch relaxed. "Then what about her? I already got a lecture from Nelson about being a jackass on the plane. I don't need another one."

"She moved from St. Petersburg to Chechnya when she was nine."

"Yeah, I know."

"How do you know? She tell you?"

"No," Mitch said. "From intel Young gave me."

Quaid's eyes narrowed. "Have you been to Chechnya?"

"No."

"Then you don't know." Quaid leaned forward, pressing his forearms to his thighs. "I *have* been to Chechnya. An assassination occurs every ten minutes. There are one hundred murders every day. Prostitution, drugs, and mafia are rampant. That move—from St. Petersburg to Chechnya—is the equivalent of moving from Jessica's plush townhome in DC to a jungle hut in Columbia run by drug cartel."

Mitch tried to absorb that, but realized he didn't have the knowledge or experience.

"I'm trained to understand people," Quaid said. "To read them, find their greatest weakness, and exploit it. I've worked with terrorists and assassins in Chechnya. Men like Halina's uncle. You need to understand that Halina spent her formative years in an environment as warm as concrete. As frightening as hell. Orphans are a dime a dozen in Russia. The reason her uncle took her in was most likely for free labor—cleaning, cooking, and someone to abuse when he was pissed off."

Mitch scrubbed his fingers through his hair. His gut ached.

"Halina was programmed to react a certain way, just like I was programmed to kill whomever Gorin told me to kill. Halina's youth effectively rendered her as helpless to her programming as the drugs rendered me to mine. She never had a choice to believe one way or another, just as I didn't."

Quaid let out a breath and pushed one hand against his thigh to twist toward Mitch. "Halina believed Schaeffer would have assassinated you. She'd grown up around men who killed professionally, and she protected you the way she learned by watching them—she blackmailed the killer. Successfully, I might add.

"It's difficult for me to describe the depth of what I'm trying to explain, but . . . you're seeing the conflict from an empowered, privileged American's point of view. Halina sees the conflict as an impoverished, suppressed, Russian underdog. You can't expect Halina to go about solving problems the same way you would.

"As far as her visions, you don't have to like what she's seeing, but they're very real. I'm telling you, that woman has a level of power caught up inside her that surpasses mine tenfold. When she learns to control the visions, there's no telling what she'll be able to predict or how her ability will expand."

Quaid straightened and pushed to his feet. "Programming can be broken. I'm an example of that. And given what Halina's done over the past twenty-four hours when she could have escaped you at any time, I'd say she's already broken it. I think she's operating out of pure emotion now—love and fear. Not programming. But hey . . . that's just me."

Quaid turned toward the house and shot a glance over his shoulder. "Get your ass inside and help us with this box. No one can read your writing. Not even your freaking twin."

Mitch didn't immediately return to the house. He spent some time thinking about what Quaid had said. It made a lot of sense. Would probably make a ton more sense if he could get Halina to talk about her childhood. He could certainly see why she hadn't. Especially given his background of American baseball and apple pie.

He dragged himself toward the house, punching his radio to tell the four guys, two here, two on guard roadside, that he was going in.

Mitch heard laughter from inside before he'd even reached the porch. Climbing the stairs, he took in the warm glow emanating from the closed blinds over the windows and a small smile turned his mouth. He loved this group—every last damn pain in the ass—and he was grateful time and again for all of them.

He knocked and looked up when Teague pulled the curtain aside from the glass and peered out at him.

"This is an asshole-free zone," Teague said and dropped the curtain back.

Mitch was too tired to be amused. "Then no one with a dick between his legs should be in there."

"Out of the way, Creek." Kai's voice melted through the glass. "He gave you a chance when he didn't want to."

"Only because Alyssa made him," Teague said.

The door opened and Mitch looked into Kai's frustrated face. His green gaze swept Mitch's face, assessing. "You look better than you feel."

Mitch cocked his head. "Excuse—" Then he realized he must be even more twisted than he realized if Kai was picking up his emotional state. Mitch sidestepped Kai. "Don't do that, Ryder. It's creepy."

Kai and Teague returned to the kitchen, where they were

cleaning up from dinner. The thought of food made Mitch's stomach growl, but his gut ached too much to eat anything substantial. He paused at the bar to grab a branch of green grapes from a bowl and popped a few in his mouth.

"How's it going in here?" he asked as he turned and glanced into the family room.

"We're all just working," Kai said. "Guys are in place. Grounds are secure. Where's Young? He's got to pick sides once and for all."

"I was just about to call him."

Mitch turned toward the family room and found everyone staring. They were all stretched out on the furniture or floor, either playing with the kids or looking through documents. Everyone except Halina. And without her, the group suddenly didn't seem complete. They were all quiet except for Kat, Mateo, and Brady. He met every adult gaze, each sending a different message, from confusion to frustration to pity.

He tossed a few more grapes in his mouth. Chewed. Lifted his brows. "Slow TV night?"

"You look like hell." Cash set some papers aside and pushed to his feet. "Go catch a nap. I'll take the radio and make rounds on the guys."

The thought of a nap instantly brought Halina to mind. Brought the idea of pulling her into his arms, feeling her against him, tasting her lips, her skin, sliding inside her, watching her arch in pleasure . . . Then *snap*. The fear kicked in, dragging him below a murky surface he couldn't clear.

Mitch handed Cash the radio with a muttered "Thanks" and turned down the hallway.

He paused at the base of the stairs, looking up, his hand covering the square head of the newel post. He didn't have another fight in him. He felt weak. Needy. Not the best time to be near her. Yet he needed to know what she'd found.

"Mitch?"

Jessica's voice startled him and he jumped, his hand falling from the post.

"Sorry," she said. "I need to talk to you for minute."

He ignored the quick beat of his heart and pushed his hands into the front pockets of his jeans. "Find something good?"

With her arms crossed over her ribs, she pursed her lips and shifted them to the side. That's when he noticed the apprehension in her eyes. "You could say that. But not what you think." She tipped her head toward the formal living room. "Can we . . . ?"

"You sound like your husband. If you're going to tell me all about the hell of Chechnya, we've already had that discussion."

"Chechnya?"

"Never mind." He turned into the formal living room and faced her. When she moved to close the pocket doors, he noticed something in her hand and a burn of alarm kicked up in his gut. "What's going on, Jess?"

She turned toward him with a look in her eyes that made him realize he'd need those defenses he was too damn exhausted to pull up.

"When I took files from the box to split them up among everyone, I found this in the bottom."

The words had his body tingling and his mind searching. She extended her arm and opened her hand to expose a familiar small blue box filling her palm. His stomach went hot just before his heart seized. But his mind tumbled backward in time, to him sitting in his office, elbows on thighs, holding the ring between his knees and staring at it while mumbling the words, "Will you marry me?" in Russian over and over until he got the pronunciation just right.

He remembered Halina coming home from work early that day . . . one of those last days . . . one of those bad days. Remembered panicking and stuffing the ring back into the nested boxes and tossing it in the nearest file box.

Then all hell had broken loose . . .

And he'd lost . . . everything.

Pain cut through him, so swift and sharp, his legs went weak and his head went light.

"Ah, fuck," he whispered, dropping his head to his hands

and turning to look for somewhere to sit before he fell on his ass.

Jessica grabbed his arm. "Behind you," she said softly, easing him back to a padded bench along a bay window.

Mitch dropped hard and fell back against the blinds, smashing them to the glass. He couldn't pull enough air into his lungs. Couldn't find the strength to even sit up straight. He closed his eyes, more to hide from his own weakness than because he needed to. "Shit."

Jessica didn't speak. She ran her cool hand across his forehead, pressed it to his cheek.

"Sorry, Jess." Automatic excuses rose to his mouth, but he didn't feel like using them. Besides, he doubted Jess would believe them anyway. "I'll be okay in a minute."

"No, you won't, honey." Her voice overflowed with understanding and compassion. "You won't be okay until you're willing to face how much Halina still means to you. You won't be okay until you decide to either let her go or go after her."

Mitch opened his eyes to stare at the corner of the gilded ceiling. Jessica was sitting beside him. "You're always so encouraging, Jess."

"Maybe I'll give up lobbying for inspirational speaking."

A smile tugged at the corner of Mitch's mouth. "Then you'll have to put that lazy-ass husband of yours to work. Somehow I don't think the pay will even out."

Jessica laughed softly.

He lifted his head from the window. The room spun for a second, then stilled. He looked down at the box. "I'd completely forgotten about it."

"Yeah, I kinda figured that out."

"Did the others see it?"

Her warm eyes met his. "Of course not. We Hill people know how to keep secrets."

Mitch smiled and covered the box and her hand with his, squeezing gently. "Thanks."

He stared at the box, holding it between the fingers of both hands, turning it around and around.

She let the silence linger a moment. "Mitch." Her voice was just above a whisper and hit him harder than any of the guys' shouts. "Honey, you can't go on like this. Halina can't go on like this. It's killing you both."

Guilt swamped him. His eyes closed and he nodded. "I know." He took a breath, opened his eyes to the box. "I don't know what . . . or how . . . I feel like I'm on a roller coaster and I'm at a total loss. I've been through enough to always find some decent way to handle every situation. But this . . ."

"You're a guy who functions with his body and his mind. You're physical and intellectual. Not emotional. That's why you're so off balance."

He nodded again, thinking back to when he'd been all three. When he'd been with Halina. And wondered if his emotional side was so damaged it was irreparable.

"In some ways," Jessica said, "we're a lot alike."

Mitch looked up from the bright blue box. Jessica had her elbow resting on one thigh, her chin resting on her fist. Those understanding eyes gazed up at him, smoothing the raw edges of his pain. "How do you figure?"

She shrugged one slender shoulder. "Halina was virtually dead to you for seven years, the way Quaid was to me. We never really got over them. Never really let them go. We've both slept with untold number of other lovers, but no one else ever satisfied. You've used your money and notoriety to buy distractions with parties, toys, and travel the way I used cocaine. You're a workaholic the way I used to be, on seven days a week, eighteen hours a day. But nothing's ever erased her from your heart or wiped her from your mind."

She paused, giving him room to argue. To tell her she was wrong. But they both knew she wasn't.

"Now that you know she's alive," Jessica said, "that the reason she left you wasn't what you thought it was, you have to decide if you could live without her if she walked back out of your life."

Mitch winced. His fingers tightened on the box.

"She lied to you. Abandoned you. Left you hurting for years when she could have eased your pain. Unlike Quaid, she had a choice, even if her choice had grave consequences for the person she loved most. If that's what you focus on, you're going to continue to feel angry and miserable."

Jessica lifted her hand to his forearm and squeezed. "You also have a lot of choices. You could choose to focus on different facts. Like the fact that she made a smart, savvy decision that everyone agrees saved your life. Or that she's here helping us when we all know she's skilled enough to run. Or that she's told you the truth when she didn't have to."

"Yeah," he said, feeling stronger about the new direction of his thoughts. "I was just working on that outside. It's . . . getting easier."

He uncapped the blue box, dumping the black velvet one inside onto his palm.

"Let me just say one more thing that might help you put things into perspective," Jessica said, "and I'll leave you alone.

"Think back to what happened just three weeks ago, with Quaid. We *all* lied to him about one of the most important, fundamental realities in his life—that he and I were married. *You included,* mister." She tapped his bicep with one rigid finger. "But I'm his wife. I had the highest duty to him out of everyone and I still lied at the most critical moment—because I love him. Because telling him the truth at that point could have ruined his recovery. Because I wanted the best for him. We all did."

Mitch's heart skipped. Sped. "Never thought about it like that."

"This is a good time to revisit your memories of the situation, then before you go condemning Halina for loving you so dearly she gave up her own happiness for yours. And remember—Quaid forgave me because he loved me more than he hated the lie."

Mitch didn't think he needed to revisit any memories. His chest was already filling with a giddy, nervous excitement at the thought of rushing up those stairs to Halina—which told him he'd already worked out the kinks in his mind.

Only, that didn't fix the problem of Halina's need to run from him.

"You can still have everything you once wanted," she whispered earnestly. "All you have to do is reach for it, Mitch. *She's . . . right . . . there.*" Jessica punctuated her words with clear, deliberate speech.

She stood, clasped her hands, and glanced at the door over her shoulder. Then turned back with her lower lip between her teeth and a spark in her eyes. "Okay, I can't leave until I see it again. It's killing me, it's so gorgeous. I've wanted to stare at it this whole time. Took you freaking forever to come in from the river."

Mitch laughed—a real one this time—and rolled his eyes. "You're such a *girl*."

He tossed it lazily to her. She caught it in both hands with an exaggerated bend of her knees and gently opened the lid. She pulled in a breath. One hand splayed high on her chest as she stared down at it. The way Mitch had dreamed Halina would when he gave it to her—but with more screaming and happy tears and kisses and a whole lot of "Yes, yes, *yes*! Oh, my God, I love you so much. Can we do it tomorrow?"

The way that dream had been slashed still made him bleed inside.

"Seriously, Mitch." Jessica shook her head, her gaze lingering on the ring as if it held her transfixed. "This is the most beautiful damn thing I've ever seen." She finally lifted her gaze and those deep brown eyes drilled into him in warning. "And if you don't give it to Halina, I'm going to hunt . . . you . . . down."

After a split second of replaying the words, Mitch burst out laughing. When he looked up, Jessica was grinning smugly. She closed the box and offered it to him.

When Mitch reached for it, Jessica gripped his hand between both of hers until he looked at her again.

"She's worth the risk, Mitch. You know that in your heart."

A white-hot jolt speared him from head to heel, but it wasn't fear. It was excitement. Yeah, he did know.

Mitch pulled Jessica close for a hug. "Thanks, Jess."

He kissed her temple and released her. She patted his chest and stepped away, shaking a finger at him on the way out the door with a half grin. "Don't make me hurt you. Oh, and if you could just mention where you got that stunner to Quaid, you know, in passing, I'd be forever grateful." Her face lit up with a grin. "He's going to buy me a new one."

As soon as Jessica closed the door, Mitch flipped open the box.

His breath whooshed out. "Damn." He pulled the ring from the velvet slot and brought it closer. "I had good taste . . . even back then."

Mitch stuffed the ring box into his pocket and slid the doors apart enough to peek into the hallway. It was empty. Conversation and children's giggles drifted along the hardwood. He darted across the hall and jogged quietly up the steps.

All the doors on this floor were open but one, and Mitch went directly there. He paused only long enough to draw air into his lungs so his head stopped swimming and knocked softly. For a second he considered calling to her and announcing himself, but didn't want to take the chance she would reject him.

He turned the knob quietly and opened the door enough to peer in. The room was huge, with a lot of furniture. A four-poster bed with a sheer canopy formed the centerpiece and papers were scattered over the shimmering gold comforter. Mitch had a sudden and savage need to make love to Halina in that romantic setting. But Halina wasn't on the bed.

He pushed the door wide and stepped into the room with a soft, "Halina?"

No answer. No Dex. His gaze skipped across the room, to a window with the curtains pushed aside. Alarm sliced through Mitch's body. He released the door handle and strode into the middle of the room, his gaze moving faster, his heart picking up speed. "Halina!"

No answer.

Fuck. "No."

Panic pushed into his throat. He rushed to the window, grabbed the sash with both hands, and threw the window open. He leaned out so far, his momentum nearly took him over the ledge and out onto the roof. *The roof.* Goddamn, the roof was right there. The window easily accessible from the ground. And when he looked down, the guard, Dillon, wasn't there.

"Halina!" Mitch screamed as his gaze scanned the darkness. *"Halina!"*

His heart pounded so fast it seemed to string out one frenzied continuous beat. Just as he pushed off the sill and turned to a sprint toward the door, Teague appeared in the hallway. A split second later, the others surrounded him.

"What's wrong?" Teague asked.

"She's gone." Mitch moved as he spoke, pushing past Teague, running past the others and down the stairs as he pulled the gun from his jeans. "Dillon's not under her window. Radio the guys."

Cash spoke into the radio before Mitch had even finished his sentence. His hands were shaking so bad, he fumbled with the locks on the front door, but finally yanked it open and darted out, yelling Halina's name and running.

He'd lost it. Abandoned all thoughts of safety, all security protocol. He didn't know if she'd been taken or if she'd run. He didn't know how to look for her and didn't know where to start. Everyone was yelling at him, but his head was filled with the memory of Halina hanging over Abernathy's shoulder like a limp doll when he'd abducted her and taken her to the harbor.

He couldn't lose her.

"Halina!" On the side of the house with Halina's window, Mitch stopped and squinted into the darkness, scanning the terrain. Fury and desperation erupted inside him when he could see nothing beyond twenty feet. "Dillon!" He dropped his head back and screamed into the sky, *"Ha-li-na . . ."*

One of the guys grabbed his arm and shook him. Anguish slowly replaced the fear as he turned to look at Luke. Dillon stood just behind him. They were both speaking, mouths moving, but Mitch couldn't hear them. He focused harder and the men's words filtered in.

"Earth to Mitch." When Luke came into sharp focus, he said. "About damned time."

"I just went to take a leak," Dillon said. "I wasn't gone more than a couple minutes."

Mitch darted looks right and left. Members of the team and a couple of the guards hovered at a distance. The bite of icy air registered, raising gooseflesh on his exposed skin and cutting through his clothes.

"That's better." Luke pulled on his arm to start turning him. "Look behind you."

Mitch's head whipped toward the house so fast, he almost toppled. His vision blurred and his head went light. It took him several seconds to refocus. When he did, he saw a small figure sitting at the base of the house, back against the siding, knees up, head down. And Dex sitting by her side.

"Oh, *fuck*." He breathed the words in such wicked relief, he almost went down again. Mitch bent at the waist, pressed his palms to his thighs and drew air. He turned his head up to Luke. "Take the others inside. I'll bring her in."

"No fucking way." Luke scowled at him. "I'm not leaving you alone with her the way you've been—"

"Come on, Luke." Jessica appeared behind him with a hand on his shoulder. "Mitch is okay. We had a talk earlier. He needs time alone with Halina. And Dex will rip his face off if he's an ass."

Luke argued but Jessica immediately cut him off with that iron streak of hers—the one that had helped her survive her husband's death, resurrection, rescue, and now kept them both going through his recovery. Halina had that same strength. And Mitch needed it. For both of them.

Within sixty seconds everyone had retreated—the team back

into the house, the guards back to their stations, and Mitch pushed the weapon back into his jeans. He approached Halina with a heart beating triple-time and muscles ready to give out. He dropped to a crouch in front of her, curved his hands around her thighs, and pressed his forehead to her bent knees. Dex whined and licked his face. "Fuck, Hali, you almost killed me."

Only when his breathing slowed and the rush of blood in his ears dimmed did Mitch realize she was shivering violently and sniffling back tears. His head came up and he slid his hands along her arms. Her skin was icy.

His gut clenched. But he didn't haul her to her feet like he wanted to. "You were running."

She nodded. Her gaze was glassy. "But I c-couldn't do it." Her teeth chattered and tears rolled out of her eyes to freeze on her skin. "I c-couldn't make myself go. I j-just . . ." She hiccupped. "I g-got here and g-got stuck."

He turned her face so she was looking into his eyes. "Why, Halina?"

"Because . . . I'm weak." Guilt swamped her expression and a flood of new tears poured from her eyes. Her voice was filled with so much anguish, Mitch felt it in his bones. She dropped her gaze and pushed the tears off her face with her fists. "Because I love you and I don't want to l-live without you anymore. But I need to g-go . . . to keep you s-safe."

Everything inside Mitch melted.

Dex whined at Halina's distress and licked her tears. She pushed his muzzle away.

"You're not weak." Mitch pulled her to her feet. "You're the strongest woman I know. I wish I was half as strong. Let's get you inside."

Mitch pushed the front door open, kicked it closed, and headed straight for the stairs.

"I should g-go," she murmured, half dazed.

"You aren't going anywhere, Hali. If you'd meant to go, you'd have been gone by the time I got out there."

He turned into the bedroom and set her feet on the ground,

closing the door behind Dex as he came in. The dog jumped into an overstuffed chair and curled into a ball. Halina slumped against the wall. "I'm sorry . . ."

"For what?" Mitch asked, combing her hair from her eyes.

"For not leaving you."

Mitch thought of what Quaid had said and smiled. "Baby, you're programmed all wrong." He leaned in and kissed her with a murmured, "We'll have to work on that."

Eighteen

Mitch slid a hand behind Halina's neck and pulled her mouth to his. He let go of all the frustration and fear and drank her in. He was starving for her after all the emotional distance he'd put between them today, and needed to close the gap. Needed to bring her back to him. Needed to mend all the tears he'd created.

He tasted her, so warm and sweet, and groaned. When she gripped his shoulders and kissed him back, he wrapped both arms around her, drew her against his chest, and devoured her as if he needed her to breathe—because he did. He realized he absolutely needed her to survive.

His emotions were running hot. And even though his mind told him they needed to talk, that they needed to understand each other to chip away at some of these walls, his body and heart were on fire. Pumping need south of his waist and telling him that driving deep inside her, bringing her to a splintering multi-gasm and immediately following would bond them on a much deeper level. And he needed to feel her lips on his. He just . . . needed her. God, how he needed her. She made him so damn helpless.

When she moaned and matched the hunger in his kiss, his mind blurred. His body exploded in heat. Need spurted over his skin and slid into his groin. Her hands fisted in his hair and pulled him closer and—damn—if he didn't stop, like two minutes ago, he'd do this all wrong.

She was too important to do it wrong.

He released her, planted his hands on the wall behind her, and leaned away. She murmured a complaint that shot a jolt of lust straight to his groin, then, as if she realized what she'd done, she drew back and covered her face.

"Shit," she whispered. "This is why I need to go. I can't do this . . ."

He pulled her hands away and pushed strands of hair out of her eyes. "Halina, explain to me what I ever did to earn such loyalty from you. Love doesn't warrant the kind of sacrifice you've made. Even people in love don't do what you've done."

She held his eyes for long moments. Her expression serious. Her eyes matter-of-fact. Just before she spoke, she tilted her head in that sweet way that made his heart squeeze. "Those people didn't live my first twenty-five years without you." She shook her head slowly, a sheen of tears growing in her eyes. "For those magical ten months you gave me, I gladly traded my remaining years of living in the open to make sure you stayed safe. I've lived countless what-ifs over the years, wished a million times I'd had other options to choose from at the time, but I've never regretted my decision. Not one day since I made it."

Emotion swelled his throat closed. His eyes burned with tears. And, shit, he didn't know what to do with it all. He hadn't cried since those dark days after she'd abandoned him. He'd been so lost. Felt like the world was against him. Now he knew his worst days had been only a tenth as difficult as hers. That not only hadn't she abandoned him as he'd believed, but she'd been watching over him this whole time.

He suddenly knew he needed to know more. Right now. He picked her up by the ass, turned, and slid to the floor with his back against the door.

"What are you doing?" She laughed the words, but sank onto his lap, her arms around his neck.

"Tell me about Russia," he said, keeping his voice soft. "I've been trying not to ask, but there are a million things I want to know about your childhood." He pulled her to him for a kiss. "I want to know everything, but just tell me one thing now."

She scraped her lower lip between her teeth and looked up at him through her lashes. "I want to tell you about Saveli."

Her voice was soft, affectionate. Fear coiled in Mitch's chest.

"Okay."

"He didn't grow up in Moscow. His family moved there when he was in high school. Until then, he lived where I grew up."

"Why didn't you get placed with his family? He turned out okay, well . . ." Mitch grinned, "except for that whole pretending to be your husband thing."

Halina laughed, but only for a couple seconds. "Saveli was a second cousin. My uncle was a closer relative, so the state asked him first. He saw me as free labor and grabbed me before Saveli's parents even knew what had happened to my mom and dad.

"I had another cousin," she said. "Saveli's age. My uncle's son, Misha. He was . . . wonderful." She nearly breathed the last word. "He hid food from the dinner table when the men ate to make sure I got something to eat. He'd claim responsibility for mistakes I'd made so I wouldn't get punished. He helped me with my homework. I'm a scientist because he was enthralled with chemistry. He was very close with Saveli. They were best friends. Like brothers. And the three of us spent a lot of time together."

Foreboding crept into Mitch's gut. "I'm not sensing a happy ending here . . ."

Halina shook her head. "I don't have to talk about this now—"

"That didn't mean I don't want to hear it." He rubbed her arms. "I was just preparing myself. Go on."

She licked her lips. Took a breath. "When he was fourteen, my uncle decided he was old enough to start going on jobs." Halina swallowed with visible effort. She flicked a look at Mitch. "You know what those jobs were, right?"

"Murder for hire?"

"Or assassinations, whatever." She looked away. Shrugged. Scraped her lip between her teeth. "Misha changed. Closed me out. Turned his back on Saveli. Didn't want to talk to us. Didn't want to spend any time with us. Avoided us at every turn. I was crushed. Sure I'd done something wrong. Now I know he did it to protect us both, but it took me a long time to understand that.

"Anyway, one night, he went out on a job and something went wrong. I never found out what, just that my uncle was livid. I've never seen him so angry. I thought he was going to beat everyone in the house to death and set it on fire."

Halina shivered, a violent tremor that snaked through her body and had Mitch pulling her closer. She stayed there as she continued, but her voice had changed. Gone weak and shaky.

"Misha groveled just like he was supposed to, promised he'd make it right. And then he disappeared. Just . . . didn't come home the next day. No one would tell me what happened. I asked once too often and got the beating of my life. My uncle never showed any concern. Not an ounce of remorse or sadness." She pressed her eyes to his shoulder. "Misha was his only son."

Mitch's heart ached. "I can guess that's when Saveli's parents moved their family to Moscow. And now I understand why Saveli was so loyal to you when you needed him to escape . . . me."

Halina nodded against his shoulder. She stayed there a minute, pulling herself together, then sat back and met Mitch's gaze. "My uncle and his men are why I understand Schaeffer. You've been around, seen bad people, bad things. Prosecuted them. But I've lived with them, day in and day out. I know how they act. How they talk. I understand the different looks in their eyes, the shift in their expressions, in their voices. What appeases them. What angers them. And what makes them snap.

"I knew after I'd worked at DoD two months that Schaeffer was a man like my uncle. But by then, I was already in love with this country. In love with the work I was doing." She lifted her hand to his face and those beautiful eyes turned so soft. "In love with you."

Mitch's heart stretched beyond its limits. He leaned in and

kissed her. Tasted her. Savored every curve of her lips, every touch of her tongue. He wrapped her in his arms and lifted her off the floor.

A strangled sound came from her throat as he carried her toward the bed. She pulled out of the kiss, panting and squirming against him. "Mitch, I can't stand to see those visions of you . . ."

He laid her back and a crinkling sound filled the air.

"Wait," she said. "The papers—"

"They'll live a little wrinkled," he murmured against her throat as he kissed her there, running his hands up her sides and beneath her shirt. "God, you feel so good."

"Did you even hear me?" she asked, her voice a little dreamy, a little breathless as her hands caressed his arms. "And did you even look at these papers?"

"Yes, I heard you." He kissed her throat. Her skin was so soft. "And no, I didn't look at them."

"Then you don't know what I found?"

"No." He ran his tongue into the V of her shirt. God, she tasted good. "Later."

"I highlighted all Classified's connections with Schaeffer— the contracts for chemicals sold to DARPA with Schaeffer's signature. The shipping invoice that lists the warehouse in the Sierra Nevada mountains as the destination for the tanks—"

Mitch lifted his head and forced a few more gears to turn in his brain. He'd been focused on taking down Classified Chemical for contamination violations. He'd planned on slamming them with enough fines to make them buckle and hammer them with enough violations to hinder their operations. Schaeffer's name had come up randomly in Mitch's research and, ironically, hadn't been of much interest to him.

"Why did they go to that warehouse?" he asked.

"Because Classified's specialized processing plant for radioactive chemicals was based out of Susanville at the time. Since then, they've grown and moved to Las Vegas. But back then, that warehouse was the closest, quietest, and least secure government facility that could house the chemicals until they were picked up and hauled to the processing plant. It was also remote, allowing fewer eyes and lower risk should the chemicals . . ."

"Contaminate? Catch fire? *Explode?*"

"I'm . . . surmising some of that, but . . . yeah."

The thrill of victory—definitely the sweetest victory he'd ever experienced—was within his grasp and it spilled through Mitch in a fiery storm.

He dropped his forehead to Halina's. "Baby, you deserve a great big present for that news." He reached into the front pocket of his jeans and drew out the ivory disk. Propped on his elbows, Mitch held it above her chest. "This is the ferrite bead I told you about. The one Quaid carved and made into a necklace for you."

"Ferrite." The inflection of interest in her voice was nearly a sexual purr . . . or maybe that's just where Mitch's mind was wedged, but it lit him up.

When Halina let go of his shoulder to take it in her hand, Mitch pulled it out of reach with a hot grin. "Say my name like that."

"Like what?"

"Like you just said 'ferrite.' "

She laughed, but the awe in her gaze was all for the carved disk, her fingers caressing the rough surface.

"It's supposed to do something with the electromagnetic energy raging through your body," Mitch said. "Insulate it or tamp it or something. But you know me. When they start talking in genius tongues, my mind goes to the ballpark."

"He mentioned it earlier in passing but I didn't know . . ." She pulled in a soft sound of surprise, then murmured, "Oh . . ." followed by a hum of pleasure that made Mitch's cock pulse hard. "I can . . . I think I can already feel it . . ." She looked up with a light of hope in her blue eyes Mitch hadn't seen in a long time. "It's so . . . I don't know how to describe it other than . . . quieting. Not calming exactly, but like all the white noise in my body has been turned down." She closed her eyes, tilted her head back, let out a deep breath. "Oh, God, that's so nice."

Oh, God . . . Mitch's gaze caressed her gorgeous face, the curve of her neck relaxed in relief . . . *that* was so nice. "Mmm-hmm."

She was smiling when she opened her eyes and met his again. And there was no missing the desire there now. Clear as sunlight sliding out from behind the clouds. And the longer she held the disk, the longer the emotion stayed. No more flickering on and off like a light. Halina looked at him like she used to. Like she wanted to eat him. Feast on him.

"I . . ." he said, a slow smile growing, a fast burn devouring him, "think I'm going to owe Quaid. Big-time."

She huffed a breathless laugh, but her gaze strayed to the disk, and her smile drifted away. "Even if this did work to control the electromagnetic power, even if we could be together without the aftermath of visions . . ."

She didn't have to say the words for Mitch to know what she was thinking. He put two fingers under her chin and lifted it until her watery eyes met his.

He cupped her face tenderly. "I need you to trust in me, Halina. I need that more than I need to drill Schaeffer into the ground. You can count on me to have your back. Always. No matter what. No one, and I mean *no one,* including the god-damned universe, is going to dictate my future. I'm asking you to *believe* in me."

Her gaze softened, but he knew that look—she hadn't changed her mind. "This isn't about you or me now. It's about . . . fate or whatever you want to call it. I can trust in you to the ends of the earth, Mitch, but that's not going to change the fact that you're asking me to allow you to put yourself in death's path."

He released a frustrated breath. "I can't argue with your visions, Halina. I've seen how deadly accurate the team's powers can be, but that doesn't mean I'm going to hand my fate over to the ether. Quaid told you that these are most likely various possible outcomes you're seeing, not the ultimate, absolute future. And you've told me yourself that every decision a person makes changes those possible outcomes."

"They're not just possible outcomes, Mitch. They're the most probable ones. When something as powerful as the universe tells you the probable outcome of your future, I think it would be wise to listen."

"Christ." He dropped his forehead to her chest just below her chin. "You should have been a lawyer. No one argues like you do."

Her fingers combed through his hair and he sighed, dropped his mouth to the cold skin above the edge of her top, and left a hot, open-mouthed kiss, followed by a lick. A sound rolled through her throat and shot right to Mitch's groin.

"You know what would be great for you?" He kissed again. Licked again. He wanted to do it all night. "Not thinking so much."

He tugged the edge of her blouse and bra down to expose one perfect nipple and closed his mouth over it. Halina drew a sharp breath. Mitch sucked hard, drawing her breast from his mouth until only her nipple remained between his lips. Then he soothed the abuse with long strokes of his tongue.

Halina dropped her head back, lips parted, and a sound of need and want came from deep in her throat.

"I have to admit," he murmured, releasing the fabric and moving his hands down the hem at her waist. "Right here, fate did real good."

While Halina's mind was still lost in a haze, Mitch pulled her shirt over her head, moving his mouth up her belly in hungry nips and licks and kisses. With every movement, paper crinkled.

He pushed up on his hands, then his knees. He sat back and tugged his shirt over his head. Unfastened his jeans. Then hers. Kissed her luscious body as he tugged them over her hips and stood to ease them down her legs.

When he straightened, she was sitting up, reaching for the waistband of his underwear. Even though he wanted to get his hands on her, he let her pull his boxers down his hips, over his erection, and push them down his thighs.

But too quickly, the fingers of her other hand wrapped

around his erect shaft. Sensation tore through his cock, rocked his balls, and shimmered through his pelvis. Mitch's legs turned into steel poles, welded to the floor, and he couldn't move. Mitch didn't remember closing his eyes. Or gripping the nearby bedpost. Or opening his thighs to make room for her other hand to stroke and tease.

Before he found the ability to open his eyes, Halina took him into her mouth. The slow, slick ride in washed his entire body with a sizzling heat wave. Stuttering in air, Mitch gripped both her hair and the bedpost and lifted his hips toward her mouth. She was hot and lush and perfect. Fire coated every nerve ending in his cock.

"Fuck, that's good." The words were a guttural growl. Not anything he would have recognized as coming from him.

She sucked him slowly, luxuriantly, as if they had all the time in the world, as if she'd never tire of having him fill her mouth, as if she'd rather have his cock on her tongue than chocolate.

"Love . . . the way you . . ." Mitch pulled in an extra breath, made a sound deep in his throat. Electricity arced from her mouth through his body. "But you . . . gotta stop . . ."

"Mmm," she hummed in complaint, before sliding him fully into her mouth again.

Mitch pulled in a harsh breath, swore. Wanted this to go on and on and on. The pleasure she brought him was so excruciating it melted his brain. But he couldn't. He wanted her too badly.

"Hali . . ." He slid a hand from her hair down to her jaw, tightened his fingers and tried to pull her back, but she was focused. Relentless. And now, Mitch could feel the roll of her tongue where his thumb rested under her chin. Could feel the indents of her cheeks where they caved beneath his palm. Could feel the rock of her head back and forth beneath his fingers as she slid his length in and out of her mouth.

Christ, that was erotic. He forced his eyes open and tilted his head down to look at her. He found her watching him, and the look in her eyes hit him like a strike of lightning. Soft yet sexual. Sweet yet sinful. Sensual, seductive, salacious. She seemed to reach inside him with a single look and wrap her hand around his soul.

He surged toward climax. Caught himself at the last second. And held her head steady as he pulled out of her mouth.

"Holy shit," he breathed, holding her shoulders as his brain came back to him.

"You still taste amazing." Her hands stroked his abdomen and rose to his chest.

Mitch stepped in, circled her waist, and moved her up on the bed. With his head still in a fog, he pulled off her panties, unlatched her bra and . . . at last . . . she was naked.

"Perfect," he said and sank every inch of his naked body against every inch of hers.

He closed his eyes, soaking in the joy of it. The sense of completion he'd missed for so long. So damn good it hurt. With his forehead against her shoulder, he groaned.

She scratched her fingernails up his back, then smoothed her palms down over the rise of gooseflesh.

"Damn, nothing has ever felt this good, Hali." He grinned. "Not even you, way back."

She slapped his back with a laugh. "Shut up."

Grinning, he pulled her into a sitting position, then lifted her onto his lap. His cock rode along her hot opening perfectly as he tied the cord of the necklace at the base of her neck. He pressed the disk flat against the skin of her chest just below the hollow of her throat and appreciated the beautiful way it contrasted with her skin.

"Sexy," he murmured.

She gasped, her hand covering the disc.

Mitch's gaze jumped to hers. "What?"

"I . . . don't know. It's . . . I'm . . . all tingly."

He grinned. Caressed her shoulders, her back. "That's me, baby, not the disc."

She laughed, but immediately stopped and gripped Mitch's biceps, her gaze distant.

"Halina?" he frowned. "What's happening?"

She grimaced, clearly in pain. "I don't know."

Panic nudged aside his excitement. "Well, shit . . . *guess.*"

"It feels like . . . the disc is drawing the energy from my body. And it's concentrating in my chest. And it's . . . hot. And tight." She was struggling to breathe. "It feels like it's squeezing . . ."

"Dammit." Mitch pushed his hands beneath her hair and felt for the knot, digging at it with his nonexistent nails to get it undone. "Shit. I shouldn't have knotted the damn thing. I didn't expect . . ."

Halina took measured breaths and clung to him, her cheek on his shoulder.

"Mitch," she said, her body relaxing. She slid her palms down his arms and covered his frantic hands, breathing deep. "It's okay. It's gone."

He brought his hands to her face. She looked a little . . . drunk. She covered his fingers with hers, tipped her head, and kissed his palm.

"You're . . . okay?" he asked.

She sighed. "I feel . . . God, I feel almost . . . normal."

Mitch sputtered a laugh. "Around here, normal is so relative."

"I feel *good* . . . in a way I haven't since I spilled those chemicals . . . Loose. Light. It's like . . ." She looked him in the eye. Pulled her hands from his and slid flat palms up his belly to his chest, brushing his nipples, making him flinch in pleasure. His fingers dug into her waist on an indrawn breath. "It's like all the distraction making me nervous and anxious and . . . scared . . . has faded into the background."

Halina brushed his nipples again, drew her fingernails down his abdomen.

"And now, all I feel is . . . *want.*" The last word came as a low, dark whisper, mirroring the desire that had expanded inside him. "Overwhelming, uncontrollable . . . *need.*"

Mitch grabbed her hands, stilling them. "I have that too,

Hali, but I want more. I want it all. One hundred and fifty percent of you, Halina. Nothing less."

She opened her mouth, but couldn't get anything out and just shook her head.

"Halina, listen to me." He slid his hands into her hair and held her head while looking deep into her eyes. "I want you, Hali—*just you*—in my life. I know I've been a total fuckup the last couple of days. I know I've done and said things that have hurt you. But it stops here. Now." So much regret and pain filled his eyes. "You are absolutely the only woman I've ever loved."

The words wrapped around her heart and squeezed. Her breaths stuttered into her lungs. The tears started up again and she covered her eyes. "Oh, Mitch . . ."

"Hali," he said, his voice deep and soft. "Just before you left I had something important to ask you. Seeing you again seven years later and realizing I love you just as much as I did then tells me it was definitely right."

She lowered her hand and blinked, suddenly exhausted and confused. "What—?"

Halina focused on the box he held in front of her—the ring sparkled up at her in the dim light, snuggled deep into the black velvet.

She gasped. Something hot and painful seized her throat. She brought a fist to the pain and couldn't tell whether it was fear or excitement. Her gaze snapped to his, bright gold and shining.

"Okay," he said, then cleared his voice when it cracked. "It's been a long time. Let's see if I can remember . . ."

His eyes suddenly glazed over with anxiety, as if he realized the seriousness of what he was about to do. He glanced away. "Um . . ." His lips moved silently a moment, as if rehearsing; then he looked directly at Halina again, but as soon as their eyes met, the sliver of confidence he'd built up vanished. "Yeah."

A laugh escaped and she lifted her hand to cover her mouth. It didn't seem to affect Mitch. He just collected himself and said, "I can do this."

A slight sheen on his forehead caught her eye and her grin grew. "Are you . . . sweating?"

He scowled at her and wiped his face with his forearm. "Only because you're so hot."

She laughed again, softly this time. "That came easily enough."

He covered her mouth with his hand. "Shh. You're making this even harder than it already is."

She bit her lip to control the nervous giddiness in her belly and he dropped his hand. When he met her eyes again, he was serious, his nerves quieted.

"Halina, *ya lyublyu . . . tebya vsem serdtsem.*"

She pulled in a breath and everything inside her liquefied. His voice speaking Russian with smooth pronunciation and inflection, telling her how deeply he loved her, stole her breath.

"Ya ne mogu zhit' bez tebya." His claim that he couldn't live without her came even smoother, his eyes conveying the truth of the words and his plea for her to hear them.

"Ty vyydesh' za menya?" The words she'd dreamed of hearing from the day they'd met, "Will you marry me?" hung in the air and showered over her, making every inch of her body glow.

"That's why you were taking Russian?" she asked, her voice a hoarse whisper.

He nodded, his grin widening until his eyes sparkled. "Bet this is throwing your universal fate into one fucking radical tailspin, baby."

She laughed, pushing out the wetness built up in her eyes.

"Say yes, love," he whispered urgently. "Say yes to me, to *us.* To taking control over your future."

She held her breath, hands tented over her nose and mouth as she stared into his beautiful eyes. The one thing, the only thing, she'd ever truly wanted for her life was being offered to her. She was terrified of making the wrong decision. Terrified of sending his fate the wrong direction.

"Jump, Halina," he urged in a quiet, confident tone. "I *will* catch you."

Her hands scraped into her hair as terror made one final sweep through her chest before she said, "Yes." She started shaking—with fear, with joy, with relief. With the hope she'd kept repressed for all these lonely years. "I've never wanted anything more than to be with you."

Mitch's eyes glazed over in shock. "Oh my God." He refocused, serious. "Did you . . . just say *yes?*"

Unable to speak through a swollen throat, Halina nodded. He grabbed her and pulled her so tightly against his body, his arms squeezed the air from her lungs. She laughed.

"I didn't know . . . I didn't think . . ." she said. "I knew I loved you with everything I had, everything I was. But I . . ." The truth hurt. "I didn't think I could ever have been enough for you to love me the same."

Mitch released her and pulled the ring from the box. Halina tightened her fingers in a fist. Stupid. She wanted that ring on her hand. But she'd spent so many years fighting to keep people away . . .

"You've always been more than enough," Mitch said, pulling her hand toward him and uncoiling her fingers. He slipped the ring on, pushed it over her knuckle, and let it settle around the base of her finger. Then he lowered his head and kissed the ring and her finger. "Perfect." His golden eyes gazed up at her with more love than she'd ever hoped to find. "You're still a perfect fit."

She wrapped her free hand around his neck, pulled him to her, and kissed him with all the love in her heart. Mitch met her kiss, matched it. And Halina relaxed into a sense of well-being. A surety that they were going to make this work.

His mouth traveled to her jaw, tongue hot, teeth hungry. Then her breast. He gripped her hips, sliding her flat on the bed and tasting his way down her body. His lips following the curve of her ribs, his teeth nipping at her hip, his tongue circling her navel, then sliding in.

Growing need made her move restlessly beneath him. His teeth bit down on the skin inside her knee then slid those hands, those giving, demanding hands, up her thighs, pushing them open, until she was spread and he was staring down at her, eyes molten fire.

He pulled her into his lap again, positioning his length to slide along her entrance. Halina lifted her hips, moving against him, needing him inside her.

"Do you want a condom?" he murmured between little bites to her lips.

She opened her eyes, tried to focus. "I . . ."

"Because I want you. All of you." He grinned and he kissed her again. "And I want a little you. A daughter. A son. One of each."

She tightened her arms around his shoulders, rose up on her knees, and let his head ease into her on a whispered, "I love you so much."

"God, Hali . . ." he groaned against her throat. "You feel so . . . perfect."

His hands slid down her back and over her ass. The way he held her, moved her to his thrusts, knew just how to bring her to climax was true ecstasy. And as she neared the edge, Mitch laid her back, tilted her hips with his hands, and let go of his own passion. Each long, deep stroke pushed her closer and closer and . . . then it was there, pleasure breaking over her, spilling through her body until her muscles clenched and her nailed scored his skin.

And he waited until the last of the orgasm trembled through her before letting go, his body driving hard, muscles clenching, every beautiful hill and valley taut and damp. Extreme pleasure washed over his handsome face, and Halina had never seen anything so beautiful. Had never been so satisfied. Had never loved so much . . . or been so loved.

NINETEEN

Halina startled from sleep. Once her eyes focused, she realized Mitch had jerked straight up in bed, his fingers clasped tight around her wrist and still holding her hand against his chest as he had in sleep. His heart beat hard and fast against her palm.

The distant sound of shattering glass ripped a path down her chest.

Dex, who'd been curled at their feet, jumped upright and growled.

Mitch released her hand and reached for his pants, sliding them on in an instant, then his shirt.

"What was that?" Halina whispered, hating the rigid fear in her voice. She pushed the covers aside and slid out of the bed beside Mitch, pulling clothes from the floor.

"Baby, stay here with Dex. Let me see what's going on first."

Silently, the door to their bedroom opened and someone stood silhouetted in darkness. Terror stabbed Halina's heart, bitter and ice cold. She fell back a step. Dex moved forward, barking and snarling.

"Dude . . ." Kai whispered.

"Tikhiy," Halina said. Dex quieted.

"Something came through the front window." Kai's serious whisper both relieved and alarmed her. She released a breath and tried to slow her heart with a hand to her chest. From down the hall, rustles and whispers drifted in. "Keira and Luke are headed there now. Teague's taking Alyssa, Jessica, and the kids to the basement. Cash is covering the back of the house."

"Where's Dillon? Nelson? The others?" Mitch finished dressing and helped Halina pull on her jacket.

"Not responding to radio calls."

Halina's stomach plummeted. Walls closed in. Mitch reached for his phone.

"Don't bother," Kai rasped. "There's some kind of signal blocker in the area. Nothing works—cell, television, radio, Internet—it's all out."

"*Fuck.*"

Mitch almost didn't have the word finished before a booming voice slammed into the house from somewhere in the surrounding hills. "This is Major Bruce Abernathy, United States Army."

Halina jumped. Mitch pulled her to his side but even his warmth couldn't keep the blood from freezing in her veins. The kind of terror she thought she'd put behind her long, long ago gripped her by surprise, a steel band around her heart, growing tighter and tighter. Halina tightened her hand on Mitch's bicep, her fingers digging in.

"We have your location surrounded," Abernathy's deep voice bellowed through the horn. "We are here to apprehend Halina Beloi for crimes of treason. Send Miss Beloi out, and the rest of you are free to go. Let me warn you now that we will not accept Beloi's research only. We will not be leaving without Halina Beloi in person, and there will be no negotiation."

A sound caught in her throat. Dex whined.

This was it. This was what had been hanging over her head like a piano on a fraying rope for seven years. All the hopes she'd had just hours ago fell to the bottom of her stomach like lead. She turned her face against Mitch's shoulder and took one more long breath of him.

But he gripped her hand and jerked her into a jog, pushing past Kai and trotting down the steps. Dex's nails clicked behind them. At the landing two silhouettes—Luke and Keira—pulled equipment from a closet. Luke swung two pieces of body armor toward Mitch and he caught it as he took the last stair. Without a sound, he secured Halina's first, then his own. Then took the weapons Keira handed him.

"Halina," Keira whispered, "what do you shoot?"

She didn't answer, but turned to Mitch, searching for his eyes in the dark and catching sight of his cold green gaze in the ambient light. "What are you doing? You can't risk everyone just for—"

"She can shoot anything," Mitch told Keira over Halina, then met her eyes again and lowered his face to hers. "Don't you *dare* expect me to give you up again. No way in fucking hell is anyone getting you away from me."

"If anyone other than Halina Beloi"—the voice sliced through Mitch's last passionate statement as if to make a point—"attempts to leave the house, they will be shot."

Two consecutive rounds of automatic gunfire splintered the thick wooden front door and lodged in the entry hall's sheetrock with a *thwffftpt*. An explosion of gypsum powder hit their faces. Dex barked again. Halina's lungs erupted in uncontrollable spasms. Mitch pulled her to the floor and held her against his chest until she'd hacked the junk from her lungs. When she found her bearings, Luke, Keira, and Kai were already crouched near the windows, peering over sills and around edges into the night through scopes.

A shadow moved on her left. She twisted from Mitch's grasp, hands up, ready to strike.

"It's Quaid." He dropped into a crouch beside them. "Is anyone hurt?"

Before Mitch responded, Abernathy's controlled voice echoed in the night again. "Be forewarned, every exit has been wired with explosive. Any attempt to escape will blow the entire building."

A series of shocked, quiet curses came from what sounded like every member of the group. Kai shifted, shined a penlight out the corner of a window, and panned it around the edge. Then sprinted past the front door in a crouch and into the dining room, repeating the scan with his flashlight.

"Sonofabitch," he murmured, then called down the hall. "Cash?"

"Here too," Cash responded in a rough whisper. "Every door. Every window."

"What did he use?" Quaid asked.

"C4. Remote switch."

Mitch turned to Quaid. "Teleport outside and defuse them."

"Can't." He was serious, but calm, as if he was completely at home in this chaotic stress. "The signal blocker he's using has totally screwed up the electromagnetic signals. I'm as stuck as all of you."

"Jessica?" Mitch asked.

"She's in the basement with the kids. I just came from asking her. She can't teleport either."

At Halina's back, Mitch's breathing grew faster, raspier, his body a wall of fire and growing sticky with sweat. This was his family. These were the people he loved above everything else in the world. And it was clear he would be forced to choose between them and her.

Halina pushed to her feet. Before she could open her mouth, Mitch's grip tightened on her arm. "No, Halina." His voice shook, but his eyes remained fierce in the dim light. "I mean it."

"Vents." Cash's voice made Halina startle and turn. "Ducts. Fireplace. Attic."

Kai took charge. "Cash, you're on vents. Mitch, ducts. Quaid, attic. I'll look at the flues. That fucker's not keeping us—"

"You have sixty seconds to send Beloi out," Abernathy's voice cut in again. "Then one explosive will be detonated every ten seconds."

Halina's breath siphoned into her lungs. Her heart thumped in her throat.

"Change of plans," Mitch said, his grip still tight on Halina's arm as if he were afraid she'd disappear if he let go. "Keira." When she turned, Mitch tossed his phone to her. "Work that photo of Abernathy and find a weakness. Kai, go sit in a corner and get into the fucker's body. Luke, don't move. And if you see him, shoot his damn head off. Cash, Quaid—find a fucking way out of this place."

"*Fifty seconds,*" Abernathy called.

So many thoughts and emotions congealed inside Halina at once, it was as if her brain detonated cells in slow motion. The realization of all she would lose when she left this circle of safety. The knowledge of where she was headed when Abernathy took her away. The certainty of her ultimate reality waiting.

Inside, she steeled herself, shedding emotion like dead skin. The transition took her back to Russia and the days she had to face punishment from her uncle.

"*Halina.*" Mitch took her by the arms and shook her. "Baby, you have to keep your head together." His voice broke and the anguish that flooded into it would have dropped her to her knees if she'd still been feeling.

"*Thirty seconds,*" Abernathy called.

"Jesus fucking Christ, you damn *super people,*" Mitch yelled, but pulled Halina into his arms and held her so tight it hurt, his mouth against her hair. "Do something with your sorry powers for a change."

Halina pulled back and pressed her hands to Mitch's face. So much pain washed his features, her body throbbed inside the steel shell she'd taken on. "Shh, it's going to be all right. You're going to be okay."

"No. You can't go," he rasped through what sounded like tears. And in the reflection of the ambient light, wetness glistened on his thick black lashes.

Halina choked with so much love for him. "I can't stay," she whispered. "You know I can't stay. Think of Alyssa, Kat, Brady . . . Mitch, let me go."

"*Twenty seconds.*"

A thin veil of ferocity glazed over the anguish in his eyes. The shadow of his jaw jumped as he clenched his teeth. "He won't take you from me again." His voice sounded like a feral growl. "Keira, Kai, *someone,* give me *something, goddammit.*"

"*Ten seconds.*"

Mitch's gaze jerked toward the door.

"Baby—" Halina started, but Mitch put his hand on the back of her head and pressed her face to his chest.

"No. No. *No!*" He screamed the last, the sound filled with so much pain, Halina winced. Her shell was cracking. "I won't do it."

"Time's up," Abernathy called, his voice carrying a new edge. "Send her out *now.*"

Someone put a hand on Mitch's shoulder and pulled.

"Mitch," Quaid said gently while Luke pried one of Mitch's arms from around Halina's back. "We'll get her back, but we've got to send her out now."

Halina went cold. She forced her mind black. Told herself this was inevitable. That he would find happiness. He would recover. But when she slipped out from beneath his arm, he broke free of the others and lunged for her.

His arm closed around her, his face pressed to the side of her head with a wrenched, "I love—"

An explosion from somewhere at the back of the house rocked the ground and tossed everyone to the floor. Smoke filled the space. Voices. Shouts. Halina looked up and found the roof spinning. Spotted the front door and crawled in that direction. She used the handle to pull herself up and managed to force the locks open.

Outside, Abernathy's voice counted down to the next blast. "Eight, seven . . ."

She swung the door wide and lost her balance. Dex appeared at her side, ready to brave the night with her.

"Ya lyublyu tebya." She leaned down for a quick hug and kiss. "Love you, sweet boy. *Ostat' sya."* She ordered him to stay.

"Five, four . . ."

Crisp, fresh air wafted over her. Her head swam.

"Halina!"

Mitch's plea gave her the strength to push herself out the door and into the night.

Slipping on debris, choking on smoke, Mitch gathered his feet beneath him and pushed off the floor with his hands. He grabbed anything to balance and slumped his shoulder against the nearest wall.

Halina was already twenty feet beyond the house. Panic churned in his stomach and made him want to puke. He pushed off the wall, lunged for the door. But came up short. Quaid caught him by the shoulders and jerked him aside just as a bullet slammed through the foyer.

"Anyone who exits the house," Abernathy reminded with a bellow, "will *die*."

Breathing hard, vision spinning, Mitch peered around the edge of the open door frame where icy night air whipped into the house. He couldn't pick out Halina on the horizon and his chest constricted even further.

"Where . . . ?" He pushed to his feet, his voice rising with terror. "Was she hit?"

No. He wouldn't shoot her. That doesn't make sense. Like any of this made sense? He couldn't think straight.

Quaid's hand remained on Mitch's shoulder, clearly as much for restraint as support. "She's crouched near the ground. You just can't pick her out from the—"

A floodlight clicked on and drenched Halina in a circle of white light. Crouching just as Quaid described, she turned her head away from the beam and lifted her arm in front of her face. Seeing her out there, completely exposed and helpless, made every muscle in Mitch's body sing with tension. Made his stomach swim with nausea. He'd never felt more utterly helpless. So completely vulnerable.

"Walk toward the light, Beloi," Abernathy bellowed. "The faster you move, the safer the others will be."

His implied meaning straightened Mitch's spine and cleared his head with the crispness of the night air. "He's going to blow this place as soon as he has her."

Mitch turned to Quaid. "We have to get everyone out." Then he turned to the others scattered throughout the front rooms of the house with weapons. "Out. Everyone out."

"Where?" Luke said. "We don't know how many guys he's got—"

"Just two." This came from Keira in that distant, dark tone she used when she'd been reading photographs. "He's only got himself and . . . Owen. Owen is the shooter."

The implications of that statement made Mitch fall back a step. His brain churned, picking at his interactions with Owen, but couldn't find anything that pegged the man clearly as friend or enemy. But something else Owen said came back to Mitch. "*I have just a little bit of pretty metal on my chest.*"

With Owen's skill, they would all be dead if he'd wanted them dead. "Luke. He knows you're bulletproof?"

"Definitely."

"Abernathy's one-hundred-percent focused on Halina," Kai said, standing in the doorway of the room he'd retreated into to sync with Abernathy's emotions. "Not an ounce of interest in any of us and already high on victory. If we're going to slam him, now would be the time. He'll be completely blindsided."

"What about Owen?" Mitch asked.

"Furious. Trapped. Belligerent."

"Ransom." Mitch swung toward Luke. "Up to being a shield?"

"You know it," Luke said.

"What kind of shield," Keira asked.

"A people-mover, from here to the in-law unit. There is a secure basement beneath."

Keira's concern reflected even in the dim light. She looked at Luke. "That's a lot of trips. A lot of exposure."

While Luke was bulletproof, he was not immune to pain, which was why Mitch hadn't just come out and ordered Luke to do it—not that he had any authority or power over the man, but . . .

"Owen's on our side," Mitch said. "He doesn't want Schaeffer or Abernathy in power. He's trapped. He wants you to get everyone out. If Abernathy's ordered him to shoot anyone who comes out the front door, he'll do it, but he'll do it his way."

"That doesn't ease my mind, but yeah, I'm doing it. I'm taking the kids first."

Luke crossed the room to Keira, wrapped her in a fierce hug, murmured a few words, and disappeared. His boots clomped down into the basement.

Cash came running down the stairs. "I've got a vent in the attic. It's small. Will need work to fit any of us out."

"Fuck! Fuck, fuck, *fuck!*" Mitch jammed both hands into his hair and fisted the strands, but the sting along his scalp didn't help him think. When he opened his eyes, he was looking out the door, watching Halina, who was almost translucent in the glare of the high-powered light. She stumbled across the open land, so totally vulnerable. So totally willing to give up her freedom, her life, for him. For all of them. Because *he* loved them. Because they were *his* family.

Mitch wanted nothing more than to run out there and take her place, but that wouldn't solve the problem of what Schaeffer had started. What Schaeffer would continue to drive once recovered and free of the hospital, or once the next Abernathy came along to take over. Besides, he didn't have what Abernathy wanted. Only Halina—

His mind zipped to the papers scattered in the upstairs bedroom. To the ones spread all around the family room where everyone had been working. To the disks.

Movement caught his eye and his gaze cut to a window in the dining room looking out onto the front yard. Dex's pointed ears and long snout were sharply silhouetted against the floodlight outside.

"Luke," Mitch yelled.

"I'm right here," he snapped.

He stepped up beside Mitch carrying a bundled, whimpering child. Mitch could tell from the size and sound it was Kat, and his whole chest seized with an overwhelming sense of impending loss and responsibility.

Mitch released a breath, pressed a hand to Kat's back and felt her flinch. He gritted his teeth against the guilt, leaned close. "Kitty Kat, it's me."

"Uncle Miiiiitch," she whined in a plea to make it all go away like she did when she woke from a nightmare. He pulled the blanket back only enough to clear her cheek and dropped a kiss there. Then caught a whiff of an unmistakable sweet, soft scent and his stomach tightened. "Is Brady in here with you?"

"Y-y-yeah."

Ah, fuck. His whole world in one little bundle.

"Wow, that's a big responsibility. Your mom's put a lot of trust in you. You sure you can take care of Brady while Uncle Luke comes back for Mateo?"

"O-of c-course."

The response was so filled with reproach for his question, Mitch couldn't help but smile. "That's my girl. Stay strong. We'll all be there real soon, okay baby?"

"H-hurry." She sniffled and laid her head against Luke's shoulder again. "B-Brady gets so c-cranky when he's h-hungry."

Mitch kissed her cheek again and covered her head. To Luke he murmured, "Go."

Luke kissed Keira at the door, backed onto the front porch, and was immediately struck in the back with a double tap. Mitch's heart stopped. Only when Luke grunted and took off running, his body twisted to cover the kids with his torso, did Mitch's lifeline start beating again. Trying to cover an adult would be far less successful. Mitch could only hope his intuition about Young was accurate.

Though Mitch tried to avoid it, he couldn't help the pull of his gaze out the door. Halina had gotten to her feet and stumbled across the grass. He doubted she was injured from her earlier fall, more likely stalling for time. Struggling for one of those miraculous moves of hers to escape.

The difference was, this time she was trying to get back to Mitch, not away from him.

"Dex," Mitch called. The dog immediately shot to his side, those golden eyes staring up at him, bright and alert.

"Kai," Mitch yelled. "What did Abernathy throw through the window?"

"A rock."

"Find it, but don't touch it."

Kai's flashlight beam scoured the living room carpet. "Here."

"Dex." Mitch pointed to the rock, the size of a small melon, pretending to tap it without actually touching it. He leaned close to the shepherd's ear and said very clearly, "Hunt, Dex. *Hunt.*" He struggled to clear his mind to bring up the Russian word . . . *"okhota."*

Dex sniffed the rock—top and sides. A low growl rolled from his throat.

"Show me the vent," Mitch said to Cash and darted up the stairs behind him, Dex on his heels.

Mitch paused at the ladder leading into the attic and turned to pick Dex up, but the shepherd darted past Mitch and climbed the ladder while Mitch watched, his mouth gaping.

"Sign him up for one of the engines," Kai murmured behind them. "He climbs better than most of the team."

Mitch ran the ladder behind the dog and found him already perched at the rectangular vent, wagging his tail, whining.

"You sure he won't break his neck getting to the ground?" Cash asked, pulling himself into the attic. "It's a much longer fall than the ladder."

"He already made it down once with Halina," Mitch said. "And it's better than the alternative."

"Hunt, Dex. *Okhota.*" Mitch leaned in, closed his eyes, and kissed the dog's fur. "Get that bastard before he gets our girl, buddy. *Okhota.*"

He gestured to release the dog and Dex jumped through the vent. He instantly disappeared into the darkness and Mitch experienced another deep jerk of loss in his chest. He turned, scrambled down the ladder, and sprinted toward the bedroom he and Halina had shared. He had to grip the doorjamb to slow himself, then catapulted toward the bed.

He was out of ideas. Had drained every last one. And he

knew each had severe limitations. So severe he wasn't counting on any of them to save Halina.

His heart beat so hard, so fast, it hammered his lungs and made it hard to breathe. Panic escaped his barriers and pushed wetness into his eyes, blurring his vision. He blindly scooped the papers he and Halina had scattered on the floor while making love and bunched them in his arms.

Kai and Cash stood near the door on his exit, just shadows shooting questions at him. Questions he couldn't even hear with the blood pounding in his ears. And by the time he'd jammed all the papers into the box they'd come from, still sitting in the family room, he slumped to his hands and knees, so dizzy from lack of air he couldn't stand.

Someone put a hand on Mitch's shoulder. Blind with terror and rage, he shook it off, jerked the box to his body as he stood and twisted toward the front door. He ran as hard as he could toward that opening and the light beyond, which pulled him like a beacon.

Just before he reached it, a body hit him from the side. Mitch stumbled, hit a wall, spun, and fought to keep the box upright while papers flew over the edge. He landed on his ass near the splintered window and stared up, dazed. Frantic.

Teague climbed to his feet, wincing. "He'll shoot you, you dumbass. How are you going to help her when you're dead?"

Mitch got his feet underneath him and stepped within inches of Teague's face. "If that was Alyssa, would your ass be in here?" When Teague didn't answer, Mitch said, "Don't get in my way again or I'll push *you* out that door in front of me."

Mitch sidestepped Teague, but instead of going for the door, sprinted toward the shattered window, stepped on the ledge, and pushed himself into a leap onto the front lawn.

Halina could have been naked and chained to a cement floor, she felt so vulnerable. With her arm up and shading her eyes from that searing beam of light, she took one shaky step after another over the uneven ground. No point in rushing, right?

Except that she might freeze to death before she reached Abernathy. Which might not be a bad alternative. Because every time her thoughts drifted backward to the house behind her, to the people inside, to the anguish on Mitch's face when he'd realized he had to make a choice between her and his family . . .

God, she couldn't take the knifelike stab at her heart. Her throat thickened with tears again. She paused so she wouldn't stumble while she blinked them away.

"Keep moving, Beloi," Abernathy screeched at her through some type of megaphone. One he didn't need any longer if the way it blew out her ears every time he spoke indicated how close she'd gotten to him.

Too close.

Her stomach did a double flip in her gut. She envisioned cement block cells and iron bars and handcuffs in her very near future. Hunger, pain, isolation, degradation, abuse.

She was no stranger to any of these things. But she had believed she'd finally escaped it. At least the kind she'd suffered most of her life. No such luck. Abernathy would throw her in a dungeon until she produced the research he wanted and then he'd kill her.

And poor Mitch. The tears picked up again. Her heart squeezed so hard she swore it would stop beating. But it just kept going. Poor Mitch . . . he would search for her. Pull out all the stops. Dedicate his heart, body, soul, and every resource. She had no doubt.

Inside, her heart broke. Her legs weakened and for a moment she seriously considered simply falling to her knees and refusing to go. She could make Abernathy come out here, pick her up, and drag her away. If it weren't for the others in the house—the others she knew he'd blow up without a second thought—she would.

She had to find enough strength to get through this. To get to Abernathy, so Abernathy would leave the others alone. Then she could take whatever chances she wanted. The kind that only involved her own life.

She closed her arms around herself as an icy gust of wind cut through the air. A hard shiver wracked her body. Her teeth chattered.

"What is wrong with you?" Abernathy yelled—but not at Halina. He wasn't using the megaphone. "Shoot him!"

Halina glanced up, but couldn't see anything past the blinding floodlight and averted her eyes. The damn thing would burn her retinas. That would teach Abernathy. He wouldn't get any research out of her then.

"I don't care where he came out, you dumbfuck," Abernathy said. *"Shoot. Him."*

Another set of twin shots sounded to her right. Halina jumped, then froze, waiting for the eruption of pain somewhere in her body. But no, he hadn't hit her. Hadn't been aiming for her. And her stomach sank a little more. She sent up another prayer that he'd missed his intended target or that the team had found a hiding place or . . . something. The only reason she held on to any hope at all was because she didn't hear anyone screaming in pain.

"Either you kill Foster or I will," Abernathy yelled to the shooter.

Fear tore up Halina's spine. She stopped and chanced a glance over her shoulder, squinting to adjust her vision. Skirting the edge of the light beam, a shadow darted toward her. Her heart jolted with both excitement and fear and she turned toward the house. In that second between losing sight of the figure and turning, Mitch appeared, out of breath and carrying that damned box from the apartment.

She gasped, half believing he was an apparition she'd conjured out of self-preservation. Then Abernathy's voice screeched again. "Get away from Beloi, Foster."

Halina instinctively lunged for him, putting her body between him and the shooter. She gripped Mitch's bare arms, his biceps hard and warm . . . and quivering beneath her fingers. "Get the hell out of here. Get back to the house. He'll shoot you."

"I don't think so." But he had a wild look in his eye. Frenzied. "It's Owen. I think Abernathy's forced him to be here. And I can't live through losing you again. I'd rather die."

He sidestepped Halina and lifted the box over his head. "I've got a deal for you, Abernathy," he yelled, raspy and breathless.

Shock hit Halina dead center in the chest and she moved again. Before she'd placed herself fully in front of him, two shots whizzed past her head. By the time she could react, the box Mitch had been holding was zapped out of his hands and spun several yards, casting out papers like a ticker tape parade.

He ducked and Halina frantically searched him for injuries. "Are you hit?"

"No." And he grinned. "See. If he could shoot that box out of my hands, he could have put a bullet in my ear."

"That's," Abernathy said over the speaker, "what I think of your deal, Foster."

Mitch tried to step away from the safety of her body again. She dug her nails into his skin. "I'm not so trusting. Humor me."

He shot her an irritated look, but stayed put, yelling, "You don't want documentation of all the research? Rostov's, Gorin's, *and* Beloi's? You aren't interested in evidence that would take Schaeffer off the map? Send him to prison for the rest of his life?"

"What are you doing?" Her mind and body finally caught up with the situation and panic flashed through her. "You can't give him everything. You *need* that. Get the hell back to that house, *right now.*"

Mitch pulled her close, wrapping her in his arms. The sheer perfection of it—his strength, his scent, his fit—shook her determination. She wanted . . . with everything she was, everything she would ever be . . . to stay with him.

Dammit, that *wasn't* a lot to ask.

"You'll never have to worry about Schaeffer catching up with you," Mitch yelled. "And he will. You know he will." Mitch slid a hand up to her head and pulled it against his chest.

Halina let herself go and leaned into him. "I'll give you everything. I only want to walk away from here with my family—including Beloi."

Between them, a circular spiral of heat built until she felt as if her skin was burning. She pulled back and looked down at the bright red circle on Mitch's chest. Lifted her hand to the area on her own chest that burned and felt the disk on the end of the leather cord beneath her fingers.

"Better tell me now, Abernathy," Mitch continued, his gaze squinting into the light. "With this wind picking up, before long your sweet evidence is going to be blown into the Potom—"

A feral growl sounded in the distance followed by several ferocious barks.

"What the—?" Abernathy's voice drifted to her ears, far less frightening without his loudspeaker, far less menacing with fear raising his pitch.

But the sound of the barks spiked the hair on the back of Halina's neck, and she pushed away from Mitch, whipping her head in that direction. The light slammed her eyes and she recoiled with her arm up. "Dex?"

She turned on Mitch for a split second, but didn't even need to ask the question when Abernathy's screams crawled over her flesh and curdled her blood. "Oh my God."

She took off running, straight into the light, dragging Mitch with her. "Dex!"

She passed the floodlight and everything went dark. Her vision took a moment to adjust, and in that moment, without her sight, all her other senses were heightened—the feral growl in Dex's throat, every heavy breath, grunt, and scream of pain from Abernathy's mouth, the rustle of brush as they struggled.

The burn against her chest grew so strong, she could barely keep her attention focused elsewhere and the disk glowed bright orange-white, creating its own light.

"There," Mitch said beside her. He pointed to the rustle of bushes.

Dex was almost at her feet when his yelp pierced the air. The sound cut through Halina's chest and she lunged into the brush.

"Don't move or he's dead."

Abernathy's voice was raspy, edgy, cut with pain. He lay on the ground with Dex in a chokehold, where he continued to writhe and growl and reach for Abernathy with his teeth.

"Call. Him. Off," Abernathy ordered, low and fierce, "or I'll shoot him right now."

Halina opened her mouth, but nothing came out. Terror hazed her mind. Everything sharp as crystal just a second ago now melted into one big watercolor. She couldn't think.

"*Tikhiy* . . . Dex." Mitch spoke behind her, breathless. "*Tikhiy.*"

Dex stilled and in the light shining from the disk, Halina could see him struggling to breathe. Could see his coat matted with something she was sure was blood. Rage ignited deep within her. A rage gathered from all the injustices and pain and loss. Emotions sizzled toward her center, channeled into the disk at her throat, and exited in one huge burst of energy, slamming Abernathy in the chest and throwing him to the ground.

The eruption blasted Halina backward several feet and into Mitch's arms. Abernathy lay on the dirt, his screams shattering the night as jagged lines of current flashed the length of his body and lit him up from the inside out.

"Holy shit," Mitch whispered. "Remind me not to make you mad while you're wearing that thing."

The whine at her feet drew her gaze. She crouched and wrapped her arms around Dex just as he collapsed against her.

"Oh, no. Mitch . . ."

"Right here." His hands closed on her shoulders.

Relief washed in for barely a split second before the urgency flowed again. "Help me with—"

"I'll help you."

The new voice cut through the night. Deep, cool, very male. Halina gasped and froze, searching for the threat, but the newcomer was nothing more than another silhouette standing on the other side of Abernathy. The energy flashing through the major's body had died out. He now rolled and groaned on the ground, emitting the horrid stench of burned human flesh.

"Or," the stranger said, "I guess I'll help him, which will be helping you too."

Mitch grabbed Halina's waist and pulled her back. A double pop rang out. The flashes from the muzzle of the stranger's weapon lit up the night for those two partial seconds. Illuminating the aim of the weapon and the jerk of Abernathy's body like a strobe.

Mitch hauled Halina around behind him. She could only sway like a lifeless doll, limp in shock.

"Courtesy of Senator Schaeffer," the man muttered.

He might have said more, but the sound of Mitch's rough breathing, the rush of blood rising like a tide in her ears, drowned out everything else.

We're next. We're next. It was all that filled her mind. That and her self-defense training.

She had no idea what propelled her forward. Didn't remember the transition from leaning against Mitch to lunging toward the gunman, only registered the reality of what she was doing after it was too late to turn back. She was in midair, sailing toward him, arms outstretched and her mind fully engaged for a battle to the death.

She hit his chest and her body crumpled against the mass of muscle like an accordion. The ground came fast, faster than it did in the light, as if it had risen to slam into her. She was completely disoriented, turned around. Couldn't see anything. Which meant he couldn't see her either—she hoped.

She groped, found an ankle, then the other. She twisted and kicked up with all she had. Her heel connected at a skewed angle with his balls, not a direct hit, but he grunted and stumbled. She readjusted, kicked again. And again. And again.

Time seemed suspended, insignificant as she kicked, hit, punched beyond the burn, beyond the fear, beyond the hopelessness. Surrounded by the night, the stench of burning flesh and gunpowder, terror stretched time thin.

TWENTY

Someone was yelling her name. Maybe more than one. Maybe it was just an echo. There seemed to be a lot of echoes. And they bled into her consciousness as her energy waned.

"I said *freeze.*" The angry voice commanded from so close he could have been on top of her. Halina's fist connected with some muscled part of the gunman and she let it drop away, went still, breathing hard, searching for bearings.

Lights floated in the dark like giant fireflies. And voices closed in.

"Mitch!" She yelled for him, turned her head to search for his shadow.

Arms closed around her and she stiffened, then his scent, his feel hit her and she sagged into him, wrapping her arms around his shoulders and holding on tight.

"Are you okay?" She fought to breathe. "Are . . . are you hurt?"

"She doesn't listen very well." A thick flashlight beam shone on the ground at their feet, illuminating dark boots and pants. Her gaze jumped to the speaker's face, but fell back to the white lettering across his chest: FBI. "What part of *freeze* or *FBI* didn't you understand?"

"Lay off," Mitch rasped alongside her head, holding her so tight she had a hard time drawing air. "She was in the middle of doing your fucking job for you, asshole."

She glanced around and the terror-filled haze faded to reveal a gaggle of what appeared to be law enforcement, some cuffing the gunman, others forming a semicircle, gazing down at Abernathy.

A wave of dizziness hit Halina hard. Her stomach pushed toward her throat. She closed her eyes and rested her forehead against the muscle of Mitch's chest. Breathed him in.

It helped.

"What's happening?" she asked against his skin. "What is this?"

"She okay?" another male voice asked behind her, this one far more concerned. Much warmer.

"What do you think?" Mitch snapped. "What about a fucking phone call, dude? For someone who's supposed to be an Army stud, you suck at communication."

"Can you answer my question, Foster? Does she need medical attention or not?"

Halina tried to lift her head, but it was too heavy. She rolled her head against his shoulder instead and peered out from behind crazy strands of hair, blowing in an icy wind. A familiar, handsome face reflected in the light.

"Owen," she breathed.

The concern etching his face eased and he smiled. "Beloi," he said in greeting. "Not a great way to meet up again."

She let out the first real breath of relief. Another person clad in FBI gear walked up. "For a little thing, she causes a lot of trouble."

The female voice startled Halina and she lifted her head. The woman was about Halina's age, dark hair, dark eyes and beautiful.

Owen laughed. "Look who's talking. I seem to remember you causing your share of trouble, Seville."

Halina didn't need to be in her right mind to see the look that passed between the two. She felt the same way about the man still holding her tight, stroking her hair.

She gasped and moved her head too fast. It spun and she pressed her hand to her forehead. "Dex. Where's Dex?"

"He's in the guest house with the others," the woman said. "One of the medics grew up on a farm and is a pre-vet student. He's looking after him. Says he'll be okay."

"The others?" She turned toward the house. "Is everyone okay?"

"Fine," Mitch said, kissing her head. "Everyone's fine."

Halina deflated once again, her body going soft against Mitch's.

"Let's head that direction," the female agent, Seville, Owen had called her, said. "We've got a lot of questions."

"So do we," Mitch countered. "You've got your share of explaining to do."

"Oh, that's right." The woman's voice dripped with sarcasm and she sighed, then glanced at Owen. "He's a lawyer."

"And you'll never forget it," Owen muttered. "I need a minute with this lawyer. Can I bring him to you in a bit?"

"Of course."

When Seville started off toward the house, Owen faced Mitch with one of those looks, the kind that doctors give the family of someone just out of surgery when there's bad news.

Halina's stomach burned. She tightened her arms around Mitch.

"She just said everyone's fine," Mitch said, his voice tight, serious, obviously reading Owen's expression the way Halina had. "Is everyone okay or not?"

"Yeah, yeah, this is about something else."

"Well you look damn uncomfortable," Mitch said. "Just spit it out."

Owen took one giant step back. "I . . . don't want to be within hitting range when I say this."

He unwound his arm from Halina's shoulders. "Well, shit, that makes me want to punch you now and I don't even know why."

Halina kept her arms wound tight around Mitch's waist and repeated words he'd said to her earlier. "You're not going to fight him."

Owen grinned, an ironic, self-deprecating grin, and huffed a dry laugh. "Hold that thought, Halina." He refocused on Mitch. Cleared his throat. "I'm responsible for Teague Creek's escape from prison. For orchestrating his partner's involvement and Alyssa's positioning for kidnap."

Halina was only half following what was going on, but Mitch's eyes narrowed dangerously. "Excuse me?"

"At that time, you were making a lot of trouble for Classified over an appeal for one of the Lejeune plaintiffs. It was evidently causing a rift between Schaeffer and Classified and Classified threatened to stop doing business with Schaeffer because *you* seemed to be a constant problem."

"Now," Owen held up his hands and took another slow, casual step back. "I didn't know this at the time. I was given an entirely different story and didn't know how this related to the bigger picture until much later."

Mitch tried to advance on Owen. Halina held him back.

"In his infinite stupidity," Owen continued, "Schaeffer decided that if your sister—your twin—was in danger, you would have to take time away from your work, which would ease the appeal situation with Classified."

"What the *fuck*?"

Owen held up his hands. "Evidently, none of the events that followed were supposed to happen. But, well, you have to admit, you do have a way of starting natural disasters, Foster."

Mitch swore and lunged. Halina had to get in front of him and put her body weight into pushing him back. "Mitch, Mitch, it's over. We have Schaeffer." He looked down at her with fury turning his eyes bright green. "Let's leave the past behind. Move forward."

"I have set up a situation that will give you a memorable payback, though," Owen said. "My small attempt to apologize and mend fences, so to speak. I think you'll be pleased. But I've got to go finalize those with Seville now . . ." Owen started walking backward . . . "and give you some, you know, breathing room. I owe you, Halina."

As Owen walked away, Halina wrapped her arms around Mitch's lean torso and held him as tight as her shaking muscles could manage. "It's over, baby. Alyssa's happy. Teague's happy. They've got everything they've always wanted. And Owen probably saved all our lives tonight. I know he could have shot you twice and didn't."

"Good thing," Mitch grumbled, finally relaxing enough to wrap his arms around her. "I'd have kicked his ass."

Halina burst out laughing.

"That's a great sound," Mitch murmured, the stress leaving his voice. "Let's get you inside before you turn into a popsicle."

"The papers," she said. "We need to get—"

"That's what FBI agents are for, sweetheart," he rubbed her arms and back. "They're experts at collecting garbage. All kinds of garbage."

She puffed another laugh against his chest.

Gooseflesh rose across his skin under her hands. "Mmm." He groaned. "Let's get questions out of the way so we can find a hotel." He leaned away, tipped her chin up with his fingers and smiled into her eyes. "Because I'm ready to put the past behind us, too. I'm ready to move on."

Mitch glanced at his watch. Again. 10:36 A.M. He rocked his shoulders to ease the electric tightness surrounding his chest.

"Thirty seconds later than the last time you checked," Owen murmured beside him in the hospital elevator.

"Shut up." Mitch shifted on his feet. Stared up at the numbers *tick, tick, tick*ing off as they traveled the floors. Sighed. Glanced at his watch. Damn thing didn't move.

"Christ, you're worse than an expectant father."

Mitch shot a scowl at Owen, but inside, his stomach made a slow roll.

Owen's gaze lowered from the numbers flashing through the floors, a grin on his face. "Where's your suit?"

"In the car."

"The ring?"

"Teague has it." He ran a hand through his hair, wiping his palm across his forehead to catch the sweat. "Or I'll choke him with my bare hands."

"Everyone's blessings?" Owen asked.

"More like threats if I don't."

"Who did you get to preside?"

"Chief Justice McMillan."

"On such short notice?" Owen's brows shot up and he whistled softly through his teeth. "You do have friends in high places, Foster."

"He's a closet romantic," Mitch said just as the elevator dinged and the doors slid open. "All it took was a two-minute rendition of our story and he adjusted his schedule to fit ours."

"Where?"

Mitch cleared his throat as he stepped off the elevator, his nerves mounting as he pulled up the frantic details he'd thrown together just hours ago. "Superior Court, main library. They're closing it for an hour."

"Apropos."

Mitch and Owen paused and turned toward the nurse's station down the hall, where four cops were staged along the corridor alongside two FBI agents, including Special Agent Seville. From the corner of his eye, he noticed Owen zero in on Seville. Saw the way he grinned.

"Are *you* planning on entering this institution again anytime soon?" he asked.

Owen started. Turned to Mitch with a frown. Then, caught staring at Seville, laughed wryly. "I'm not opposed to marriage. I just didn't have the right match first time around."

"Should have been matched to her all this time?" Mitch asked.

Owen lifted a shoulder. "You're getting a little intrusive, counselor. And we need to focus elsewhere right now. I've never seen you so distracted at such a critical moment."

Mitch smiled, straightened his blazer, and started forward alongside Owen. "I've never had the right match waiting for me at the altar, changing all my priorities. So let's just get this over with."

"Foster," Owen said, his voice lowered, "hold your tongue, will you? We don't need to give this guy any loophole—"

"Believe me, he won't get any. Anything I say will either be legally binding or inconsequential in a court of law. You'll know which is which. Relax, Colonel. I know the law the way you know a battlefield."

Agent Seville stepped forward, gave both of them a professional smile, then met Mitch's gaze. "Ready to slay your demon, counselor?"

"Born ready," Mitch said. "And I'd like to slay quickly."

"Understood."

She turned to a man dressed in a black suit, black tie, and white dress shirt. The earbud tucked into his ear and the line hugging his neck nailed him as Secret Service. He met Agent Seville's gaze, nodded and murmured into his microphone. Three of the four police officers and the other FBI agent set their stances wide, shoulders back. The second FBI agent pulled out a small camera and pushed buttons. The fourth officer pulled cuffs from his duty belt and stepped toward the still-closed hospital room door with Agent Seville. All the nurses vanished but for one who stood off to the side.

"I want to go straight home." Schaeffer's grouchy order penetrated the door and made Mitch smile. "And I don't want to be bothered. There will be reporters and FBI and others calling. You're to tell them my doctor ordered me on bed rest and I can't be disturbed. Do you understand?"

The door opened and another Secret Service agent stepped out first. He glanced at the man Mitch assumed was his boss, who nodded; then the first agent moved forward and stood beside the other.

Schaeffer waddled through the door, still looking back at the agent behind him. "Has anyone called my chef to tell him I'll be back at home? I don't want any delay in my meals."

He turned, then took one more step into the hallway and stopped short with a startled look and a gasp. Widened eyes made one sweep of the people in the hallway, his gaze lingering an extra second on Mitch. Blackness fell over his gaze, pure vivid fury lit the mud beneath his eyes, and he exploded.

"What the hell is this?"

Seville spoke first. "Senator Schaeffer, I'm Senior Special Agent Seville of the FBI—"

"I don't give a fuck who you are." He approached her as if he planned on mowing her down. Owen stepped forward, but the police officer was closer and stopped Schaeffer first with a hand flat against his chest. Schaeffer pushed against it as he yelled at Seville, jabbing a pointed finger at her as he barked. "This is an invasion of privacy. I'll have your ass up on harassment charges. I'll have your badge. You'll never work in law enforcement again. If Foster put you up to this, you'll be sorry you ever met the man—"

"Senator," Seville said, her voice remaining congenial, but authoritative, "stop now or I will add threatening a government agent to the long list of charges I'm here to arrest you for committing."

"You little bitch." That's when the spittle started to fly. When his face turned red and the veins on his temples bulged. When the whites of his eyes pinked up. "Who the fuck do you think you are? You don't have the authority to—"

The cop restraining him dropped his free hand to Schaeffer's wrist and swiftly twisted the man's hand behind his back. Then grabbed the other and did the same. "Yes, she does."

Schaeffer howled in fury, twisting and jerking from the cop's grasp. Two others stepped up and pushed Schaeffer's round belly against the wall. He actually bounced off, still ranting about all those jobs that would be lost once he got done taking names, et cetera, et cetera.

Mitch crossed his arms, more irritated than amused. As long as he'd been drooling for this chance to feed Schaeffer his own head on a stick, all he wanted to do now was get back to Halina. Mitch couldn't care less about this waste of oxygen other than putting him away for the rest of his natural life—times three.

Mitch shot a God-the-drama look at Young. Young slanted a what-a-psycho look back at Mitch.

By the time the cops had linked three pairs of cuffs together to accommodate Schaeffer's sausage-like arms behind his back, the man was huffing and puffing as if he could barely draw air.

Mitch turned to the nurse whose name tag read Peggy and murmured, "Can you put a pulse ox on his finger, please?"

She nodded and clipped a portable monitor to one of Schaeffer's index fingers. The red LED readout was clearly visible to everyone, and registered ninety-nine. The bastard had plenty of oxygen in his blood.

"You're not faking your way back into a hospital room, Schaeffer," Mitch said. "No passing go, no collecting two hundred dollars. *No way out.*"

When the cop turned Schaeffer around, his face was a sickening fuchsia. "That's it, Foster. This is the last straw. I'll have you up before the bar by week's end. You'll never practice again."

Mitch pulled his phone from his pocket, framed Schaeffer in all his irate, indignant glory in the viewfinder, and clicked the image. He slid the phone back into his pocket and said, "That would be difficult to do." Mitch remained relaxed and maddeningly calm, knowing it would only infuriate Schaeffer further. "The bar doesn't respond to criminals, Gil."

Schaeffer sputtered, spit spraying in an arc. Agent Seville took a step back with a disgusted frown.

"You don't know anything—" Gil started.

"Yes," the cop said. "He does. You have the right to remain silent. Anything you say or do may be used against you in a court of law—"

"I demand an explanation, right *now!*" Schaeffer yelled.

"You're being arrested, Gil," Mitch said with excess patience as if explaining to a three-year-old.

"You have the right to consult an attorney," the cop continued over him, louder, "and to have an attorney present during questioning."

"I'm available," Mitch said. "If you ask *real* nice, I could probably get the jury to consider one death sentence instead of three. I'm good like that."

"If you cannot afford an attorney—"

"You can't, by the way," Mitch interrupted. "All your assets and bank accounts have been frozen."

"—one will be appointed for you," the cop continued. "If you decide to answer any questions now—"

"Beware . . ." Mitch let the wickedness beneath his grin show. "Because I'll twist everything that comes out of your mouth."

"—you can stop answering at any time."

"You also have the right," Mitch added, "to get strip-searched by District of Columbia's finest. You have the right to become Big Bubba's latest bitch. You have the right—"

"Do you understand your rights?" the cop asked Schaeffer, shooting a glare at Mitch.

"Dead, Foster," Schaeffer growled. "You're dead."

Mitch chuckled darkly. "With your track record and all these witnesses, you'd better hope I don't turn up dead anytime soon."

"Do you understand your rights, Senator?" the cop asked.

"Of course I do, you ridiculous civil servant, I'm a United States Senator, for God's sake. Now tell me what I'm charged with or get these cuffs off me."

"I'll start, Senator," Agent Seville said. "You are under arrest for the murder of Army Major Bruce Abernathy—"

"That's ludicrous," he yelled. "I've been under twenty-four-hour care here for weeks."

"But when conspiring to commit a crime, Senator," Seville said sweetly, following Mitch's lead in tone, "the conspirator is as guilty of the crime as the perpetrator. Which leads me to the charges of conspiracy to commit said murder and murder for hire."

"Insanity," Schaeffer said. "Absolute insanity."

"You ain't heard nothing yet, Gil." Mitch slid his hands into the pockets of his slacks, rolled back on his heels, and grinned. The thick, sweet, decadent slide of vindication and vengeance coated his insides. Vindication for the team. Vengeance for Halina, and yes, for himself.

"Pull up your big-boy pants, Gil, you're gonna need them. I'll try to keep it simple for that teeny-tiny brain of yours."

He paused to savor the sheer joy of witnessing justice in action. Then he let loose on the charges the Attorney General had given him permission to disclose.

"You are charged with multiple counts of campaign fraud, multiple counts of misuse of public funds, and multiple counts of bribery." Mitch grinned. "Can't wait to see those photos of you at the Alibi Club splashed on *World News Tonight.*"

"You set me up," he wheezed. "This is a conspiracy."

Mitch waved him off. "Hold on, that's coming. Let's get a few others out of the way first. So impatient." He glanced at the ceiling as if he needed to think to remember the charges. "Where was I? Oh, right." Staring Gil directly in those muddy eyes, he said, "You are charged with two counts of false imprisonment for the illegal—not to mention despicable, animalistic, unethical—incarceration of Teague Creek and Cash O'Shay. There will be many more charges coming related to the two men, but I don't want to confuse you. You're already starting to pale, Gil."

"He's fine," Peggy said from behind the senator, where she monitored his pulse ox, a disgusted look on her face. "Finish up. I want to get him out of here."

"You are charged with multiple counts of mail and wire fraud," Mitch continued. "You are charged with multiple counts of extortion. You are charged with multiple counts of fraud and conspiracy to commit fraud. You are charged with multiple counts of biological and chemical weapons trafficking.

"If it were up to me, I'd have a slew of other charges, but the attorney general is a little more conservative. Don't worry, as more evidence surfaces, there will be plenty more to tack on. We're doing our damnedest to round all this into a package worthy of your . . . stature."

When Gil only stared at the floor, his face as white as the plaster wall, mouth hanging open, bent at the waist, Mitch crouched, tilted his head, and said, "Do you understand the charges as I've outlined them, Gil? Your court-appointed attorney will get everything in writing. Shit, dude, I hope you didn't screw him too at some point over your last twenty years in office. That would suck."

Mitch straightened. "Hey, Gil, would love to stay, watch you rant and writhe, but I've got to run. Halina and I—you remember Halina, right?—yeah, we're getting married today. Crazy, right? Who'd have believed? I'm living the dream, man." He reached out and slapped Gil's arm—hard. Gil pitched forward. The cop kept him standing with a hand against his chest. "Living. The. Fucking. *Dream*."

Mitch pressed his hands to his thighs and stood. Turning to Owen, he dusted his hands and said, "My work here is done. See you at the courthouse, right?"

Owen offered his hand and Mitch took it with a familiar sense of accomplishment and goodwill flowing through every inch of his body. "Wouldn't miss it."

Mitch started toward the elevator, then turned back with a thought, still moving backward as he spoke, pointing between Owen and Agent Seville. "Feel free to bring a date."

Halina paced the library's anteroom. She rubbed her damp hands together. Took a deep breath to try and slow her heart. She glanced at the clock over the door again.

"Is that clock right?" she asked, more to herself than the others milling in the room. "Did the second hand stop?"

"Sweetheart," Alyssa said. "Relax. He wouldn't miss this for anything."

Halina turned. Searched the gazes of the men in the room, each dressed in a fresh dark suit Mitch had purchased for them that morning. The same way he'd sent Alyssa, Jessica, Keira, and Kat out to buy the women crimson gowns and instructions for Alyssa to help Halina choose the wedding dress of her dreams.

This was one attractive group—the men oozing charm and testosterone, the women simply breathtaking. A photographer crouched unobtrusively in the corner, shooting pictures of Kat trying to teach Mateo how to dance, each dressed in miniature versions of the adults' clothes. Dex sat watching the kids, wearing a ridiculous-looking bow tie. Halina still didn't know whose idea that was, but if she had to guess, Kai would be the main suspect.

Mitch had thought of flowers, candles, even a cake and champagne. The only thing Halina had to consider was a ring for him. She'd picked up a thick, solid platinum band when she'd chosen her dress and now spun it around her middle finger, where it was still too big.

"Has anyone talked to him?" When they shook their heads, Halina turned her gaze on Alyssa and pressed a hand to the sudden roll of nausea in her belly. "He's . . . he's okay, right? Nothing could happen to him. Owen was with him. The police and the FBI were there, right?"

"He's fine." Alyssa wrapped her in a hug. "Just long-winded. You know him."

Kai pulled his phone from the pocket of his slacks, set his stance wide. "I'll call—"

The door opened and Mitch sauntered in, followed by Chief Justice McMillan, who'd introduced himself earlier. Then another couple—Owen Young and the FBI agent from the night before? Owen wore a handsome navy suit, Agent Seville a deep eggplant-colored dress.

Mitch spoke to the judge for a moment in a low voice, and once Halina's gaze strayed back to him, she couldn't tear it away. He wore a black tuxedo, with a white shirt, cummerbund, and tie, and when he shut the door behind the judge and turned toward the group, all Halina's air slipped from her lungs.

His black hair shone, and the few hours' worth of stubble on his jaw gave an edge to that polish that made her heart beat quicker. And then he met her eyes, his filled with life and love and so much excitement, they shone liquid gold.

She let her gaze slide down his lean body and took in the perfect way the tux fit every inch.

"About damn time," Kai muttered. "Figures he'd be late to his own wedding."

Mitch either didn't hear Kai or didn't care. He didn't take his gaze from Halina. And she'd never felt more beautiful. Or more loved. He conveyed it all with one look.

He put a hand over his heart and groaned. "Thank God there's a doctor on-site." Without taking his sweeping gaze from her, he said, "Judge, we should hurry. I don't think I'll able to stand much longer."

Halina crossed to him and took his hands, searching his gaze. "Are you all right? Are we . . . all right?"

He slid his arms around her waist and slowly pulled her against him. Oh, he smelled amazing and her lids went heavy as she breathed him in and instantly calmed.

"Never better," he murmured, low and sexy. "And you've never looked more beautiful. I'm the luckiest man on earth."

He lowered his head to kiss her.

"Ah-ah." The judge drew their attention. "None of that just yet."

Mitch pulled back and beamed down at her. Halina's heart overflowed with more love and happiness than she'd believed possible.

"You clean up pretty good, brother." Teague stepped up next to Mitch, acting as his best man, and pushed him away from Halina. "Put your eyes and your tongue back in your head, dude. You've still got a few words to say."

Alyssa came up beside Halina and handed her the flowers she'd set down twenty minutes ago. Keira took Brady from Alyssa's arms and gave her a bouquet of her own.

Halina went a little hazy for the next several minutes, floating through the formalities of a ceremony she'd convinced herself she'd never experience, to the man of her dreams she'd believed could never love her with equal depth. The whole thing was such a fantasy, she was sure her feet didn't touch the ground.

"Halina," Alyssa whispered behind her, tapping her arm.

She was lost in Mitch's warm eyes, his bright, lively smile, thinking she couldn't ever remember seeing him so happy. "Hmm?"

"Your flowers." Alyssa was grinning at her as if Halina had

missed something, then leaned close and even more quietly said, "Do you remember your vows?"

"Oh." Halina's stomach did a triple flip. "Yes."

As soon as Alyssa took her bouquet, Mitch's hands slipped over hers and she was absorbed in that golden gaze again.

"It is my honor," Judge McMillan's smooth, confident voice filled the room, "to be with you all today to unite Mitch Foster and Halina Beloi in the blessed union of marriage. Mitch, are you here of your own free will to join your heart and soul with Halina's in the eyes of our Lord and the law?"

His gaze never left hers, but his fingers tightened and his grin grew. "I am."

"Halina, are you here of your own free will to join your heart and soul with Mitch's in the eyes of our Lord and the law?"

She swallowed, licked her lips, held his gaze. And sighed out a "Yes."

"Mitch," Judge McMillan said, "I understand you and Halina have your own vows."

His gaze darted to the man between them for a split second as he made a quick nod, then looked back at Halina. He repositioned her hands in his and held on tight. Took a breath that raised his shoulders and blew it out quick. The first flash of nerves lit his eyes, but he went very quiet and still. The way he sometimes did before he delivered an important closing argument.

"I choose you," he said, low and smooth, "Halina Heather Raiden Sintrovsky Dubrovsky Beloi—"

She burst out laughing, dipping her head as her face flushed with embarrassment. But everyone else was laughing along with her and Mitch's eyes twinkled with pleasure.

He waited until the room quieted to continue, serious, sincere, painfully sweet. "—to be my wife, my partner, my best friend, my soul mate," he paused and squeezed her hands, "above all others."

Halina's heart swelled to painful proportions. Tears glazed her eyes.

"When you need encouragement," he said, "turn to me. When you need a helping hand, let it be mine. When you need someone to trust, look to me. When you long for love, know it will always be here." He lifted one of their joined hands to his chest.

"I believe in you. I believe in us," he continued with so much conviction, Halina was lost in his words. "Together, we are strong. Together, we are eternal. You are the only woman I have ever loved, the only woman I have ever needed, the only woman I have ever truly wanted. And I promise you . . . all of me . . . from this day forward."

The tears spilled over. Her air stuttered into her lungs. The judge allowed a moment of silence to linger before he murmured, "Halina."

She swallowed, held on to his hands tight for reassurance. For a second, she closed her eyes. When she opened them, she couldn't fathom the depth of love she saw gazing back at her. And as always, he gave her the strength to push the words forward.

"Mitchell Raiden Foster," she said, "you are everything I've ever wanted or ever needed, and at this moment I know all my prayers have been answered, all of my dreams have come true. I promise to always be truthful with you. I promise never to run from you, never to hide from you, always to believe in you and to never, ever, take another false name."

His grin broke into a laugh. Wetness glistened in his eyes.

"In sickness," she continued, "I will nurse you back to health. In health, I will encourage you on your path. In sadness, I will help you to remember. In happiness, I will be with you to make memories. In poverty, I will do all that I can to make our love rich. And in wealth, I will never let our love grow poor. I vow to share with you everything I have and everything I am. You are the only man I have ever loved and forever will."

Emotion washed over Mitch's face, so potent, so rich it gripped her heart and squeezed hard.

They exchanged rings with simple vows and Mitch pulled

her hand to his lips to kiss it before he threaded his fingers with hers and lowered them again.

"Halina and Mitch," the judge said, "with quite possibly the most eloquent expression of love and commitment I've ever witnessed here in front of God, friends and family, by the power vested in me by the District of Columbia, I now pronounce you husband and wife."

Halina broke into a giddy smile. Her heart floated in her chest.

"Mitch," the judge said, "kiss your beautiful bride."

They were both laughing as he drew her into his arms, his gold eyes open and on hers as their lips pressed the first time. Then Halina let her eyes drift closed. Lost herself in their new and thrilling fantasy come true.

Mitch held her tight and kissed her as if he hadn't kissed her in months.

They broke apart to the urging of the others for hugs and kisses and laughter. With their limited time, cake and champagne quickly followed. And with the room filled with more happiness and love than Halina could have ever hoped for, Mitch pulled her aside.

He slid one arm around her waist, kissed her temple, and murmured, "I want to smear you with cake and lick you clean."

She laughed, kissed him. "Okay."

"I have something to show you," he murmured.

She pressed her hand against his chest, felt the quick beat of his heart beneath her hand, and leaned into his hips. "I think I already feel it."

He laughed, low and deep. "That's for later." He lifted his phone. "A wedding present."

She turned her head and glanced at the picture of Schaeffer, red-faced and indignant, eyes bugging out, arms cuffed behind his back. He looked so ridiculous, she burst out laughing. Then she turned to Mitch, wrapped her arms around his neck, and pressed her face to his shoulder. Her laughter turned to tears. And he held her tight, stroking her back.

"Hey, baby," he crooned. "I'm sorry, I thought you'd be happy."

She nodded, pulled back, sniffling. "I am. I am. My emotions are just . . . kinda all over the place." She put a hand to his face, drawing his gaze to hers. "I have something for you too." She leaned close and whispered, "I'm pregnant."

He gasped. Stilled. His hand closed around hers. "Really? For sure?"

She nodded and pressed her forehead to his jaw. "Teague felt it when he was healing some of my cuts."

Mitch dropped his mouth to hers and took her in such a searing, passionate kiss, she had to fist her hands in his jacket to keep herself from swaying right off her feet. He pulled away, holding her face in both his hands. Tears lined his lashes.

"Oh my God," he said, breathless. Then a heated smile came over his face. "Maybe we can work on perfecting your skills with the ferrite bead. See if our kid's going to be a Supreme Court judge or the next Nobel Peace Prize–winner or . . ." His brows rose. "A pitcher for the Padres like his . . . or her . . . old man once upon a time?"

Halina laughed and shook her head. "I think I'd rather enjoy watching our baby follow his or her very own path, choice by choice."

"Agreed." He kissed her again. Pulled back and pressed his forehead to hers. "Hali, God. I love you so much. You've filled my life beyond my wildest dreams."

She smiled and whispered against his lips, "That makes three of us."